PRAISE FOR

The Goose Walter

"Every character in this surprising book carries the past like a burden, as does the small New Jersey town in which their lives all intersect. Miller unspools this quirky tale of everyday magic and human connection at a skillfully controlled pace, leading readers alongside them on their unexpected, interconnected paths to redemption. This deeply humane novel is an antidote to cynicism and a lovely debut."
—C.B. Bernard, author of *Ordinary Bear* and *Small Animals Caught in Traps*

"A moving, richly-drawn testament to the power of human resilience against unimaginable loss. Impossible to put down, *The Goose Waltzer* will restore faith in humanity to even the most hard-hearted of cynics."
—Reuven Fenton, author of *Goyhood*

"If you enjoyed the whimsy and wisdom of Fredrick Backman's *A Man Called Ove* and Shelby Van Pelt's *Remarkably Bright Creatures*, you'll love *The Goose Waltzer*."
—OverBOOKed in Pottstown

"*The Goose Waltzer* is worth every moment of your reading time—full of mini-criminals, gut-wrenching moments, and all-encompassing love."
—Kristan Ryan, *A Woman's Write*

"Complex themes, intriguing characters, and intense moments in history."
—Florence Ann Romano, *The Bookhive Bookclub*

"Beautifully explores the complexities of loss, redemption, and the healing power of unexpected connections…Deftly weaves together adventure, suspense, and heartwarming moments in a well-paced plot that develops into an unforgettable end."
—K.C. Finn, *Reader's Favorite*

"A hopeful story with characters to fall in love with…"
—Teresa Sarsted, *The Bimbos* (Beautiful Intelligent Maladjusted Bookworms of Seattle)

"*The Goose Waltzer* is a testament to Miller's ability to craft a narrative that is both compelling and thought-provoking, making it a noteworthy addition to contemporary fiction."
—*Literary Titan*

"*The Goose Waltzer* is a beautifully written and insightful view into the human mind, post-traumatic stress, and our linked humanity."
—Grant Leishman, *Reader's Favorite*

THE GOOSE WALTZER

A Novel

By Samantha Leigh Miller

Sleigh Books

Sleigh Books
Pottstown, Pa 19464

ISBN-13: 979-8-9900206-3-4 (pbk)
ISBN-13: 979-8-9900-2061-0 (ebook)

Cover design and photography by Matt Mossholder
Cover image(s): www.freepik.com

Printed in the United States of America
First Edition

In Memoriam H.A.S.M.

WAWA
BUS STOP
TO NEW YORK CITY
SIXTW STREET
KINDERKAMACK NEW JERSEY
ALBERT'S HOUSE
CLARE'S HOUSE
JARED'S HOUSE
SWALOTT DRIVE
CEE-CEE'S HOUSE
LENNY'S MAIL ROUTE
SCHLINGMAN'S DOGS
PATWMARK (A&P)
TRINITY STREET
FOOT PATH
PENELOPE'S HOUSE
TIROL FARM
CEE-CEE'S HIDE-OUT
OLD CLEVEDON ROAD
OLD CLEVEDON ROAD
GRAVEL DRIVE
ALBERT and CLARE'S BENCH
GRASSY MEDIAN
HONOCK POND
VIOLET'S ISLAND
KITANE CREEK
TO NEWARK
DE VRIES CROSSING
HUNTING LANDS

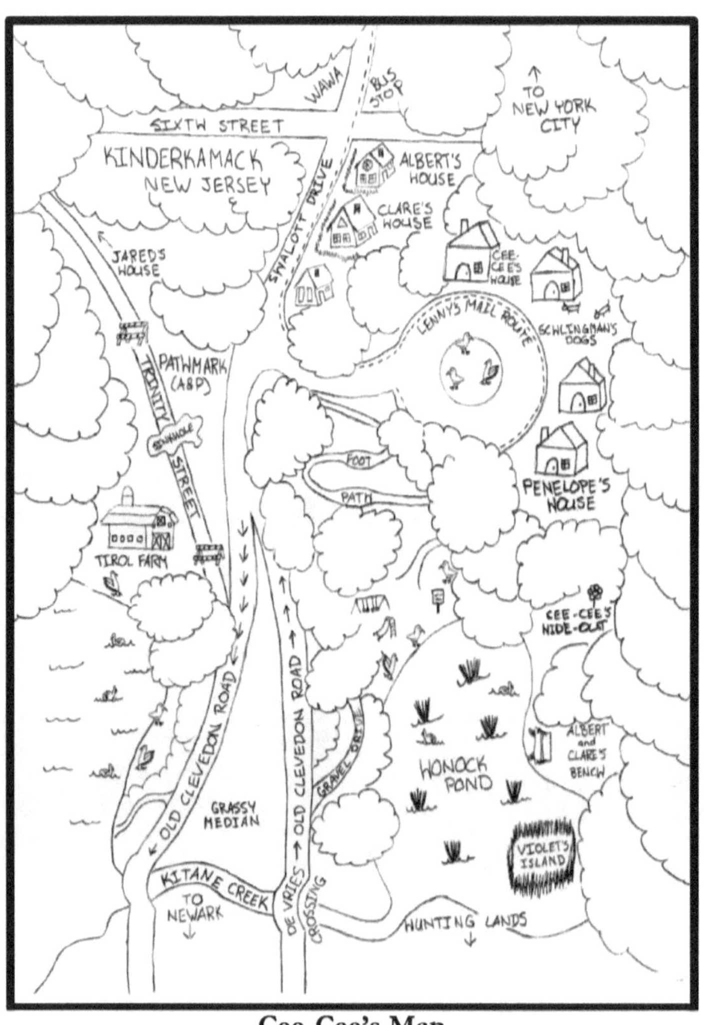

Cee-Cee's Map

PRÉLUDE

Let Love clasp Grief lest both be drown'd,
Let darkness keep her raven gloss:
Ah, sweeter to be drunk with loss,
To dance with death, to beat the ground,

Lord Alfred Tennyson,
"In Memoriam A. H. H."

VIOLET

(You hope your last day together would be perfect. But it never is.

It was dark and fuggy with summer rains, and he'd left early that morning without telling me where he was going. I was determined to be about my business and not think about it, but the more I specifically didn't think about it, the more I absolutely thought about it, and by the time he returned, I'd managed to gather something of a rage toward the both of us. He presented me with a small gift, a tasty treat to add to our lunch, and my body filled with hot shame. Of course he returned. He always returned. It was me who never believed he would. Who still couldn't relax into a relationship that had already spanned seven winters. Once you're abandoned in this life, the loss never leaves you. Maybe that's why we orphans are often single.

We spent the day in parallel. He doing his work, me trying to focus on mine. His foot was bothering him. I could tell from the way he favored it as he moved from one task to the next. When his foot acted up, it caused him to stumble sometimes, the pain shooting up his leg in a fiery arc. It was a childhood injury, a bite from a snapping turtle in a pond that he and some friends frequented. As I watched him hobble, my guilt warmed again. He'd been hurrying this morning. Rushing to get back to me. Worrying about me, knowing me too well.

I'd meet his eyes at times, and I saw the love in them. Quiet, strong, constant. He knew that once I'd wound myself up, it took some time for me to come back to him, and so his eyes let me know we were okay. And his silence, his presence, close, but not too close, let me know he didn't mind waiting.

At the end of the day, he suggested a walk, and I didn't hesitate to fall in beside him. The sky, which had been gray and churning all day, cleared just enough to see the first few lights in the darkness, and we paused at the edge of the road to admire the glory above.

He moved closer and I leaned against him. Together, we breathed in and then out, and in that moment, I felt all the burden of the day slip from my shoulders like it was nothing but a bit of fluff.

I didn't see what happened. I think there's still a part of me that doesn't believe it happened, since I have no memory of it. We were walking together, crossing the road, he at my side, maybe a little behind me because of the limp. And then, he was gone.

Later, I would remember the sound of wet tires screaming against slick pavement. I'd see, from the corner of my eye, the sudden, disorganized jumble that was his body. I'd hear the sickening, sloshed thud as he landed in the grassy median between the lanes of traffic.

He couldn't move, and there was a redness spreading beneath him, so that it stained me too, where I lay in the grass beside him. But his eyes were open, and they stayed on mine. Clear, focused, holding my gaze. Telling me not to worry. Telling me he wasn't in any pain. Telling me he would love me long after he was gone from this world. And I held his gaze too, even as I quivered in fear, in grief, in the great pain that would grab hold of my heart and take years to let go. If it ever did. I held his gaze as the cars continued to pass by, as the rain started to come in great gusts of pellets, as memories of our life together stormed through my mind. As thoughts of the future I thought we would have with each other threatened to drown me. I held his gaze until every last bit of light was gone from it.

And then, finally. Someone came. A figure in a yellow raincoat and hat. A big man with a soft voice who stooped down and put his hand on me to help me to my feet. I pulled away from him, scratching, biting, beyond reason, beyond sense. I'd hurt my leg in some way I would never remember, and it buckled beneath me. I crashed down in the grass and laid there, panting, no longer caring what happened next.

I watched him scoop up the body at my side. Watched him shift the dead weight between his arms. And then he stood there, watching me.)

PART ONE

And one far-off divine event,
To which the whole creation moves.

Lord Alfred Tennyson,
"In Memoriam A. H. H."

23 DAYS

**Monday, June 7, 2010
7:34 p.m.**

At seventy-nine, Albert Henry Hallam was prepared to go to jail. He thought it preferable to a nursing home where the bars were made of bingo nights and tapioca pudding. He worried, though, that his age would land him in a minimum-security facility with some soft-bellied roommate named Montgomery or Chase and with whom he might still be forced to play bingo and eat tapioca pudding. His skin color, however, could mitigate the situation. Over the slow decay of dementia, Albert thought he might happily choose a good shanking. *Or was the verb form shiving? Does one shiv with a shank? Or shank with a shiv?*

Albert stared thoughtfully into the mirror, mulling over this syntactic puzzle. A bit of white in his beard caught the light. Darkened lines carved ruts from his eyes. When he was young, he measured his time in years. Plans made for years even decades in advance. Now, he thought in terms of months, days even. Thirty-two left? Twenty-three? No matter. There wasn't much he had left to do. Just this one last thing.

Albert turned away from his image in the glass, one he recognized less and less these last few years and opened the tiny drawer of the table beneath it. Shadows gathered in the soft corners of the room, but Albert, not wanting to draw attention from the street, continued his search in the dark. After a lifetime in the house, Albert could find his way easily along its narrow halls, through its tidy rooms, beneath each of its arched doorways. The sigh of a loose floorboard in the upstairs study, the lingering ghost-scent of cinnamon in the bedroom closet that should have been three years gone, the irregular stone flooring in the kitchen that cooled beneath his bare feet at different temperatures. Albert knew the house's intimate details like those of a close friend. His last friend.

Checking beneath stacks of paper and tossing aside dried-up pens, Albert reached farther into the drawer and banged the back of his injured hand. Blood seeped, unnoticed, beneath the poorly wrapped gauze, as Albert continued to search. He knew he should have had his hand checked by a doctor days ago, but that would have required an explanation. Some sort of story. And Albert, storyteller he may have been, was not at all willing to provide or create a tale that would justify what the doctor would find. Worse still, the wound told its own story, one Albert was determined to keep silent.

Several minutes later Albert found his house keys half-buried in the dirt of his potted peperomia. He never would have found them at all if not for an errant ray of light that glinted off the metal. Albert had no memory of placing the keys in the plant, nor had he reason to do so. He fought a chill, an image of cold fingers creeping over his brain, plucking items out at will. The vision was strong, compelling, but Albert had no time. Sunset was coming. He had to hurry.

Albert's yellow slicker and matching rain hat hung in their usual place on the hook behind the front door. His disguise, or so he called it. Albert was raised on radio drama; Orson Wells' portrayal as The Shadow would unwittingly inform many of his adult predilections. Albert knew all criminals needed a disguise. A mask, glasses, or even just a well-placed hat. Nothing too elaborate, just enough to throw off police and any potential witnesses. A good criminal needed his tools too. And Albert had these handy. He picked up the brown paper bag from the table and hefted it, a loud rattle in the darkened house. A disguise, tools, and a good cover story. Albert had them all.

Parting the curtains at the living room window, Albert peered outside. Most days Officer Light stopped at the Pathmark after his shift and picked up a frozen dinner or a bag of chicken and rolls for one. Albert had a retirement gig distributing samples at the Pathmark—a little booth set up in the freezer section, tiny plastic cups—and the officer passed by often. The man never turned down a free sample. Everyone knew that on Mondays, though, Officer Light liked to treat himself to the Crab Shack's weekly special—a surf n' turf burger and a to-go cup of crab bisque. The restaurant closed at 7:30 on Monday nights since Pete, the owner, made it clear to all his patrons that barring an act of God, he would never miss an episode of Dancing with the Stars. The Crab Shack was seven minutes from Albert's house, and so that meant…yes, here came the police cruiser now, rolling down Shalott Drive, right on time.

The police car hesitated as it passed Albert's house. Albert leaned away from the window, holding the curtain open with the tip of his finger, his heart galloping in his throat. A moment later the car was gone, disappearing around the tree-covered bend at the end of his street.

Albert let out his breath. Before he let the curtain drop, however, he noted movement along the walkway of the house next door. A flash of purple. A switch of short blond hair that dashed behind the hedges that separated the yard from the street. The girl never turned to show her face, but Albert knew that purple cloak anywhere. It was his papergirl scuffling into the shadows, her bag banging against her legs, a bag Albert could clearly ascertain did not hold newspapers inside.

Albert moved away from the door, chuckling at the little thief.

Potting soil clung to the grooves of his keys and Albert gave them a shake. In fifty-two years, Albert had never locked the door to his house, and it had been fifteen years or more since he'd parked a car in his driveway. Still, Albert never went anywhere without his keys. The keys were his routine, like putting on his watch or brushing his teeth. He found more and more these days that routines kept him focused, safe. They grounded him in the man he'd always been, not this shuffling old geezer he was quickly becoming.

It hadn't taken much to turn Albert to a life of crime. In truth he'd been searching for a while now, for a reason, a cause, a hill on which he might die. If someone had asked him just a few days ago, Albert would have said his absence would go unnoticed. With the exception of the peperomia, which seemed intent on living if only to spite him, plants and dog had all withered and died in the absence of his wife's loving care. It seemed death came easily to the broken heart. Albert often wondered why the same had not happened to him. There were no children. No nieces or nephews, cousins, siblings, in-laws. Even his colleagues at the school had all passed away. Albert taught history and American government at Kinderkamack High School for 41 years and upon returning to the school 5 years ago for some ridiculous "meet your elders" senior project his wife had guilted him into, Albert had recognized no one. Not one single soul. So yes, a few days ago, Albert was content with the fact that aside from the papergirl, there was no one to mark his absence if he should suddenly up and disappear. This was June. By July, the crime-spree Albert was orchestrating would be over and he could vanish, either to jail or more heavenly regions, without incident. This fact bothered Albert very little, the irrelevant nature his life had taken on. He was ashamed to admit, even to himself, that it was something of a relief. The idea of slipping away, unnoticed. It was alluring.

But then Memorial Day came, and everything changed.

Albert had been watching the house next door since last fall when it had become occupied again. In the beginning—was it twenty-five years ago now?—renters had come and gone in the house next door, and every so often a garden would appear in the front yard, grow for a season, and die when the house went vacant again. The renters never stayed long, spooked by the rumors, or so Albert had heard. The house next door was something of a legend, neighborhood lore that had grown only darker and more wild with time. But Albert was not one to spread stories, even if the tale Albert could tell was much, much worse.

Painters came every five years to repaint the house. Purple, from roof to foundation, shutters to shingles, and the homeowner's association would kick up their usual fuss. Bergen County New Jersey had a take-no-prisoners approach to community management, though the older neighborhoods, like Albert's, had grandfather clauses on their side. With the painters came renewed hope. A possibility of return. But for years, the painters had come, and she had not, and Albert had begun to believe he'd lost his chance forever. Then late one night last November, Albert saw a light go on in the house. There had been no moving van, no truck of any kind. Just that single light. He waited. He watched. Just to be sure. And then he was. Clare Lyndsay had come home. And so, Albert began his watch, sitting up nights in his second-floor study and peering into the purple house below. For months, Albert had watched, waiting for a sign, not knowing what that sign would be, but having faith that he'd recognize it when it came. And then last Monday, Memorial Day, it finally did. It seemed Albert might get a second chance to right a very old wrong.

But time was running out.

"I'll listen to you this time. I promise," Albert said, his words catching only a stray cobweb in the corner of the darkened room.

Albert lingered a full minute after the police car rounded the corner before he opened his front door. As he waited, Albert shoved the paper bag up under his arm and slipped his hand inside the breast pocket of his coat. The feather was there, tucked into the pocket, warm and soft against his heart, just where he'd left it. Albert had two stops to make tonight, and it was getting late.

Wrapping the tape tighter around his damaged hand, Albert pressed firmly to stop the freshly opened wound and counted the minute out loud. Forty-two, forty-three, forty-four…amazed again at the vigor and force his days had suddenly taken on. It was as if he'd returned to the stage after years of sitting and watching from the wings. So easily he'd slipped back into the leading role of his life, his hero's journey not quite over, perhaps. There were still adventures to be had. Dragons to defeat. A maiden to rescue. He might just earn an honorable death yet.

Albert stepped into the last light on the porch, a hint of night already sharpening the air. He chuckled at himself as he shut the door behind him and started down the sidewalk. Such hubris. Conceit. He knew better. Hadn't he taught his students better? Didn't every character in history think he was the protagonist of the story?

7:37 p.m.

Officer Benedicto Light slowed as he turned the cruiser onto Shalott Drive and approached the house. It was still early, a cool orange sun holding steady at the horizon, and cold for June, all the yards in the neighborhood were empty. Memorial Day barbecues pulled back into garages, half-planted gardens anxiously waiting, children huddled around television and computer screens behind closed windows. The chilled scent of pond water leaked through Ben's cracked window to mix with the fishy vapors seeping from the bag beside him. The smell stirred Ben's empty stomach.

The Lyndsay house wasn't hard to spot. Some said it was Alice Lyndsay herself who had originally painted the house—stayed up all weekend with a bucket and a single brush. Neighbors swore they saw the woman in her nightgown, straddling the peak of the roof between her knees, covered in purple paint, and singing at two in the morning. They also swore they saw her light candles and perform rituals in the backyard. Missing pets were alluded to. A possible orgy.

After the woman's body was discovered, the stories multiplied, became darker and more fantastical with each year. It was the eighties, and Satanism was as popular as Rubik's Cube and He-Man. Backmasking, recovered memory, and whatnot. Children across the nation were spinning tales of occult activity and ritual abuse. Two children had come forward in Ben's neighborhood. First was a Helen something and then little Penelope Baker who still lived in the area, the cul-de-sac down the street in fact, though she was Penelope Homerton now. The little girls had pointed fingers at the Lyndsay house with teary faces and terrifying generalities. But by then the woman was dead, and the criminal investigation never got off the ground. This lack of fact only propelled the rumors in more bizarre directions.

The story about the house was true, though. Ben remembered that day. He'd sat with Clare in her backyard, and they'd both watched her mother on the roof of the house. Watched until the sun disappeared, and lightening bugs glowed against the dark. Ben and Clare weren't friends then, not exactly, not anymore. She'd let him walk her from the bus stop sometimes, if only to deter the taunts and name-calling from a gaggle of girls, Penelope

Baker/Homerton among them. When he and Clare were young, and his mother did house cleaning in the neighborhood, they would dig for worms in the blackberry bushes by the Lushington house or climb the oak in the backyard—Clare always daring to reach the higher limbs that frightened Ben. Sometimes they would watch cartoons at Mr. Hallam's house after school or play Battleship on the three-legged card table by Clare's back door. Clare allowed Ben in the yard or on the porch, but not in the house. Never in the house.

On the day Clare's mother painted the house, Alice Lyndsay wore sweatpants and a t-shirt, though, not a nightgown. And she was talking, not singing. She was, indeed, covered in purple paint and either did not notice or did not care. The woman was lecturing, Ben remembered, as if she stood behind a podium at one of her anthropology classes at Columbia, and he and Clare sat in audience. The lecture was something about Native Americans that Ben had long forgotten, though the sight of Mrs. Lyndsay straddling the house and wielding a paintbrush was one Ben would never forget. (Alice Lyndsay's lecture had actually been about the Kwakiutl tribe and a Bear dancer who kept watch over a cannibal. Though Ben had forgotten the details of what Alice said that night, the image of a bear dancing over a man who ate human flesh stayed with him, especially later, after Ben heard the story of what happened to Clare's mother. Throughout his life and in times of great stress, Ben's mind often lighted upon this bloody scene, though he would never remember from where such a disturbing image came.)

A car pulled to a stop behind Ben. Then another. The narrow street and parked cars made it impossible for the drivers to pull around him. As yet though, the sight of Ben's cruiser had inhibited any urge to honk. Ben pulled forward, creeping past the low hanging branches of the old oak tree until the house came fully into view. The muddy yard beyond the overgrown hedges. The ruined porch. The rhododendrons climbing nearly to the roof. He stopped again.

They were twelve the night Alice Lyndsay painted her house. The night Clare caught him on his way home from helping his mom at the Carlyle's. Clare took Ben's hand, and he felt her whole body vibrate through his palm. She didn't say a word, but there was a wildness in her eyes that changed her whole face. Ben had nearly pulled away.

The Lyndsay house was quiet tonight. Curtains drawn. Light on in the front room. Car in the driveway. Ben had checked the parked cars up and down the street, but Jared Croker's black tow truck wasn't there. It wasn't at the garage, and it wasn't parked at the man's mother's house either. Ben had had another unpleasant exchange with the woman that afternoon. All wispy hair and gnarled teeth, Croker's mother. Even without the profanity, Mrs. Croker was a vile little woman.

The curtains at Mr. Hallam's house next door suddenly fluttered, catching Ben's eye. Ben could feel the man watching him.

"I'm after bigger fish tonight, Mr. Hallam," Ben murmured with a small smile.

Satisfied that Jared Croker's black tow truck was nowhere in the vicinity of Clare's neighborhood, Ben steered his police cruiser toward home. Circling the block slowly, Ben's mind went on cop mode as he searched the sidewalks, noted the makes and models of the cars parked like sardines on the side of the street, and sifted through the other erroneous details of the neighborhood. One roving dog, a blown-over trash can rolling toward the gutter, a couple of kids who ducked behind a fence when they spotted Ben's cruiser, one of them wearing a purple Halloween cape whom Ben knew well, but still no black tow.

Elizabeth Landryes. The name rose again in Ben's thoughts as he drove home. *Lacy*, the blood-mottled necklace in the evidence bag had read.

The woman was brought to Hackensack Regional Medical Center three days ago with a broken wrist, multiple lacerations to the face and neck, and a severe subdural hematoma. The blow had come from her right, striking her zygomatic and shattering her nose. It had been a single blow from a left-handed attacker. A closed fist, based on the knuckle pattern still visible below her swollen eye. The force had driven the woman backward and to the right. She'd spun, thrown her hands forward to break her fall, and snapped her left scaphoid when she hit the floor. Her skull broke the glass coffee table when she landed, slicing her face, and nearly severing her left ear.

It was the coffee table's steel frame that caused most of the damage to her brain.

The case was not Ben's, it wasn't even in Ben's district. He'd overheard some officers talking about it in the hospital. The woman's tiny apartment was cluttered with glass tubes, burned balls of aluminum foil, and corner-cut plastic bags. Narcotics was all over it, but their only lead was a complaint call made the night of the attack—"loud rock music" coming from the apartment parking lot around midnight. The house next door had contacted the police, said the music came from a black tow truck parked behind the dumpster. By the time an officer arrived, long after dawn, the truck was gone.

There was only one left-handed meth addict Ben knew who also drove a black tow and had a history with "clumsy" women. Jared Croker. He'd been in the same class as Ben and Clare when they were kids and had a reputation for cruelty. A reputation largely earned from a dead-kitten-in-a-bag incident for which he'd gained much notoriety among their elementary-school peers, the details of which Ben had never cared to learn.

Adulthood had not imbued the man with any more sense. Croker worked some sort of animal control business with his brother and repoed cars on the side. In the last year alone, Ben had been to the Croker house three times to take the man away in handcuffs. And three times the woman had either "misunderstood" the situation, or simply disappeared before any formal charges could be filed.

But Ben was a patient man. He kept an eye on his old classmate. He made a round of the neighborhood after each shift, kept a log of where and when he spotted the man's black tow around town. It was only a matter of time, Ben figured. Until recently, he'd been content to wait.

Lately, though, Ben noticed Croker's black tow parked in Clare's driveway.

Ben stopped at a traffic light three blocks from his apartment. As he waited for the green, he held his hand out, watched the shadows from the streetlight play between his fingers. It had only taken a single blow. An explosion of violence. Over in a second. Lacy had probably never seen the man lift his arm. Ben made a fist, straining the tendons of his fingers. His hand shook. Something sour filled his stomach.

The light turned green.

An hour later—after not returning home but instead, checking in with dispatch and bringing Marcy a coffee, sending Chasseur home for the night, and completing a dozen little tasks that could have waited for morning—Ben was back at the Lyndsay house.

The lab was still processing dozens of prints found at the apartment, but Ben knew that would take days. In the meantime, Ben decided a quick visit to Clare's house was in order. A knock on the door. A heads-up on the situation. Nothing that would get him in trouble with the D.A., just a friendly warning. *Your boyfriend's a psychopath.*

There had to be a better way to word that.

As Ben chewed on this dilemma, he caught sight of something that made him slam on his brakes. Veering the vehicle to the left, Ben flipped off the headlights, and slid into the driveway beside the Lyndsay house. He was out of the car, flashlight in hand, with one smooth movement. His other hand covered the service weapon at his side.

7:46 p.m.

"Do you think he saw us?"

Cecilia Anne Lushington peeked between the slats of the fence and watched the police car roll by, ten feet away.

"Did he? Cee-Cee?"

"No," she lied. "C'mon."

They emerged from behind the fence, moving quickly along the crumbling sidewalk. The neighborhood was quiet, empty, only the occasional radio from a passing car broke the silence. Cee-Cee divided her attention between the uneven sidewalk and the awkward weight of the bag on her shoulder. The policeman had gone, but Cee-Cee still felt eyes following the two of them. She fought the urge to turn and look behind her and instead, pulled her purple cloak tighter around her arms.

Her cell phone hummed in her pocket.

Dad: ???

Cee-Cee's fingers flew over the keypad.

Me: coming now sory!!

She slipped the phone into her pocket and reached to flip the hair from her neck. It was a thoughtless gesture, one she performed a hundred times a day. But this time, her fingers caught only air. She'd cut her hair short for her twelfth birthday last week—ten inches on the floor, a shocking sight that nearly brought her to tears. But Cee-Cee had hid her panic with a big smile. And her father smiled back, pretending to believe her.

Grabbing Freddie's elbow, Cee-Cee propelled them faster down the sidewalk.

"He was right there, no way he didn't see us," Freddie moaned. He yanked his arm from Cee-Cee's grip but kept the quick pace beside her. "Is he coming back, Cee-Cee? You think he might come back?"

It was a cold night, but the cloak had a thick silk lining and high collar that bundled her in warmth. Cee-Cee's father had ordered the cloak online from a costume shop in New York after she had explained in passionate detail that it was the only cloak in existence that captured the spirit of her Halloween costume—not Harry Potter or some sort of witch, but rather a wizardess, more powerful than any make-believe nonsense. She'd emailed her father the link and it had arrived just two days later. Sometimes Cee-Cee felt guilty about the ease with which her father ordered things for her online. Or how quickly he agreed to drop her off at the roller rink or pass her $20 for an afternoon at the movies. Cee-Cee's mother had been gone a year now and mostly her father still walked around with a stunned expression on his face. She sometimes wondered how long a person could hold onto an expression before it simply became who they were.

"What about *her*, what if *she* calls the cops?"

Cee-Cee pulled the bag higher on her shoulder, its contents banging against her leg. It was her newspaper carrier bag—*The Record* printed in bold letters across the side. Since Cee-Cee was only twelve, the route technically belonged to Dylan Schlingerman next door. Dylan, who was Freddie's much older brother and who would much rather smoke pot in the basement while playing video games with his friends than chuck newspapers to the last few houses in the neighborhood who refused to succumb to the age of technology. Technically, the route paid $63 a week, of which Dylan paid Cee-Cee $20-$25, depending on the price of weed that week.

And technically, you weren't supposed to put anything in the bag except for newspapers.

Technically.

Cee-Cee and Freddie walked in silence for a few minutes. She could feel her friend fidgeting beside her. Freddie's nose squished up into his head whenever he got upset. It made him look like a pig. She didn't need to look.

"Seriously, what if she calls the cops?"

"Who, Mrs. Homewrecker?" Cee-Cee glanced down the street, then back at Freddie. "Pssh. She can't see anything from there."

"No, the *Lyndsay* lady. What if *she* calls the cops?"

"She won't."

"How do you know?"

"Because. I know."

Another block passed as Freddie sighed and fiddled with the strings of his jacket hood. Freddie smelled like nervous sweat and the Fritos they'd eaten earlier at his house. Cee-Cee moved to put more space between them as they walked.

"Yeah, but what if she finds out it was us?" Freddie turned around to walk backwards, looking toward the Lyndsay house which was already out of sight. "What if she puts a spell on us or something?"

"Don't be stupid."

"She could. She could turn us into frogs or something."

Freddie almost fell, and Cee-Cee caught him. She spun him around and pulled him forward.

"—toads or *cennerpedes*, you don't know."

"She's not a witch."

"How do you know? That crazy old bat was her *mom*, you know."

Cee-Cee shot Freddie a sharp look. "That doesn't mean anything."

"Of course, it does," Freddie babbled on, leaping over a large chunk of broken curb. "Her mother was bat-toons crazy and a mean old witch."

Until recently, Cee-Cee had never considered the relative meanness of mothers. Mothers were mothers, and by default they were neither mean nor crazy. But last week Cee-Cee saw pictures of her mother and her mother's new boyfriend on Facebook. They'd gone to Ocean City, ate fried ice cream on the boardwalk, bought matching crab-head hats, splashed each other in the waves. And then posted 47 public photos of their happy time together.

Had her mother's work plans changed at the last minute? Had she simply forgotten Cee-Cee's end-of-school recital? Or had she forgotten the lie she'd told Cee-Cee?

"Just because her mother was mean and crazy, doesn't mean she is."

"But that was her mother, you know? Her actual mo-ther."

Cee-Cee fought a sudden urge to shove Freddie into the street.

"And now she lives in that creepy old house and never goes out and no one comes over. Ever. And you know Dylan said he saw her at the window that one time. She could be doing anything in there—chants or spells or carnations."

"You're an idiot, Freddie."

"It's true. You don't know. We could just wake up one day and have spiders for hands and then you'll know I was right."

"Fine."

Cee-Cee stopped walking, causing Freddie to jostle into her. She finally looked Freddie straight in the eye. He had to look up to meet her gaze, since, having just turned twelve, she had three inches and two years on her friend. Cee-Cee was feeling those two years more and more lately, struggling with moments of confusing sadness when the two of them were together. ("Nostalgia" might have been how Cee-Cee described the sense that their friendship was coming to an end as she entered her teen years, but Cee-Cee wouldn't incorporate this particular word into her vocabulary for another year.)

"You want to see it again?"

Freddie's face instantly de-pigged itself. He grinned. "Yes."

Shrugging the strap of the bag off her shoulder, Cee-Cee caught the canvas strap in her hand and looked around. They were still alone on the street. The feeling of being watched had subsided.

She lowered the bag onto the sidewalk and parted the opening at the top, spreading the bag out to reveal its contents.

Freddie's grin widened and a passing car lit up the gap between his teeth. "Cool."

She nodded, letting herself smile. "Yeah."

Her heart had felt so big against her ribs as she climbed the steps of the Lyndsay house just minutes ago. She'd thought for sure it would burst through her chest, felt her whole body rock with its force, her sight turning dark at the edges. But then, that's how it always felt, just before. She just had to push through because once she'd done it, the fear dissipated, leaving behind a wonderful lightness in her limbs. Her trip back down the stairs had felt like flying, her cloak lifting behind her in the breeze as she raced toward the hedges to meet Freddie. She couldn't feel the ground beneath her sneakers. She felt only the rush of adrenaline that surged from her heart to her arms and down to the tips of her fingers. She could still remember how it sounded, humming in her ears.

It was that lightness in her limbs and that rush in her ears that started her collection in the months since her mother had left. It was stealing, Cee-Cee knew that plain and clear. What worried her was that she didn't seem to care.

"Hang on, I want to send it to Bobby." Freddie slipped his cell phone from his pocket.

Cee-Cee slammed the bag shut and lifted it back to her shoulder. She started walking again. "We're not showing it to anyone."

"What? Why not?" Freddie ran to catch up. "Bobby won't tell. C'mon, let me send him a picture, I'll tell him to delete it right away."

"I shouldn't have let you come. I knew you couldn't keep a secret."

"Keep one better than you," Freddie grumbled.

Cee-Cee turned so Freddie wouldn't see her face. She and Freddie had been friends as long as Cee-Cee could remember, but for the first time in their relationship, she was keeping a real secret from Freddie. Well technically, it was Mr. Hallam's secret Cee-Cee was keeping. And technically, it wasn't anything he'd told her, but rather something Cee-Cee had discovered on her own—Mr. Hallam's sunset walks, his paper bag, his yellow raincoat. But most of all, it was what happened at the pond that she was bursting to tell someone. She'd seen it three times now and still couldn't quite believe what her eyes were telling her. The first time she saw it, Cee-Cee went straight to Freddie's house afterward, dodging the dogs and running right up to his front steps before stopping herself. It was that feeling again, that sadness (nostalgia), her intuition, urging her to protect what she had witnessed, advising her that Freddie wouldn't understand if she told him and, more importantly, something precious would be destroyed in the telling.

"I'll make him swear. Please?" Freddie was saying. "I'll tell him what you said, and he won't say a word—"

But Cee-Cee wasn't listening anymore. There was a man in the truck parked across the street. Its headlights were off, but the engine was running. The truck was big, bigger than the pick-up truck her dad brought home from work sometimes. There was a row of lights on top and a metal cross in the back with heavy chains attached. She stood still, dumbly staring, her hand gripping the strap of the bag. With Freddie's constant chatter, she hadn't heard the music until it was right beside them on the street.

Cee-Cee and the man behind the wheel of the truck stared at each other as Freddie prattled on about Bobby and the picture. The lights from inside the truck lit the man from below, drawing long shadows across his face and casting his eyes in deep hollows beneath his knitted cap. He'd been watching her for a few minutes, Cee-Cee felt this instinctively. And now that she saw him, now that she was looking directly at him, he didn't look away. But he didn't smile or wave either. He stared at her. As if he knew her. As if he were *thinking* about her.

Cee-Cee was grateful for the cloak, and she pulled its thick material tighter around her body. (It was her midsection she was protecting, an instinct as old and visceral as it was unnoticed. Cee-Cee covered her heart, the softness of her belly, the newly sprouted buds of her breasts.)

With one hand gripping the cloak's material in a knot at her chest, Cee-Cee used her other hand to drive Freddie forward. "C'mon, we gotta go."

7:51 p.m.

Jared Wilson Croker held the girl's gaze, unblinking, unmoving, daring her to break it off first, which of course she did. Grabbing the scrawny kid by the shirt, the girl in the purple cape rounded the corner at nearly a run. Jared tracked her progress for another few seconds, a flash of fire-gold hair flickering behind the hedges.

Fiery, flaming, flaring, fierce, ferocious, vicious…

Jared popped open the glove compartment as he spun the knob of the truck's sound system, lowering the Nine Inch Nails track he'd been listening to on repeat. He dug around the empty bottle of hand lotion, mouthwash, spare set of truck keys, rusted box-cutter, and shoved aside the glass pipe and some dirty straws to retrieve a wrinkled notebook. As he freed the notebook from the glove compartment, his .22 revolver fell onto the carpeted floorboard of the truck with a dull clatter.

Opening the notebook, Jared flipped toward the back before coming to an empty page. He started writing:

VICIOUS
PERNICIOUS
SUSPICIOUS
DELICIOUS
LUSCIOUS
CURVACIOUS
RAPACIOUS

Jared looked over his list, tapping his pen against the steering wheel. A cool breeze slipped through the cab's broken window behind him, tickling the back of his neck. The sensation reminded Jared that the tape he'd used to cover the broken window with plastic had failed yet again.

His tongue found the sore spot at the back of his mouth. He traced the area, flicking inside the rotted tooth, prodding the gum with the tip of his tongue until he sent a bolt of pain into his ear.

After a moment's consideration, Jared crossed *suspicious* from his list. Another moment, another throb of pain, he added *lascivious*.

Still not entirely satisfied, Jared turned off the dashboard lights and the cab of the truck settled into darkness. He tossed the notebook onto the seat, where it landed on top of his binoculars and bent to retrieve the revolver. After checking the gun's safety, he placed it back in the glovebox. Jared tried to remember the line he'd once read about putting a gun in the first act of a play. That Russian prick, Jared thought. He'd read the first two stories of some long-forgotten book after stumbling across a Wikipedia article and talking himself into a passion for Russian literature. (The Wikipedia article had actually been about the dueling Pushkin, not Chekhov's gun.) What was his name? Cheevsky? Some cheeky bastard who wrote like a two-year old. At first Jared thought the guy was on to something. Sardonic humor. Smart, and in a way not many people would understand, which Jared appreciated. He felt smarter, in fact, just holding the book in his lap. "Went home and died." That was great.

But the more Jared read, the less intelligent he felt and the more he became convinced that the little Russian prick was laughing at him. The stories were a joke, simple enough to fool you into thinking they were something more. But they weren't. They weren't about anything at all. And Cheevsky and his Russian prick friends probably got a good laugh about it, sitting around a fire up in some icy Russian castle, drinking their goddamn vodka and laughing at him—*Ameriki spasibo! Bolshoye spasibo Ameriki!* (Which Jared believed meant something like "fuck them, fuck the Americans!"—a phrase he'd learned from a late-night cable movie in which a minor character—a prostitute from Taganrog, coincidentally—expressed mocking gratitude to an American soldier who had failed to leave her a tip, *thanks a lot!* Thus, Jared ironically expressed the exact sentiment, if not the exact words, intended in his Russian-ice castle-Chekhov-drinking-buddy fantasy.)

Jared had been dating the chick from Hunter at the time, the one who thought everything in the world was either "clever" or "quite," as in "that was such a clever movie" or "it certainly is quite cold out tonight." She probably thought it made her sound British and, by some sort of verbal osmosis, made people think she was smart. He'd found the Russian bastard's book on her shelf propped up by two wooden ducks. She used the ducks as bookends, their blank eyes staring into the room. Jared spun them tail first whenever he fucked her (their empty stares elicited a wilting effect), but the ducks were always back at attention when he visited her again. Jared had liked to sit up with the book, long after she'd gone to sleep, so that when she woke in the night, she might find him browsing her Russian literature.

That Hunter chick, what was her name? Jared tried to remember. She was the one who said he looked like Thomas Kean Jr., the senator, for fuck's sake. The little wanker who blamed 9/11 on the CIA. All his life people said Jared was a dead-ringer for Ray Liotta, and here this little twat comes along and compares him to some Gumby-faced, no-balls politician. They'd fought about something after that, Jared couldn't remember what, but he did remember that he'd slapped her. She'd been quite surprised.

He probably should have stayed with that one, *Christ, her name!* He might have avoided that whole business with Lacy. Even Jared had to admit, that was some bad shit.

Jared's tongue slipped into the spot at the back of his mouth, and he winced.

It was the girl in the cape that had distracted him, Jared decided. He'd seen her around the neighborhood, of course, riding her bike and slinging papers, but tonight he hadn't recognized her at first. It was her hair, Jared realized now. She'd cut it short. Close to her chin, flipped up at the ends. When she'd turned toward him, Jared thought he'd seen a ghost. Suddenly he was twelve years old again and it was Clare on the sidewalk. Clare in the pink Strawberry Shortcake t-shirt she'd worn all that summer. Clare at the bus stop, staring at him silently, horror tightening her eyes, but beneath that, something…else. Even after all these years Jared couldn't name that look in Clare's eyes or understand why it had such an effect on him.

C'mon you pussy, just do it!

He heard the boy's voice and Jared felt the episode coming on, but as usual, he was powerless to stop it. It came on like a wave, approaching swiftly and from nowhere, drowning him in moments. It was his brother Elwin's voice Jared always heard first. And then came the smell of urine, the phantom stench of it curling into Jared's nostrils. And finally, the blood. Clare's cropped blonde hair, matted with blood, clotted with it, sticking against her cheek. Slick like tentacles where it slid across her closed eyes.

Jared shuddered, pulling his hat down tight over his head, making fists at his ears with the material, threads of yarn snapping over his skull. He slouched back in the seat and squeezed his eyes shut, groaning in the pit of his throat. Jared was familiar with the memories. Familiar with the splanchnic reaction of his body—the roiling stomach, the rise of bile in his throat, the sweating, the pounding in his ears. After so many years, Jared knew there was nothing to do but ride the wave of imagery to the end. Hope it passed quickly. Hope he didn't vomit.

But when Jared opened his eyes, what he saw through the windshield of the truck was startling, enough so that the sequence of memories rolled back abruptly, interrupting their cycle, and disappearing into whatever flimsy recesses of his mind that kept them at bay. Jared's body released, and for a moment he sat, slightly stunned, at this unexpected reprieve.

Earlier in the evening, Jared had spotted the cop back at Clare's house, and so he'd turned off Shalott Drive into the cul-de-sac to wait by the park trail while he decided what to do. This had been the third time in as many days that Jared had nearly crossed paths with Officer Light. First there was the hospital where Jared had ended up hiding in a stairwell outside of Lacy's room, his fistful of wilted flowers tossed in the trash. Then yesterday at his mom's house as he cowered in the basement while the beaner cop banged at the front door. And finally, today at Clare's, where Jared had gone knowing she'd turn him away again, knowing she'd be angry, furious even, but not caring. He had hoped to find a little sleep there, if not sex. Jared hadn't slept since that night at Lacy's. Three nights now.

And so, from where Jared had parked in the graveled shoulder of the street, he had a clear view of the man who turned quickly off the pavement and dodged into the woods.

It was Mr. Hallam, Jared realized, his old teacher who lived next door to Clare. The man had passed close enough to Jared's truck for Jared to see the print of the man's plaid shirt. The cab of the truck was dark, and the moon was full, so Mr. Hallam had not seen Jared as he passed, shocking Jared out of his unpleasant reverie.

Jared watched Mr. Hallam glide into the woods, briefly admiring the old man's unexpected agility. What was that black bastard doing out at this time of night? Jared wondered. And what the hell was he *wearing*?

8:38 p.m.

Clare Alice Lyndsay heard the knock clearly as it sounded again at the front door. Nine staccato raps that pounded out a sense of urgency. Authority.

Clare swallowed, set the tiny glass on the table, but didn't look up. The liquid burned into her chest, bloomed like fire through her empty stomach. She grimaced, holding her mouth closed. Heat radiated down her limbs, prickled her fingers. Clare lifted her hand from her lips. Wiggled her fingers before her eyes. Imagined licks of flame at the tips. (Clare was a terrible drunk, she knew this about herself. Alcohol tended to dull all the wrong thoughts in her head. But even so, Clare would have rather not been the sort of person who did what she planned for tonight, stone cold sober.)

The kitchen light flickered above the table, a fluorescent bulb burning too brightly in its last hours. The old refrigerator kicked off in one dark corner of the room. There was a clang of metal as the motor died. A soft thud.

Clare reached over the carefully arranged items on the kitchen table for the bottle, her fingers sliding along its wet sides. The knock came again. She counted. Thirteen raps this time.

Clare thought it was interesting how people usually knocked in odd numbers. Even numbers—2, 4, 6, and so on—purported a sense of balance, ease, Clare supposed. Matching lamps, coordinated bed sheets, two's company—three's a crowd and whatnot. Odd numbers were jarring. They demanded attention.

The flickering light overhead suddenly went out altogether and Clare looked up. Blackness. A void that could have extended through the kitchen ceiling and into the empty night above. An icy universe beyond. She stared, swaying into the vertigo of her imagination. *This is the way the world ends*, Clare thought. *...a fluorescent whimper.*

The bulb flickered back on, and a bolt of light shot through the back of Clare's skull.

Clare lost count of the knocking when it came again. The raps were hard, shaking the old wooden door on its hinges. The carcass of her Ficus shook where it sat in its dry pot in the living room. Its emaciated limbs trembled.

When she finally turned toward the front door, Clare saw she'd left the lamp on in the living room. It lit up the curtains with a falsely cheerful glow. She'd also left her car parked in the driveway.

Details. At least two missed.

Jared would be at the back door next. Was it locked?

Clare splayed her fingers across the table's surface, moving her wobbly thoughts toward an alternate scenario of the next thirty minutes of her life.

It was possible.

Even in Clare's altered state, she recognized the opportunity to have the business finished off by someone else. (Beneath Clare's thought, the image of a mountainside rose sluggishly to the surface. The way the car had spun like a skater on ice.) Jared certainly had the violence for it. It was as engrained in his DNA as his thick wavy hair or ruddy, slightly Mediterranean complexion. Wasn't that why Clare had invited him in in the first place, all those weeks ago? Even when they were young, back when he was *Jay*, the skinny boy with the big sad eyes who sat behind her in music class, Clare had always sensed in him a certain...recklessness. Even before that awful day at the bus stop, when he'd ultimately proven her intuition correct, Clare had sensed in Jared some potential for explosion. If given just a few minutes, three at most, Clare knew she could come up with a sentence that would drive him to it. Some poisoned phrase. It would be easy. Jared clung to rational thought as a stranded man might cling to the side of a cliff in a hurricane. One targeted blow would send him off and into the raging storm.

But it was precisely Jared's recklessness that turned Clare against the idea. He couldn't be trusted. And there would be a mess. And noise. But more than anything, Clare hated the idea of a mess.

Sighing, Clare pushed down on the arms of the chair and backed away from the kitchen table with a terrible scrape against the worn linoleum floor. She brought herself carefully to her feet. Anger wouldn't work. Neither tears. Clare hesitated, searching for her play.

When the knock came this time, Clare was certain the hinges would give.

She crossed the living room in a series of well-thought steps and stopped at the front door. What was that? That flutter in her stomach? Not the alcohol... Fear? Whatever it was, Clare felt it as something foreign to her being, this flush of adrenaline. Some phantom limb pain, nearly unrecognizable, barely remembered. Like the twitching leg of a decapitated chicken.

Her hand was on the knob. Not at all sure of what might happen next, Clare swung the door open wide.

"I'm sorry to bother you," said the man on Clare's porch. "But I've got something of an emergency."

The man smiled, a flash of white in the dark. He held a casserole dish against his chest, clutched awkwardly in his left hand. A bandage covered his other hand, hastily rolled and held together…was that duct tape?

Not Jared. Clare's mind was slow to catch up to this new information. It wasn't Jared at her door, but this older man. A tall man who stared down at her with the crooked grin of a six-year-old.

Clare gripped the doorknob to steady herself. "I'm sorry, but I don't—"

"It's my oven. I think it must have popped a fuse or something. We've had this cold snap, you know? And I woke up this morning with an idea for my Shepherd's Pie. What do you think of chili?"

He waited, but Clare only stared at him.

"I had a pot of it leftover, so I dumped it in with some sweet tomatoes. The first of them turned last week, delicious, and then I thought, green peppers would be just the thing, but the store was out, so I took a walk up to Tirol Farm and wouldn't you know, they had just the loveliest, plumpest peppers you ever saw—"

Clare stepped back as he continued speaking, seeing the man more fully now that he'd moved into the glow of the porch light. He wore cheap shoes and the cuffs of his khaki pants were high enough to reveal dark dress socks beneath. His wrinkled plaid shirt was tucked neatly into a belt that lifted his pants up and over his rounded belly. Clare glanced up long enough to discern broad facial features covered in rolls of skin that slid away from the center of his face like melted butter. His ears hung in large folds just above his jaw line and a crop of salt and pepper nubbles grew unevenly across the top of his head.

Clare looked down again. Faces tired her.

(Had she been less drunk, the editor in Clare might have noticed the safety pin holding together the man's shirt in the middle where a button had gone missing. Or the mustard stain at his collar. Or how stubble sprouted in patches across his sagging cheeks where he'd missed with the razor that morning, but how his fingers were perfectly manicured, nails clipped, clean. Clare might have also wondered why the man wore no jacket, though the night was chilly, or how the man wasn't actually looking at her, but repeatedly, and somewhat anxiously, glancing at the kitchen table behind her.)

As it was, Clare was distracted by the mental image of rolls and melted butter. She wondered vaguely when she'd eaten last.

"I guess I'm hoping you'll take pity on a hungry old man?" He was smiling again, sloping eyes disappearing into deep black crevices.

"I'm actually…" Clare glanced behind her. "I'm in the middle of something."

"Thirty minutes, tops."

Thirty minutes.

"I'm sorry," Clare said, starting to close the door.

"I won't even come in. Here." He held out the casserole dish, blocking the doorway. There was a note on the lid of the casserole dish, soft stationery etched in purple flowers. Cooking directions fastened with the same duct tape that held the man's bandaged hand. The script was precise, familiar.

"Just pop this in the oven at 400 and I'll be back in a half hour. I'm Albert, by the way. I came by when you first moved in, but you…probably don't remember. I live next door."

Mr. Hallam. Clare remembered. Of course she remembered the old man who lived next door when she was growing up. Clare knew him now as she'd known him the day she moved back into the house, but she saw no point in making the connection. Clare felt these memories of Mr. Hallam, of her childhood, of…that life, her life, as she felt everything else—foreign and not at all belonging to her. They were removed…untethered. The twitching leg of a headless chicken. The instinct remained, but the meaning was lost.

It had been the wrong decision, coming back home. Clare felt it the moment she stepped across the threshold last November, but by then it was too late. She'd cut her ties in Seattle, moved herself to the online division at *Running Brook*, and fired the renters. Since then, Clare had been putting in time (waiting for a sign, though she'd be loath to describe it as such). So when Jared showed up at her door a few weeks ago, Clare recognized him for the character he would play in this, her final scene. Jared was the omen, the harbinger of doom that would bring about the end. And Jared had every bit played that part.

Clare stared at the casserole dish. Then she looked again at the old man's footwear. Saw something on the side of his shoes, something so incongruous to her meandering thoughts that they halted altogether. There were sea creatures swimming along the sides of his feet. Tiny white cetaceans that grinned up at her.

Was it the ridiculous whales that changed her mind? Clare would never know.

Thirty minutes.

Clare opened the door.

8:46 p.m.

After depositing his casserole into Clare's hands, Albert left the porch. He turned once to offer a quick wave to Clare, but she'd already closed the door. The porch light switched off, and a moment later the living room window darkened as well.

At the end of the front walk, Albert paused, holding his chest with his good hand. He looked up the street to his right, looked down the street to his left, looked across the street at the row of houses that lined Shalott Drive. Every house flickered with the glow of a television. The garage doors were all closed. The sidewalk was empty. It was June and either too early or too cold for the locust serenade Albert usually listened to summer evenings on the porch. Even the Schlingerman's dogs slumbered early on the night Albert brought the casserole to Clare's door.

As was always the case however, two unbroken lines of cars moved along the narrow road that wound through the neighborhood. These were the commuters. One line of traffic headed north to New York, while the other headed south to Newark. When he and Emily first bought their little brick house on Shalott Drive, only the locals used the road. It was sometime in the eighties that the road became a way to avoid the turnpike, though back then, rush hour only came twice a day and only went in one direction. Now the traffic was constant and in both directions, something Albert never understood. Farther south of town Shalott Drive split into one-way roads—Old Clevedon north and Old Clevedon south—as it circled through the woods behind Honock Pond and over the Kitane River. Through those woods traffic often swam upwards of seventy miles an hour and around more than one blind curve. Through Albert's neighborhood, though, the cars traveled bumper to bumper, gliding, nearly silent along Shalott Drive, as if boats on water.

Albert pushed hard with his palm against his chest, trying to slow the organ's beats. He walked as quickly as he could manage through the damp grass in the side yard that separated his house from Clare's. A moment later, instead of relaxing in his own warm living room, congratulating himself on another successful night of criminal mischief, Albert was standing in Clare's backyard, heart pounding, jacketless and shivering.

Albert had known something was coming, hadn't he? Maybe not how or when, but definitely coming. That was why he started watching in the first place, wasn't it? (But the Shepherd's Pie? Well, that was just good timing. Albert had been craving comfort food all day.) After weeks of watching Clare's house from his second-floor study, the time had finally come, and here Albert had nearly missed it. It was Memorial Day that something changed. Some…shift. Clare was a solitary person with a simple routine—coffee, work on laptop, bit of lunch or dinner, work on laptop, water the plants, lights off by eleven—but last Monday that routine abruptly ended. The lights started staying on until long into the night. And there was suddenly no more work on the laptop. Instead, Clare had started to pack. And while packing by itself wouldn't have caused Albert concern, what she did with the plants did. The plants Clare watered every day, without fail. The plants she lingered by, untangling their vines, turning their pots in the sun, lovingly pruning their dead leaves.

The day after Memorial Day, Clare packed the plants into her car and drove away. When she returned, the plants were gone.

And of course, there was that scene with the Croker boy…

And here Albert had returned home this night, later than usual and with thoughts of Officer Ben distracting him. He'd hung up his coat, stashed the paper bag under the kitchen sink, and placed the rescued garden gnome on the floor of his closet, before shuffling past the study room door toward the bathroom. He had actually already crawled into bed before he remembered to check in on Clare. Albert felt a chill suddenly, one that had nothing to do with the cold. He'd come so close to sleeping through this particular night…

Taking some cover behind a tangle of blackberry bushes, Albert moved closer to the house. He now had a clear view through Clare's bare kitchen window. He waited.

Clare sat at the table for a few moments longer and then rose slowly and came to the window. Albert didn't move from his position behind the blackberry bushes, though, confident as he was of the bright, if flickering, glare of the kitchen light and of his submersion in the deep shadows of the backyard. Clare stood at the window without moving, facing what could have only been her own reflection in the glass.

And Albert faced Clare.

To say that Clare had changed from the little girl he remembered was both an obvious truth and a lie. Clare was Clare. Same frizzled, slightly Afro-textured hair that was not quite blonde, but not quite brown; same round, European eyes that picked up whatever color she happened to wear; same tiny nose and slight flatness to her cheekbones that echoed some far-off Asian line; same Baltic skin that burned easily in the summer and turned a raw pink in the cold.

Albert had never met Clare's father, the man whose genes had mixed so strangely with Alice's. Alice Lyndsay—whom Albert assumed had "passed" all her life, but whose thick, unruly hair told its own story—would speak of Clare's father to no one, would have the town believe in an immaculate birth, but Albert knew better. Emily had inquired once, gently, as was her way. Emily was a nurse, and skilled at setting others at ease, but to this question Alice had gone cold. The woman froze, stopped speaking, stopped breathing, as if the machinery inside her body had jammed. A moment later she was back, moving forward in the conversation as if the question had never been asked. Emily never tried again.

But Clare was *not* Clare. And this demonstrated itself so plainly, so starkly in the clear view of the woman at the window. Albert had to look away for a moment to reorient himself. He remembered a footpath he'd traveled behind his father's farm and along the creek when he was young. It was a path that changed dramatically with the seasons. Wildflowers and honeysuckle in the summer, bramble and ice in the winter. Whether June or January, though, there were always the same winding curves, the same landmarks that told Albert how far he was from home. It was this type of change Albert had expected to find in Clare, the change of simply growing up, evolving.

Instead, Albert encountered this altered Clare. It was as if some non-indigenous species had planted itself within the girl Albert remembered, had choked out the native flowers and invaded the territory to such degree that the geography of the landscape had been irrevocably transformed. Lost.

Or stolen. Albert knew something about the thieving ways of grief. How grief stole everything for itself—memories, moments, habits, small pleasures forever tainted—and left very little behind. Just some odds and ends that no longer fit together properly.

And yet…how could Clare not remember him? Or Emily? The lemonade summers spent on their porch? The childhood years when Clare had used their home as a refuge? It was a question Albert tried hard not to ask. Such questions inevitably led to others and if Albert chose to follow such a trail of thought (which he did not, most definitely did not), he would quickly find himself back at a time he never wished to live again (and yet there it was, rushing to the surface like a submerged balloon—Clare's twelve-year-old face, screaming at him from under the bed, blood speckled across her cheeks, dried tears and mucus plugging her nostrils, terror turning her into a whitened fear-thing, a changeling that Albert barely recognized as he ripped off his jacket and covered her body with it, already knowing this moment would haunt him for the rest of his life, already knowing he would fail her.)

Albert physically shook himself, throwing off the memory.

"Not this time," Albert said softly.

Clare stared a moment longer at her own face in the glass and then moved toward the living room. Albert gave up his spot behind the blackberry bushes and crept closer to the house, taking care as he stepped across the uneven ground. He stopped a few feet from the window and saw Clare, now standing motionless again in the living room entryway.

"Mr. Hallam? Is that you? What're you doing back there?"

A beam of light momentarily blinded Albert. When the flashlight lowered, Albert saw a police cruiser parked on the sidewalk, haloed in a ring of light. The car had pulled into Albert's tiny driveway, headlights off, and stopped without Albert ever hearing it. *Damn new cars and their stealth technology—*

"Mr. Hallam?"

"*Me?* What are *you* doing here?" Albert replied without hesitation this time.

There was a pause from the cruiser. Albert fought a smile.

"Mr. Hallam, you can't be back there," came the voice again a moment later. Albert had already identified the man in the cruiser as Officer Light, one of Kinderkamack's finest. And most tenacious, it was turning out. Albert had already had one near miss tonight, why was this man suddenly popping up everywhere he went?

"What do you mean, I can't be here?" Albert stepped away from the window and spoke in a loud stage whisper. Clare had gone into the living room where Albert could now see only the very top of her head.

"Mr. Hallam, you—"

"Don't you 'Mr. Hallam' me. A man's got rights, you know? Least last time I checked. Or does Bush's war on terror now preclude the right of a man to do a little stargazing in the privacy of his own backyard?"

As Albert spoke, the officer began walking toward Albert through the side yard. He was a big man, thick in the face and neck. This always took Albert aback, that his students grew up, became adults, and that it happened again and again and always so quickly. Ben had been a skinny kid, light of limb, but he'd always had that swarthy look about him. Pirate ancestry, Albert had assumed.

The officer approached Albert, swinging his flashlight in one hand. "Mr. Hallam—"

"So this is what they've got you doing now, Benny? This is what you signed on for? It's not enough, you coming after me at the park, now you're harassing an innocent citizen for standing out under the stars in the privacy of his own backyard? How much they pay you for that, Benny? What's the going rate for a man's conscience these days?"

"Please calm down, Mr. Hallam. That's what I'm trying to tell you. This isn't *your* backyard."

Albert stopped abruptly. He turned in a quarter-circle, scratching the back of his head. He continued turning until he faced his own backyard. Completing the rotation, Albert again confronted Ben. Albert arranged his face into a look of confusion, furrowed eyebrows, a slight opening of the mouth. Albert waited for his feigned bewilderment to impact the officer's course of action, and...*yes*, there it was. That small flicker of pity on Ben's face. That quick, upside-down smile of embarrassment for Albert. Oh, how Albert loathed that expression, the one that usually came with a lot of touching and a quick shift to the plural form. *Let's have a seat, shall we?* Though Albert had to admit, being seventy-nine had its advantages, especially when caught trespassing.

"And it's Obama now, right? Hope and change, remember?" Ben asked in a way that people lately had, one that always seemed to necessitate some show of pride from Albert. *Oh yes, we're all very proud of our boy, Barack.* But it was an annoyance that would end soon, Albert figured. Albert had lived long enough to see that pendulum swing many times…

"Come on, let me walk you back to your place, Mr. Hallam." Ben held out his arm and suddenly noticed the bandage on Albert's hand. "What happened there?"

Albert scratched the back of his head again. Looked back toward his own yard. He could tell the kid was uncomfortable. Albert lingered, enjoying the moment.

"You've had enough trouble lately, haven't you? We wouldn't want to add trespassing to the list."

"What? Oh, no. We wouldn't want that."

Head down and with a slight shuffle, Albert let himself be led out of Clare's backyard. With one hand on Albert's slumped back, Ben guided Albert along the sidewalk and up the little path to his house. Albert took the stairs to the porch one at a time, pausing for a breath at the top.

"You all right?"

Albert nodded, holding his chest. "Just runs out on me sometimes."

"Especially in this cold, I'd imagine. Hard to believe it's June."

Ben looked out over the darkened street. Albert stood beside the man, supporting himself on the porch rail. Evening had passed into full night. An even deeper silence had descended on the neighborhood in the nearly half-hour since Albert left Clare's house. All was quiet, save for the low drone of the cars. Always the cars.

The light in the house across the street winked out as Albert and Ben watched.

"There's been cloud cover all day," Ben said mildly. He stared ahead. "Not a star in the sky."

Albert was silent, watching the street.

"You sure you're all right, Mr. Hallam?"

And for an instant, Albert considered confessing all. In truth, he was old and he was tired and he wanted only to take his old, tired body upstairs to bed. And here, here was an officer of the law, for goodness sakes. If Albert were looking for help, here it was, standing on his front porch. And Benny was a good kid. A bright kid. Albert might dump the whole mess and be done with it tonight.

It was Emily's voice that stopped him, though. Emily, who'd played the role of his conscience for 54 years while they were married and in the last three years had yet to let something as minor as death usurp her part. Albert had ignored her once before when it came to Clare and paid too high a price. He wasn't going to make that mistake again.

"You have yourself a good night, Ben. Don't work too hard."

8:46 p.m.

Clare shut the door without saying goodbye. The old man's footsteps creaked along the old wooden boards of the porch and then went silent. Clare turned off the porch light.

Back in the kitchen, Clare stood at the table with her back to the oven. Inside the oven the old man's Shepherd's Pie was just beginning to heat up. The timer on the microwave read 28:34.

As she waited, Clare rearranged the items on the table. She picked up each one, turned it over, and set it back down so that the items formed a straight, neat row. There was her Washington driver's license (*ISS 12-20-2004 SEX: F HGT: 5'4" WGT 113lb EYES: HZL EXP 12-20-2009*), her social security card, the deed to the house, the title to her car, her keys (the keychain, courtesy of her former assistant, read *Has a sleeping dog got your tongue?*), and her birth certificate. Clare held the faded document for a moment, her right thumb nearly covering one tiny footprint.

CLARE ALICE LYNDSAY
Born this day on Monday, January 22 in the year 1973
Father's full name: UNKNOWN
Mother's maiden name: ALICE LYNDSAY.

For as long as Clare could remember, she knew she had been born on the day women "took back their bodies." Clare's mother celebrated this event by sketching out a draft of what would become the *New York Times* op-ed, "What Have We Really Won?" on the back of some hospital menus and which managed to enrage both sides of the *Roe v. Wade* debate. Alice enjoyed telling this story, especially the part where the nurse brought the baby to her in an attempt to trade the notes Alice had strewn across the hospital bed for her newborn daughter. Alice had then taken one look at the misspelling of Clare's name on the bracelet they'd snapped around her baby's tiny ankle and deftly shifted rhetorical gears from railing about a woman's right to work to lecturing the nurse on the innate sexism of orthography around the world. "There's something so ridiculously feminine about the letter *i*,"—she told the trembling nurse, who had the unlucky happenstance to be named "Ivy." This was why, Alice explained, she'd chosen the more masculine letter *e* for her daughter's name. All the while, of course, her mother ignoring the *i* in her own name.

While Clare's mother often took the liberty of educating the uneducated masses, she would never consider herself a teacher. Instead,

Alice Lyndsay knew herself as a researcher and scientist first, regardless of the varied roles she'd taken on during her career—women's studies professor at Wellesley and then Columbia; cultural anthropologist who'd studied and traveled in the steps of Ruth Benedict; second-wave feminist whose theories on rape and sexual politics influenced and enraged the likes of Kate Millett, Robin Morgan, and Shulamith Firestone; close friend and sharp critic of Margaret Atwood whom she'd called "Peggy" and met when they were both fiercely competitive graduate students at Radcliff.

"Question everything," Alice had told her daughter from the time Clare could remember. "See the world through the lens of inquiry. 'The trouble with life isn't that there are no answers, it's that there are so *many* answers.'" Conversations with Clare, if in fact that's what such activities could be called, were more akin to brainstorming sessions. Clare learned early that her role during such sessions was to play the part of the empty notebook, the blank sheet, the sounding board whose sole existence was for the impression of her mother's ideas.

Clare also learned that "question everything" didn't actually mean asking her mother anything. Alice would often respond to Clare's inquiries with a litany of philosophical challenges. Or, sometimes, Alice would simply wander out of the room, still talking.

And when it came to the date of her birth there was, of course, one question Clare would never ask.

Above this neat row of items on Clare's kitchen table lay a single sheet of notebook paper. Clare laid down the birth certificate and picked up the notebook paper, the noise her fingers made against the sheet obscenely loud in the room. She read the sentence she'd written in pen across the top of the paper, suspended in white space, as if even the sentence itself knew it had no place on those straight, clean lines. The sentence was short—ten words, nine of which were just one syllable. Clare started writing the note on Memorial Day, had whittled it down from nearly a page, and then to a paragraph that ended with, *I glimpsed my life and was underwhelmed.* No matter how she tried, Clare could not scrub the maudlin from her words. Finally, she arrived at this:

I do this of my own free will and volition.

The last item in the group was a three by five photograph. It lay by itself now, slightly askew. Clare reached for the photograph to place it at the end of the row, but her fingers stopped an inch from its surface. She pulled away, leaving the photo where it lay.

Moving to the other side of the table, Clare picked up the bottle of pills, peeled off its plastic ring, and set it next to the bottle of vodka. She threw the plastic into the garbage under the sink.

Clare stood at the sink for a moment, in front of the big bay windows that looked out over the backyard. She saw only her own face in the black glass. She looked pale, barely there. A shadow, half sick, fluttering in the failing fluorescent. (A quote passed through Clare's mind, mostly unnoticed. *A ghost, dying in the night and with no language but a sigh…*) It felt very late. She thought she'd be asleep by now.

The timer on the microwave now read 19:46 and Clare thought about sitting back down at the table. She imagined herself sitting in the chair, hands in her lap, bare feet pressed together. Then Clare imagined sitting on the couch in the living room. Legs crossed beneath her, leaning against the pillows like she used to. Clare next saw herself sitting on the porch steps out front, knees tucked under her chin, arms wrapped around her legs. It was June, but it was cold. Maybe she would get a sweater from one of the boxes. Finally, Clare imagined herself standing at the big bay window in the kitchen. She saw herself looking out into the yard, seeing only her own moon face fading in the glass.

A hiss came from the oven and Clare startled. The timer now read 13:09. Another six minutes lost. But Clare was used to losing time now, used to looking up from her thoughts (which were not exactly thoughts, but simply a smooth, barren expanse across which she glided effortlessly) and seeing an hour or even two had gone by. Even after coming back to herself, it often took several more moments before Clare could move, during which time she felt entirely disconnected from a body that refused to obey any of her commands. When this first began to happen to Clare, it caused her some concern, but over the last few days (since Memorial Day, to be exact), Clare began to embrace this missing time. She didn't think about it much, but when she did, she assumed this was her body's way of preparing itself. Of readying itself for what was to come.

Clare moved away from the window and went to the living room. She stood by her couch. She'd removed all the pillows from the couch and stacked them in the far corner so that she could lie down, fully reclined and in full view of the front door.

The framed pictures from the end table were gone, packed away into a box and hidden in a far corner of the attic where the house's future owners would surely find them. There was nothing to do about that. Clare could not give those photos away, any more than she could throw them out.

The bookcases at the far wall and along the staircase were empty, wiped clean of dust and other debris. Her books, which she'd procured from several thrift stores in the area, filled six boxes that were stacked behind the front door, each labeled with a fat marker—*Kinderkamack Library*. There was another box beside her books into which she'd folded the last of her clothes and with the same marker, written *Hope House*. There were folded, unused boxes stacked beneath the window. She hadn't had as much to pack as she'd thought.

Walking through the living room, Clare went up the stairs, clutching the wooden banister and pressing her palm against her thigh to climb the steep steps. Her body felt heavy, already half-asleep.

At the top, Clare passed a closed door on her right without pausing. She'd opened the door only once since November—just to see that the room was indeed empty, stripped bed in the center, bare dresser in the corner, benign, just a room like any other—and quickly closed it again. She hadn't touched the door since.

Clare's bedroom was at the end of the hall, where she'd slept ten feet from her mother for the first twelve years of her life. On her second day back in the house, Clare had kicked aside the baseboard at the back of the closet and retrieved the pet rocks she'd hidden back there, some of their googly-eyes still attached. Nearly thirty years of renters had not found the little family Clare had kept safe in her closet. Two large, smooth rocks and their smaller, brightly-colored children. The paint had mostly chipped away, and the smallest rock, the baby, was nowhere to be found. Clare's throat had filled with tears, and she'd choked a little, there on her knees in the closet, holding those rocks.

Instead of returning them to their hiding place, Clare had left the rocks on the floor of the closet, where, weeks ago, Jared found them. The rock he chose was about the size of an egg, round and beveled at one end with a sharp edge at the other. After flicking off a plastic eye, Jared used the rock to crush some of the larger crystals in his spoon. Jared remarked how finely the rock turned the meth into powder. Clare had watched silently, a dull ache in her chest, as Jared slipped her rock into his pocket.

Now the closet was empty, and Clare's single mattress lay in dim moonlight beneath a bare window. She'd stripped the bed of its sheets and blanket this morning, then washed and folded them into boxes as well.

At the bathroom, Clare turned on the light. She'd spent the afternoon scrubbing the room, floor to ceiling, emptying the vanity, bagging up bottles of shampoo, and bath creams, and body soaps, and hand lotions.

She'd thrown away her toothbrush.

When Clare returned to the kitchen, the microwave timer read 8:23. She sat back at the table, hands in her lap, watching the timer. The heat from the oven warmed the room. The refrigerator clunked off again. Smells filled the kitchen—sizzling beef and browning vegetables. In the seven months since she'd moved into the house, Clare had not once used the oven. Breakfast was coffee and toast, lunch was usually skipped, and dinner spent at her laptop eating a can of something she sometimes didn't bother to heat.

The timer was counting down its last two minutes when Clare finally rose from the table and went to the oven. She hunched down, balanced awkwardly on her toes, and opened the oven door. Heat fanned her face. Liquid bubbled under the glass lid. Reaching for the crocheted potholder the man had left with her, Clare lifted the lid from the dish to peek inside. The juices boiled softly. She could almost taste the rich aroma. Clare couldn't remember the last time she'd been hungry.

"Hello? You here, Clare? "

Clare dropped the lid back on the dish with a clatter and shut the oven door.

22 DAYS

Tuesday, June 8, 2010
7:03 a.m.

Before Clare opened her eyes, she lay listening to the *swush* of the trees. The sound, *swush*, was specific to June and July, Clare remembered. It was only the plump summer leaves that made such a sound when they slid against each other as the breezes lifted their branches. The hard buds of May and April were too small, too much air filled the spaces between them and the winds that blew between them made a thin whine. Fall gusts clattered and shattered the drying leaves. And the blustery squalls of winter wheezed like death rattles through the bared branches. Clare remembered all these sounds from her childhood as she lay with her eyes closed on the side porch of the old man's house.

As Clare lay listening, an old feeling of exhilaration crept over her. Some forgotten voice seemed awakened, was whispering in her ear...there was so much to do, so much that could be done, and every moment contained within it a secret, some hidden surprise that Clare had yet to discover. It was this voice that used to rouse her summer mornings as a child, set her off on her bike, or wading through the pond, catching tadpoles before the sun had fully turned from pink. With the voice came the old notion that she had only to open her eyes and the world would come to her—big, bright, beckoning. *Open your eyes Clare.* But Clare kept them closed.

Swush.

She almost smiled.

Pieces of the night before began to settle in her mind. They formed an eclectic collection of images that fit together in no particular order, but that, each in their own right, were emblazoned permanently upon Clare's memory. There was the ceramic mug with a hand-painted starfish on the side that the old man had brought to her on the porch saying, *You have to steep it for at least five minutes to get the full flavor;* the swollen water bug that had scuttled out

44

from beneath the refrigerator after they'd finished eating, and which the man caught in a yellow plastic tumbler and set free outside; the crocheted potholders he used to pull the casserole dish from her oven; the smooth spines of the books she'd run her fingers over as she waited in his living room, a slight fragrance of vanilla emanating from the massive shelves; the sight of the old man standing in her living room beseeching, cajoling, and the sound of her own voice, incredibly, inexplicably—*Okay. Yes, okay*; the scent of the fresh linen pillowcase, embroidery pressing against her cheek; the steady creak of the porch swing where she'd slept—they were a mass of impressions, a post-modern painting that contained more idea and emotion than actual reality.

Clare understood none of it. Not why the old man had invited her over, and certainly not why she'd said yes. Clare knew only that it was strange to wake up to this morning, to this sunrise she'd never expected to see. To this stolen day. This eighth day of the week.

Clare had slept through the night beneath a mound of blankets on the wide, cushioned swing bench on the old man's side porch. The porch was screened on all sides, keeping bugs out, letting air and light in. The swing (in which she'd slept more hours the night before than she had all week) swayed with the trees in the breeze that threaded through the backyard. The cold had broken sometime during the night. The sun had already begun to burn off the morning mist.

Through the sounds of the neighborhood, Clare heard a squeak of brakes and a rattle of chains. She rolled onto her stomach to see a girl of maybe ten or eleven with cropped blond hair, wearing a long, plum-colored cape, who pedaled down the sidewalk along Shalott Drive. The girl withdrew a rolled newspaper from the sack around her shoulder and slung it unto the front walk of Mr. Hallam's house. As she rolled by, Clare heard the girl's soft humming, a lilting tune, almost a lullaby, one that Clare recognized with a warm prickle across her neck...*talkin' bout hey now, hey now, Iko-iko un-day*... Their eyes met for an instant, through the shrubs at the front yard. Wide, pale eyes beneath dark brows, a wisp of hair caught at the corner of her mouth.

Then she was gone, pedaling away, weaving into the slow-moving traffic, the long material blowing out behind her, golden silk lining flapping in the breeze.

"You're up, good."

Clare twisted in the swing to see Mr. Hallam leaning from a screenless second floor window. He was already dressed in another plaid shirt, buttoned at the neck and wrists. He poured a palmful of something onto the metal gutter that made a sound like sleet falling. Clare heard a flutter of wings, a scuffle of feathers, excited chirps.

He chuckled at the birds, brushing his palms together over the gutter.

"Come on in, when you're ready. I've got banana bread…and an errand for you."

6:13 p.m.

Lenny had two kinds of houses on his mail route. Indeed, Lenny believed that the populous of the world as a whole could fall, more or less, into two, easily distinguishable categories—the Christmas-tippers and the non-Christmas-tippers.

The Carlyle's, for example. Green lawn all summer, pinwheels big as your head lining the front walk, crisp fifty-dollar bill in the mailbox come December. The Homerton's—twinkle lights on the fence, playful garden gnomes by the hydrangeas, thirty-five-dollar check tucked beneath a stack of outgoing Christmas cards. The Hallam house—red rose bushes out front, hanging begonias on the porch, a stack of wrapped sugar cookies waiting in the mailbox every December 23rd. Or, at least that had been the case, before the wife went and died. Lenny wasn't heartless, though. Once a Christmas-tipper, always a Christmas-tipper, was his philosophy.

But the Arnold's? Weeds in the marigolds, rusted bike in the side yard, and barely a wreath hung above the door before the snow flew. The Lushington's? Drooping daisies, birdbath filled with muck, zipidy-nada in the mailbox come the end of December. And the Schlingerman's? Ha! Forget about it.

But Lenny prided himself on not treating the non-Christmas-tippers any differently from the Christmas-tippers. They all got their mail on time, nothing dropped in dirt, no boxes left in rain. He made sure of this, went out of his way sometimes to ensure that his tolerance and his charitable open-mindedness were out there and available for all to see. Lenny waved his 'howdy's and 'how are you doing's' with a smile and humble nod of his head with what no one could argue was anything less than impartial, unbiased, unabashed friendliness. Christmas-tipper or non, 364 days of the year, Lenny considered himself tipper-blind.

Lenny stopped his mail truck on Shalott Drive and pulled as far as he could off the narrow street (just so people could see that he'd tried), but was still blocking traffic. The sidewalk was empty, just a few kids making noise at the end of the block. At the other end of the block a black tow truck was parked with a man sitting inside. Lenny took a quick look, ascertained that the man wasn't from the neighborhood, and so held back his usual "how do you do" nod. (That this was the second time in a week that such a sequence of observation and decision had taken place with the man in the black tow truck was something that registered on a lower level of Lenny's awareness but never made it any higher. Lenny wasn't one to meddle in others' affairs. In fact, he took pride in his philosophy of noninvolvement and believed the world in general would be a better place if everyone just minded his own business.)

Lenny sifted through the bins in the back of his mail truck, shoving envelopes into his bag, tucking a package under his arm, and walked up the sidewalk toward the Lyndsay house. This was the oldest neighborhood on Lenny's route. Houses here may have been built near the turn of the last century, but most of them had been maintained beautifully. While not among the most affluent neighborhoods of the area, Shalott Drive in particular was known among the mail carriers for its pristine cobblestone sidewalks and spectacular gardens.

The Lyndsay's house, however, was in need of an intervention. The yard was all dirt and hollow-out pit, straggly dandelions taking over the front walk, sagging fence, and not a speck of furniture on the front porch, not even a welcome mat. And the house was purple. Can you imagine that? Someone had actually painted the whole thing purple—trim, doors, gutters, everything. And not some faded lilac, either. Big, in-your-face, freaky-deaky, full-on purple.

Tipper-blind as Lenny may have been, what irked him the most was when a non-Christmas-tipper started *acting* like a Christmas-tipper. And here was a perfect example. Lenny had met the lady on Shalott only once since she'd moved into the ugly purple house last fall—all stringy hair and sunken eyes. Christ. Once was enough.

Lenny blew hard through his lips and climbed the steps to the front porch. He was already three hours late on his own route after picking up half of Frank's. He'd had to gas up the mail truck after *someone* forgot yesterday, he'd hit a traffic jam on Old Clevedon Road…and now this. He'd be lucky to catch the last half of *Dancing with the Stars* by the time he got home.

Lenny rapped on the front door.

Leave it inside, the woman had said. Not in the mailbox, not on the porch, but *inside*. Lenny remembered this request very well, but heck if he was going to open some stranger's door without at least knocking first. He just wasn't that sort of man.

Lenny rapped on the door again and waited, taking in the broken porch rails, bird nest in the rafters of the porch roof, peeling purple paint by the door. And where the heck was the woman's mailbox? Lenny saw the lightened square by the door where the box had hung only yesterday. Now, though, there was only a rusted streak in the paint, but no mailbox. Of all the insults the house inflicted on the neighborhood, Lenny suddenly found the lack of mailbox to be the worst.

Lenny gripped the package tighter under his arm, not caring if his sweat stains rubbed off onto the brown wrapping. He was reaching for the doorknob when it suddenly turned by itself.

"Yes?"

The woman slouched against the door frame and leveled her eyes so that her gaze fell somewhere around the tuft of chest hair that poked through the top of his work shirt. She wore a sweatshirt that hung to her knees, ratty jeans, no shoes. She'd obviously just woken up.

"You're here," Lenny said.

"Yes."

"You were supposed to be gone?"

The woman flinched, a quick tightening of her shoulders, a twitch at her hand. She finally looked at him, and Lenny saw eyes as washed out as the sweatshirt she wore. She said nothing, just stared at him like some hungry dog.

Lenny began to think he'd imagined their conversation from a few days before.

"You said you'd be gone," Lenny repeated, embarrassed now for no reason at all. He held up the package. Shook it slightly, hoping to rattle her memory.

"You were traveling? The package was coming today, you said. You were going to leave the door unlocked?"

"Oh."

"You said to leave it inside. That you'd leave the door unlocked and that I was to come in and leave it inside." Lenny sighed, a big breath that blew a limp strand of hair off the woman's shiny forehead.

Nothing. Just a slow blink.

"Well, here." Lenny shoved the package at her, his embarrassment quickly dissolving into anger. "Next time, you can put a hold on your mail, you know. You don't have to—"

But she'd already closed the door and Lenny was talking to himself on the empty porch.

Rude. But what could you expect?

Non-Christmas-tipper.

6:16 p.m.

Jared watched Clare's front door swing shut. He watched the mailman trundle back down the front walk, knees jiggling beneath boxy shorts. A car approached on his left, and Jared raised his hand, pretending to scratch his face.

If anyone asked why Jared was parked on the street outside of Clare Lyndsay's house, Jared had his story in place. There was a repo right around the corner, a 2009 Hummer H3 SUV, 3.5 liter, 220 horses, cherry-popping red. The skip tracer found it a few days ago. The owner was parking it at a friend's house, as if Jared hadn't seen *that* trick a thousand times. For anyone who happened by, it would be the repo story Jared would spin. It was the goddamned cop Jared had to watch for, that officious son of a bitch.

The mailman strode into the street, barely acknowledging the car that jittered to a stop to let the man pass. He climbed into the mail truck, slammed the door harder than necessary, and slid into traffic with a puff of black smoke from the tailpipe.

Repoing cars in broad daylight actually proved for many fruitless hours for Jared, whole days wasted sometimes, waiting on side streets and eating cold ham sandwiches. Jared used to work at night. Back in the day, he'd loved the empty streets, loved walking up to a house filled with laughter and light behind the curtains and claiming something of that life for his own. It was such a high, that sense of power that filled him to the toes when he slipped into a repo and disappeared into the darkness. And he was good at it, excellent even. For the first time in his life, Jared was better at something than those around him. And he was making decent money, thanks to the lingering effects of the 2008 recession, not that Jared had much to show for it. Cash under the table melted fast in the basin of a spoon.

It was the darkness Jared had enjoyed the most, though, the seeing, but not being seen. The knowing, but not being known. Jared went through a Raymond Chandler phase a few years back and still enjoyed thinking of himself as the hardboiled detective, Philip Marlowe. Dark. Brooding. Filled with sadness and yearning. Handsome as hell. "Dead men are heavier than broken hearts." Jared loved that line. All his computer passwords were still set at Marloweman69. (Jared knew very well that he was no Philip

Marlowe, that he was not, in fact, the hero even of his own life story. If Jared were honest with himself, he'd admit that he identified stronger with the character of the murdered chauffeur Chandler left in the trunk and then so famously "forgot all about.")

Jared hadn't told anyone but his brother that he'd switched to days, and he regretted the telling immediately. Elwin had laughed at him, just as the guys at the garage would have laughed at him. But the cover of night had just become too hazardous for Jared's liking. After years of dogs, knives, baseball bats, a fire poker, and not one but *two* separate chainsaw incidents, it was finally a 2008 Jaguar XJ, platinum silver, 4.2 V8 from the previous summer that changed Jared's mind about nighttime repos. The owner of the Jaguar had surprised Jared, had snuck up behind Jared in the driveway as Jared worked the air wedge in the driver's side window. Jared heard a click and then felt a hard coldness against the back of his neck. "You're on my property with suspicious intent," the owner had said, perfectly calm. "Get the fuck out of here before I blow your goddamn head off."

And so Jared had got the fuck out of there, cursing the psycho with the gun, cursing himself, but mostly cursing Elwin for not showing up that night and making Jared go it alone.

Jared spotted a white car through the bushes, and he reached for the gear shift, ready to peel out from the curb. As the car turned the corner, Jared relaxed his hand. It wasn't the cop's cruiser. Officer wetback must have found someone else to protect and serve up his bullshit this afternoon. How a spic like that ever found a job in the force, Jared would never understand. (That some of his animosity toward Ben might stem from Jared's long-forgotten childhood fantasy of becoming a police officer was not a connection Jared would ever make.)

Jared had returned to the house of the 2008 Jaguar a few days later and with a piece of his own. Elwin had had a good laugh over Jared's purchase, snatching up the .22 from the package and twirling it around, calling it an "old-lady's fart," but Jared ignored him. Jared's gun was cheap and easy to use, even if the ad on the website had said it was a popular choice for "the disabled and elderly."

On the day Jared returned for the Jaguar, he parked his rig beneath a low-hanging sugar maple and watched the front door of the house through the fluttering branches as the sun came up. At 7:08, the door opened and the psycho with the gun stepped onto the porch—pin-striped suit, shiny shoes, shiny bald head. A woman followed, bare feet, wrapped in a man's bathrobe. She gave him something, square-ish, black—a cell phone, a wallet, a remote-control detonator—leaned up to say something in his ear. Psycho-gun-slinger patted the woman on her ass, his hand hardly reaching purchase through the thick robe and then turned to wave at the doorway. One, then another small, blonde-headed child appeared. They bounced up and down in the doorway for no apparent reason, like whac-a-moles at the carnival.

Jared leveled his new .22 at psycho-gun-slinger's head. "Pow," he said softly. Moving toward the woman, "pow." He shifted the barrel of the gun toward the doorway.

"Pow. Pow."

Jared let the white car pass, fumbling in his pocket for the garlic cloves he'd stuffed in there that morning. The garlic was his only relief from the pain these days. The ice didn't touch it anymore and the pills he'd pilfered from his mother's nightstand were long gone. Jared crunched a clove carefully with his front teeth, using his tongue to shove some of the mush into the decaying tooth at the back of his mouth. The throbbing worsened for a moment and there was a sharp sting as Jared pressed with his tongue. Then the pain eased.

It was a 2007 Nissan Altima hybrid Jared was after the day he saw Clare Lyndsay. Jared had been sitting in his rig just off Old Clevedon Road, late April, stereo blasting, waiting for the owner to show when Clare simply drove past him in a green 2000 Kia Sportage. If the sight of Clare had not been so brief, so clouded by passing shadows, her image recognized only in afterthought, Jared would never have identified the woman behind the wheel as the girl he'd known when he was a boy. The Clare that Jared remembered had been soft, round in the face and shoulders, bright in the eyes, a deep smile. He'd had a schoolboy's crush, perhaps, and the strength of it, the raw force of his feeling had startled Jared after all these years.

The Nissan forgotten, Jared had driven home immediately, showered, shaved, and returned a few hours later with a bottle of tequila and no agenda other than reconnecting with an old friend. (That he and Clare had *not* been friends, quite the opposite in fact, and that he'd bought a fresh pack of condoms with the bottle of tequila were incongruities Jared's mind easily dismissed.) Clare met him at the door already half-toasted, by the smell on her breath. Surprisingly, incredibly, Clare welcomed Jared inside, shared a can of soup, even drank with him. He slipped a little helper into her glass when she went to the bathroom, just to speed things along, and overall, Jared couldn't believe his good fortune.

Later, on the couch though, nothing about Clare seemed familiar. Not the bony angles of her hips, the hollowed line of her stomach, the sallow tint of her cheeks. But the lemony scent of her hair and the taste of her salted skin was fucking delicious—a synesthesiac high more powerful than the meth. Jared's mouth roamed hungrily over her neck and shoulders as his body pressed hers. Her panties were silk, his favorite, as if she *knew*, as if she'd planned the whole thing!—and soft as cream when he slipped his hand inside.

It seemed she changed her mind halfway through (as many of the women Jared was with seemed to do, though Jared was unaware of any pattern, choosing instead to interpret their "no's" as flirty female behavior), but by that time Jared had Clare on the kitchen table, and it was too late. They'd tussled a bit and the noises she made turned him rock hard, forcing him to finish quicker than he liked. They ended up on the floor, and she'd whimpered a little, nothing too dramatic, thank god. He hated it when they got dramatic (Jared rubbed at his neck without thinking, where Clare's scratches had long faded), and when it was over—she, sprawled across the linoleum, he, leaned against the wall, smoking a cigarette—she mumbled something, drunken, slurred. Something that sounded like "how's the other guy," but Jared couldn't be sure. Honestly, he hadn't cared.

It had gone on like that for a couple of weeks. Sometimes she drank with him, sometimes she fought him, sometimes she cried, other times she fell asleep on his naked stomach when it was over. Jared enjoyed the sex either way. It was a good thing they had going.

Was.

A week ago, the bitch threw him out. Out of nowhere. No warning. Caught him off-guard and just drove him out the door before he even knew what happened. Jared had blundered about like an idiot, had had to button his pants on the goddamn porch. On fucking Memorial Day no less, when he'd taken off early just to see her. No one had ever done that to him before. No one.

Jared waited in his rig, watching Clare's door long after the mailman had driven away. He didn't have a plan yet. Only a memory and an idea. Until he had a plan, he would wait. Jared moved his hand from the faded scratches on his neck to the .22 on the seat beside him.

After a long while, Jared picked up the pen and began to write in his notebook:

BLUNDER
PLUNDER
PILLAGE
DESECRATE
DEVOUR

6:16 p.m.

Clare shut the door and sat back down in the kitchen. She set the package on the table and stared at it. The fluorescent light was off, but the late afternoon sun that lit the backyard shone through the windows over the kitchen sink, brightening the area where Clare sat at one end of her kitchen table. The items she'd placed on the table the night before were still there, lined up together in a neat row, photograph askew. Clare focused only on the package.

Clare Lyndsay
1842 Shalott Drive
Kinderkamack, NJ 07640

She ran her fingers over her own neat script, tracing the careful curve of the *C* with her nail, the elongated tail of the *Y*. Clare peeled back the packing tape and unfolded the brown wrapping paper. She placed the book on the table without a sound. *Blind Man and the Elephant* by Jivraj Syed. Clare read the title and the author once, twice, ten times and then pushed the book as far away from her on the table as she could reach. *Jivrah, like "gibberish" but with a v instead of a bah sound, and an "ah" of enlightenment at the end,* she could still hear him say. Clare sat, staring at the book.

The refrigerator stumbled on, rattled off. Knocked on again. And off. Clare's mind was blank, her thoughts a benign hum she could safely ignore. She tipped the prescription bottle on its side and rolled it back and forth with the tip of her finger. The plastic bumped each time over a large knot in the old wood grain, jostling the pills inside.

It was only when the light shifted in the kitchen and Clare could no longer actually see the book at the end of the table that she remembered the clock on the microwave. 7:57. Clare set the bottle upright. Pushed it back into its lineup.

She was late.

Clare checked the numbers on the side of the house against those written on the folded piece of lavender stationery she pulled from her pocket. *Homerton 1833. 7 o'clock. Don't be late.* This was the place.

It was still dusk at 8:15 in mid-June and the cul-de-sac was enjoying its extra hour of daylight. A shoeless toddler riding a plastic bus rolled down the driveway at the next house. A man on a cell phone washed his car in an identical driveway at the house across the circle. The odor of detergent and chemicals laced the air. Someone was barbecuing and beneath that, Clare detected the greenish scent of the pond that lay just south of the housing development.

Clare opened the screen door, held it with her foot as she struggled with the object in her arms, and then stopped. What was she doing? Clare suddenly felt foolish on her errand—idiotic perhaps, in the reckless connotation of the word. Better to simply leave what Mr. Hallam had given her on the woman's porch. Or on the front walk by the garden—

"Can I help you?"

The woman who opened the door looked like she'd been crying. Her gray eyes held a strange, blurred look and the skin beneath them was swollen, tender. A rash reddened the area beneath her bulbed nose, around her swollen mouth, and spread down her squat neck to her chest. She wore a lilac-colored bathrobe, nappy at the hems, and tennis sneakers with no socks. Her hair was drawn away from her face and pulled tight, so tight it seemed to raise her eyebrows at their corners. She gripped the folds of her robe across her bosom and frowned at Clare as much as her taut skin allowed.

Clare took a step back and completely forgot what she was going to say.

The frown opened into a look of surprise and curiosity. "Clare?"

That this woman knew her name struck Clare as surreal in some way, which only worsened her ability to speak. She took another step away from the door.

"Clare, wow. I heard you'd moved back to town. It's Penelope, remember? Penelope Baker? Well, it's Homerton now, but—oh my god, you found it!"

The woman rushed forward and plucked the ceramic garden gnome from Clare's hands. Her breath briefly warmed Clare's cheek, fruity, rich, an undertone of alcohol. "Oh, thank goodness, it's okay. I don't know what I would have done." She turned the little troll upside-down several times, checking for damage.

"It's part of a set, you know. You can't buy these anymore."

Penelope gestured toward the hydrangea bushes at the side yard where a gnome holding a wheelbarrow stood beside another gnome who brandished a shovel. A browned spot in the grass beside the couple suggested a spot for the gnome holding the yellow flower that Clare had just delivered. Further along the bushes, Clare saw more gnomes. One holding a lantern, another riding a motorcycle, still more lounging in a hammock, others gathered around a mushroom table playing poker. Walking up to the house, Clare had spotted a koi pond in the backyard with several gnomes fishing beside a musical band of gnomes complete with banjo, ukulele, and squeezebox players.

"Thank you so much, you have no idea," Penelope was saying, polishing the buttocks of the gnome with the cuff of her bathrobe. "But where did you find it, I looked all over."

"Oh. Well, I uh—"

Penelope suddenly stopped rubbing the gnome and stared hard at Clare. "Never mind. I know exactly where you found it."

"You do?"

Penelope's voice had changed, and the woman was now looking over Clare's shoulder as she spoke, her swollen eyes narrowed into pinkish slits. "I appreciate your returning it, Clare, really. We'll have to catch up sometime."

Slamming the door shut behind her, Penelope brushed past Clare and hurried down the porch steps toward the sidewalk, bathrobe bouncing. She gripped the gnome around its neck in one hand, swinging the little troll wildly with each of her strides.

Clare stared after her. "Okay…"

The man on the cell phone took one look at Penelope storming across the cul-de-sac and quickly ended his call.

"*Cecilia!*"

"I want to speak with your daughter," Penelope said. "Right now."

The man dropped the hose on the driveway and shoved his cell phone into his pocket. He raised both hands to Penelope in either a gesture of calming or defense. "I know, I know. She's coming. *Cecilia!*" He called again.

"And then you and I are going to have a conversation, Mr. Lushington. This absolutely cannot continue." She waved the gnome at the man, punctuating each word.

"I know, Mrs. Homerton. Trust me, we'll figure this out."

A blond girl in ripped cut-offs and an Eagles football jersey that hung nearly to her knees emerged from the back of the house. She was missing her cape, but Clare recognized her all the same. The girl stopped short when she spotted Penelope with the gnome in the driveway. She slipped behind one of the bushes beneath the side windows of the house and crouched down, hidden, watching.

"*Cee-Cee!* Get out here!"

ALBERT

Until the summer of 2010, Albert had committed only three acts of criminal activity in his life. First, an arrest for stealing a car when he was sixteen. That the car was his father's, and that Albert was driving it to pick up his sister from their aunt's house was of little importance to the Bergen County police officer who pulled him over. The officer heard the red bumpers of Henry Hallam's Diamond T truck rattling from a half mile away and was convinced the boy was trouble when he saw the driver, one hand flung out the window, beating out a drumbeat on the truck's door and singing loudly to a tune that apparently played only in his head (Sarah Vaughan's *Perdido*, whom Albert had seen perform a few years prior when she opened for Ella Fitzgerald at the Apollo in New York City). The entire matter was cleared up within a day, which included seven hours in a holding cell. As Albert and his father left the police station, the chief of police himself shook young Albert's hand and assured father and son that Bergen County welcomed peoples of all color *and wasn't it just something that Jackie Robinson would join the Dodgers for the '47 season? Just something...* It was Albert's father who propelled him quickly out of the building before Albert actually did commit a crime.

When Albert was 21 and on semester break from Temple University, he accidentally packed a library copy of Edmond Hamilton's *Horror on the Asteroid* into the back of that same Diamond T, borrowed again from his father. His girlfriend, nursing student, Emily Nosynnét (soon to become Emily Hallam) read the book while they drove along LR 164 (today's US 209) through the Pocono Mountains of Pennsylvania. They were on their way to Shawnee on the Delaware, where Albert would caddy for the summer and Emily would make beds (one of which would be Lucille Ball's, whom Emily met briefly in the hall one morning, reporting only a red sparkle wrap, a faint scent of almonds, and a dismissive nod from her encounter). Emily hated every story she found in *Horror on the Asteroid*, believed Hamilton to be a deranged man, and—though she continued to read—

threatened to sling the book out the window several times between Wind Gap and Stroudsburg. Albert finally rescued the book from Emily, returned it to the box in which he would mail it back to the library when they reached the inn, and made it up to her in kisses. They found a warm, secluded swatch of meadow off the road and swayed barefoot in the grass to a little waltz Albert hummed deep in his throat. Emily laughed softly in Albert's arms and then whispered his name over and over against his ear, as he made love to her with a soft breeze tickling his bare behind.

In December of 1969—after the Stonewall Riots quieted in lower New York and a half million people descended on the Yasgur Farm in upper New York, after Neil and Buzz met Kennedy's goal with five months to spare, but before the Jackson Five made their first appearance on the Ed Sullivan Show—Albert was 39 and teaching American history to twelfth-graders at Kinderkamack Senior High. He and Emily had been married sixteen years the night Craven Hawtrey pounded at their door, half-drunk at two in the morning, out of money, out of friends, and out of ideas. Hawtrey had dropped out of Albert's fifth period US government class earlier in the year and Albert recognized the boy immediately through the split in the living room draperies—boney fingers raking through his clumped hair, purple Nehru shirt billowing over his bell-bottoms, bare feet shoved into a pair of dirty sandals. Before Albert could object, Emily had opened the door, shuttled the boy onto the living room couch—*they read my number first thing, man, first thing*—and hurried to the kitchen to make him up a plate of leftover chicken. Emily would hear none of Albert's protests, only ordered him upstairs for extra blankets and a pair of Albert's old shoes, while she emptied their yellow sugar bowl into Hawtrey's open hand, all $347. *He came here, Al. He came to us.* In the morning, Hawtrey was gone and a day later, Albert learned the boy was dead. He'd leapt from the bushes where he'd been hiding and was accidentally run down by the bus that would have taken him into Canada. Albert never saw any reason to tell his wife.

For all of Albert's seventy-nine years, this had been the cumulative extent of his run-ins with the law. That is, until the summer of 2010. But Albert learned that sometimes people change. Desperate times and all that.

Tuesday, June 8th 2010 (continued)
9:03 p.m.

It was full night by the time Albert returned to the house. He fumbled his way along the fence in the dark, stopped at the rose bushes, and turned into the little path through the side yard, clutching his brown paper bag under one arm and holding out the other to steady his walk. He reached the unlit back door of his house and used the railing to pull himself up the steps.

Once inside, Albert placed the paper bag where he kept it under the kitchen sink and tossed his yellow slicker on the couch. Standing in the darkness, Albert waited a few breaths until the pounding in his ears subsided. Then he turned on the lamp in the living room and opened the front door.

"You're just in time."

Albert stepped away from the door and gestured for Clare to come inside, but she only continued to sit on the porch steps, staring at him. She looked so surprised, so utterly at a loss. The experience had an opening effect on Clare's face. Her eyes widened, nostrils flared, mouth drooped into a little 'o'. Albert held back a chuckle.

"But…I knocked."

"Come in, come in. You're letting in the bugs."

Clare got slowly to her feet, still staring. Albert gestured her inside, reaching behind her to shut the door. "You like seafood, right? Here, make yourself at home."

He motioned toward the sofa and left Clare in the living room while he went into the kitchen, still talking. "Pathmark had a sale on Saturday, buy one pound, get one free. Should have frozen it, I guess." He waited, but there was no response. "I'm a sucker for sales, it's a retirement thing, I think. Last time it was bananas. Nine cents a pound, if you can believe that. Ate them for a week."

Albert returned to the living room, drying his hands on a dishtowel. Clare still stood by the front door, hands tucked in her pockets. Her gray t-shirt fell like a drop cloth from her shoulders, hanging loosely over her jeans. She'd tied a ponytail at the back of her neck—frizzled hair dipped in ash at the roots—and wore flip-flops, revealing chipped bare toenails. What was she now, thirty-five? Thirty-eight? Albert couldn't remember.

Clare had showered and changed her clothes since that morning, which Albert took as a good sign.

"So what do you think?"

"What do I think?"

"Snow peas and shrimp. Sound good?"

Clare shook her head and turned toward him. Her eyes were wide and full of curiosity. Another good sign.

"What is this?"

"Dinner?"

"No, with the...with that stupid gnome. She thinks the papergirl took it."

"Ah. You were late," Albert said, clicking his tongue.

"No, I was, well—"

"Was it schnapps? Sangria? No, no, definitely schnapps." Albert answered his own question, scratching under his chin and muttering toward the ceiling as he thought about it. "Peach or maybe strawberry, she seems like a strawberry—"

"What? What are you talking about?"

"Silent sufferer by day, combative after the drinking hour. It's classic alcoholic-in-training. I told you not to be late."

But Clare had stopped listening. She looked behind Albert and took a step into the room. Albert moved aside, silent. Clare had spotted the photograph. Earlier, Albert had moved the clutter from the desk and placed the photograph on one corner, highly visible from the doorway. He'd found the photo in a box upstairs and had dusted off the picture's wooden frame before setting it on the desk that morning.

Without speaking, Albert crossed the room, picked up the photograph, and handed it to Clare. The photo was one Albert remembered well. Albert had taken it himself the night Emily helped him chaperone the senior dance at the high school, the night that had ended with the two of them parked by the pond and making out in the back of the station wagon like a couple of teenagers. (Albert drove an AMC Ambassador at the time, after the AMC Pacer had broken down beyond repair. They'd traded in his Diamond T long before for a family car, back when there had still been hope for children.)

Before the dance, Albert had driven home from the school to change and pick up Emily. The Nikon FE2 he and Emily had taken on their trip up north the previous weekend was still on the car seat beside him, and the scene Albert had found on the porch caused him to pick up the camera without thinking.

Emily and Clare were rocking on the porch swing bench together. Clare was sleeping, and her hair had still been long that day, long, blond braids that trailed across her sunburned shoulders. A book lay open on her chest, its spine broken, its cover frayed at the edges. That was the summer of *Tuck Everlasting*. Clare went everywhere with that book, Albert had even seen it tucked into the waistband of her shorts as she sped by the house on her bike. Albert had taken to calling her Winnie that summer, to which Clare had responded with a toothy grin.

Clare's head rested on his wife's lap. Emily was already dressed and ready for the dance (in all their years of marriage, she had never made him wait.) Her skirt was frothy lace, her bare legs were crossed at the ankles, and her skin glowed like amber in the dusky sun. Her eyes were closed. She'd been 43 that day on the porch and Albert had watched Emily for a long while, savoring the moment. She had never been more beautiful. But in truth, he'd had such a thought about his wife many times before.

"You must have been eight or nine there, I think." Albert watched Clare carefully. He kept his voice casual. "You loved to play in our yard with your little dolls, and you had that giant yellow bike."

Clare didn't respond. Her mouth had softened, and there was a wetness gathering in the corner of her eyes.

"You zoomed up and down the street and did all these crazy tricks, feet on the handlebars and such. Emily and I, we were always afraid you'd fly off that thing one day. Just go soaring into the sky."

"I loved that bike."

Albert let out a long breath. It had been just before Thanksgiving last fall when Clare moved back into the house next door. He'd seen her through the window that Tuesday afternoon, knew her immediately, and gone right away to greet her. She was pulling a box out of the back of her car when Albert stepped up behind her with a hearty greeting. But when she turned, there had been no recognition at all in Clare's pale eyes. Instead, the look Albert found on Clare's face chilled him to silence. Albert had watched six years of footage from Vietnam on his television set; he'd seen the blanket devastation caused by bombs that fell and flattened everything—trees, buildings, people—caught within the radius of the explosion. This is what Albert found in Clare's look. It was a look as blank as a blast zone. Total destruction. Nothing else.

Albert watched Clare now, standing in his living room with the photograph in her hand and he let out a single, long-held breath in response to what she'd said. So she did remember. Of course she did.

"Let's get some dinner, shall we?" Albert lifted the photo gently from her hands. "And there's ice cream for dessert. Hope you like mint-chocolate chip."

Clare looked up at Albert and began to speak. Her mouth worked anxiously, and she frowned, trying to form her thoughts into words. But Albert knew this wasn't the time. He shook his head, stopping her.

Relief loosened all the muscles in Clare's face. She let out a breath, dropped her shoulders. "Okay."

Albert crossed the room to return the photo to the desk, noting the change in Clare's voice. It was subtle, wedged within just that one syllable, but it was there. With the change, Albert also noticed something different in the room. Something had shifted between them. A space had opened up, wide and wonderful. *You were right again, Emily*, Albert thought. *Now we can get started.* And as he set the photo on the desk, bumping a stack of papers and sending them sailing to the floor, Albert knew that Clare felt the change as well.

Clare reached down to help him retrieve the fallen papers from beneath the desk and sofa. She flipped through the small sheets, but Albert plucked them from her hands before she could read what was written on the tickets.

When Clare looked up, Albert saw she was almost smiling.

"Parking or speeding?"

"What do you think?"

Clare thought a moment. "Definitely not speeding."

Albert grinned. "Oh, you'd be surprised."

8:47 p.m.

Clare knocked again, leaning toward the door to listen. After a moment, she moved to the window and cupped her hands by her face to peer inside. The lights were off in Mr. Hallam's house, not even the porch light was on. Clare shook her head and paced back and forth on the porch—paused at the steps, back to the door. Finally, just as Ben thought she would return to her own house, Clare sat heavily on the top porch step, thrust her clenched hands between her knees. She stared over the rose bushes that lined Mr. Hallam's front yard, toward the street.

Ben watched her through the windshield of the cruiser. He'd parked on Fifth Street, a block away, but he still had a clear line of sight through the hedges, down the sidewalk on the east side of Shalott Drive, and along both the Hallam and the Lyndsay house. Ben watched Clare take a deep breath and turn her face up to the night sky. She rubbed her arms, hugged herself, let her shoulders slump forward.

She was smaller than Ben remembered, which of course, made no sense. The last time he'd seen Clare they'd both been twelve years old. She'd been a child, still round in the face, chubby arms, a sturdy quick gait. But she'd been tall for her age, two inches taller than Ben. And she'd had a way of moving that took up all the space around her, a confidence that seemed to reach out in all directions. Ben remembered a day on the bus home from school when he'd said something to make her laugh—he was always trying to make her laugh—and the sound felt warm and wonderful, expansive and generous in ways Ben was far too young to understand at the time.

This Clare appeared shrunken, though, folded into herself in a way that happens to some people over the years, Ben thought. The effects of a lot of time and a lot of life.

Ben knew something about the withering effects of time. It had been eight, no, nine years already since Ben himself had been dealt a blow that made him feel as if he'd grown smaller in ways he was still discovering. Ben blew slowly through his mouth as that number settled around him. In September it would be nine years, yes. It was one of those "before and after" dates, or at least that's how Ben thought about it. One of those events in life that splits your storyline in two—your life before something happens, and then the life you have to lead after. The split for Ben had started with a scream, one so wild and so guttural Ben had not, at first, recognized it as human. Before that moment, Ben had been unaware that the human body could summon such a sound. Sometimes Ben thought about his life before that scream, before his world had transformed so enormously, so grotesquely. Ben could barely recognize the smiling, easy-going man he used to be. Ben's life had simply divided in two. There was the Ben he'd been before that night, and person he became after.

Clare lowered her head, bringing her face down to meet her knees, her arms still wrapped tightly around herself. The longer Ben watched, the more he began to understand that Clare had probably stumbled into more than one split in her storyline so far.

You nobody hero.

In his memory, the words were always tangled with the scent of tomatillo sauce and incense, the voice was a warm breath filled with worry and disappointment. As Ben watched Clare from his parked police cruiser, he heard the words as clearly now as he did when he was a child. There was a time when he planned to prove that voice wrong. But now he knew it to be true. For nine years he'd known the truth. For nine years he'd played the part of the hero, put on the uniform, said all his lines. For nine years he'd hidden the secret of his failure inside the costume. (But what Ben would learn, and in just a mere 22 days, is that his hero's journey is far from over.)

The prints had come back on the Landryes' case that morning. Croker's hit, of course, but so had a dozen others. The print match wasn't even enough to pick up Croker for questioning, according to the investigator in charge. With no eyewitness accounts and scant evidence at the apartment, it was the DNA that would seal the deal, the bits of skin they'd scraped from beneath Elizabeth Landryes' fingernails, the strand of dark hair they'd found on her body (Lacy was blond), the rape kit they'd performed on the unconscious woman. Ben's contact believed it could be thirty days, even sixty before the DNA results would be finished. "But it could be sooner, if the vic dies," the man added, as if to reassure Ben. "Everything moves faster for a murder investigation."

There was movement on the sidewalk, a flash of yellow in the dark. Ben sat forward, watching the figure of a man appear beneath a streetlight. Tall, African American, mid-seventies, medium build, wearing a yellow raincoat and carrying a brown paper bag. The man stopped short, having spotted Clare sitting on the porch steps. Stepping quickly off the sidewalk, the man hurried through the side yard and disappeared behind the house.

Ben shook his head. "Oh, Mr. Hallam. What am I going to do with you?"

A moment later, the lights came on in the living room, followed by the light on the porch. Clare spun around as the front door opened. There was conversation, some hesitation, but Ben never saw what happened next.

Headlights had come to rest on the side street where Ben was parked. The vehicle had been traveling south along Shalott Drive and had turned left in front of Ben. It parked, and its red taillights winked out just as Ben reached for the door handle of the cruiser.

Ben got out of the car, crossed Shalott Drive, and approached the vehicle in a wide angle at the back left bumper, avoiding both the driver's side and rearview mirrors.

The vehicle was Jared Croker's black tow truck.

21 DAYS

Wednesday, June 9, 2010
10:27 a.m.

The next morning Clare rolled the big yellow bike out of the shed in the backyard. Twenty-five years of renters had not disturbed the shed, oddly enough, though there was damage to the roof in the back corner and evidence that a family of squirrels had made their home among the water-ruined boxes. Clare found a bag of toys—a faded Speak & Spell, a stuffed Curious George who looked less curious and more tired, one strap-on roller skate, Garfield playing cards, a rotting Strawberry Shortcake doll that had long lost her fruity scent—the wooden rails to her old bed, framed prints stacked against one wall that included both a Judy Chicago and a Hannah Wilke, a rusted push lawnmower, and a plastic snowman that stared at her menacingly from its remaining eye. Beneath the dim window and buried under a crate of books was an old steamer trunk. Inside the trunk were her mother's journals.

(Had Clare read her mother's journals that day, she would have found that Alice Lyndsay arranged her journals geographically, rather than chronologically. She'd written no dates on the journals, only the place or country name in large block letters across the weathered covers: BRAZIL—six months of graduate research, RUANDA-URUNDI—her dissertation work, URUGUAY—the two years of independent research, where she had a brief fling with a member of the *Tupamaros* and fled the country after he was tortured and killed, and NEW MEXICO—her research fellowship with the Zuni Pueblo, many of whom spoke kindly of the great Ruth Benedict who had visited them only a generation before.

The journal Alice labeled with only a small CA in one bent corner chronicled her year in northern California. This was the year before Alice Lyndsay finally returned home from her travels, four months pregnant with Clare, thirty-three years old, already published twice in *Current Anthropology* and gaining a name for herself in the circle of woman's theory. The California journal was empty. Not blank-page empty, but sheets-ripped-from-the-spine-in-tears-and-rage-leaving-only-jagged-edges empty. The California journal laid deeply buried beneath the other journals, but wrapped in a scarf, the empty book carefully preserved over the years.)

But on the day Clare rolled her old yellow bike from the shed, Clare entirely ignored the trunk that held her mother's journals. Clare knew only, Alice Lyndsay, professor of woman's studies at Columbia University; author of *Vagina Dentate and the Fallacy of Rape*, a satirical work that nearly got her fired and in which she described a barbed device a female might insert into her vagina to protect against unwanted invasion (a device, coincidentally enough, very much like Rape-aXe, an anti-rape condom which was distributed to more than 30,000 South American women during the 2010 World Cup, with the tagline: *If men can use their bodies as a weapon, it's time for women to do the same*); Alice Lyndsay, single mother and occasional obsessive personality who once wrote with Clare's red finger paint, *"CULTURE IS PERSONALITY WRIT LARGE"* in foot-high letters across her blue bedroom wall; Alice Lyndsay, who transformed their entire house into a Midnight Plum fantasy-castle one frenzy-powered weekend; and Alice Lyndsay, under whose bed Clare would often crawl at night, long after the woman fell asleep, just to be close to her mother during the only time of day it was safe to do so.

Clare leaned over the crates of books, banged her shin on the trunk filled with journals and grabbed the bike pump from where it sat in the windowsill. Finding the yellow bike was a whim, really. Some leftover from her conversation with Albert the night before. Clare hadn't put much thought into what she was doing. She knew only that she suddenly wanted to see her old bike again and, upon having found it, wanted to restore its banana-yellow chrome to its previous radiant shine.

"What are you doing?"

Clare turned and saw the papergirl on the sidewalk behind her, one foot on a pedal of her bike, one foot on the sidewalk, purple cape hanging around her ankles. Clare had heard the girl approach, since the screeching chain of her bicycle could be heard from down the block. Now that she'd met the girl's eyes, Clare saw clearly that the bravado of her voice did not match what Clare found on the girl's face.

There was fear there, and some suspicion. Clare remembered the father calling her Cee-Cee, and Cee-Cee lingered on the sidewalk, taking care not to step onto Clare's driveway.

Clare turned back to the bucket of soapy water.

"What does it look like?"

"Is that *your* bike? Cool."

Clare didn't respond. A moment passed. Then another. A car horn sounded down the block.

"Hey, I was wondering if you, I mean, I was gonna ask you if maybe…"

Clare came around to the other side of the bike and sloshed the sponge up and down its back fender. She watched Cee-Cee through the wheel spokes. The question Cee-Cee wanted to ask was so plainly written in the girl's eyes. Clare wondered how things had gone for her after Clare delivered the stolen gnome yesterday.

"Yeah?"

"Never mind."

Cee-Cee wheeled her bike a few feet down the sidewalk and then stopped again, brakes squeaking. Cars passed by in a steady stream along the street behind the girl. There were dogs barking somewhere and a heavy beat thudded from a passing car window. It was late in the morning and the sunlight made Cee-Cee scrunch up her nose when she turned again toward Clare.

"You wanna get the paper?"

This was not the question Cee-Cee wanted answered, and Clare almost smiled. Clare dropped the sponge in the bucket. Reached in, squeezed it.

"We have a sale. New customers get a free month."

"I don't read the paper."

"But he said…"

"Who said?"

The girl shrugged, fidgeting with the cape, pulling at a loose thread.

Clare finished wringing out the sponge and went to work on the bike seat, watching Cee-Cee from the corner of her eye. The girl's little blond head lowered, she dragged one foot thoughtfully across the pavement.

"Hey," Clare called. "That cape. Doesn't it ever get caught up in the tires?"

"Nah, not if you do it right."

Clare nodded and turned back to the bike.

"It's a cloak."

"What?"

Cee-Cee sighed, clearly having explained this to more than one adult. "It's a cloak. You fly with a cape. You do magic with a cloak. I was a wizardess last Halloween."

Again, Cee-Cee failed to pedal away. She fiddled with her bike pedal, spinning it with her toe. Clare had another thought.

"The man next door, he gets the paper, right?"

"Mr. Hallam? Oh yeah. He always pays six months up front. We get extra for that."

"You know him?"

Cee-Cee nodded vigorously and pedaled forward onto the driveway. The gears of her bike groaned loudly. "Yeah, he's been here forever. He used to be a teacher. He gave me this book one time. Grena... Grenadine Brooks?

"Gwendolyn."

"Yeah, anyway, my mom said it was 'over my head,' which is what she always says." Cee-Cee blinked suddenly, like something caught in her eyes. "Anyways, I understood all of it, so she was wrong about that too. My favorite was about the sun-slappers and the self-soilers, which made Freddie laugh so hard he almost—"

"'Even if you are not ready for day, it cannot always be night.'"

"Yeah! I remember that part." Cee-Cee was quiet for a moment. "Mrs. Kinsley at my school said Mr. Hallam was the very first black teacher there. Now we have three. Oh, and Miss Diaz. She's from Puerto Rico." Cee-Cee cocked her head at Clare and frowned suddenly. "Are you Puerto Rican?"

"He used to be married, right?"

"Yeah, Mrs. Hallam, she died a couple years ago," Cee-Cee said. "It was sad. They had a funeral and everything, but I wasn't allowed to go."

"Oh."

"And Mr. Hallam, he didn't come out of his house all year almost. I mean, *nobody* saw him. He didn't go on his walks, he missed the Fourth of July picnic, and I heard Mrs. Homewre—, I mean Mrs.

Homerton tell somebody that the ladies from the church had to make meals for him."

Cee-Cee shrugged. "But I knew he was okay."

"Yeah?"

"Yeah. He never let his papers pile up."

4:05 p.m.

"But what're we gonna do without Norman? It won't work without him."

"Shut up, Freddie. We gotta hurry."

"But what if everything else is gone too? What if they took our—"

"I said *come on.*"

Cee-Cee shoved Freddie forward and together they ran through the yard and into the woods that separated the pond from the housing development where she and Freddie lived. It was late in the afternoon and her father would be back from the store soon. He'd worked from home that day, keeping Cee-Cee virtual prisoner in the house. They didn't have much time.

"How'd they even find it anyhow? We hid it good."

"I don't know. Spies, I guess," Cee-Cee said, thinking of Mr. Hallam. And had he seen them just now? Would he tell her dad?

Freddie's eyes grew large. *"Spies?"*

Grabbing Freddie's arm, Cee-Cee dragged the boy behind her, both of them trampling over the thick vines and piles of dead leaves and debris at their feet. The sky in front of them illuminated brilliantly for and instant, lightening playing behind the clouds, followed by a low rumble. Cee-Cee wasn't worried, though. It had been cloudy all day, but had yet to rain one drop.

As she walked, tugging occasionally at Freddie's shirt, Cee-Cee mulled over the situation. Freddie had a point. Norman the Gnome had played the part of the wizard perfectly. He was mysterious and friendly, powerful and just a little bit evil. Where were they going to get another wizard?

"So how long you grounded for?"

"The rest of my life, my dad said." Cee-Cee let go of Freddie's arm to navigate a seeping mud puddle. "Maybe till Friday."

"So you can come to the movie on Saturday? My mom said she'd drive us, but—"

"Shhh," Cee-Cee hissed. "We're almost there."

Cee-Cee and Freddie came upon the place cautiously, stepping lightly, falling into whispers, searching for signs of the enemy invaders who had captured Norman. Cee-Cee half expected to find the log overturned and all of their collection smashed or stolen or strewn about the ground. She had already decided not to cry. Freddie would. Freddie always cried. But along with the not crying, Cee-Cee had also decided she would tease Freddie only a little this time. He *was* only ten, after all, and the loss of Norman *was* something of a tragedy. She could hardly blame the kid.

But upon arriving at their log, Cee-Cee and Freddie found that nothing had been disturbed. The pinwheel Cee-Cee had swiped from the Carlyle's yard was still out front, marking the spot, and when they knelt down to peer inside the log's hollowed innards, they sagged against each other in relief. It was all there—Freddie's snow globe they used as a crystal ball, the stock pot her father was still looking for and that doubled as a cauldron, the giant orange fur ball inside the stock pot that Freddie had spent two months collecting from his cat, the Pathmark glow necklaces she'd stashed under her shirt, the broom snatched from the Arnold's back porch, the broken yard flag rods they'd colored with a black sharpie and used as wands (which stained their palms and required much re-coloring), the stuffed dragon from the kindergarten room that barely fit inside her backpack on the last day of school, the plastic water bottles filled with rainwater potions—it was all there. Even the mailbox they'd taken from the Lyndsay house the other night. They planned to use the mailbox as a sort of talisman, a portal, perhaps, transporting messages to a secret realm and drawing its power from the haunted Lyndsay house. (Cee-Cee still maintained the house was not haunted, but she was not above allowing this bit of possibility, if only for the thrill of the theft.)

"But what're we gonna do without Norman?" Freddie was saying. "Can we find another one, do you think? Maybe one of those big Halloween pumpkins? My mom's got a bunch in the attic, no way she'd figure one was missing."

Cee-Cee wasn't listening. She'd spotted something at the far end of the log, behind their mound of treasures. It was propped up against the side of the log in the small clearing she'd made for Norman the Gnome.

Freddie followed her gaze and immediately dropped the plastic water bottle he'd been swishing in circles. "Cool! What's that?" He lunged forward, but Cee-Cee pulled him back.

"No, wait."

It was a feather. But it was a feather unlike either of them had ever seen. Cee-Cee knew instantly that the feather belonged to some ancient mystical creature. How else could it be so big? As long as her forearm, longer maybe. But what was most fantastical about the feather was its extraordinary color. The feather obviously had special powers, powers far greater than Norman's ever were. And as if proving the veracity of its magic, a beam of dazzling sunlight suddenly broke through the thundering clouds to shine down through a rotted-out hole in the log. A mist of dew sparkled like crystals on the feather's soft down, catching the ray in a million brilliant drops.

The feather was purple.

And as quickly as she knew where the feather came from and what it could do, she knew also that the feather was meant for her. Cee-Cee grinned and turned to Freddie.

"New game."

4:04 p.m.

The mail truck pulled up to the mouth of the cul-de-sac and stopped at the sidewalk with a tiny rattle of its engine. The truck's door swung open and a pudgy man in a short-sleeved work shirt and walking shorts got out. He was perhaps forty-five or fifty, if one could count jowl rolls like tree rings. He wore black leather shoes, black socks over his swollen calves, and a cricket cap with the words "United States Postal Service" scrawled across the front.

Albert moved further into the shadows of the elm tree and checked his watch. Rain waited in the clouds above. A ribbon of cool air wound through the neighborhood.

A door slammed to Albert's left, and he watched Cee-Cee, and the kid whose name Albert could never remember, tumble out of the house and onto the sidewalk. The papergirl was all business, pushing the kid from behind and steering them southward to the pond. Instead of taking the path, however, the two children cut through the yard and behind the Homerton house into the thick tangle of woods behind.

Albert had a feeling Cee-Cee had spotted him. The girl was sharp. But Albert knew where she was headed. And he knew she'd be happily distracted by what she found there.

The mailman filled his tote bag with envelopes and weekly circulars from the bins in the back of his truck, slammed the door shut, and walked into the cul-de-sac. Making short work of the first house, the mailman pulled an envelope from the box, slipped a circular inside, and lowered the metal flag. At the second house three geese were lounging in the side yard between a koi pond and a group of ceramic gnomes wearing plaid overalls. They were Canadian geese, round gray bellies, white stripe like a horse's bridle wrapped around their heads. The mailman flipped through the contents of his tote, withdrew a few white envelopes, folded one of the circulars in half and shoved everything inside the mailbox.

The geese never looked up.

Moving along the sidewalk, the mailman stepped around an overturned plastic bus and filled the next mailbox. The first few notes of Whitney Houston's "I Will Always Love You" suddenly filled the quiet cul-de-sac and the man pulled a large cell phone from his shorts pocket, read something on its screen, frowned, slipped it back into his pocket, and continued on his way.

A burst of lightening opened the sky to the south, on the other side of the pond. Several moments later thunder erupted slowly in the distance.

As the mailman neared the next house, the door to the second house opened and a woman in a bathrobe stepped onto the porch. She watched the mailman for a moment, then walked to her mailbox and withdrew the contents inside. As she turned, Albert saw her face alight in rage.

Shoving the envelopes back into the box, she picked up a garden hose from the grass, pulled the trigger, and aimed the nozzle at the lounging geese.

"Shoo! Get out of here, shoo!" The water came out in a fine mist and the geese only fluffed up their feathers and tucked their beaks into their bodies. "Shoo!"

Albert took note.

The mailman had by now reached the fourth house on the circle and as he approached, two massive Great Danes waited for him from behind the yard's whitewashed fence. They wagged their tails and panted in anticipation as the mailman drew near. In the house behind the two dogs, an orange cat curled against the window, watching with some interest. The mailman crossed over some invisible boundary line and the dogs let loose in a volley of enthusiastic barks. They jumped at the fence, and as the mailman walked by he gave wide berth to the massive barking canines.

The ruckus finally roused the lounging geese and in a flutter of flightless wings, the geese ran from the yard and disappeared behind the back of the house.

The woman in the bathrobe dropped the hose. She wiped her wet hands on the front of her robe and reached into the mailbox to retrieve her mail.

The mailman finished the last house on the cul-de-sac and returned to his truck. He raised his hand to Mrs. Homerton in greeting as he passed.

She blushed.

Albert took note.

8:37 p.m.

"Evening ma'am. Are you having some trouble?"

It was raining hard, but the policeman who stood at the back of Clare's hatchback was illuminated sharply in the headlights of his cruiser. He clutched a small pad of paper in one hand and held an umbrella high over his head with the other. As Clare drew closer she saw that the officer wore a long-sleeved blue shirt, navy tie, and black pants with a broad band of gold down each leg. A thick strap lay diagonally across his chest and held the pistol by his hip. There was something faintly German-army about his uniform, Clare thought, and it oddly juxtaposed the squared Hispanic face beneath his saucer-shaped hat.

The man watched her approach and, as she came up along the cruiser, he tipped his head, touching the brim of his hat with the pad of paper in a gentlemanly greeting that made Clare suddenly conscious of her bedraggled state.

"Is it engine trouble?"

"No, I, well…"

"There's no parking along this road except for emergencies." The officer glanced down at her muddy shoes and pants, and then up at her soaked shirt, her dripping face and hair. "Are you experiencing some sort of emergency?"

A half hour before, when Clare had first set out on her failed venture through the woods, it hadn't been raining and there was still some light left in the sky. She'd been driving north along Old Clevedon Road, headed back to town after an afternoon at the farmer's market in Paramus. Mr. Hallam had given her a list, another soft sheet of purple stationery, along the margin of which he'd written detailed notes— asparagus (*green down to the root, fluffy, some spring at the tips*), wild mushrooms (*light, not dark*), garlic (*2-3 cloves, large bulbs, skin intact*), and so on. Mr. Hallam was tired, he said—old men and their naps, he'd joked—and would rest while she shopped and then make them dinner when she returned.

Why Clare had agreed to such a thing—going to the store for the old man, agreeing to another dinner at all—was something Clare still didn't understand. The only rationale that made any sense to her was that she simply had nothing else planned. Two days ago, she'd had a plan. Two days ago, Clare had known exactly what the future held for her. The road ahead had stretched out in a narrow, clear, and short line. One that ended at the bottom of a pill bottle. Now…that road had disappeared. The way forward had vanished, obscured by Shepherd's Pie and garden gnomes. *Now*... Clare had planned nothing for this *now*. Nothing at all.

Clare had been on her way back from the farmer's market when she spun the volume down on the CD player (Eva Cassidy's Live at Blues Alley on replay) and pulled her car to the side of the road. She leaned over her purse and the heaping canvas bag of vegetables, and peered through the passenger side window.

The woods were dark. (Lovely and deep...) Even with the lingering light, Clare could see only a glistening flash of water through the thick summer undergrowth. Honock Pond lay directly east of Old Clevedon Road, south of the new housing development, and north of the public lands (where, in the fall, businessmen in camouflage and thermal onesies hunted anything unlucky enough to fly into their sights). The Kitane River fed the pond, traveling beneath the two bridges of Old Clevedon Road—one northbound, one southbound—two miles south of Kinderkamack. A half a mile north of where Clare had pulled to the side of the road, the grassy median between the north and southbound lanes of Old Clevedon Road disappeared and both lanes merged into Shalott Drive.

Clare and Albert lived in the older neighborhood on Shalott, just north of the housing development, but still within easy walking distance to the pond. The pond was fifteen walking minutes away at most, even for an eighty-year-old man in whale sneakers.

A truck had blown by as Clare peered out the car's window, spraying road grime across the windshield and rocking her tiny hatchback on its tires. She hit the car's HAZARD button and looked back toward the woods. There. A flash of yellow. She saw it again. That was no trick of light. If she hurried, Clare thought she might catch him. Checking her rearview mirror, Clare waited for a break in the traffic, opened her door, and slipped out of the car. After a moment's hesitation—*catch him and do what?*—Clare half ran, half slid down the steep embankment on the side of the road and then took off at a brisk walk into the woods.

Twice in the last few weeks, Clare had spotted Mr. Hallam pass her house in his yellow raincoat. Both times the sight of the old man in a raincoat, without a drop of rain in the sky, had barely pierced any level of her awareness. But last night, after she'd waited on the porch for half an hour, after the old man had somehow slipped into his house without Clare's notice, Clare saw the raincoat on the old man's couch. It had been tossed there, quickly, hastily. Later, he'd snatched it up and hung it on the hook behind the front door. Clare would have thought nothing at all about the coat, if not for the expression on the old man's face when he spotted it on the couch.

It was guilt.

Only a few minutes after she exited the car, Clare—out of breath, shoes soaked in mud, hair clumped against her cheeks—gave up and turned back toward the road. It had begun to rain by then, quickly become full dark, and so Clare had easily turned herself around in the wet, windy woods. For the next twenty minutes or so, Clare stumbled through muck, tripping over fallen tree branches, and had generally succumbed to the quiet panic that manifested itself in a string of mumbled obscenities…*a descent into the maelstrom, the goddamn, freaking Moskoe-ström*… She found the road only after spotting the flashing red and blue lights from the police cruiser. The lights circled the canopy of trees, spinning salvation, and Clare plunged through the woods, toward the lights.

Standing now, beside the officer by her car, Clare was grateful the man couldn't see the spot on her pants from where she'd slipped and fell on her ass.

"Do you need some help?" The officer repeated when Clare didn't answer. He moved closer, holding his umbrella so that it covered them both.

"No, I just, I thought I saw—" Clare gestured toward the woods, wet hair slapping her mouth. *I thought I saw an old man in a yellow raincoat. I think maybe he's...stealing a garden gnome? Burying a body?* Clare turned back to the policeman.

"I think maybe I saw a deer?"

"A deer?" His eyes softened. "You went looking for a deer in this rain?"

"No, I'm sorry," Clare mumbled, stepping away and back into the rain. She started for her car. "I'm going—"

"It's Ben. You probably don't remember." Again, he stepped forward to shelter her with his umbrella. He smiled, a little shy, his head lowered. "Ben Light? You and I, we use to…"

He paused in the silence she offered.

"We had Mrs. Browning's class together, fifth grade? Wow, has it been that long?"

A truck passed by, nearly drowning out his last sentence and throwing a mist of grimy water over the two of them on the side of the road. Ben guided her further toward the gravel shoulder as several cars passed in quick succession, each tailgating the other behind the slower moving truck.

Clare looked up at the officer. Headlights moved across his face in steady rhythm with the passing vehicles. Ben. Yes. Clare could see the boy he'd once been, beneath the mature angles on his jaw, the faint lines deepening around his mouth and eyes. A memory came, flashed brilliantly in Clare's mind—Ben's mother at the school, bending at the waist to speak into Ben's ear, something in Spanish, him smiling, her patting him softly on the head, something sharp twisting Clare's stomach as she watched the two of them together, his mother's long fingers brushing back a strand of Ben's hair, the two of them passing her in the hall, the scent of something damp and spicy—then the image vanished.

Clare took a step back, directly into the mud puddle behind her.

"We'll have to catch up some other time, I think," Ben nearly shouted above the noise of the traffic.

"Sure, okay," Clare said because she could think of nothing else to say.

Ben withdrew a business card from the breast pocket of his shirt and handed it to Clare. It read *City of Kinderkamack Law Enforcement* in gold letters across the top and had a website and multiple phone numbers below. The card was damp from the rain.

"My cell's at the bottom. If you ever have any trouble, just give me a call."

Clare nodded.

Ben dipped his head to look directly in her eyes with an intensity that confused her. A stream of water poured off his hat. "Anytime. I mean that."

"Okay."

"Alright now, we better get your car off this road," Ben said. "You be safe out there, Clare."

Albert held the door open for Clare, then caught sight of her muddied shoes and rain-soaked hair and clothes. He started to laugh. "What did you do, go out in the fields and pick everything yourself?"

"You have to tell me what's going on."

"Come on in, I've got tea."

"I'm not going anywhere until you tell me what's going on." Clare pulled the canvas bag of vegetables higher on her shoulder.

"You're holding my asparagus hostage?"

Clare's eyes suddenly widened. Albert followed Clare's gaze to his yellow raincoat where he'd laid it across the desk chair to dry. Rain droplets still glittered on the vinyl. *Oops.*

"You weren't napping, I *knew* it!"

"Well, I did lay down for a bit this afternoon—"

"Tell me what's going on here. With the gnome and the sneaking around and your *oven*, oh!" Clare stamped her foot as another thought occurred to her, and Albert did laugh out loud this time. "Your oven wasn't even broken, was it? You made that banana bread yesterday—"

"That oven's a tricky little bastard. It comes and goes—"

"Tell me now, Albert. Or no more favors, that's it," Clare said.

Oh, so it's "Albert" now, eh?

Clare pulled Ben's business card from her back jean pocket and held it up. "I'll call up Officer Light right now and tell him all about your gnome-stealing and god knows what else you've been up to."

"You saw Benny? Huh..."

"I don't care if you *are* old and senile, after he hears about this, you'll have more than some parking tickets to worry about."

"Parking tickets?" Albert wiped his mouth with his good hand, but he couldn't stop his smile. He hadn't had this much fun in years.

Clare stopped. "What?"

"I don't even own a car, Clare," Albert said, nodding at the empty driveway behind her. "I expect you'd have noticed that by now. Why do you think I asked you to do the shopping?"

"Albert!"

"Okay, okay. If you really want to know, I'll tell you. But we have to close this door. These bugs'll eat us alive."

Clare folded her arms across her chest, still grasping the canvas bag.

"I can show you, Clare, but not now. Tomorrow. At the pond. 8:15." Albert held out his hand. "Now can I have my asparagus?"

"Just tell me, Albert."

"8:15. And don't be late this time. Now we eat and no more talk about this."

Clare waited a moment, staring back at Albert. She finally handed him the bag.

"Oh, and Clare?" Albert had started for the kitchen, but he turned back to Clare.

"Yeah?"

"You'll need to find yourself a yellow slicker."

CLARE

It wasn't until Clare was thirty-four that she came around to her mother's way of thinking. Or, rather, that Clare became the sort of thinker her mother was when she died. Not the "extraordinary" thinker, as listed in the gushing reviews on the backs of her mother's books. Not the "revolutionary" thinker as her mother was called by her colleagues from the university who occasionally came for wine and Chinese takeout and splayed about the living room furniture until sunrise—*the No-bel, Alice, this year it's yours, you just watch*—while Clare listened upstairs. And not the "subversive" thinker as told in the hushed words and side-glances of neighbors who never crossed the boundary of their front walk, but stood a pace away, smiling crookedly if paths happened to cross while dog-walking or baby-strolling. Clare once asked her mother what "subversive" meant, after hearing the word uttered in a sizzling tone by a teacher when her mother came to pick her up from school.

"What's the context?"

Clare quoted, "'that woman's subversive drivel set the feminist movement back fifty years.'"

Without looking up from her book, her mother flicked one long finger toward the bookshelf behind her. "Look it up."

"Subversive" led Clare to "subvert" (as dictionaries tend to do) which led her to "to pervert or corrupt by undermining morals, allegiance, or faith" and also "to overturn, or overthrow from the foundation." It was this last characterization which spoke most convincingly to Clare. She set the heavy-bound book aside and daydreamed about her mother walking through the streets of Manhattan, tall as a skyscraper. Her hair blue like night, her eyes green like earth, her hands big as bulldozers. In Clare's imagination, Alice Lyndsay walked at the same slow pace she always did, hurried by nothing. And in Clare's imagination, her mother plucked buildings like daisies, ripped one from its foundation, turned it upside-down and shook out all the people before tossing the building aside and moving on.

It was only awe Clare felt for this image of her mother. Awe, and a special kind of terror that helped Clare understand the enthusiastic human sacrifices of the Aztec people of Mesoamerica (Clare found Harner's "The Enigma of the Aztec Sacrifice" on her mother's desk and spent a Saturday afternoon stumbling through the text), a people who so willingly slaughtered each other to appease a god they could no more describe, than comprehend.

Clare summoned only one word to articulate the type of thinker her mother was, and it was this type of thinking that swept through Clare's mind the winter of 2007 with a force and autonomy completely free (seemingly) from her own will. Young Clare had known her mother to be a *powerful* thinker. Alice Lyndsay was not an authoritative woman (in truth, she had little reason to be since her colleagues, students, and daughter acquiesced all in her company), and she was not a controlling woman, since rarely would Clare receive from her mother any direct guidance—a "faithless transcendentalist" is how her mother referred to herself. *Truth lights her torch in the inner temple of every woman's soul*—Alice told her daughter often, feminizing Brownson's quote as she did all her quotes. Clare's mother was the sort of thinker who shook the very ground upon which one stood, so that to be in her presence was to be in a constant state of securing one's own footing. Alice Lyndsay believed in truth, not fact. In choices, not coincidence. In luminescence, in the cool connections excited by internal thought, not in the heated sentiments of external love.

In theory, her mother's way of thinking opened up philosophical pathways to lands of ideas that waited to be pillaged and plundered. It provided fodder for her research and facilitated a distance between herself and the world in a way only the Intellectual could afford. Life, as a hypothetical, could be neither cruel, nor joyful, nor lived.

In practice, however, this thinking wreaked havoc upon Clare's childhood. Once, when Clare was in kindergarten, her teacher sent a note home regarding an incident at craft time between Clare and another girl. The girl had used most of the paint they were to share to make their project (Clare's painting was of her mother, standing taller than the clouds and clumped treetops). When Clare asked her for the paint, Clare's classmate happily dumped the last of it onto Clare's paper.

"Did you mean to kick her?" Clare's mother asked. She stood by the porch rail, a damp blue sky and billows of white creating a background very much like the one Clare had painted earlier in the day. She did not look at Clare as she spoke, but instead, gazed out over the yard.

"Yes," Clare said without hesitation. At five, Clare already knew lying to her mother was not an option.

"Did you say you're sorry?"

Across the yard, Mr. Hallam was backing his car into the driveway next door. The car stopped and Mr. Hallam got out, did a quick jog around the front of the car to open the door for his wife, and raised his hand in greeting toward Clare and her mother. The Hallam car was a bright yellow, *lemon yellow, but doesn't drive like one,* Mr. Hallam always said with a chuckle, though Clare never understood why. There was a fading "Unity is Strength" Jimmy Carter sticker peeling from the bumper and a colorful knitted scarf draped across the backseat. The car itself was dome-shaped, and it reminded Clare of The Jetsons cartoon. Often, after watching it round the corner at the end of the block, Clare imagined Mr. Hallam flying the car off into the sky.

"Yes."

Alice Lyndsay lifted her fingers from the wooden rail, fluttered them briefly in response, then clasped her hands together as if to restrain herself from more grandiose gestures.

"Why," her mother said after Mr. Hallam and his wife went inside the house. "Why did you tell her you were sorry?"

This made Clare pause. "Because the teacher said so."

"But are you sorry?"

Another pause. "I don't know."

Her hands clasped tighter, whitened at the knuckles. "How about if I tell you to say, 'I can fly.' Try it."

"What?"

"Say it. Say, 'I can fly.'"

Clare looked at her buckled shoes. The straps across her feet hurt, but then again, they had always hurt, so Clare thought this was the way shoes were supposed to feel.

In a mumbled voice Clare said, "I can fly."

"Like you mean it now."

"I can fly."

"Better. Come on." Grabbing Clare's hands, her mother pulled Clare to her feet and swooped Clare's arms up and down, up and down. "I can fly! I can fly!"

"I can fly!" Clare shouted with her mother, giggling. They danced around the porch, from one end of the house to the other, arms flapping. "I can fly! I can fly! I can fly!"

When they reached the porch steps again, Clare's mother suddenly let go of her hands.

"Now go jump off the roof."

Clare's arms fell to her sides. She looked up at her mother, golden hair lit from behind, ten feet tall against the afternoon sun. Her mother's peasant dress fluttered in the breeze like soft drapery pinned and hung around a statue.

"Come on. You said you can fly. What are you worried about?"

"But," Clare paused, confused, frightened, for the first time considering the possibility that her mother really *wanted* her to jump off the roof. Clare knew there was a lesson here (there was *always* a lesson), but she could not discern exactly where the lesson ended. With Clare on the roof? In the air?

"But," Clare said again, her heart beating so hard it made her head ache.

"Yes?"

"I can't fly."

"No," her mother said, bending down so that Clare could feel her mother's words on her skin. There was anger in her mother's green eyes. Fury. "You *can't* fly."

Clare didn't understand the lesson at five, but at thirty-four her mother's point had crystalized: the world is not a thing we can rewrite into whatever we wish it to be. No matter how hard we might try. No matter how honorable our intentions. No matter if our very lives might depend on it.

20 DAYS

Clare stepped onto her porch and shut the front door quietly behind her. She tightened the knotted string across her chest and checked the street. After ensuring that there was no one on the sidewalk, no one at the windows, no one to see how ridiculous she looked, Clare tiptoed down the creaky porch steps and slipped onto the sidewalk. She walked quickly, head down, hands clenching the material at her sides.

After a few minutes, Clare left Shalott Drive behind and turned left onto the sidewalk that made a long loop along the newer development of houses. From there, she stepped onto the path that led a winding way down and into the woods.

A brief heat wave during the afternoon and the evening's sudden chill had left a whitish haze at the base of the trees, which rose like cold smoke from the trunks. The sky at the zenith had already circled into night, early stars flashing, but the horizon still burned with light. A soft wind rocked the branches of the oaks and the last of the sunset appeared as firelight, flickering between their fluttering leaves.

Clare smelled the pond long before she saw it and had a sudden memory of riding her bike along this same path as a child. The image rose up from an ash-bed of her memory with such speed and clarity that Clare startled and nearly misstepped. She thought she could hear the sound of gravel crunching beneath bike tires, feel the sun too brightly in her eyes, sense that she was flying down this hill instead of walking and would soon lift off the path altogether and ascend to the heavens. She remembered now, how she flew on that bike, away from her house, away from her mother's narrow gaze. How she closed her eyes and saw clouds gliding beneath her, feet off the pedals, arms open wide like the wings of a bird, soaring over the treetops. Clare's heart quickened, but as quickly as it manifested, the memory disintegrated and was gone.

"Wow, look at you."

Albert stood by the wooden sign that was staked into the ground at the entrance to the pond, *Welcome to Honock Pond. Please Respect Our Wildlife.* He was fully dressed—yellow slicker, matching yellow rain hat, and blue whale sneakers. He took off his hat, held it to his chest, and bowed dramatically as Clare approached.

"Your majesty," he said with a chuckle.

"I feel like an idiot, Albert."

"Ah, but you look like a princess." He gestured to the cloak with his hat. "What was the price?"

Clare lifted the yellow drapery from around her legs, revealing its purple underside. She'd turned it inside out. "My old three-speed."

"The indomitable Cecelia. She drives quite a hard bargain."

"And she worked in a three-month subscription."

Albert laughed, the sound rumbling up from his belly like warm bubbles from a geyser. He picked up a large paper bag from the top of the wooden fence, and something like gravel rattled inside.

He held his arm out to Clare, the last of the smile turning his mouth. "Shall we?"

But Clare caught something else on Albert's face, a sense he was holding his breath. Waiting. Watching. She understood that Albert was not at all sure Clare would follow him into the woods.

And why would she? Clare hesitated. There was something new to these last few days, these stolen days she'd been living since that night at her kitchen table. Clare felt it as something carefree, sweetly wild, something that made her feel as if anything were possible. (The word Clare circled, but never landed on was "curious." For the first time since Clare could remember, she had no idea what the day would hold. No clue as to what might happen next. What she might do next. And rather than cause anxiety, this uncertainty filled Clare with warmth and excitement.)

Clare took Albert's arm.

Clare walked with Albert down the winding path and deeper under the forest canopy where the light scattered beneath the trees and the sound of their voices was dampened by the mist. The air was wet and cool, as only air chilled by a nearby and large body of water can be. Clare's cloak swayed like a bell as she walked.

She was surprised to find herself at ease with Albert, her arm linked with his, her stride matching his slowed gait. All the questions spinning in her mind were quieted just like their voices, hushed by the mist or the coming night or the closeness of the trees. In the calm that had unexpectedly filled her mind, Clare was able to simply slip into the moment. Her thoughts gathered only on the easy talk in which she and Albert exchanged—the capricious summer weather they'd been experiencing, the freshness of the strawberries they'd had for dessert the night before, Albert's late-blooming roses. Clare's mind was, for the first time in a year or longer (perhaps much longer), at rest. She had neither concern for where Albert was leading her, nor worry for how she had come to such an odd place from where she had started, alone and drunk at her kitchen table only four days before. It was the light, perhaps, that held Clare in such a place and within such a moment. It was a gloaming kind of light that filled one's head with magic and mystery, that stole from the world its tangibility, its concreteness, its belief in itself. It was the kind of light that made little children see pixies in the hills or caused a driver to veer dreamily off the road. It seemed nothing existed outside of such a light and though Clare was not aware of this as she walked along the path with Albert (as one can never be aware of thoughts, unthought), it was the first time in a year that her mind unclasped the sorrow in her heart. (Soon enough, Clare would grab hold of it again of course, before she and Albert reached the pond in fact, but from this moment and in the weeks that followed, Clare would never grasp her grief quite as firmly.) Unaware of this as she was, however, Clare felt an unnamed relief lift her body and a weight released from her bones. She felt lighter, nearly floating, tethered to the earth by only Albert's arm.

They walked slowly, and Clare lost all track of time, so that she couldn't be sure if a few minutes, or maybe an hour had passed. They chatted about nothing, of small things, enjoying the sounds in the trees, the tiny creatures that crossed the path, the intermittent smooth bands

of silence between them. It was only when they had almost reached
the pond that Albert began to tell Clare his strange and beautiful story.

8:13 p.m.

Albert paced back and forth along the gravel pathway, kicking small stones into the brush. He became aware that he'd been nervously bumping the brown bag against his thigh and stopped at the fence to place the bag on the wooden post. He took a deep breath. She would come. It was early yet.

But when Clare did appear—rounding the corner in dazzling gold and a flash of purple, a cautious smile—Albert couldn't help but release his breath in relief. His plan would work. His plan *was* working. Emily would be pleased.

"Wow, look at you."

They walked together along the meandering path, down toward the pond. Albert had walked this path alone these last few years. The silence had been loud at first, a painful and constant reminder of conversations from the past, of the voice he'd lost. Eventually, though, Albert heard other voices in the woods, birdcalls, the whispering trees, animals that tittered overhead. His walks to the pond slowly became a comfort again. And the conversation started back up, even if it was mostly one-sided.

As he walked with Clare toward the pond that evening, chatting about nothing, both of them knowing the real dialog had yet to begin, Albert struggled to find the place where his story started. There was so much to tell, so much to explain so that Clare would understand, and it was so important that she *did* understand. Albert floundered in his thoughts, lighting on and rejecting one idea, then another, but the more they walked, the more Albert felt Emily with them. Emily's solid assurance, her complete and unwavering faith. And as Albert relaxed into the moment, he suddenly knew exactly where to begin.

"Do you remember flight 1549?" Albert said. "The one that went down in the Hudson last year?"

Clare shook her head, her words, like her stride, moving just a bit more slowly. "I think so. They thought it was terrorists, right? But it turned out to be birds."

"Geese, actually," Albert said. "I used to come down here all the time. Feed the ducks, sit by the water, watch the kids play, but after 1549, everything changed."

They had finally reached the pond, which was, actually, more of a lake during the month of June. Spring rains filled the banks to brimming, and at the pond's widest point, only the strongest of swimmers could have safely spanned its body. The water was dark, full black toward the middle, and nothing could be seen swimming below, or floating above. Lightening bugs flickered in the darkening twilight like fire sparks thrown along the shore. Lush trees glowed at its western edge, burning in the lingering sunset.

Albert did not pause when they came upon the clearing, but instead, led them along the path which wound around the water.

"You'd think it *was* terrorists who brought that plane down," he continued. "All of a sudden it was all about the geese. 'They're ruining our parks,' people said. 'They're pooping on our benches, they're scaring our children, polluting our water.'" Albert waved his hand in disgust. "Geese causing pollution, can you believe that? Not the burning of fossil fuels, not tanker spills, deforestation. Oh no, let's talk about geese. A bunch of horse manure, excuse my language, but that's what it is. Here we are."

They had come to a children's play area with painted benches surrounding a jungle gym and swing set. Clare turned around. "Where?"

"There," Albert said. "The plane went down, and that sign went up."

Albert pointed to a metal sign affixed to a wooden pole at the edge of the play area. The sign was glaringly white, with thick red and black letters. Across one corner of the sign, bird feces had dropped, dripped, and dried.

Feeding Geese or Other Wild Fowl
Strickly Prohibited
$1000 Fine and up to 90 days in Jail

Albert stood on the path and stared up at the sign as he had many times before. He shook his head. "Not sure what irritates me more," Albert muttered. "What it says, or how it's spelled."

"Yeah, but those signs are everywhere."

"Yes, but this one," Albert wagged his finger at the sign, "this one only went up after 1549."

Clare looked down the shoreline the way they had come and then across the water to the line of trees at the north end of the pond. Albert followed her gaze, knowing what had caught her eye before she did. Shrubs and bushes crowded at the base of the trees and there, winking slowly in the low light, a brilliant flash of color, blinking now and then in the breeze. Albert knew the odd sight to be a stolen garden pinwheel, its spokes catching the sun as they rotated in the breeze.

Clare frowned at the flashing colors and Albert watched her gaze continue to lift, up along the steep slope that led away from the pond. At the top of the hill, an outline of a house was just barely visible in the low light. Albert waited, knowing the question that would come next. The angular lines of the house's modern construction, along with the enormous satellite balanced on its roof, made the house impossible not to recognize.

"Albert, is that…" Clare frowned again, "Is that that woman's house? The one with the gnome, Penelope?"

"Ah, yes," Albert said, hustling past Clare who continued to stare up at the hill. "But now you're jumping ahead in the story."

He moved away from the sign and returned to the path that would lead them further along the pond. There were some things Albert would not be able to explain. Some things Albert knew that Clare would have to see if she were to believe. But he had to hurry, time was running out. Something pressed down hard on Albert, quickening his pace, squeezing his heart, telling him it wasn't only the sunset he was racing to outrun. (Albert, of course, did not appreciate that his death was now just twenty days away from this evening at the pond. But Albert felt the urgency of it, however, the imminent nature of his time growing short.)

After a moment, Albert heard Clare take a few running steps to catch up with him.

8:04 p.m.

The little blue car drifted aimlessly to one side of the lane, then to the other, slowing to several miles below the speed limit. Brake lights flickered. As the road straightened out, the blue car began to pick up speed. Then the road curved to the left, and red lights flared steadily until the car was nearly at a crawl.

"Fuck! Fuck! Fuck!" Jared pounded the steering wheel of the truck with each word. "Fuck!"

Downshifting into second gear, Jared brought the truck within punching distance to the blue car's back bumper. He flicked on the truck's wrecker light bar, head and tail light flashers, LED dashboard strobe, and the flood light mounted to the hood. Old Clevedon Road was suddenly awash in flashing, spinning color.

The blue car slammed on its brakes and veered crazily toward the shoulder of the road. Narrowly missing a tree and blowing into some low-hanging branches, the car bounced over the uneven ground and skidded to a stop in a cloud of gravel dust.

As Jared roared past the blue car, he caught a quick sight of the driver—*a woman, of course!*—eyes wide, one hand over her mouth. He laid on the horn shouting, the sound of the horn drowning out his voice. "Get off your phone, you dumb bitch!"

With the blue car behind him, Jared relaxed into the gas pedal, turned up the speakers so that the sound shook the windows of the truck—*slave screams! he thinks he knows what he wants*—and brought the truck up to nearly sixty miles an hour in the empty stretch of pavement created by the slow-moving car he'd just forced off the road. Jared gripped the steering wheel, feeling the force of the truck's engine thunder through his body, envisioning all eight cylinders grabbing hold of his muscles, diesel power flooding his veins. He could hear the beauty of the engine's components, shifting, spinning, thrusting. He could smell the gears working, hell he could *taste* the gears—the sharp metallic flavor smothered in a golden honey-oil. It tasted fucking delicious. Jared pushed the truck toward seventy.

It was a good day. Finally, a truly good day. It had been a while since Jared could remember having a good day. The ice he'd smoked with Elwin before he left had helped. This batch had even obliterated the pain in his tooth (and just in time, that garlic was making him heave). Elwin had made him promise to clean out the dog pens before he'd shared his stash, and to check in on Satan, who'd injured a paw on a run earlier in the week. Elwin had also made Jared promise to pick up the Hummer, which was just more big brother bullshit that Jared had forced himself to overlook as he reached for the pipe. In fairness, it had been a few weeks since the skip tracer had found it. There was only so long he could use the Hummer as an excuse for hanging around Clare's neighborhood. Not that the cop had bought that story anyway.

Jared felt his sense of ease slip as he remembered his conversation with Officer Fuckface two nights ago. The cop had appeared out of nowhere, sneaking up to the truck, scaring the shit out of Jared so that he couldn't think straight. The cop had a lot to say, but Jared didn't hear most of it. Instead, Jared stared at the glove compartment as the idiot prattled on and on with his idle threats and ultimatums. Jared thought the cop would have had a lot less to say if he'd known about the .22 inside the glove compartment.

The one fact that did penetrate, however, was that Lacy could die. *Was* dying, in fact. It was only a matter of time, according to the cop. Jared was determined not to think about that. The ice had helped in that endeavor.

Jared finally slowed the truck as he came up on the traffic heading into town. He coasted along Old Clevedon Road feeling almost calm. Patient. After days of confusion, days of asking himself what he'd done wrong, why Clare had cut him off like that last week, thrown him out of the house without cause, without explanation, Jared had finally figured it out. He'd taken one hit from Elwin's pipe that afternoon, and the answer had simply come to him. Clear, simple. Clare had already given him the answer. She'd told Jared that first night, without meaning to or even realizing it.

How's the other guy? is what she'd said, or something like it. Her drunken, slurred words had been nearly whispered, and Jared had ignored her at the time. But now…now it all made sense.

So Jared was feeling a smooth sort of calm that evening because he wasn't on his way to the garage to take care of the dog pens. Nor was he planning to pick up the Hummer as he'd promised Elwin. Jared was on his way to Clare's house because he'd finally figured out why Clare had thrown him out.

Clare was fucking someone else.

8:27 p.m.

"Albert, is that that woman's house? The one with the gnome, Penelope?"

Clare gazed across the pond and up the hill. When she turned back to Albert, Clare saw that his eyes were full of mischief. He smiled that secret bursting smile of a young boy with a frog hidden in his pocket.

"Ah, yes. But now you're jumping ahead in the story." Albert turned again toward the path, hobbling along the pavement without waiting for Clare.

After a moment, Clare followed.

They walked in silence for a few minutes along the water. The temperature had dropped with the setting sun and Clare thought of her sweaters, still packed away in boxes, along with her other clothes. Would she unpack them now? Clare found the idea somehow unappealing. Would she buy new sweaters? It had been three days since she'd brushed her teeth. Clare ran her tongue over the fuzzy surface of her back molars. She thought of her cell phone, thrown from her car window a week ago. What happens now? Clare still wasn't sure.

"First you need to know about Prospect Park."

"Prospect Park," Clare repeated, rejoining the moment—the water, the walk, Albert. "In New York?"

"That's the one. They've got about three-hundred or so geese living out there."

"Okay."

"They've been there for as long as anyone can remember," Albert continued. "And they're all headed for the gas chamber in a couple weeks. I've been reading about it in the paper."

"The gas chamber?" Clare almost stopped walking, but Albert didn't pause. "They're going to kill them? Why?"

"The official word is the geese will sacrifice their lives for the sake of air traffic safety, which is more horse manure," Albert said, not bothering to apologize this time. "It's not about air safety. Or parks or pollution. It's about the tourists."

"Tourists?" Clare frowned. "Why would tourists care about a bunch of park geese?"

"They don't," Albert said, and Clare noticed he was walking even faster now. She kept falling behind. "The point is, it's a process and it always ends the same. First, they bring in the signs, like the one we just saw. They put up signs to keep people from feeding them, from seeing them as actual living things. They call them 'fowl,' not birds. Venison, instead of deer. Pork, instead of pigs. We have the French to thank for an entire vocabulary of animals that are easier to kill because they're food first."

Clare was silent, thinking. Was there a difference between "ground beef" and "ground cow"? Yes, she decided. Yes, there was.

"The signs are always the first step," Albert continued, "then they bring in the dogs to chase them out of our parks, away from our view. And finally, when they can tell the public they've exhausted all possibilities, they bring in the gas."

"You make it sound so…"

"Methodical? Diabolical? That's because it is. It's what's happening at Prospect Park, and it's what's starting to happen here."

Albert continued walking without looking up, and Clare recognized a change in his tone. It was her mother's tone, her lecture voice. Albert was speaking to the class.

"Every mass slaughter in history follows the same process. Every genocide. Every massacre. It always amazed my students, how we could track the trajectory of such incomprehensible death. I had them graph it on the board. First, you identify a group of people and blame them for something, some problem that impacts a large percentage of the populous. It might be unemployment, bad economy, even terrorism. At the root, though, it's always money. Then, you diminish that group's value in some way. Change their name, tell them they're only allowed to use certain bathrooms, maybe give them a yellow star to wear. Next, you start rounding them up, create camps or reservations, separate the families, take away all of their support systems. You strip them bare, make them vulnerable. And finally, the process completes itself when there isn't enough room or the money runs out, and it seems as if the only logical solution to the problem is to exterminate."

"The Germans, the U.S. South, the Hutu's in Rwanda—they weren't monsters. They were regular people, just like you and me. *Regular people.* That's what the 'banality of evil' means. Evil is boring. It's committed by regular people who get swept up in the process, the policies. The propaganda. It's the only way to get otherwise normal human beings to commit insane acts of violence."

Albert had stopped walking. He took a deep breath, and when he turned toward her, Clare saw pools of moisture in the folded creases by his eyes.

He nodded at a group of long reeds growing out of the water near the center of the pond. "But that's not why we're here. We're here, because of her."

Clare looked up and down the shoreline, saw only a few ducks bobbing along the dark surface of the water, and turned back to Albert.

"Have a seat and be patient," he said, smiling. He gestured toward the bench by the water. "I'll tell you a story while we wait."

After Clare sat down, Albert lifted the folds of his slicker and settled himself beside her, taking care not to let the slicker wrinkle beneath him. It was a quick motion, one he'd obviously performed many times before.

"I'm not exactly what you would call the law-breaking sort, even if the law *is* a brainless one," Albert began, gazing out onto the water. "So when the signs went up, I did as I was told. I stopped feeding the birds. Broke my heart, though, to have them come to me and not be able to give them anything. So eventually, I stopped coming to the park. That was, oh," Albert paused. "Maybe five months or so back.

"A couple of weeks ago," Albert continued. "I was working at the Pathmark. I had this job as a sample man. You know, the guy who stands by the little table... 'you want to try a bite, there's a sale' and blah, blah, blah."

Albert sat back, holding up his arms to straighten his yellow coat. He smiled. "Can you guess what I was handing out?"

"Ah," Clare said. "Fish."

"Grilled shrimp, to be exact." Albert nodded. "So this one day, two guys, both in hunting caps, they come over to my table. And they're talking about a goose they'd just seen in the road on the way in. A pair of geese, actually. One of them had been hit and was dead, but the other one…"

Albert shook his head at the memory. "They said she was wandering back and forth across all four lanes of traffic, scared out of her mind. They were laughing, you know. These guys, they thought it was funny. People were honking, yelling from their cars, but this goose, it just wouldn't get out of the way. 'Playing chicken,' one of them said. When she was really a goose. Like it was all a joke."

Albert wiped his face, rubbed the corners of his eyes with the palm of his hand. "So I left. Just walked out. Slicker and hat and all. I kept walking until I reached the road and Clare…it was terrible. I won't describe it. The cars, the honking, the yelling. Poor thing was terrified. That was plain to anyone. She was scrambling back and forth, completely in a panic. She kept going back, you see, to the…the other one."

"The dead one."

Albert nodded. "Geese mate for life and that was her mate, there in the road. She couldn't stay there, but she couldn't leave him either. And she was about to get herself killed."

Holding up his hand that was still bandaged in gauze and held together with duct tape, Albert gave a rueful smile. "I tried to pick her up. Dumbest thing I've tried for a while." He pulled away the gauze to reveal a swollen, scabbing bite mark in a telltale triangular shape. "It would have healed up by now, but I keep bumping it."

Albert gestured to a little grove behind them at the base of the tree line. In the lingering light, Clare could see a fresh mound of dirt with bits of new growth at its center.

"So I did the only thing I could. I picked up the dead goose from the road and I buried it. And she followed me, which was the most amazing thing. All the way across the road and then on into the woods. She waited by his side while I went up to the house to fetch my shovel. And then she stayed close and watched me until it was done."

A wind fluttered the tiny clovers growing in the loose dirt of the grave and then flowed down the slight hill, lifting Clare's hair and rippling the water's edge. There was a long silence in which Clare watched the darkening pond. Flickers of light continued to spark along the shore. New stars appeared overhead.

"I came by the next day, but she was nowhere to be found," Albert finally said. "I came the day after that and after that. I thought she was gone. But then one day, about a week or so later, I stopped by on my way home from work. It was around sunset and everyone at the park had gone home for the day. She spotted me immediately. Probably saw me coming from way up the path, like a yellow beacon. Some lighthouse on the shore. And you know what?"

Clare shook her head.

"She never comes out now unless I've got my yellow slicker. They're holding my last paycheck ransom for it, but they're never getting it back now."

Albert was silent for a moment. He smiled. "So what do you think, am I crazy?"

Clare returned his smile. "You don't care if I think you're crazy."

"And I haven't told you the half of it yet."

Albert's grin deepened and then broke into a chuckle. He turned to watch the water again. They were quiet for a few minutes, enjoying each other's company, enjoying the dwindling twilight.

Then Albert leaned forward on the bench. "Here she comes."

His eyes sparkled brilliantly with the water's light.

8:41 p.m.

"Oh, she's not home."

She shouldn't have said it. The moment the words left her lips, Cee-Cee wished she could take them back. She wished, in fact, that she'd never left the house at all. She should have gone over to Freddie's to watch X-Men on DVD or just hung out on the couch with her dad. If she had chosen either of these activities, Cee-Cee would never have encountered the trembling stick-man at the Lyndsay house. Years later, Cee-Cee would remember that evening as a turning point—the point where she began to turn away from childhood. (Ben might have named it a "before and after" date.) It was the moment that struck the first blow to her childish bravado, her youthful confidence. More of these moments would come for Cee-Cee, of course, but it was this particular June evening that Cee-Cee would remember as the first time she understood the world was truly a dangerous place.

It was the feather that started it. Cee-Cee had taken the magnificent purple treasure from the hideout and brought it home to hide in a shoe box she kept in her closet. That evening Cee-Cee had sat with the feather on the floor, leaned up against her bed as her father watched TV in the living room. She spun the feather between two fingers and petted its smooth barbs with her palm. An idea was forming. Cee-Cee smiled.

A few minutes later she was grabbing her change purse from her book bag and rushing out of the house.

"Hey, hold up, where are you going?"

"Wawa for a soda. Do you want anything?"

"No thanks. Maybe grab yourself a banana with it at least," her dad said, turning away from the racing cars on the television. He caught sight of Cee-Cee at the door and frowned. "Why, I mean, what—"

"Do you like it?"

Cee-Cee turned so her dad could see how she'd slipped the base of the feather into her ponytail. Her hair was so short that it'd been difficult to wrap the band around the ends, but she'd managed it after several tries.

"I'll be back before dark, promise," Cee-Cee said, before he could say anything else. She shut the door behind her and bounded down the porch steps.

It had been just past eight o'clock when Cee-Cee grabbed her new bike from the garage and stepped onto the sidewalk. She was just getting the bike up to speed, reveling again in its smooth, silent velocity, when she'd spotted the Lyndsay lady. It was the brilliant yellow color that caught Cee-Cee's eye. For a reason Cee-Cee thought she might have been able to guess, the Lyndsay lady had turned Cee-Cee's cloak inside out so that the cloak's golden lining shone deeply in the setting sun. Cee-Cee fought a pang of regret to see her beautiful wizardess cloak on someone else, but then she remembered her purple feather. (Freddie would call her an Indian princess when Cee-Cee showed him the following day, but he would be wrong. With the feather jutting proudly from the back of her blond ponytail, Cee-Cee felt imbued with more than royal power. The new game was "medicine woman" or maybe "sha-woman," Cee-Cee had yet to settle on an appropriate title). Much better than casting spells was the power to heal.

Cee-Cee was returning from the convenience store, having enjoyed more than a few curious stares, and was walking her bike along Shalott Drive, sipping her grape soda, and swinging her plastic bag with the obligatory banana inside when she saw him. (Cee-Cee had actually just walked across Fifth Street, directly through the spot where, twenty-five years earlier, the stick-man and the Lyndsay lady had waited for the bus on a stormy, fateful day in September.) There was a man at the Lyndsay house. He was tall, shaggy hair poking beneath a dirty brown hat, baggy pants, black t-shirt that was too wide at the neck. He was pounding at the front door of the house with an open palm.

"Oh, she's not home," Cee-Cee said.

Maybe it was the feather, maybe it was the carbonated sweetness on her tongue, but the words just popped out of her mouth before Cee-Cee even realized she was going to speak.

When the man on the porch turned, Cee-Cee knew him immediately. She'd only seen him once—the night she'd stolen the mailbox from the Lyndsay house. He'd been sitting in his truck watching her and Freddie on the sidewalk. In the dark, through the windshield of the truck, and from across the street, Cee-Cee had not appreciated the full force of the man's appearance. Now though, the sight of the man on the Lyndsay porch made Cee-Cee stop short. The banana banged against her leg.

He seemed a skeleton in human skin. It was the only way Cee-Cee could understand what she was seeing. The shape of his skull poked through his face so that his mouth protruded oddly from his sunken cheeks. There were sharp angles beneath his clothes where the bones came together and bent in various directions. The skin beneath his neck draped deeply before meeting his collarbone. The darkened skin around his eyes seemed to squeeze the orbs so that they bulged. Reddened. Wild.

Before the scarecrow man turned, Cee-Cee had seen something else—a glimpse of dulled metal, a gun shoved sloppily into the back of his pants. It was the briefest of sights, just an instant, but enough for her animal instincts to identify it and react. It was a sight not unlike a flash of bared teeth, a low growl in the darkness. Time to fight or flee.

And then he spoke, and the word flew at Cee-Cee from the man's cracked lips. The word hit Cee-Cee like a punch in the gut.

"Nobody *fucking* asked you."

Cee-Cee dropped the bike and ran.

8:41 p.m.

"Here she comes."

Clare heard the anticipation in Albert's voice and her heart beat faster for it. She was entirely caught up in the old man's excitement. And it *was* a sort of craziness, Clare understood. But it was a joyful craziness, one of the harmless variety, she decided. A craziness related to the flights of fancy in which only the very old and the very young are able to indulge. It was a way of thinking Clare had not exercised in many years. Loose, malleable, fuzzy at the edges. And the longer she sat next to Albert on the bench by the pond, the more Clare felt the hardened boundaries of her thoughts soften. It seemed fairies might appear at any moment to hover above the water, or the trees might suddenly grow faces and smile down on the two of them where they sat on the bench. Clare's mind no longer required a reason for what she was experiencing, but rather, it was simply letting her experience.

Albert stopped talking and both he and Clare were completely attuned to the movement of the reeds in the water. *There's something out there*, Clare thought. And on the heels of this thought came another, just as strong. *And it's beautiful.* Clare was standing suddenly, with Albert beside her. It would happen any moment now.

There was a shape moving behind the reeds, which, Clare understood by now, were not simply reeds, but rather tall grasses that grew around and along the shore of a tiny island. The island was completely hidden from those who passed along the banks of the pond, and also from any who swam along the pond's surface, secreted away as it was among many similar groups of tall grasses which sprouted throughout the water. The island was *terra nullius*. It belonged neither to the waters of the pond, nor to the paths of the park. It was unsovereign territory, with a heritage shared by both, but claimed by neither.

"Here she comes," Albert said again. His voice was whispered, reverent.

The solidity of the island was proven only by the shape that moved behind the grasses, since the shape did not float, but waddled. The figure disappeared for a moment and then returned, rustled the reeds, withdrew again. Clare quieted her body, palms open and hanging loose at her sides. Her breath let out and she rested in the quiet space before her next inhale, watching.

The grasses parted and a bird slipped into the water in a single, swift motion. It was a slender creature, its body pillowed in soft down, its willowy neck curved toward the sky. It floated along the surface of the water, barely creating a ripple as it contemplated Clare and Albert at the shore. Clare felt its gaze. She sensed its hesitation. The bird dipped its head into the water and then raised its beak and swallowed, tiny ripples threading down its long neck.

Clare watched it silently for a moment before whispering to Albert. "Is that…a *goose?*"

"An American Blue Goose, maybe," Albert whispered back. "But I've never seen anything like her."

"But she's, I mean, is it the light? She looks like she's—"

"Purple, yes. Isn't she wonderful?"

The goose continued to float along the water, now cocking its head slightly toward Clare and Albert, as if straining to hear their conversation. She was, indeed, a purple goose, drawn as if from the pages of a children's book. Brilliant color ringed each of her feathers. Her body was like a silk petal, silver-white at the base with peaks steeped in a deep plum. She was lovely in the truest sense, in the sense that Clare felt lovely just to be watched by her.

"And in my breast spring wakens too," Albert recited, his voice soft, watching the bird, "and my regret becomes an April violet."

Clare looked up at Albert and saw that he had changed since they first arrived at the bench. His voice, even in a whisper, was more powerful now. His eyes, brighter. His body hummed with energy. In fact, Clare realized, Albert had been changing ever since they started walking toward the pond. His stiff movements now flowed. He stood up straighter, taller. Every muscle in his face had opened, revealing a glimpse of the younger man he had once been.

Albert smiled, still watching the goose.

"I named her Violet."

8:41 p.m.

Jared watched the blond girl run away. The plastic bag she held swung wildly and liquid slopped from her can of soda in an arch across the sidewalk. It was only in retreat, when the silly girl had spun around to flee, that Jared noticed something in her hair. Some raggedy piece of purple ribbon that flopped up and down as she ran.

The rage had flared quickly, immediately overtaking him, spreading like fire through his body, incinerating his thoughts. It was an odd anger, an *old* anger, mixed with a panic he hadn't felt since he was a boy. Those dark, childhood days spent cowering from his father, hiding from his brother. Those days he spent mostly alone smashing bottles in the alley behind the Pathmark, or in the laundry room where he sometimes slept, or burned patterns into his arm with the faulty wire behind the dryer.

It was the fucking girl, Jared decided. Every time he saw her now, this blond kid that kept reminding him of Clare, his body reacted violently. And suddenly the little doppel-fucktrip was everywhere. Just like the cop, she was in his face, giving him shit every time he turned around. Following him? Was she *spying* on him? Why? Jared took a step to go after her as this paranoid thought occurred to him, but the girl had already rounded the corner and was gone.

But she wasn't wrong, Jared, realized. Clare's car was parked in the driveway, and so he'd thought she was home. Jared had been banging on the front door for the past ten minutes, thinking she was inside, refusing to answer which had pissed him off. But then another possibility occurred to him that *really* pissed him off. She was out with *him*. Tooling around town in *his* car, while Jared had been pounding on her door like an asshole.

"Fuck," Jared muttered, kicking the door. The steel toe of his boot left a satisfying dent in the wood. Jared kicked the door again.

Two minutes later, Jared was at the back of Clare's house pulling aside layers of vegetation—weeds as big as small trees, thick ropes of green ivy, the rubbery branches of some flowering plant—until he found what he was looking for. Casting a quick glance around the empty backyard, Jared clasped the mossy handle of the cellar door and let himself into Clare's house.

8:43 p.m.

The grasses on the island began to move again and one by one, five goslings appeared. They had none of their mother's hesitation and simply plopped into the water and bobbed along the surface like tiny corks in a bottle. Also unlike their mother, the goslings' thin pinfeathers were a bright yellow. In the dwindling sunset, the little birds seemed to glow from some unknown light source that radiated deep inside their miniature bellies. They gathered around Violet in a clamor, bumping into each other and into their mother, splashing water and shaking it off their heads.

One of them sneezed.

Albert took a step forward and gave the paper bag a shake, rattling its contents. As if on cue, the goslings began to swim toward the shore. Violet circled around and began floating toward Albert, but she hung back, making sure her young stayed together.

Within seconds the first of the goslings reached dry land—a scruffy little bird with a black mark across one eye like a patch. The other four goslings quickly followed and then Violet emerged from the water. She stretched out her legs tentatively, as if testing the ground to ensure it would hold her. She walked carefully, each step methodically planned, movements performed in sequence as one who has learned to perform the action again after a long illness. The goslings ran around and through her legs, tripping over each other and rolling on the dirt. Now that they were closer, Clare heard the sounds they made—tiny squeals, like the plastic squeaker of a dog toy. The goslings were ecstatic it seemed, running in directionless, euphoric circles by their mother's webbed feet.

Clare stepped up beside Albert.

Albert opened the paper bag, reached inside, and pulled out a handful of seed. "Cracked corn and barley," he said, showing Clare. "Bread's bad for them."

Albert sprinkled some of the seed onto the ground and the little birds ran forward, the one Clare had already named Patches in front and leading the others. Violet again hung back, limping heavily, grunting softly, letting her goslings eat first.

"When it first happened, she could barely walk. I figure she'd been grazed by more than one car before I ever got out there that night. And within a week, she'd wasted away to somewhere near half her body weight," Albert said, spilling another handful from his palm. "She lost a lot of feathers and had this big bald spot on her neck. At first, I thought she was sick, her eyes were dull like that, but then I noticed how she never comes out to graze with the others during the day. Spends all her time on the island with the babies. I think she only comes out when I'm here. Sometimes…well… Albert paused, reaching into the bag.

Clare watched Violet. There was something familiar about the way the bird swung her head low to the ground. Something Clare recognized in the bird's hesitant movements, her furtive, sidelong glances.

"Sometimes I think maybe she isn't sick at all," Albert was saying. "At least not in the illness sense of the word. Foolish maybe, but I think she's been—"

"She's grieving," Clare said.

8:47 p.m.

Jared remembered exactly where to find the camouflaged door to the Lyndsay basement, a door no one had used for many years since it was disguised not only from the outside by overzealous undergrowth but from inside as well, the exit hidden behind the ancient furnace and blocked by stacks of dusty milk crates and cobweb-tangled wooden pallets. Jared himself had pulled the iron bolt from the inside of the door weeks ago, leaving it unlocked in case a need such as today's should ever arise.

But it was also a door Jared had spent much of his life trying not to remember. Jared had chased a twelve-year-old Clare through these cellar doors, after she saw what he did at the bus stop, after Clare had also pounded on the front door of her house only to find it locked. Clare had screamed at him through the tears that choked her voice, but Jared had followed her around the house and into the backyard, unthinking, wanting only for her to stop, *just stop, goddamn it will you STOP* (but this was where Jared's memory ended. In fact, this was where the storyline of Jared's life first split in two. There was his life before that day at the bus stop when he chased Clare into the house, and then his life that came after. Ben's "before and after date," though Jared would never call it so. And in the middle of the split was an empty hole. Jared had no recollection of pounding down the cellar steps after Clare, up to the kitchen, crashing through the living room, thundering up to the second floor where he finally caught up with her at the door to her mother's bedroom. He'd collided into her, in fact, because Clare finally *had* stopped. They had both stopped—stopped running, stopped breathing, stopped thinking—as they stared for that eternity of a moment from the doorway. Then Clare screamed and ran into the room. Slipped. Landed with her face in the blood. Seconds later, as Jared ran from the house, Jared's brain had done its job—it deleted the entire scene of the bedroom, along with most of the day. Wiped it clean. Or, at least, mostly clean. Traces are always left.)

C'mon you pussy, just do it!

Jared stepped softly onto the wooden steps, spongy with age, and pulled the metal door shut behind him. The stench of ammonia threatened to overwhelm him and for a moment, Jared had a vision of blood-clotted hair, but he fought through the darkness, feeling his way to the basement floor, kicked aside the milk crates, shoved the pallets against the wall, and brushed a spider from his neck that had rappelled down from a low-slung beam in the ceiling. The smell of urine gave way to the scent of minerals and wet soil that were strong beneath the years of dust and decay, as if the earth had begun the process of reclaiming the basement space.

Once upstairs, Jared took a few minutes poking around Clare's kitchen, investigating empty cupboards, peeking in the refrigerator—dried out bottle of mustard, half a loaf of molding bread—and the ice-encrusted freezer, pulling open empty drawers, and more empty cabinets beneath the sink. The plants by the window were gone, and when Jared spun around toward the living room, he saw the rows of boxes by the front door.

She's moving out... Jared struggled to assimilate this new information, and then another thought, a tiny explosion in his head...*with him! She's moving in with him, the whore...*

Jared went to the cupboard beside the stove and was relieved to find his bottle of whiskey still tucked away on the top shelf. Helping himself to a swig, Jared let the liquid do its slow-burn thing in his gut. As he stood there, rage and alcohol creating a poisonous elixir with the meth still thundering through his veins, Jared caught sight of something else on the shelf where he'd found the bottle. Taking another swallow, and coming up on the toes of his boots, Jared reached into the cupboard, back toward the wall. His hand closed around a smooth, cool object that Jared scooped into his palm. It was a stone, smooth, and with a weight that fit pleasantly in his hand. Turning it over, he saw chips of yellow paint around the edges and one plastic eyeball hanging by a few threads of glued felt. It stared, dead-eyed, up at Jared. (Jared had a flicker of a memory. Clare's bedroom and a similar rock he'd found on the floor of her closet, but the connection failed to take hold.) Jared flicked the eyeball free of its felt with his thumb, sending it into the shadows of the kitchen with a soft clatter, and tossed the stone onto the counter. Losing interest as quickly as it came, Jared moved to the living room to set his plan into motion.

The idea had come to Jared a few days ago as he'd sat in his rig, watching the mailman waddle away from Clare's porch. It was simple really, something he'd seen again and again in many of his favorite movies. A man sits in the quiet darkness of a living room. He watches the protagonist arrive home, watches her toss her coat on the back of a chair, slip out of her heels, turn on the lamp and *wham!* She screams to see him there, a honey-pure, high-pitched tone that only the milky-smooth throats of beautiful women can create. (Oddly enough, and despite all evidence to the contrary, Jared did not cast himself in the role of antagonist in this scene, but rather as the deeply misunderstood co-star). To set the stage Jared needed only the empty house, the rapidly-falling darkness as the sun set behind the curtains, and a single prop.

Jared settled himself on Clare's couch, facing the front door. He planted his feet firmly apart on the carpeted floor, his right hand resting on his thigh, fingers spread. His left hand grasped his single prop. The .22 revolver.

8:52 p.m.

"It's molting season, so she won't be ready to fly for a month or so. She and the babies all. Four weeks. That is," Albert added, with a sly grin, "if I can keep myself out of jail until then."

"Can I try?"

Albert held open the bag and Clare scooped out the seed with both hands. She scattered it along the ground and the goslings crowded around her feet. Their tiny squeaks grew louder as they tumbled over each other to get at the food.

"You're moving up from accessory to accomplice, you know." Albert stood to the side, watching Clare with the goslings.

"How much do you owe, altogether?"

"Nearly three grand," he said with a chuckle. "Nothing would please me more than to go to jail over this. I already have the headline—'Elderly man thrown in slammer for feeding birds: Community cries fowl.'"

Albert lifted the bag and Clare took another handful of seed. "I've already decided who should play me in the movie."

"Morgan Freeman?"

Albert huffed. "Denzel!"

"They would never do that, could they? Actually put you in jail?"

"If Mrs. Homerton had her way, I'd already be in shackles. Snarky woman's got one of those cards our buddy Ben gave you," Albert said. "She watches me out here from her living room window. Nothing better to do than hassle people with her binoculars. She calls and he comes, just like that."

"Really?"

"Yes, well, I've been working a way around it."

"*Really.*"

Albert met Clare's eyes and broke into a grin. "You've been helping."

Albert poured another handful of seed onto the ground and this time Violet came forward, stepping slowly, hedging the bench and ducking her head. She dipped her beak low and ate a few bites. Clare and Albert continued dropping the seed until the bag was empty and the goslings had returned to the shore to paddle around in the shallow water. Violet sat nearby, feet tucked beneath her body, watching her young. The sunset was nearly gone, only a single layer of embers glowed along the horizon.

"Okay," Albert said, just as Clare thought they were about to leave the park. He carefully refolded the paper bag and placed it on the bench. "Are you ready to see something?"

"What do you mean?"

Albert smiled and left Clare standing by the bench. He walked a few paces toward the water and then stopped in front of Violet. Violet had watched as he approached and was getting to her feet, shaking off her feathers in a shudder that began at her shoulders, traveled down through her chest and spun out through her tail. Her black eyes flashed with excitement, and she bobbed her head several times.

"Okay ol' girl," Albert said. "Come on."

When Clare went to bed that night, she tried to remember what it was Albert said after that. He'd left her by the bench, went to the bird and said something, but the memory was lost in the extraordinary event that followed. Or perhaps Clare never heard what Albert said to the goose at all. In the end, it didn't matter.

Clare and Albert walked home some time later, arm in arm, two yellow figures moving quietly through the dark. As they walked, Albert told Clare about Cee-Cee and the gnome and about Penelope and her pond-watching ways. He explained about discount movie night that Penelope went to on Tuesday evenings, her visits to her mother in Philadelphia on Saturdays, and her trips to the outlet mall on Thursday afternoons.

"She has church Sunday and Wednesday nights, so we have only Fridays and Mondays to concern ourselves with."

"You're a stalker, Albert."

When they had nearly reached their neighborhood again, Albert stopped on the sidewalk and turned toward Clare. All the light had gone from his eyes and the lines in his face had again deepened with age. He looked tired.

"So what do you think, Clare. Are you in?"

Back in her house, Clare turned off the light and fell asleep in her empty bedroom within minutes. It had been a year or more since she had fallen asleep before the wee hours of dawn. Longer, since she'd slept more than two or three hours at a time. When

Clare collapsed onto Albert's swing bench four nights ago sleep had come, mercifully enough, like an ocean wave that fell on her and washed her mind, drunk and sick as it was, clean away from her body. It was as if Clare had been holding on to the side of a great precipice and had finally let go. She plummeted into the depths of the abyss below and had no impression of time passing, or of herself as she slept. In the morning, she had the sense that the place where she woke was foreign to the place where she had fallen asleep. She had been carried far by the wave during the night but had no memory of the journey.

(That Clare had avoided catastrophe when she arrived home after meeting Violet and her babies was not something Clare would ever be aware of, since we generally do not see the catastrophes averted, only those encountered. In her state of wonder over the event she had witnessed at the pond, Clare failed to notice several telling details upon her return home. The first of these was the return of her yellow bike that had been left where Cee-Cee had let it fall in Clare's front yard. Another, that the front door she'd locked on her way to meet Albert had been unlocked and even left slightly ajar. Clare also never entered the kitchen where she might have found a member of her hidden pet rock family face down on the counter, its remaining eye ripped off. Likewise, she never perceived the state of the door that led to her mother's bedroom. It was an old door that normally rattled in its latch when closed properly. When the door was slammed, however, and especially in the summer when the humidity was high, the heavy wood collided with the old paint of the doorway and held fast. Had Clare not been in such a state of wonder, she might have imagined the force of such a slammed door. She might have imagined the intruder who couldn't help but sneak a glance at the bedroom that held such a devastating, if forgotten, memory. She might have felt the fear that struck the intruder as he'd stared again at her mother's bed. She might have heard the sound of the door bang against the frame as it was slammed shut in terror, or felt the old house shake as the intruder thundered down the stairs and escaped out the front door, leaving it unlatched behind him.)

On the night Clare met Violet, sleep came as floating, rather than falling. Clare slipped from the precipice in a single, swift motion and was carried through the air, riding a gentle swell of wind. Her thoughts softened, became malleable, and finally dissolved. Her journey became her experience and she, her dreams. And in her dreams, Clare saw a man. An old man and a purple goose.

And together, they were dancing.

19 DAYS

When the doorbell rang again the woman muted the volume on the television and turned toward the foyer. The curtains by the front door were closed, so even with the light on inside, there was no way anyone on the porch could see where she sat on the living room couch in her bathrobe. The mailman had already come and gone and at any rate, she wasn't expecting any packages. She wasn't expecting anyone, in fact, and aside from the woman who had returned her garden gnome a few days ago, Penelope couldn't remember the last time she'd heard the doorbell ring.

Ding-dong.

Probably just kids. There had been a time, last fall, when some of the neighborhood children had been doorbell-ditching Penelope's house. *Horrible children*, Penelope thought, *with their cell phones and their music pads and their $700 of technology falling out of their pockets, and they still haven't come up with anything better than ding-dong-ditch.*

Penelope turned back to the living room and stared through the open picture windows that overlooked the pond. The sun was setting. She waited.

Within seconds, whoever was on her porch rang again.

Ding-dong. Ding-dong. Ding-dong.

"Fine," Penelope said to the empty room. "Fine, fine, fine."

She stuffed the bag of barbecue potato chips into the drawer beneath the end table, rolled the empty bottle of strawberry schnapps under the couch with her foot, grabbed the chocolate bar from her lap, and threw the blanket from her legs. Standing, she looked around the room for a moment, then rewrapped the chocolate bar and shoved it between the cushions of the couch.

"Yes, what?"

It was that woman again. The one who had returned her gnome. Clare, with the scrawny legs and big dark eyes. Had she thought Penelope was actually serious when she'd promised to catch up sometime? Surely not.

"Penelope? I'm so glad you're home, I was worried when you didn't answer the door."

"Yes, well. I was upstairs."

"I'm sorry to bother you. I hope it's not too late?"

There was something different about the woman. Her hair? She seemed taller, maybe.

"I was just going to bed, so if you don't mind…"

"I hate to ask, and I wouldn't, really, except that it's sort of an emergency."

Clare's hair had been long when they were children, past her hips, Penelope remembered. She had a flash suddenly, ten years old, chasing Clare down the sidewalk, she and Helen Argoson together, both of them yelling, *witch!*, and grasping at Clare's long blonde strands that flew out behind her as she ran. The old guilt rose in her throat, but over the years, Penelope had become skilled at swallowing it back. The last time Penelope had seen Clare Lyndsay, prior to her showing up with Penelope's garden gnome earlier in the week, was twenty-five years ago. She'd spotted Clare from the sidewalk on a wet afternoon following that business with her mother. Off to her aunt's, was the rumor at school. Penelope had glimpsed just the back of Clare's head, shoulders slumped, arms wrapped around her body, getting into a car. Clare's hair had been cut short by then.

Penelope suddenly understood what was different about the Clare who had shown up on her doorstep a few days ago and the Clare standing before her now.

The woman was smiling.

"I'm really hoping you can help me out here." Clare held up the white casserole dish in her hands. "It's my oven. I think it must have popped a fuse or something.

PART TWO

We have but faith: we cannot know;
For knowledge is of things we see;
And yet we trust it comes from thee,
A beam in darkness; let it grow.

Lord Alfred Tennyson,
"In Memoriam A. H."

18-12 DAYS

Week of June 13, 2010

A week passed as it usually does when it's summer in suburban New Jersey. Long days stretched into warm nights and vegetation grew wild in a land that was suddenly full of plenty. Backyard gardens became feral territory where butternut squash, lettuce heads, and beet plants strained the limits of their wire fencing. Tomatoes and cucumbers grew too fat on their vines and fell to the ground where fatter creatures chewed off and dragged juicy chunks back to their nests. And everywhere it was green, layers upon layers of green, from the tops of the trees to the moss-bottomed pond rocks. It was a world that knew no winter, that held no memory of cold, and contained no vocabulary for ice or snow. It was a life, however brief, of collective amnesia, shared by all.

For Clare and Albert, it was a busy time. After that first casserole, a classic Chicken Divan served over brown rice, there was a four-cheese baked ziti, a seafood pilaf with saffron cream sauce, a fresh vegetable lasagna, and a blueberry strata pie—this last enjoyed by Clare and Penelope over vanilla ice cream on Penelope's front porch. Albert helped Clare with the recipes; they shopped together, then chopped and peeled throughout the afternoon, while listening to Albert's collection of LPs on an old record player that opened up like a suitcase, and which Albert kept under the desk. Albert introduced Clare to Herbie Hancock and Miles Davis, but also Freddie Hubbard, Mary Lou Williams, and Cecil McBee; the female forces of Etta James and the lesser known Etta Jones, Sarah Vaughn, Shirley Horn, Carmen McRae; and the free jazz of Ornette Coleman—all music not to passively listen to and enjoy, but rather "to experience and to live," as Albert put it.

For Albert it was also an inspirational time. Watching the changes in Clare made Albert come alive in a way that was similar to how he felt at the pond when he was with Violet. Each new day revealed a

121

new facet of the transformation Clare had begun. It wasn't only that she looked better, that her face had regained some of its color and roundness, or that she moved differently, as one who now had purpose and determination. For Albert, the greatest indicator of Clare's transformation (but what truly came to his mind was not the word *transformation*, but rather, an image of Clare returning to herself) was her smile. It was not a smile of happiness, or laughter—there were some of those—but rather, a regular placement of her mouth that was now ready to smile. There was joy available to her now, a joy that could come at any moment and for which Clare was now ready. And on the night Albert watched Clare through the window as she unpacked the boxes in her living room and placed her books back onto their shelves, he knew his time of vigilance was finally over.

As for Clare, she was aware of these changes, or at least she was aware that something was different. She felt, at the same time, both more and less like herself, as if a film of grime had been lifted from a painting—the image was still there, the colors were true, but suddenly the hues were vivid, powerful. Clare no longer lay in bed before rising, rehearsing in her mind what she would do that day, imagining herself performing the actions of brushing her teeth, or getting dressed, or making a meal. She no longer needed to talk herself into getting out of bed at all. At night, Clare no longer lay listening to the noise her breath made in her ears. She stopped visualizing her lungs collapsing, her stomach shrinking, her heart growing dark and decayed in her chest. And during the day, Clare no longer lost large amounts of time during which she stared at a book, or the computer screen, or her own hands in her lap. In fact, Clare found that her time was now filled with movement, energy, every moment building onto the next so that she no longer thought about her days in terms of time, but rather in terms of action and, more importantly perhaps, in terms of interaction.

While Albert watched the paper for the outlet mall sales, Clare talked Penelope into joining a book club that met Monday evenings at the Kinderkamack Library. At the first meeting, Clare sat at the back of the room beside a silent Penelope, who had changed from her lavender bathrobe to a fuchsia sweatshirt and leggings for the occasion. But by the end of the night, Clare sat at the table between Penelope and a grocery store clerk, got angry enough to nearly kick someone under the table, and laughed so hard her stomach hurt. Even Penelope joined in, revealing to the group her love of the Romantics, the response to which was a club decision to add one nineteenth century poem a month to the reading list.

While Clare kept Penelope busy and away from the sunset scene going on outside her living room windows, Albert continued to make the journey to the pond in his yellow slicker. He was now free to feed Violet and the goslings without worry of an appearance by Officer Light. Clare joined Albert on the nights Penelope was away at church or out of town, often bringing a snack she shared with Albert while they waited on the bench for the sun to sink into the horizon. The pond would darken, the grasses would part, and Violet and the goslings would come out to eat. When the feeding was finished, the night always ended the same.

"Okay ol' girl," Albert would say to the goose. "Come on."

Violet would shake herself, bob her head in excitement and the two would then begin their slow way around the pond. Albert took the lead, arms up, elbows slightly bent, palms facing out. Violet followed close behind, her limp somewhat improved, her long neck straightened to its uppermost height, head erect, beak pointed at the back of Albert's yellow slicker. The goslings tumbled in behind her, and then the procession began.

Albert stepped forward with his left foot, stepped out and to the right with his right foot, then brought both feet together. He then stepped back with his right foot, back and to the left with his left foot, and again brought both feet together. Repeating the sequence again and again, Albert moved in a clockwise circle around the pond, two steps forward for every one step back, cocking his head and moving in perfect time, listening only to the music of his body. Violet stayed close behind Albert as he moved, and the goslings stayed close behind Violet. The goose waddled forward with Albert, she waddled backward with Albert, and the goslings stumbled about, making sure to stay within their mother's general proximity. Clare noticed that during this nightly routine, Violet's steps were more secure and unwavering; the goose walked with barely a trace of her limp. It seemed that moving in dance made her forget the uncertainty of her abilities. Violet fluffed up her feathers and shook herself every few repetitions as if she could barely contain her thrill. If a goose could experience emotion, Clare believed it could be nothing but pure joy that Violet was feeling.

It was an evening a week or so after Clare first met Violet that Albert asked Clare to join them. He had been preparing for his walk with Violet when he suddenly turned toward Clare and stooped down low in an exaggerated bow. Still bent at the waist, Albert looked up at Clare, grinned, and offered his hand. They had gone together to take care of Albert's wound at the urgent care in Paramus. The dog bite story had been Clare's. The new white bandage gleamed in the low light.

"Lady Clare."

"Oh, no," Clare said, backing away when she realized what he was asking. "I can't. I don't know how."

"There's nothing to know," Albert said. "Some things you just *do*."

Albert took Clare's right hand in his, picked up her left wrist, placed it on his shoulder, and then began moving them along the pond. Clare did her best to match his steps, but very quickly she stumbled over Albert's feet, got her own foot caught up in the folds of the cloak, and nearly brought the two of them to the ground.

"Stop thinking, Clare. Just let it come." Albert laughed as he righted them both and lifted her arm to begin again. "Two steps forward, one step back. Just like life."

Clare took a breath, let her shoulders relax, and stepped back with Albert. She tried not to think about her feet, and then she tried not to think about how she wasn't thinking about her feet. This thought made her laugh and Clare's laugh made Albert laugh as well. Violet bobbed her head behind them. The goose knew well enough to stay back a safe distance.

"You know your whole face changes when you smile," Albert told Clare as they stepped together in the wet grass. "It's quite beautiful."

11 DAYS

Saturday, June 19 2010
2:03 p.m.

Clare and Albert walked back to the pond the next day. It was early in the afternoon, far too early for Violet to make her appearance, but Albert had invited Clare to a picnic lunch he'd packed in a canvas bag—ham sandwiches, potato salad, and peanut butter brownies he'd baked from scratch that morning. The day was warm, as all the days in the last week had been warm. Brilliant pools of light gathered on the ground between the trees.

"What's Guardians of Freedom Day?" Clare asked. They'd passed two flyers, red papers stapled to fence posts at the switchbacks of the trail. At the bottom of the flyer it read, *Come celebrate with us on July 4th! Now in our fortieth year!*

Albert made a snorting noise in the back of his throat. "Our annual celebration of erroneous history."

Clare frowned. "I don't remember anything like that."

"Well, your mother wasn't one to…participate."

Clare was silent. It was the first time either of them had mentioned Clare's mother and Clare wanted to let Albert's comment settle before she responded. She knew Albert was aware of what he'd said. Albert looked away, suddenly very interested in a wet leaf that was plastered to one of his whale sneakers.

They had reached the pond and were walking along the water before Clare spoke again.

"It says there's going to be a cook-out."

Albert hesitated only a moment before responding. "Roasted wieners, no doubt," he said with a childish grin.

"You don't approve?"

"Of celebrating the day a bunch of men sat around for a weekend and waited for a British army that never had any intention of showing up? No, not as such."

"I've never heard the story."

"Probably because there's none to tell," Albert said. He shook his head as they passed the playground. There was another flyer, this one taped to the bottom of the 'strickly prohibited' sign that Albert so despised.

"It was bad information that led to a waste of time for a lot of people who were fighting over land that didn't belong to any of the parties involved. There was a mayor a while back," Albert added, "thought it might bring in some revenue."

They walked quietly for a while and had nearly reached their bench when Albert suddenly turned and stopped. Clare heard it too. It was only the sound of a truck, but it was an odd sound, nonetheless, incongruous to the soft space of the pond. Within seconds, a brown pick-up truck with a camper shell appeared from the shadows of the trees at the west end of the park, where Old Clevedon Road zoomed by only a quarter mile away. The truck turned off the tiny gravel road and drove over the lawn toward the pond, leaving two deep trails of tread marks along the spongy grass. It circled the northern tip of the pond where it skidded to a shuddering stop at the base of the walking path.

Two men got out of the cab of the truck and walked toward the camper shell in the back. Both men wore work boots and long-sleeved shirts, even though the day was warm. The driver—shaved head gleaming in the sun, full beard, fast hands—unlocked and opened the camper shell, and the other man, the passenger, reached inside. The passenger was taller, but scrawny in the legs and hips. He wore a knitted beanie pulled low over his ears, a brown hat that Clare recognized immediately. As Clare and Albert watched, this second man jerked the camper door open, and in one twitching moment, lunged out of sight.

"Come on Neptune, get on out here."

A moment later, two black and white Border Collies jumped from the truck and ran toward the pond.

"What is…?" Clare began moving toward the truck, but Albert put his hand out to stop her.

The two dogs reached the water's edge and crouched down close to the ground, noses pointed like foxes, tails dragging in the dirt and gravel. A group of geese grazed by the shore, picking through the thick blades of grass; other geese curled up in soft pillows on the lawn under the trees, beaks tucked into their backs and sleeping. When the first goose sounded the alarm, the others quickly followed, honking furiously and flapping their flightless wings in fear. The dogs fanned out, one dog circling behind the group of geese, while the other dog moved toward them. The geese ran south along the water in a mob of horror, directly across from where Clare and Albert stood by the bench. Wings spread, feathers flying in all directions, the honking soon reached panic levels. One of the geese in the front tripped and was trampled by the rushing herd behind it. The goose rolled into the mud by the shallow water, its body colliding with another goose who pitched forward and landed beak-first in the muck.

Shoulders hunched, slinking along the ground, the dogs followed the terrified birds, stalking their prey.

In between this frenzied scene and where Clare and Albert stood by the bench was the pond. And on the pond was the hidden island.

The grasses on the island shuddered.

Clare turned around, looking for Albert and found that he had left her standing by the bench, while he strode toward the men from the pickup truck. Clare ran after him, but Albert had already reached the men by the time she got there.

"—only our job, man. They call us, we come out," the bearded man was saying. Clare searched her memory for a name. Jared had mentioned his brother often during their brief time together, but he usually used the term, *bald fuck*.

"Are you telling me that someone actually *pays* you to come out here and terrorize these animals?"

"Back off, buddy."

Jared had stepped between his brother and Albert, pitching forward awkwardly, to stand nearly nose to nose with the older man. Jared's voice had lowered to a dangerous pitch, but it was Clare he was looking at when he spoke. There was something in Jared's eyes that Clare at first mistook for sunlight, then for a flicker of a smile. It was neither, however. It was a glitter of violence that shone on Jared's face. A hatred so strong that Clare caught her breath, her stomach filling with something sour. She looked away.

Albert moved closer to Jared, attempting to block the man's view of Clare. Albert's fist was clenched and for a moment Clare thought

Albert might actually strike Jared. Jared stared down the length of Albert's trembling body. His eyes moved lazily back to Albert's face. Jared smiled.

"You wanna go?" he whispered.

Albert swung his arm toward the pond and raised his voice louder to be heard over the honking geese. He stepped closer to Jared. "Are you deaf? Are you blind? How can you not see what's happening here, you simple-minded—"

Jared's smile widened. There was a broken toothpick clenched between his teeth. "Careful there. You're gonna give yourself a heart attack, old man."

Jared's brother—*Elwin*, the name suddenly appeared in Clare's mind—tossed an open container of raw ground beef on the seat of the truck and turned back to Albert. "Hey now, let's everybody just settle down."

Elwin put his hand on Jared's shoulder, but Jared shrugged it off, walking back toward the truck. "We're doing our job. That's all. We have permission to be here, permits, okay? We're licensed professionals."

"So were the Nazis," Albert said.

By now Clare had read the logo written across the side of the pickup truck in white letters. *The Goose Guard*, and below that, *Preserving our Parks since 1987*. There was a cartoon drawing of a dog dressed in army fatigues who chased a smiling bird.

"The dogs are trained not to hurt the birds," Elwin explained. The man's speech had slowed, each word carefully pronounced, as if he were talking to a child. "Iago and Neptune, they don't even touch them. They just chase 'em away and make sure they don't come back."

"What does that mean?" Albert said. "They're birds. How can you keep them from coming back?"

Elwin shrugged. Clare realized he was also smiling. He just hid the expression better than his brother.

"We bring in the dogs for as long as it takes. Until they get the hint, you know? They're birds. They're lazy. They don't like all the running. They stay away eventually."

A fresh volley of honks rose from the far side of the pond as the dogs launched another attack. The birds had settled in a nervous group by the base of the tree line but were quickly roused to renewed panic when the dogs advanced. Again, the geese were flanked by the dogs and were pushed further from the water and into the woods.

The grasses on the island were still.

"Away where?"

Albert addressed the question to Jared, who leaned against the hood of the truck, arms crossed over his chest. Jared watched Clare. Even when everyone else startled at the sound of the geese cries, Jared never took his eyes off Clare.

"South, you mean," Albert said. "Toward the hunting lands."

In the silence after Albert spoke, Jared pushed off the truck and crossed to stand before Clare. The roll of his ski cap shaded his eyes. His grizzled mouth pulled into a tight smile. Clare caught a whiff of decay from Jared's breath as he spoke.

"Sure. Goose meat is fucking delicious."

10 DAYS

Sunday, June 20, 2010
9:37 p.m.

The pond was silent. Only a few lightening bugs flickered by the marsh where the water met the land. The bugs made slow, looping circles. Up, then down, then up again, going nowhere in the dark.

It had been dusk. For an hour it had been dusk and Clare had stood by the water's edge, cloak draped at her knees. Clare watched the island grasses. And Albert watched Clare. For an hour, he had watched the unmoving line that was Clare's back. The sky turned orange, then flamed red, then drained of color altogether. The sun set, the stars emerged, and suddenly, it was night.

Violet and the goslings never appeared.

"We'll come back tomorrow." Albert sat on the bench while they waited for Violet and had now come to join Clare at the water's edge, to join her gaze over the blackened water before them. "She's just shaken. Really can't blame her."

Clare nodded.

All day Albert had waited. And all evening the day before. Violet had vanished, much like Clare had after their encounter with the Croker brothers the day before. Holed up inside her purple house with the lights off and the shades drawn. When Albert rapped at her door that night, he hadn't been at all sure she'd join him. Though if Violet didn't show again, Albert worried he should have let Clare alone.

"Tomorrow. She'll come out. You'll see."

Clare was silent.

"We can fix this," Albert continued when Clare did not speak. He jiggled the paper bag, shaking the seeds against the bottom.

"I've been thinking, been working on something. A plan. We can fix this."

Clare nodded again and sucked in a harsh breath. When Albert turned toward her, he saw Clare's cheeks were bright and her eyes

130

shone, but there were no tears. Her face remained unchanged. Lips pressed together, eyes unblinking, just as Albert had found her that first night.

But there was more, something gathering behind Clare's eyes that made him want to ask a question. An old question, twenty-five years now, Albert thought. Clare had carried the secret long enough, and Albert wanted to relieve her of it, but he couldn't see a way through. The words wouldn't come. And this wasn't the time.

So Albert turned back to the water and watched the island that had disappeared into the night. A long while passed between them before he spoke again.

"It was Memorial Day," Albert said, choosing a different question, but at its heart, they were one and the same. "Is that right?"

Clare nodded. "Her…birthday."

"Anniversaries are tough."

Albert said nothing else. Grief was a burden, he knew. It was an actual weight on the body. Albert had seen that weight in Clare's eyes that first night in the driveway, when she'd moved back into the house. He'd felt that weight, stepping into her house on the night he brought the casserole. Just sharing the same air with Clare had enacted a heaviness in Albert's chest. He'd felt her struggle to simply breathe.

And he'd seen the photograph on her kitchen table.

When Clare said nothing else, Albert spoke again.

"How old was she?"

The night deepened around the pond. The lightening bugs circled.

"Eight months," Clare finally said, her voice a whisper. "Nineteen days."

He was still on top of her when she woke, his bulk pressing on her lungs in a way that should have been alarming. Spindly legs tangled between hers, one meaty bicep pressed against her neck, stale sweat rising from his damp head. They'd fallen asleep on a ratty sleeping bag in an older wing of the mausoleum, where the shadows had been so thick the night before, Clare had almost felt them against her bare skin.

The light in the stained-glass windows in the ceiling told Clare she had missed sunrise by at least an hour. She'd be late to the grave site. Late to meet Lance. Late to see that look on his face that made her wish the earth would swallow her whole.

When Clare reached to disentangle herself, however, she found she couldn't move. Her right arm was pinned behind her back, her left, trapped at her stomach between their bodies. She'd slept mostly on her back, her cheek pushed up against a crypt front, and when she rolled her head away, shoving against his arm, she felt its raised letters pull from her skin. Her body twisted at her waist, her hips at a slight angle beneath him, creating a small space in his midsection that allowed her only the shallowest of breaths.

Clare opened her lips—dry, sticky, tasting of ash—meaning to speak, to wake him, to move him off her before she suffocated, but then realized she didn't know his name. Instead, Clare stared up at the ceiling, at an unfamiliar saint, his arms open wide, his robe fluttering, colors crisp in the sparkling glass. He looked down at her with an empty smile, and it was then, held within the saint's glassy gaze, that Clare shifted her hips. She straightened her right leg so that she now lay flat on her back. The dead weight of the man on top of her settled. And the weight squeezed the last of the air from her diaphragm.

Earlier, he'd been surprised when she came upon him, but later he'd been game enough. Clare had been visiting the cemetery for three months by then, and she'd seen him on the grounds a handful of times, the first of which had been the day of the funeral. He'd been clearing snow from a walkway at the edge of the property, swinging the shovel easily, carelessly, tossing it to the ground when he finished with no more thought than flicking a cigarette butt. Clare found that same carelessness in the way his eyes flicked over her body when she approached him the night before. She also recognized something in the callous set of his jawline as he tossed back shot after shot at the bar they'd gone to a block from the cemetery. Sensed a certain potential for cruelty in the way he grabbed her wrist and not her hand as he led her on a drunken, midnight tour of the cemetery, one that ended at the mausoleum, at a storage closet from which he'd pulled the sleeping bag with a familiarity that told Clare this was not the first time he'd done so.

He was tentative at first, fumbling with her clothes, laughing nervously on her ear, not quite as drunk as she. But then he grabbed the back of her neck and scraped her face against the cold stone floor with an angry grunt, and she'd known she'd chosen correctly.

A dark, spectral fog had crept into her peripheral vision before Clare decided she disliked the idea of being discovered naked and crushed to death by a gravedigger in a mausoleum. Unable to pull her left arm free, she instead shoved it further between their stomachs, reaching lower, lower, her head pounding now, the darkness blotting out the saint's face.

Finally, her fingers found his flaccid member. She gripped the loose skin. Twisted. Pinched hard. Gasped air like fire into her lungs.

9 DAYS

Monday, June 21, 2010
1:04 p.m.

Ben slipped his pad of paper into his back pocket and decided to try a different approach. It was hot outside the cruiser. He'd sweated through his shirt by mid-morning but had taken care to roll down his sleeves and straighten his tie before knocking on the door. Overgrown honeysuckle vines had taken over the porch of the old house, grabbing at his legs and face when the wind blew. Bees buzzed from a nest beneath the depths of the rickety wooden steps. The stench of manure wafted up from somewhere nearby.

"I'm not saying he's in any trouble ma'am." Ben was nearly shouting, straining to be heard over the frenzy of the dogs that were penned in the yard around back. He swatted at one of the flying insects. Ben could tell from the way the tiny woman had opened the door only far enough to poke her face through that he would not be going inside the house.

"You gonna 'rest him?"

"I just need to speak with him."

"And I told you, my boy ain't here."

Unlike Ben's last visit, when the black tow truck was parked beneath the aging willow tree out front and the basement window glowed with betraying light, Ben knew well enough that Jared wasn't home. But Ben wasn't coming for Jared today. Not yet.

"Well, it would be helpful if you could tell me where I might find him, Mrs. Croker. It's important."

"Lot of things in life be helpful."

"We've had complaints, Mrs. Croker, about explosives..." He let that last word hang in the air between them for a moment. Ben's hope was that it was this message, the one about explosives, that Mrs. Croker delivered to her son. Everyone in town knew about the illegal fireworks the Croker boys sold every Fourth of July from their shed at the edge of the property, so Ben landed easily on the idea. It was a

134

weak misdirect, he knew, but Ben was hopeful Jared would be desperate enough to take it. Ben worried he'd overplayed his hand during his most recent confrontation with Jared outside Clare's house. He worried Jared might be thinking about fleeing.

"My only concern is for your son's safety."

The woman's nose twitched, and a bit of color rushed into her patchy lips. She wore a housecoat and stained slippers. Where she gripped the edge of the door, Ben saw her knuckles were swollen and twisted with what looked like painful arthritis. Every one of her many years had marked her face, carving deep grooves along the sides of her mouth and beneath the wispy hair at her forehead. Something must have flickered in Ben's eyes, some look of pity perhaps. She looked away.

"I want to help."

Another twitch. Ben waited.

"You come back when you gonna 'rest him," she said and slammed the door.

Ben waited on the porch for what he hoped was an appropriate amount of time to convey his disappointment. Then he made his way down the porch steps, taking care to avoid the rotted wood on the last step. Instead of heading back to where he'd parked the cruiser on the dirt driveway, though, Ben circled around the house. He counted on the honeysuckle brush obscuring Mrs. Croker's view of Ben trespassing onto her property.

As Ben approached, the barking rose to a near deafening pitch. The biggest dog, the black one with the bandage around his front foot, rose up on his massive hind legs and banged again and again against the rusted chain-length fencing. The entire structure wobbled and swayed, and Ben felt a turn of fear in his stomach. Two other dogs raced a path back and forth behind the black dog, tearing up the bald earth and kicking dirt in all directions.

"Hey there, buddy. Hey there." Ben said.

His voice sounded calm in his ears, steady, reassuring, and Ben was relieved to see the dog at the fence respond. Coming down on all fours now, the dog continued to bark, though Ben saw a spark of interest in the canine's eyes. Ben reached into his pants pocket and withdrew the half-eaten package of crackers he'd saved from lunch.

"You like cheese?" Ben showed the cracker to the dog, holding it at his side, close to the fence. "Well, it's not quite cheese, but I think you'll still like it."

The black dog nosed through the links in the fence, sniffing Ben's hand, mouth closed now, suddenly curious. The two other dogs soon quieted as well, crowding around the black dog in an effort to see what had captured their pen mate's attention. Ben crouched by the fence and opened his hand. He felt a warm tongue against his palm. The cracker disappeared.

Ben emptied the contents of the wrapper onto the ground, spreading it out so that all three dogs were able to enjoy the Ritz Bits he'd picked up at the Pathmark on the way to the Croker house. The crackers were eaten quickly, and the dogs were looking for more within seconds. Ben allowed the black dog to lick the crumbs from his fingers, while he reached around with his other hand to cautiously scratch the dog's neck.

"That's a good boy."

Ben pulled his hand back and held a few strands of fur up to the sun. Then, standing, Ben pulled a baggie from his other pants pocket and deposited the fur inside.

The DNA tests had yet to come back, but his friend at the lab in Paramus had texted Ben that morning with the preliminary results from the dark hair found at the Landryes' crime scene. Results that determined the hair was not human at all, as they'd assumed. Nor was the sample hair.

It was dog fur.

8 DAYS

Tuesday, June 22, 2010
2:56 p.m.

Penelope suddenly stopped digging and looked up from where she and Clare knelt at the base of the fence. Clare lowered her trowel and leaned forward, following the woman's gaze. The mailman was at the house next door. And, just as Clare was hoping, the mailman wore a red rose tucked into his shirt. Clare watched Penelope watch the man as he walked up the front steps of the house and began tucking envelopes inside the metal box that hung by the front door. Penelope was still, but alert, her whole body attuned to the happenings on the porch next door.

"So what do you think?"

Penelope continued to stare past Clare, her voice soft when she spoke. "About what?"

Clare smiled. "What do we start with? Pansies or marigolds?" She picked up two plastic boxes filled with plants.

The mailman finished at the house next door and Penelope was suddenly on her feet, brushing off her sweatpants, and straightening her t-shirt. She stood beside Clare's open hatchback, ran her palms over her hair, smoothing out the frizzy bits and tucking a stray piece behind her ear.

During the short time that Clare had known the woman, Clare had seen her new friend in only two conditions. Penelope was either tearful, as when Penelope spoke about the loss of her husband, Odis (who was not at all "lost," though Clare could not have known this at the time), the children she and Odis would never have, and the domestic life she had imagined for herself that had vanished. Or Clare experienced Penelope's anger, as when the woman railed against the war in Iraq that she told Clare had claimed her husband, or the employer who'd fired her for no reason (her chronic absences had, according to Penelope, just been an excuse), or the friends who had drifted away in the wake of her loss (and bitterness). And also, of course, Penelope complained about the geese who trespassed onto her property. The dirty, lazy, pond invaders that crapped all over her gnomes and honked loudly at all hours of the day and night. To hear Penelope tell it, the geese were no better than terrorists, plotting to destroy her way of life.

Always the geese.

But here was a different Penelope, one Clare had not met, even during those brief lapses Clare had witnessed either at the book club, or chatting on the porch where some amount of good humor momentarily interrupted the woman's unending parade of misery and grief. Clare was more than a little amazed at the change she witnessed in Penelope as the mailman walked toward them. Like a wave rushing over ruined sand, leaving it soft and gleaming again, Penelope's happiness at seeing the mailman washed over her face, pinkening her cheeks and smoothing her swollen eyes, leaving them bright and dazzling. From where Clare knelt at the base of the fence, she looked up at her new friend, back-dropped against an ocean-blue sky, dark curls waving in the breeze. Penelope looked younger. Pretty. Clare felt her own heart lift at the sight of her.

As the mailman approached, Penelope suddenly turned to pick up one of the flower boxes from the back of Clare's car.

"Afternoon ladies," he said, nodding. "Mrs. Homerton."

The mailman looked down at Clare where she sat on the ground with the plant boxes in her lap and dirt smeared across her hands and arms. Clare thought she saw a flicker of a frown pass over his face, but it was gone in an instant. He moved to stand between her and Penelope, his back toward Clare.

"Hi Lenny," Penelope said, turning. Her eyes skipped from the mailman's face, down to the red rose at his shirt, and back to his face. Her cheeks deepened with color.

"Planting flowers?"

"Yes," Penelope said.

Though Clare could not see the man's face, she noticed Lenny's posture straighten in response to Penelope's voice. The sagging material in the flat backside of the man's walking shorts shifted.

"Well, it's a beautiful day for gardening, that's for sure."

"Yes," Penelope repeated.

There was a moment as Lenny said nothing and Penelope stared at the flower box in her hands. The sagging material where the mailman's buttocks should have been was moving again. It shifted back and forth loosely as the mailman fidgeted. Clare turned away from the view.

"Well, I'm off, I guess," Lenny said.

The mailman walked a few steps down the sidewalk toward the next house, tote bag swinging from his shoulder. A moment later, though, he turned back to Penelope.

"Oh, sorry," he said, handing Penelope her stack of mail. "The new coupon book came out today. Don't want you to miss that."

Penelope beamed. She took the stack and said something that might have been *thank you*, but Clare wasn't sure, her voice was so soft. Lenny nodded, backed away a few steps and then left.

She just needs a little push, Albert had said. *Someone to move her story in the right direction. Everybody needs a little push once in a while.* Clare set the plant boxes on the ground and got to her feet. It was time to see if Albert was right.

"You really should do something about that," Clare said, standing next to Penelope.

The two women watched the mailman finish at the next house, turn with a little wave, and continue across the cul-de-sac.

"What do you mean?"

"He likes you."

"What?"

The dogs at the Schlingerman's house began to bark as Lenny drew closer. They lunged at the fence, tails wagging, mouths open, grinning. Clare raised her voice above the noise.

"He likes you."

"Lenny? No, it's not like that."

The mailman moved on to the last house in the cul-de-sac where Cee-Cee was sitting cross-legged on the front lawn, pushing buttons on her cell phone with one hand and eating an apple with the other. The girl's thick blonde hair was pulled into a messy ponytail at the back of her head and Clare startled to see the object poking up out of the rubber band. It was a feather jutting up from the back of Cee-Cee's head.

A purple feather.

Cee-Cee looked up when the mailman passed her on the walk and the two exchanged a few words that were lost in the noise of the barking. Lenny dropped the mail in the slot of her door and then headed back toward his truck. With one last glance at Penelope, he got inside the truck, started the engine, and drove away.

"He's been leaving me roses," Penelope said, her voice low but brimming with delight.

"Yeah?"

"Red roses, in my mailbox," she said. "The first one was a few days ago. It was just sitting there, on top of all the envelopes. No note or anything, just a single red rose."

Clare turned back to the plant in her hands. She smoothed the rich dark soil over its roots, patted gently around its base. She smiled.

"At first, I wasn't sure it was him. Like maybe it was a mistake, you know? Somebody got the wrong mailbox or something. But then they kept coming."

When Penelope moved closer to fence, Clare saw that behind the woman, down the sidewalk, and only twenty feet or so from where Clare and Penelope stood, was a goose. It was one of the Canadian geese that lived at the pond, one of the many geese that frequented Penelope's yard that was unable, as they all were, to differentiate between the lush grounds of the park and the sweet grasses of the housing development. The other geese had been lounging in Penelope's side yard, which was why Clare had suggested they start planting out front, and had flapped off toward the pond when the dogs began to bark. This lone straggler, however, had become separated from the group somehow and instead of following the others down the hill and back to the pond, was now wandering up the sidewalk toward Penelope.

"There was just one the first day, a Saturday," Penelope was saying. "I remember because it was waiting for me when I got back from my mother's. And then there were two that Monday. And three the next, I think it was Tuesday or maybe it was Wednesday—"

Clare watched the goose over Penelope's shoulder as it walked along the sidewalk. It ambled to the left, to the right, and then dipped its head anxiously and paused, as if considering its options.

"Yesterday I found *six*," Penelope continued. "I have a vase of them in the kitchen. And then today, he shows up with that rose on his shirt." The woman clutched her hands together with a little thrill. "It's like he wanted me to say something."

"Well, *are* you going to say something?"

"What? No." Penelope looked down and smiled into her chest. "No, what would I say?"

Across the street, Clare saw that Cee-Cee had gotten to her feet and was walking toward the sidewalk. She'd finished her apple and now held the core in her hand by her waist. She flipped the core with her fingers like a baseball player preparing for a pitch.

"Well, you like him, don't you?"

"Yes, but, oh, I don't know. Don't you think it's too soon?"

"Wouldn't Odis want you to be happy?"

The goose was walking again, and its halting stride brought it closer and closer to where Penelope and Clare stood on the sidewalk. Clare saw Cee-Cee raise her arm and before Clare could react, the apple core shot through the air.

"Oh, I suppose. But it's hard to think about. Moving on without him. It's been so long, and all this time, feeling like…I don't know, like maybe I don't belong here anymore. Maybe not anywhere. Even if we weren't happy all the time, me and Odis, at least when I was with him, I knew where I was supposed to be."

Cee-Cee had dead aim and the apple core landed on the sidewalk, a foot in front of the goose. The bird jumped back, wings up, feathers out, and flapped off in the opposite direction, disappearing behind the house a moment later.

Clare took the woman's shoulders in both hands, and all at once, she knew exactly what to say. "You're supposed to be here, Penny. You don't need a mailman to tell you that." She bent closer to her friend and smiled. "You belong wherever it is you're happy."

Penelope reached out suddenly and grasped Clare in a strong hug. When Penelope let go, her eyes were wet and some of her hair stuck to her face, but she was smiling. "Let me drop this mail inside, and then we'll get back to work."

Clare watched Penelope hurry down the front walk and then up to the porch, feet springing on each step.

When she turned, Clare found Cee-Cee standing beside her. For a moment, the two were silent, watching the house together.

"You've got a good arm."

"My dad taught me."

Another few moments passed.

"I'm pretty sure it was Mrs. Homerton who called those dogs on the geese," Cee-Cee said, still watching the house.

"Yeah."

"She really hates those geese."

"She does."

And somehow, what Cee-Cee said next didn't surprise Clare at all.

"Do you think Violet and the babies are okay?"

7 DAYS

Wednesday, June 23, 2010
9:02 p.m.

The light went on in Clare's kitchen, spilled through the windows and lit up half the backyard behind the house. The bulb had been replaced. It burned steady now, casting the room in an easy glow. Clare set her bags on the counter and unpacked the groceries, stacking items in various cupboards and into the refrigerator. When she was finished, she set a head of lettuce on the cutting board, pulled a knife from the drawer, and began making herself a salad.

They were only a few days into Albert's plan, but he felt it was going well. Lenny was the easy part. Albert had merely to mention Penelope's name and the man nearly dropped his mailbag. Albert smiled, remembering. It always amazed him to see the effects of love.

It was Albert who'd been clipping the roses from his garden, of course. Albert, who'd stripped the thorns and tucked the stem into the mailman's lapel yesterday. Albert who'd been slipping the same roses into Penelope's mailbox the previous week. Now, *that* was the hard part. The Homerton woman was a watchful little bird.

"For your lady," Albert had told Lenny that afternoon, holding the bunch of roses toward the timid man.

"What? No...I don't—"

Albert took hold of the man's hand and pressed the bundle into his palm. "It's time. Trust me, she'll love them."

Lenny turned the roses over in his hands and spoke the next in a soft voice to the flowers. "What if...what if she doesn't?"

"Then she doesn't," Albert said steadily. "But you'll never know if you don't try."

After asking the man to wait on the porch, Albert had gone back inside the house for his pad of paper, which he'd found on the top shelf of the refrigerator. Over the past few months Albert had compiled a list of strange places to look whenever he'd misplaced

143

something. The rice cooker and refrigerator were at the top of the list, followed, of course, by the potted peperomia. He knew it was only a matter of time before he also misplaced the list, but Albert had decided not to let it trouble him for now.

Albert returned to the porch with the folded piece of lavender stationery. Inside he'd written, *To Build a Fire* in neat script. Albert slipped the paper into the mailman's breast pocket. He left his hand on the man's chest for a moment as he spoke.

"London knew something about living in fear. Don't be the fool who freezes to death in the woods."

Feeling satisfied with the day's accomplishments, Albert leaned back in his chair, still ignoring the book in his lap. From where he sat in his second-floor study, he could see directly into Clare's kitchen through the bay windows above her sink. He had watched Clare move back into the house, right after Thanksgiving, some seven months ago now. She'd set three plants in the bay window, unpacked one box of dishes into the cupboards, and plugged in a coffee maker on the counter. At the end of the day, she sat at the table and ate something cold from a can. Clare had sat at the table every day since then, working on her laptop and drinking coffee, usually late into the night. Sometimes, Albert saw her water the plants. Once, he saw her talking on a cell phone. No one came to visit. She rarely left the house. A month ago, the laptop disappeared from the table. Soon after that, the liquor bottles appeared.

But now there were fresh greens on Clare's kitchen table. Love transforms, Albert thought, remembering Clare's face that first night at the pond, hearing her laugh as they danced together in the dark. Love, in all its many shapes and designs, transforms.

The second-floor study was Albert's favorite room in his house. Some of his favorite authors—Du Bois, Tennyson, Hurston, Blake, Hughes, Frost—lined the shelves on every wall of the room, his entire record collection was housed in the cedar chest beside his desk, and for thirty-three years it was where he came to read his students' essays and grade their exams. Sometimes Emily would bring him green tea in a mug while he worked. Other times they made love on the chaise lounge. Long, sweet afternoons when the papers went ungraded and her soft words—*oh, Al, yes,* warm lips against his ear—filled all the spaces of his body. In the fall, the cassia tree in the backyard exploded in yellow blossoms, and in the spring, the cheery tree beneath the window burst forth in pink. He and Emily had watched ice and snow and thunderstorms blast through the neighborhood from the very chair where he sat now. During the blizzard of '96, they had huddled together beneath piles of blankets, she on his lap, after the winds had ripped down the power lines. In the summer of 2003, they enjoyed the aurora borealis flame across the night sky for more than a week. And in September of 2001, they watched smoke rise from New York City. Two gray plumes that lasted nearly a week. The scent of ash reached them through the open window.

"Nothing will ever change," he had told Emily. She'd come to check on him when he'd stayed too long at the window during that long week in September. "Seasons change," he'd said bitterly, his voice cracking with emotion. "People don't."

Emily set the mug on the windowsill and then sat beside it, facing him. Sunlight and smoke rose from behind her silhouette. Her scrubs were pink that day. Albert remembered his wife's career in color—blue when she worked at the hospital, orange for the doctor's office, green when she volunteered at the nursing home. Pink was the clinic next to the homeless shelter on the edge of town.

She rested her hands on his knees, a firm, gentle pressure.

"People do change, Al. When the world around them changes, people change." She leaned forward and then Albert could see her eyes. So beautiful, her eyes. He'd believe anything those eyes told him. "That's how it's always been. We just...we have to be patient."

Standing, Emily had pulled him to his feet. "Now come down, I have dinner." She led him through the study door.

"I hear you. I'm coming."

And Albert had followed her.

9:06 p.m.

Clare felt him in the room with her. There was no sound, no breeze, no telltale gust from an opening door, just the sudden realization that she was no longer alone in the kitchen. Before Clare spun around, a flash of understanding lit her mind: our bodies recognize each other. Like magnets, the human body reacts to another human body, somehow, even without our awareness.

But this intriguing thought and all her others were obliterated by the sight of Jared standing in her kitchen.

It had been a good day. A good day among many good days that Clare had had in a row now. There was a time when Clare counted her good days, balancing them precariously one atop another until something came along to knock them all down. But Clare wasn't counting anymore. She'd gone to the pond with Albert that evening, dewy grass cooling the pads of her bare feet as they'd fed the goslings and then, as always, danced with Albert and Violet around the water. The fresh night air, the swaying, the happy chortling of the goose behind them had such a powerful impact on Clare. There was a warmth that spread through her limbs, a pleasant loosening in her chest. It was a difficult experience for her to define. (Clare might have described this experience as one of *love*, but, unlike Albert, Clare was still in the early stages in her exploration of the many facets of this emotion.) There was easy conversation, a bright moon on the way back up the path, and now a quick snack before she went to bed. A good day.

"Where the fuck have you been."

It was warm in Clare's kitchen. She'd taken off the cloak and blouse she'd worn to the pond and had been preparing her salad in only the thin tank top she wore underneath. But Jared was shivering, and Clare couldn't understand why. Clumps of hair hung beneath Jared's brown ski cap and trembled by his chin. Great shudders rode along his thin arms, his long legs. An odd light glinted at his side. It appeared as if something powerful vibrated inside Jared's body. Some terrible internal machine, it seemed, had slipped its track.

Clare stood without breathing on the other side of the kitchen table. She gripped the knife she'd been using to cut the lettuce.

Aside from his sudden presence in her house, the editor in Clare was also thrown by Jared's statement. Despite its syntax, what Jared had said was not a question. This much was clear by the tone of his voice—flat, asking nothing, only demanding. But without a question, Clare was confused as to what, exactly, was being demanded. Jared's statement pinned her in a tight rhetorical corner where silence seemed her only option.

The refrigerator kicked on, breaking the spell, but when Clare tried to say the only word that occurred to her—*what?*—there was no air left in her lungs to make the sound. All at once, Clare's lungs expanded, filling with a great, gulping gasp, oxygen washing cool relief over her rigid spine and down into the tips of her fingers.

For all the time they had spent together over the last few weeks, Clare had known the violence that lurked within Jared. During her more lucid moments, Clare had even remembered Dr. Johnson's words that last day in his office—*You chose a stranger, a 'gravedigger.' Why do you think that is?* Clare had always known why, of course. Knew, also, why she'd chosen Jared, allowed him into her house, into her bed, all those weeks ago. But until this day, Clare had only experienced hints of Jared's violence. A lashing out here and there, a slippage of the mask.

Now though, here in the kitchen, Jared's murderous potential was laid bare for all to see.

Again, Clare tried to speak, but then she suddenly understood something about that glint of light at Jared's side, at the end of Jared's twitching left arm. An ugly buzzing began in her ears.

Half hidden in the folds of his baggy chinos, Jared held his gun. Clare knew about the gun, of course. Jared was chatty when he was high. (Jared had, in fact, nearly told Clare about his experience with psycho-gun-slinger and his whac-a-mole children, but stopped himself just in time. Later, he was angry with Clare, feeling that she'd tricked him, somehow, into nearly revealing this embarrassing piece of information.) Clare knew that Jared kept his gun in his truck, but she'd never seen it.

"He's coming here, then. Meeting you here. Fucking you here."

Again, Clare's mind swarmed with confusion. Jared gave her no questions to answer, and yet he stared at her, his eyes shrunk to dark crystals, waiting. He'd lost weight since Clare had seen him last. She hadn't noticed the other day at the pond. Shadows played across the deepened hollows in his face. A sore oozed at the sharp line at his chin. Something foul emanated from his mouth.

"How…" Clare struggled, her voice too scratchy and dry around the word. *How did you get in?* was the question Clare was trying to ask, even as she noticed the open basement door behind Jared. Something fluttered in Clare's memory (the unlocked front door on the night she returned from first meeting Violet), some knowledge she hadn't been fully aware of. *This isn't the first time he's let himself into my house…*

"You think…Albert?"

"Not that old fuck," Jared said, twisting the curse like sour milk on his lips. "You think I'm stupid. That I wouldn't figure it out. That you're the only one with a *fucking* brain."

As he spoke, Jared had been moving toward her. He advanced in jerks and starts, gesturing around the room, the gun swinging wildly. On the word, *fucking*, he shoved her hard in the chest. Clare stumbled backward and banged into the sink. Grasping the edge of the counter, she managed to stay on her feet. The force of Jared's shove landed on her lungs, and Clare coughed hoarsely. Tears wet her eyes.

Jared's eyes opened in shock. His arms dropped back to his sides, the gun dangling by two fingers, his mouth worked as if he was speaking. The sound that came out of Jared's mouth, however, was some soft, strangled screech that reminded Clare of a squeaky hinge, or a dying bird.

In all their time together during the weeks preceding that evening on Memorial Day when Clare finally threw him out, Jared had never struck Clare. They'd scuffled a bit sometimes, usually when his high wore off or during those brief moments when Clare allowed herself to catch a glimpse of the woman she'd become. Jared had no qualms with tossing her around a bit or even silencing her if she protested too much. But in all their scuffles and ugly late-night tossing, Jared had never hit Clare.

As the pain in Clare's chest blossomed into her stomach, the strange, strangled noise continued to whine through Jared's parted lips. The moment lasted only a second or two, but as Clare stood, grasping the sink, staring up at Jared, she felt the world slow its rotation around the kitchen. With a nearly audible shutting down of machinery, she felt the old gears stutter and skip, chips of rusted metal flying in all directions. The pulleys stretched taught, spokes slowed, cogs grinding against a wheel and finally beginning to catch, and then slowly, painfully, the world stopped. And the memory emerged.

Clare is twelve years old, standing at the corner down the street from her house. She is waiting for the bus, but the bus is late, and she is getting anxious. Clare doesn't understand why she is alone at the bus stop, when normally there are half a dozen middle schoolers shoving and laughing at each other on the corner. It is late in the morning, heading toward ten o'clock, and Clare has been waiting nearly two hours. The sky grows darker the longer Clare stands at the corner, as if the sun rose and then changed its mind.

It is September, still warm and green all around, but the wind that skeins through the streets over the past few minutes has a brisk edge. The chilled air flutters the hem of Clare's Strawberry Shortcake t-shirt (her favorite, worn thin and soft), then feathers at the back of Clare's neck, the skin newly exposed from a haircut the week before. Goosebumps rise along Clare's arms. The air is cool, but also tainted with an odd odor. Something sharp like bleach, or the oily scent of grease that sometimes leaks from the gears of Clare's big yellow bike.

"C'mon you pussy, just do it!"

Clare hears the voice as if it were shouted directly into her ear. The acoustics are skewed from the wind, dampening Clare's own breath in her ears, yet carrying this voice as if the speaker stands just behind her. Startled, Clare spins around.

Jay stands on the street about a half a block away from Clare. His brother, Elwin, stands behind him, taller, darker, leering down at Jay with a nasty grin. Clare knows the brothers only by reputation—Elwin mainly, who had already been suspended, and this being only the third week of the new school year. Clare knows them both on sight and has perfected the art of avoidance over the years—ducking out of sight in school halls, crouching behind shrubbery in the neighborhood—knowing that crossing Elwin's path rarely went unnoticed.

Elwin's younger brother, Jay, is still a question though Clare avoids him all the same. Caution seems best, even if Jay has yet to give Clare reason to fear him. Jay knows who Clare is, nonetheless. Clare has often caught him staring at her during music class, watching her on the swings at recess. He never smiles, though. Only stares, his eyes huge and rimmed red. Jay makes Clare nervous.

Jay stares at Clare now. From half a block away, Clare sees that the boy is shaking. He clutches something in his left hand, a cloth sack, a pillowcase perhaps, its material bound around his knuckles. The sack is damp at the bottom—water, or maybe something else— and it moves by Jay's knees. Squirms. Mews. Another sound buoyed preternaturally along the whipping wind.

"Ha-ha, he's gonna cry!" Other boys are gathered around Jay and his brother, but only Jay has spotted Clare at the bus stop. "Pussy girl's gonna cry!"

Clare is too far away to see Jay's tears, but she sees the boy's mouth moving, his face flayed open, anguish twisting his features. The sound comes again, a mewing, or a screeching, an awful noise that hurts Clare's head. This time she isn't at all sure the sound comes from the sack in Jay's hand.

"C'mon you pussy, just do it!"

Clare steps forward, both arms raised in an effort to reach him, to stop him, comfort him, to do whatever she can to take away the awful thing she sees on his face. Clare has taken just two running steps before Jay squeezes his eyes shut, swings the sack with both hands in a wide arc over his head, and brings it down on the pavement. The mewing stops.

The kitchen is still.

Jared is silent now, trembling, one eyelid spasming, a pool of spittle collecting at the corner of his open mouth, but silent. He stares down at Clare who is still crouched and panting at the kitchen sink, and for a moment, Clare feels as if it is *she* who stares down at Jared. At a doomed man, slipped from some high, narrow ledge, and plummeting to his death. This is where Jared lives, Clare understands, between that slip and the bottom. Clare watches Jared from above, falling out from below her, just out of her reach. *He could kill me,* Clare understands without a trace of panic in her heart. *Right now, right here in this kitchen.* It would only take a single blow. An explosion of violence. Over in a second. Clare would probably never see Jared lift his arm. And it would destroy him. And it's at this moment, that Clare also understands it's for this destruction that Jared yearns, that he has yearned for it for years now. One wide swing to have it all done and over with. Finally.

Clare is intimately familiar with the freefall that is Jared's entire existence. An unending plunge into an infinite hole that sucks in and destroys anything that comes near.

Like attracts like, as they say.

Clare loosens her grip on the knife. Starts to close her eyes.

But before either Clare or Jared can discover what comes next, Albert appears in the open basement door.

6 DAYS

Thursday, June 24, 2010
3:12 p.m.

Cee-Cee pulled her hair away from her face and retied it with the rubber band. She took the feather from Freddie and shoved its shelled tip into the back of her hair. Several of the short strands broke free immediately to float around Cee-Cee's face.

"How come you always get to be the shaman?"

"I told you, I'm a sha-woman. I heal people."

The day was hot, and aside from Mr. Carlyle, who had been up at seven, mowing his lawn, the circle had been quiet all day. Most of its residents were either at work or huddled in front of window air conditioners that did little to cool the steamy cloud that had settled over the neighborhood the last few days.

Cee-Cee had spent the better part of the afternoon sucking on freezer pops and flipping through a library book. Cee-Cee passed by the Kinderkamack Library, nearly every day of her life, but had never been inside. She'd found the book in the mailbox yesterday, along with a slip of purple paper tucked inside the front cover. *Cecelia, meet Annie,* was all it said, but there was only one person Cee-Cee knew who called her Cecelia. (She had lately been thinking she would introduce herself to her teacher next year as such.) Cee-Cee had already read through chapter four of *Annie John,* finding a kindred spirit in the thieving protagonist whose complicated mother-daughter relationship she recognized.

"Shamen are stupid. I wanna be a werewolf."

Cee-Cee ignored Freddie and turned toward the sound of a door banging shut. Freddie's brother came out to the sidewalk. He had a slight swagger to his walk that Cee-Cee had noticed in many of the high school boys that year—it seemed a cross between a limp and a trip that reminded Cee-Cee of the time she'd accidentally caught Freddie between the legs with her remote while playing Wii Sports. Freddie hadn't walked the same for a week. As he approached, Dylan pulled off his t-shirt and threw it around his neck. Sprouts of dark hair grew randomly along his chest with a line of soft fur tracing down his stomach and disappearing into the low waist of his cargo shorts. Dylan passed without a glance or a word for either of them.

"You're stupid," Cee-Cee said, kicking Freddie's cell phone across the grass with her foot. Her chest felt hot, tight, for no reason Cee-Cee could understand. "Shut up and hide so I can heal you."

Freddie picked up his phone, shoved it in his shorts pocket, and slouched off toward the trees. He was headed for the shed behind his house, or maybe the crawl space beneath the back steps. There were only a few places Freddie would hide, and even fewer places if it had rained recently. Cee-Cee had spots all over the neighborhood and into the woods, undaunted as she was by things that might slither or skitter in the dark, or by grown-ups who might catch her on their property.

Cee-Cee flopped on her back and looked up at the sky, breathing deeply the scent of wild onion grass. Spreading her arms out wide, she closed her eyes and imagined she felt the earth spin beneath her. She saw the stars whirl by, felt a lurch of vertigo in her stomach. Cee-Cee dug her fingers into the lawn, holding on.

"Watch you don't get bit by ants."

Arching her back, she balanced on the top of her head, crushing the feather, to look behind her. The mailman stood upside-down. His knees were swollen and hairy.

"In Australia they have spiders that crawl into your ear and eat your brain while you sleep."

The mailman made a noise like *harumph*, left the envelopes in their box, and continued down the sidewalk to the next house. Cee-Cee rolled over on her stomach to watch. The man had a funny walk, a kind of side-to-side waddle that took him twice as long to move in a forward direction. And his legs bowed out in the middle—one sad mouth, one happy mouth. Cee-Cee squinted and held her thumb and forefinger up to her eye, positioning the mailman's figure in between. She squished him.

The dogs began to bark as the mailman approached Freddie's house and Cee-Cee giggled when the man gingerly reached out to shove a few envelopes into the box, while keeping his feet as far from the fence as possible. Freddie's dogs were big. Even Freddie was scared of them.

At the noise of the barking, the geese that had been sleeping by the fountain in Mrs. Homerton's front yard startled, flapping off behind the house, safely out of sight. A few moments later, Mrs. Homerton appeared on the front porch with a tray of drinks and Cee-Cee lowered her head, taking cover behind the long sprouts of grass. The woman was watching only the mailman, though. Setting down the tray, Mrs. Homerton went to the porch steps to wait. He hurried up the walk and the two exchanged a few words Cee-Cee couldn't hear. Mrs. Homerton lowered her head and smiled.

"Oh, Mista Mailman, what a big bag you have." Cee-Cee giggled quietly.

No roses today. Maybe Mr. Hallam was out. But Cee-Cee didn't think Mrs. Homerton minded. She was too busy drawing the mailman deeper into the shadows of the porch, where the two would sit and drink iced teas for a while. Too busy to notice Cee-Cee spying, and too busy to notice the sudden absence of geese in her front yard.

Mr. Hallam's plan had worked perfectly.

Cee-Cee's side vibrated and when she pulled her cell phone from her pocket, she saw Freddie had finally texted her.

Dork: IM REDY U SUK JK

Cee-Cee quickly texted back.

Me: OMW

Scrambling to her feet, Cee-Cee checked that the feather was still firmly tucked into her hair, then ran off toward the shed.

3:16 p.m.

Penelope stood at the top of the steps, yellow sundress fluttering by her knees, dark hair loose at her shoulders. After the mailman completed his reversed route through the cul-de-sac, he set his empty tote bag on the steps and joined Penelope on the porch. She handed him a glass, which he took from her, his hand lingering on the back of hers. She smiled. He lowered his head. They moved away from the steps toward the shadows of the house.

The geese had been driven from Penelope's front yard by the barking only seconds before Penelope came out of the house with the tray of drinks.

Clare turned to Albert. "I can't believe that worked."

"I'm sure the Schlingerman's dogs are glad to have served the greater good."

"Those geese are bound to come back, though. What if she calls again?"

Albert winked. "Happy people are tolerant people. Let's wait and see."

In the yard across the cul-de-sac, Albert watched as Cee-Cee suddenly jumped to her feet and ran toward the back of the house. The purple feather tucked into the back of the girl's hair waved up and down in the breeze as Cee-Cee ran.

The cul-de-sac was now empty. Only the sound of locusts hummed in the distance. Albert and Clare left the shade of the elm tree and began walking again toward the pond.

"You know she knows," Clare said. "About Violet."

"Cecelia? She's a compatriot, a little wild maybe, but loyal to the cause." *And she knows about more than just Violet*, Albert added silently to himself. "She's a good heart. Just too much time on her hands with Mrs. Lushington gone and her father all the time in New York."

"Oh, did her mother…"

Albert peered down at Clare. "I thought she would have told you by now."

"I've hardly spoken to the girl."

"Mrs. Homerton, I mean. It's her husband that Cecelia's mother ran off with."

Clare stopped walking and looked up at Albert.

"What? But that's…Penelope told me her husband was dead."

"Did she? Huh."

"Yes," Clare said. "She said…well, she said that the war took her husband."

Albert thought about it. "I suppose that's true. Maybe more true than anything else. The man came home from Iraq and told his wife he'd had an awakening. That he needed a 'change.' Convenient his 'change' lived right across the street. Why do you think the girl's been torturing Penelope? That garden gnome you returned wasn't the first thing to disappear from her yard. Bit of misplaced rage there…"

"I had no idea."

"Well, that's how Lenny tells it, anyway."

A car horn sounded somewhere, a fleeting squawk quickly smothered in the quiet, humid air. Albert turned back to the cul-de-sac, the tidy arc of houses, matching doors and shutters each.

"Forty years, I tried to explain to my students—history isn't fact, it's story. It's right there in the word, nothing ambiguous about it. The past is much more than simply what happened. It's what we *tell* each other happened. And what we tell ourselves. That's what counts."

They walked a little while in silence, Clare a pace ahead of him. The sun simmered behind a white New Jersey sky and Albert's collar stuck to the back of his neck. He could smell the water rising in humid vapors from the pond. The noise of locusts rose and fell around them, a buzzing chorus that rolled over the path in waves.

When Clare spoke, she didn't look up.

"Thank you again for…for last night."

"I wish you'd have let me call the police."

They'd fallen into step beside each other again, but Clare kept her distance, walking along the far edge of the path, her eyes at her feet. The tips of her fingers wandered along the buttons of her shirt. Albert saw a mark on her chest, just above the top button, reddish at the edges, darker toward the center. Albert looked away.

"I don't think he'll be back," Clare said quietly. "He was just…confused." But they both knew this was not the word Clare meant. "What did you do with—"

"In a safe place."

Albert could see that Clare was still shaken by what had happened after Albert appeared in the kitchen the night before. She'd watched the old man take a long stride to come up behind Jared, slip the gun from between Jared's trembling, sweaty fingers, and turn into the space between Clare and Jared in one fluid move. (It was a move that had struck Clare as so familiar at the time, though she didn't know why. Later, much too late to tell Albert about it, Clare would remember this moment and connect it to the many moments they shared with Violet at the pond. It was a waltz step Albert had performed, one that had disarmed Jared and protected Clare in one graceful motion.) Jared, shocked—both at the sudden appearance of the old man in Clare's kitchen, and also by the sudden weightlessness of his left hand—made the only choice his racing mind allowed him. He simply ran, leaving Clare's front door open behind him.

Albert and Clare walked a while longer along the path, taking the sharp switchback at the midway point, heading deeper into the trees where the light fell in fading pools that disappeared as they approached. Albert waited for the question he knew was coming.

"I was wondering about something…"

"I'd been keeping an eye out."

Clare nodded but kept her head down. Albert watched the path, taking his steps carefully. *I'm going to need some help here, Emily*, Albert thought, and for a moment, the loss was sharp again. Twisting and hot in his chest, just as it had been in the weeks following her death. As it was every time Albert circled around again to find it still there, still fresh, still that open, tender wound. He took a deep breath, filling his lungs with damp, green air.

"I've got a chipmunk," Albert said. "She comes by my window around three in the morning every night. She's got a bit of a sweet tooth, actually, she eats up all the dried pineapple and apricots. Leaves the peanuts and sunflower seeds in a pile in the gutter. Picky little thing."

Albert slowed to step around a leafy mud puddle. Clare walked a pace ahead again. Her fists were tight, her whole body keened toward Albert's words.

"I can see into your kitchen from my second floor," Albert continued. "So I kept an eye out. Not at first, but then there were some things…the insomnia, for one." Albert turned the wedding ring between his fingers. "I'm familiar with that particular demon."

They were coming up to the darkest part of the footpath, where the way narrowed and the branches of the trees met overhead. The sunlight blinked out entirely, and suddenly it was five degrees cooler.

"Mostly though, it was Lenny," Albert continued, lowering his voice. "Lenny told me you were expecting a package. That it was an important package and that it was coming on a certain day. He said that if he knocked and you didn't answer, he was to go on in. He was pretty bugged up about it." *And even then, I almost missed it.* Albert shivered, remembering.

Clare folded her arms across her stomach, silent.

"Heck of a thing, you know. For Lenny to find. Might have stopped his ol' ticker for good," Albert said.

When Clare looked back at Albert, he knew she saw the bit of humor in his eyes. Her face softened in return. She slowed her pace and within a few strides, they were walking side by side.

3:21 p.m.

"Is this the same stuff from last time?"

"I told you."

"Yeah, but it looks different."

Jared had been sitting in the truck for nearly five minutes by the time the shirtless boy showed up—an open, endless, excruciating expanse of time during which jitters made their way from Jared's right foot and traveled up his leg which bounced and jangled against the keys he'd left in the ignition. He had parked the tow just north of Fifth Street, behind the massive branches of an overgrown azalea at the bend in the road where Shalott Drive began to wind toward Kinderkamack proper. (The same bend where, some forty-one years earlier, draft-dodger Craven Hawtrey had hidden himself within the brush and bramble and newly sprouted wild azalea of what had been a vacant lot—Mrs. Hallam's sugar bowl money a bulky, reassuring presence in his back pocket, Mr. Hallam's shoes warming his feet—when he'd realized the approaching bus was not slowing down since the driver saw no one at the stop and had jumped out late, too late, to flag it down.)

Jared ignored the bare-chested kid who stood at his driver's side window and watched the scene happening at the corner. He was more than a block away, but Jared could just barely make out Clare and the old guy. They stood in the shadows beneath a group of shade trees, talking, plotting, scheming…something. Their heads bent in conspiracy. The old guy put one of his gnarled hands on Clare's shoulder.

"It was greener before, wasn't it?" The kid continued to argue. "This stuff looks gray, I don't know, man."

Was Clare fucking the old guy? Jared hadn't thought so, and truly couldn't imagine it. (Well, actually he could imagine it and really didn't want to.) But there they were, cuddled up on the corner together. And what other reason was there for the man to be in Clare's house last night?

"There's no buds here," the kid said, holding the baggie up to the sky to peer at the contents at its bottom, in full view of anyone passing on the sidewalk. "The other stuff had some serious buddage."

Jared hadn't slept at all after returning home from Clare's house the night before. He'd had sleepless nights in the past, more and more often in fact, but usually there were at least a few lost moments during the night, some floating spaces of consciousness during which time lurched ahead toward dawn. The hours were long last night, however, and Jared watched the blackened depths of the basement ceiling until the first pinpricks of light appeared between the warped hardwood floor above—a constellation of sunrise. Jared couldn't stop thinking about the moment the gun disappeared from his hand. There was a moment, a sense of absence (but *relief* was the word Jared refused to acknowledge, a sense of lightening in his body, as if some burden had been lifted, a fleeting moment of self-enlightenment that vanished as quickly as it came), an absence that ate away at Jared even as he sat in the truck, watching Clare and the old guy talking quietly in the shade. And there was anger, oh yes, there was anger so bright and hot and acidic Jared was afraid to touch it. He felt it roiling through his body, breaking through his skin in a slick sweat along his back, pooling and festering in the rotting cavity that had once been a lower molar in the back of his mouth.

"Do you think they're fucking?"

The kid stopped mid-sentence, the baggie still held up to his face. "What?"

"Them, right there," Jared said, gesturing wildly at the windshield. "Do you think they're fucking?"

Glancing down the street, the kid began to laugh. "I don't know what you're on about, man. Maybe you need to lay off your own product, you—"

Jared grabbed the kid by the ends of the t-shirt that was slung around his scrawny neck and yanked him forward, the kid's head just barely missing the roof of the truck. "Right there, you jerkoff," Jared growled, his lips flicking against the boy's ear, "those two, *do you see them now?*"

"Yes! Ok! Get off, yes, I see them!"

The kid was battering Jared, all lanky arms and sharp elbows, the smell of sweat mixing with the scent of maple syrup and cheap cologne filling the cab of the truck. He slipped in the gravel outside the truck and fell against the door, but Jared had balled up the t-shirt into a one-handed fist beneath the kid's chin which prevented him from slipping through. Jared pulled the kid back into the truck by the neck, all the while hissing quietly over the boy's choked screams—*"I said do you think they're fucking!"*—as spittle sprayed across the kid's face and onto the steering wheel. Jared dodged what could have been a heavy blow to his left temple as the kid's hands flew wildly against him. The anger was with him now. Jared had brushed against just the tip of it when he'd grabbed the ends of the kid's t-shirt, and now that rage he'd been holding in since the night before had burst wide open all over the cab of his truck.

Pussy girl's gonna cry!

Later, Jared would wonder what might have happened, had the kid's fist not finally banged against the truck's horn with a sharp, loud blast. The noise seemed to flip a switch in Jared somewhere, and he suddenly saw himself, hot-faced and grunting, strangling a half-naked fifteen-year-old boy with his own Kanye West t-shirt.

C'mon you pussy, just do it!

And for a moment, it wasn't the floppy-haired kid in Jared's grasp. He felt the soft dark curls of a woman's hair wrapped around his fingers, saw Lacy's stunned gaze meet his just before she fell into that coffee table, heard Clare's startled gasp when he punched her in the chest...

Horrified, Jared let go, and before the kid took off at a galloping run down the street, Jared saw that the boy's lips had turned a dusty gray.

5 DAYS

Friday, June 25, 2010
2:06 p.m.

On the day of the first two deaths that summer, a sinkhole opened up in the far parking lot of the Pathmark grocery store. A week before, the rotted wooden fence that quartered off the sidewalk from the pavement had collapsed into a soft heap with little notice from either patrons or employees. Two days before this hole opened in the earth, a large crack appeared in the pavement, one that originated at the base of the fence and drew a jagged line across five parking spaces. "It's teeth, look!" a little boy said the day before to his mother who neither saw nor would have appreciated the anthropomorphic image of a grinning monster with parking curb eyes. When the sodden limestone beneath the asphalt finally gave way at 6:13 that morning, the parking lot had been empty, and, save for a small colony of carpenter ants thriving happily beneath a moldering Wawa coffee cup, the entire incident had been victimless.

By the time the ground would settle, just before the fourth of July, this new aperture in the earth would be large enough to comfortably gulp down a mid-sized SUV. Work crews would measure the sinkhole at nearly twenty feet deep, though it was difficult to be precise since the belly of the hole had filled with water and sludge and all manner of planetary innards. The street behind the Pathmark would close indefinitely as the town council and the Great Atlantic & Pacific Tea Company argued over property lines and responsible parties of terrestrial happenings. In the meantime, with Trinity Street access to Old Clevedon Road shut down, all traffic rerouted to Sixth Street and then funneled through Shalott Drive.

Ben had heard about the sinkhole. Already the event had caused a stir in the community, speculation that would quickly sprout into rumor, but he had yet to see it for himself. When Marcy gave him

161

the news, Ben had been standing outside Room 504 of Hackensack Regional Medical Center's ICU. The view through the patient window seemed to foreshadow the event at the Pathmark that morning. The earth collapsing into itself and swallowing anything in the vicinity was a fitting metaphor for death if Ben had ever heard one.

The gravel road twisted hard around an ancient oak tree, and Ben braked into the turn, then released, letting the tires of the cruiser spin back to purchase as the road straightened out. He maneuvered expertly, bouncing along the narrow way that led from Old Clevedon Road to Honock Pond, the flat of his palm guiding the base of the steering wheel. He drove a bit faster than was necessary, perhaps, letting the crunch of the tires and the attention required to navigate the sharp turns pull his mind from the sense of foreboding that had settled over him at the hospital and lingered this afternoon. The St. Michael medal that always hung against his chest, bounced softly against the collar of his shirt, keeping time with the dips in the road. Ben had slipped the chain from his shirt as he'd waited in the hall for the doctor to finish her efforts, rubbing his fingers raw on the silver, the old prayer passing his lips—O *San Miguel, Arcángel, defiéndenos en la batalla*—in a quiet breath he'd barely noticed.

Ben's Catholicism was a thing from his childhood. It had been many years since he'd attended a mass, though he did visit Our Lady of the Visitation in Paramus on a near monthly basis, if only to make deliveries. Virgin of Lourdeses, Our Lady of Guadalupes, Virgin Marys, Baby Jesuses, Our Lady of San Juan de los Lagoses, and many others that Ben's mother had been shipping across the border since she'd moved back to Cholula. (Worried about the crackdown, his mother's employer had turned in their housekeeper in the last days of 2001, after 17 years of service. Ariana left the country without a word.) Milagro charms, wall crosses, ceramic pots, painted masks, prayer cards, rosaries, quilts—the boxes came once, sometimes twice a month and Ben didn't have the heart to ask her to stop. He donated most of what she sent to the church and didn't know whether to be glad or frustrated that so much of the money he sent south supported his mother's local artisans.

The St. Michael medal never left his neck, though, even in the shower. His mother had laid this gift in his hands after Ben graduated from the academy. *For to protect you away the evil,* she'd told him, her broken English shy and soft when they were together in public. Her eyes were wet. The metal, warm, heavy. Her trust in Ben was the same, warm with a mother's blind love, and equally heavy. A weight across Ben's shoulders that grew by the year.

Ben was her golden child, her greatest accomplishment and for whom she had committed painful acts of sacrifice. Ben was her first and only child. The first American in the family, the first to graduate high school, the first to earn a comfortable living. When Ben was younger, he had secretly enjoyed his status as her American Dream, but as the years wore on, especially these last nine years, Ben had watched his failures pile up as one might watch a multi-vehicle car crash in slow motion. Ben's most recent failure had sent him an email just yesterday, in fact—a pathetically kind review of the relationship he'd been stumbling through these last few months that ended, *you're just not here, Ben, literally and figuratively...* a point with which Ben could only sadly agree, incapable as he was of explaining why he repeatedly left her bed to go home. The nightmare didn't come every night, but the fear of it made it so that Ben could only sleep when he was alone. As he'd explained during his mandatory counseling sessions, Ben could never remember what happened in the nightmare. But it always ended the same, with a scream, with that inhumane noise that Ben knew well and that often followed him into his waking hours.

You nobody hero...

Ben made the final turn into the grassy area and stopped the cruiser at the entrance to the pond. Across the water and just past the playground area, Ben saw two figures on the path that led down from the housing development. African-American male, medium build, 5'10" or 5'11", dark slacks, red plaid shirt, slight leftward limp. Caucasian female, small build, 5'3 or 5'4", shorts, blue t-shirt, dark blonde hair. At this distance, Ben could discern no distinguishing features, but he knew well enough who this pair at the pond was. He'd need to be careful with his questioning, since Ben was unclear about Clare's relationship with Jared at the moment. But time was a factor. It was inevitable that word would get around about what had happened that morning at the hospital. Ben couldn't risk Jared finding out before Ben found him.

Ben slipped the chain back into his shirt where the St. Michael medal settled comfortably against his chest. He took a deep breath, seeing again Elizabeth Landryes's mother collapse on the floor beside the bed as her daughter died. Ben played the scene again and again, examining each tragic detail as he drove slowly over the long grass.

The woman first went to the floor in a kneel that reverberated throughout her body, then, in shuddering stages, she bent at the hips, and finally buckled entirely, falling to the floor in a rubble of anguish and defeat. It reminded Ben of seeing the first tower fall. He'd witnessed this event on the tiny television mounted to the wall of the locker room as he and the rest of his unit scrambled to gear up. They had watched together in stunned silence while thousands of pounds of steel screamed in protest as the tower collapsed upon itself. For all its engineering and innovation, the building simply hadn't been built to withstand the impact of a 767 colliding into its ninety-second floor.

After Elizabeth Landreys's mother fell at her daughter's bedside, Ben had leaned over her crumpled figure, holding the woman as she screamed in long, aching breaths. He held tight to her quaking body, trapping her fingers that tried to rake a path of destruction down her face. Rocking her, soothing her as best he could, thinking all the while that we aren't, any of us, build to withstand this kind of pain.

2:11 p.m.

Albert and Clare turned the final corner of the footpath and arrived at the pond. A group of geese and ducks chortled quietly by the jungle gym, taking some shelter from the sun beneath its wooden platform. Beyond the birds, green lawn stretched over rolling hills, pushing back the tree line and keeping the woods at bay. Above the pond the air was still; the water below shimmering like a pool of sky, spilled from the heavens and poured into the earth.

Clare stood beside Albert, stopping to take in the sight, as they always did when they arrived at the pond. (She would remember this moment later. When all their other trips to the pond blurred together in her memory, she would recollect this day with a kind of photographic clarity. The birds, the light on the water, the smell of pond leaves heated in the sun. It was a moment she would file away, something to remind her of how things had once been.)

"You know the Lenape named this pond," Albert said. "Masters of onomatopoeia. You know what it means?"

"Honock Pond?" Clare thought for a moment and then smiled. "Goose Pond. That's good."

A hawk crowed in the distance and Clare watched as the bird circled the far end of the park, swooped down and cut diagonally across the pond. It circled again in the sky above Clare and Albert, soaring back toward the water, completing a nearly perfect figure eight.

"There's going to be a protest at Prospect Park," Clare said, still watching the sky. "It was in the paper this morning. They're going to try and save those geese, I guess. Bunch of silliness, probably. But I was actually…I was thinking, maybe I would go."

Before Albert could respond, they both turned toward the sound of a car approaching. A white police cruiser rolled out of the woods and along the gravel drive at the western perimeter of the clearing around the pond. The car stopped on the other side of the jungle gym and Office Light sat behind the wheel, talking into the microphone at his shoulder. After a few moments, he got out of the car and walked toward Clare and Albert.

"He's a good man, Ben," Albert said, as she and Albert watched the man approach. "Comes from good family. Ariana never missed a parent teacher conference, not that I remember. Brought me cookies."

"Your student?"

"For a year. Would have been two if not for that woman. She wouldn't let him fail." Albert smiled faintly.

Albert stopped talking as Officer Light drew near to where Clare and Albert stood at the base of the footpath. The officer touched the brim of his hat and nodded at Clare as he had that night on the road, but there was a darkness in the man's face that Clare didn't remember. His eyes skittered across the horizon above them before he turned to Albert.

"Miss Lyndsay, Mr. Hallam."

"Officer Ben," Albert said with a grin that folded every wrinkle in his face. He spread his arms dramatically. "You may frisk me if you like, but I assure you, you'll find no contraband here."

"I'm sorry about that, Mr. Hallam. I was just doing my job."

"As was I when I assigned you all those Saturday detentions." Albert's grin deepened. "Tell me Benny, how much do you remember of the good Reverend King's thoughts on unjust laws?"

Ben smiled, looking down in a surprisingly boyish gesture. "Maybe you can explain 'moral responsibility' to Captain Raglan. He won't listen to me."

"Ah, you do remember! Well, perhaps I'll write the man a letter myself one day. Better yet…" Albert took a pad of lavender paper and a pen from his shirt pocket, wrote silently for a moment, and ripped off the sheet.

Clare leaned over. *The Trumpet of Conscience*, written in a flowing cursive hand.

"Leave this on his desk." Albert tucked the paper into Ben's shirt pocket, gave it a pat. "In the meantime, what can we do for you, Officer?"

"I'm looking for the Croker brothers, Jared mostly. There's been some trouble."

Clare's stomach turned at the mention of Jared's name and she threw a glance at Albert. She couldn't understand the urge she felt to protect Jared, but there it was, nonetheless. (The urge existed outside Clare's ability to articulate it, as so many do, but an image fluttered just below Clare's consciousness, as if from some forgotten dream—a soft covering, a shield, spread wide, with long downy ridges.) Clare was still scuttling through her thoughts for a reply that would lead Albert away from telling Ben about the last time they'd seen Jared, when Albert spoke.

"Weren't enough Saturdays in the year for those two, sadly enough," Albert said steadily, not looking at Clare. "Drugs again?"

"Explosives." Ben pulled out his notepad and flipped through a few pages. But he'd glanced at Clare before doing so, and again, Clare saw something dark in Ben's eyes. This time it looked like fear.

"Homemade fireworks, pipe bombs, M-80's, various rocketry. Apparently, he's selling them online. 'Tis the season—"

Again, the hum of a vehicle rose from the western perimeter of the park and Ben stopped talking as they all turned toward the sound. Within seconds, a brown pickup truck with a dirty-white camper shell drove out of the shadows of the trees and onto the lawn. The truck circled around, passed the police cruiser and drove by the base of the footpath where Clare and Albert stood watching.

Ben held out his hand and walked toward the truck. "Afternoon," he called.

The truck came to a stop and the man behind the wheel rolled down the window. Today Elwin wore a green camouflage cap over his bald head. He looked past the officer to where Clare stood beside Albert. He stared at her without acknowledgement.

"Hey, Elwin," Ben said. "Who do you have with you today?"

The man's gaze shifted to the officer and his eyebrows lifted, moving his cap further back on his head. He smiled. "Got all three of 'em back. Satan's paw healed over good as new."

As the man spoke, a torrent of barks suddenly rose from the back of the truck, echoing inside the camper shell. Clare heard the click of claws against metal.

"Sounds like Iago and Neptune are glad to have him back."

"Yup. Rarin' to go."

"No Jared today?"

"Naw, he had a thing up in Clifton. Gave him the day off."

Even Clare could tell Elwin was lying as she watched the man blink hard and shift his gaze away, but Ben only nodded and turned toward the tree line, surveying the park. "Well, I'll let you get to it then."

"Will do."

After banging twice on the side of the truck door with his open palm, Ben backed away. Elwin shifted the truck into gear and rolled toward the pond as the barking resumed in the camper shell.

Clare and Albert had watched this exchange silently from the footpath, but now Clare moved forward. Albert shook his head sharply at her, spreading his hands toward Clare in a calming gesture.

"I'm wondering," Albert said, once they'd reached the spot where Ben stood on the lawn, still watching as the pickup truck circled the widest bank of the pond and continued south along its eastern edge. "How it is that the Goose Guard was called out here today?"

Ben turned, as if startled from his thoughts. He nodded toward the truck. "Elwin's not one of your favorite people, I gather."

Albert smiled sheepishly. "Was it…a neighbor complaint, perhaps?"

"We haven't had complaints, not lately, anyway. The Goose Guard, they come courtesy of the tourism council of Kinderkamack Township."

"Town council?" Clare said, stepping forward.

Ben nodded, slipping the notepad into his pants pocket. "Yep. They're hoping all the geese will be gone by the fourth."

"Guardians of Freedom Day," Albert said slowly.

"Last year's attendance was way down," Officer Light continued. "Hurt the town pretty bad, though I don't see how some birds had much to do with it. Guess everyone needs a scapegoat."

"Or goose."

By now the pickup truck had stopped and Elwin was at the back of the camper shell, opening the door. He fed the dogs something from an aluminum package—raw ground beef, Clare guessed from the distance where she watched—then set the Border Collies loose in the park. Where the first two dogs had been white with some black markings, the third dog was mostly black with only a few white areas around its legs and the base of its tail. Silent now, the dogs fanned out in three directions and immediately surrounded a group of geese that had gathered in the shade of a tree by the edge of the pond. Noses down, bellies and tails dragging on the ground, the dogs advanced in strategic movements and before the first bird managed to honk an alarm, the dogs had cut off all avenues of escape. When the honking started, it spread quickly through the group, panic jumping from one goose to the next until the entire park was on alert. The dogs paid no heed to the noise and proceeded in their attack, flanking the birds on the right and driving them away from the water and into the woods.

Clare stood beside Albert, watching the dogs stalk the geese, unable to force herself to look away. The dogs preyed on the birds, their desire for the kill an obvious strain against their training. They pulled against this control as if at the end of a leash that might break with any sudden movement, any reasonable opportunity. The geese ran and when they fell, their bodies continued to tremble. When they honked, the sound broke the air like screams. There was a latent brutality to it all, a terror stirring beneath the surface, visceral and barely restrained. Clare saw that Ben sensed it as well, where he stood slightly apart from Clare and Albert, brow furrowed, his mouth slightly ajar. The horror of the birds was palpable to any who experienced it.

When it happened, it happened fast. Clare would look back on that afternoon and remember it as a cascading series of events that began with a shout—*Neptune!* Elwin's voice cut through the din of honks after the dog jumped into the water and it was the urgency behind his shout that alerted Clare he would soon lose control of his animals. Clare never knew what made the first dog suddenly turn toward the island—a sound, perhaps, a frightened rustle of grasses—but once spotted, Violet and her goslings were quickly targeted by all three of the Border Collies.

It was her color, Clare guessed later, Violet's strange and stunning purple hue, which built up such a frenzy in the dogs that they began to bark for the first time since they'd exited the pickup truck. Quickly, the dogs' barks became growls and snarls, as they shed any traces of the highly-trained canines that had been stealthily creeping through the grass only a moment before. The dogs came from the east, so Violet gathered her young and paddled frantically away from the island in the only direction she could, toward the shore. West. Toward the road.

Clare didn't remember deciding to chase after the dogs. She knew only that she was suddenly running through the park with Ben close behind. Past the footpath, as Violet and the goslings made it to shore, around the pond, as the dogs cut across the narrow end of the pond and scrambled back on dry land, and through the grassy field, as the noisy stampede disappeared into the trees. Clare didn't slow when she reached the woods. The underbrush scraped her bare legs and leaf-covered mud puddles soaked her sneakers and splashed up on her shorts. Only the sounds of barking and the terrified honking of the geese filled her mind. She lost track of Ben but kept the dogs in sight. And the dogs kept Violet and the goslings in their sights. They were rapidly closing the gap.

When she fell, Clare went down hard and all the breath in her body exploded through her mouth. She pushed up off the ground and found herself staring deep into the muzzle of one of the dogs—the black one, aptly called Satan. It snarled at Clare from the pit of its chest and brought back its lips in a grin that was all wet teeth and black gum. Clare and the dog heard the squeak at the same time and when Clare turned, she saw a gosling stumbling over a pile of dried leaves, yellow feathers flying all around its head. In the flash before she sprung back to her feet, Clare saw the darkened spot over the gosling's eye. It was Patches, separated from Violet and racing blindly through the woods.

Then the dog was gone, and Clare was running again. She stumbled over a tree root, caught herself, and staggered a few steps before hearing the first sounds of cars on Old Clevedon Road. Bursting through the tree line and onto the shoulder of the road, Clare never saw the gosling cross onto the pavement. She remembered only the sight of yellow feathers shooting into the sky. For a desperate instant, Clare thought what she saw was flight. The gosling bounced off the bumper of the car and flew toward the center lane of the road.

"Clare, no!"

Clare leapt forward and was suddenly face down on the ground again.

All went black.

CLARE

In the summer of 1985, it seemed that every day the newspaper brought stories of bombs exploding and airplanes falling from the sky. In May, the City of Philadelphia dropped a bomb from a helicopter onto a residential neighborhood to flush out members of MOVE—an anti-technology group who, among other misdeeds, were allegedly (and perhaps ironically) stockpiling weapons to promote their cause. The ensuing fire destroyed more than sixty homes and killed eleven people, including five children. *Testosterone crossed with accessibility. Men with guns can always find a reason, if not reason, and this world provides those in spades.* Clare couldn't be sure if her mother was talking about the members of MOVE or the Philadelphia police. Most likely, though, her mother would not have seen the need to differentiate.

In June, Sikh militants detonated one bomb on Air India Flight 182 over the Atlantic Ocean, killing 329 passengers, and placed a second bomb intended for Air India Flight 301 at the Narita International Airport in Tokyo. The second bomb killed two baggage handlers when it exploded an hour early, due to a daylight savings time miscalculation. *Such literary symmetry,* Clare's mother mused while she read the article, *that an arbitrary Western construct should play both the cause and the downfall of their plan. Life answers so many of its own questions.*

In July, the French government ordered the bombing of the Rainbow Warrior, a ship that sailed for Greenpeace and was bound for a protest against nuclear testing in Moruroa. *The Rainbow Warrior, only a man would choose such a name for a ship of peace.*

And in August, Alice Lyndsay sat at the kitchen table, laughing until tears streamed down the sharp corners of her face over a newspaper article describing the rainy microburst that had caused the crash of Delta Air Flight 191. *Brought down by nature's bomb,* her mother said between gasps for air, *oh I love it when she kicks a little ass.*

That her mother wasn't sleeping was evident by the pile of books that grew all around and on top of the kitchen table and had, by September, spread like growing mold into the living room and halfway up the staircase. That her mother wasn't eating meant Clare was forced to forage in top cupboards for half-empty boxes of stale rice and dusty-tasting crackers, or linger until dinnertime at the Hallam house, though Clare often preferred an empty stomach to the crawling sensation created in her chest under the pitiful gaze of her kind-hearted neighbors.

When her mother did remember to bring home food, it was an elaborate affair—pots of boiling oil-tainted water, casserole dishes filled with only milk and flour finding space on top of the refrigerator or in the windowsills, chopped and bloodied meats arranged in strips on the cutting board. Clare's mother ripped open bags and poured ingredients, wiped baking soda into her hair, and swayed to her Doors LP that replayed deep grooves in the vinyl from the living room cabinet (...*waiting for the sun...waiting for you to tell me what went wrong...*) long into the night. In the morning Clare found the raw meats tanning beside empty wine bottles on the counter, cold and swollen pasta congealing in the pots, stalks of rubbery celery, forgotten and wilting on the table.

Her mother wandered down from her bedroom one afternoon after one such night, darkness bruising her eyes, silk robe slipping off her shoulder to reveal ashen, angular bone beneath. She watched Clare clean up the kitchen through a tangle of dark bangs. When she spoke, her tone was tentative. Hurt, mixed with a confusing intensity that Clare couldn't understand and so tried to ignore. It was rare that her mother would address Clare directly. Alice Lyndsay spoke more easily to a crowd of hundreds, than an audience of one, and so Clare grew awkward under her mother's attention, banging her shin into an open bottom cupboard, fumbling with a pot and splashing herself as she dumped its contents into the sink.

"That idiot, Bob Grant is on."

Clare heard the radio drone softly from the cabinet in the living room. She had scooped the soddened pasta from the sink and thrown it in the garbage before realizing her mother's words were an invitation. Clare turned, dropping her hands to her sides, water dripping from her fingertips to the linoleum floor.

"I have homework."

"Some trifling housewife just called in," her mother continued.

She turned away from Clare, crossed her hands behind her body, and leaned against the chipped doorway that led to the living room. In profile, Alice Lyndsay's features sharpened—a steep jaw line sloped to a point beneath small hard lips, the precipitous rims of her eyes bordered unplucked brows at the summit and shadowed wastelands at the base. Her mother had a way of holding her face that reminded Clare of the nativity statues that went up every Christmas at the Kinderkamack bus station (every year there were threats to take it down, yet every year, there it stood). That Clare's mother resembled the frozen features of the Virgin Mary was not an irony lost on Clare, even at twelve years old. There was something resolute about the way the mother of Jesus pressed her hands together and tilted her head toward her son, while the men gaped stupidly about her. A dynamic Clare thought her mother might appreciate.

"She called up to tell half the eastern seaboard about her daughter's date rape. The fool." Alice Lyndsay let her head roll back to rest against the door frame. Her tone had changed, and Clare knew her mother was no longer addressing her, but rather an imaginary lecture hall where students bent over notebooks, taking furious notes, and hoping like hell to have an intelligent question to ask if the opportunity should arise.

Clare turned back to the sink.

"What is that, anyway? 'Date rape.' A term created to achieve an effect opposite to what it actually renders. As if violation by an acquaintance is somehow preferable to that of a stranger. Don't they see that qualifying the type only drains any veracity the word actually contains?"

Her mother paused, letting the idea form in her audience's mind. "She's starting a support group, out there at Hunter College. Daft woman."

Some of the pasta had burned into the bottom of the pot and Clare used a steak knife to loosen the crusted dough from the metal. When the knife slipped, she pierced the tip of her finger and bled into the pot—bright red drops splashing onto pale, cold pasta. The cut was deep, and Clare felt its pain shoot up her wrist and into her arm.

"Imagine this," her mother said, using a phrase that was a favorite for launching one of her hypotheticals. Clare recognized it as a preamble for a "what is wrong with the world" speech, which she could safely ignore. That afternoon, however, Clare heard none of the energy that usually accompanied her mother's rhetoric. And when she sneaked a glance, she saw that Alice Lyndsay gazed at the ceiling as she spoke, appearing almost disinterested in what she was saying. The intensity was there, but it sparked, failed to catch, and went dark. Her mother's voice was tired, flat. It was as if she were reading a script, one that held no more surprises, no new plot twists. One that now bored her.

"Say a man goes into a bar and gets into a fight. His fault, or not, it doesn't matter. Maybe he hits on another man's girl, maybe he did nothing but sit in the corner and drink his beer. The point is that this man gets the living shit beat out of him. Broken nose, busted eye, broken arm, concussion, the works. He wakes up in the hospital the next day. What's the first thing he says?"

Clare continued working on the pot, one-handed now as she held her wound closed between her thumb and middle finger.

"'How's the other guy look?'" her mother let out a sound that could have been a laugh but wasn't. "That's what he says. No one offers him counseling. No one gives him literature on how to 'take back his power.' Christ. All he gets are high-fives from his buddies, one of which is probably the guy who beat the crap out of him in the first place. Where are the self-help books for men who survive bar fights?" Her mother shook her head. "An entire genre in need of third-rate authors. What a shame."

"But rape? Rape is tragic, they say. Oh yes," her mother continued in the same tired, slightly sarcastic voice. "Rape is violation. Rape is betrayal. Rape is worse than death. It makes death preferable in fact, because it is rape and rape alone that can seek out and scorch that secret, sacred sanctum that solidifies the very soul of sisterhood."

Where other, lesser orators lapsed into trite metaphor, Alice Lyndsay lapsed into alliteration. Clare often found herself listening less to the meaning of her mother's words and more to their lilting, rhythmical sound.

"The real tragedy of rape is that it is perhaps the most powerful piece of penile propaganda perpetuated on our society since the invention of the war machine. Language has been and always will be our most potent weapon, ever since Adam named the animals. 'This, here, is a sheep and not a horse or a cow,' they say. Men build their walls and draw their maps and pretend they create the world by naming it."

"Because you see, it's not the act of rape, but the invention of the *word* itself and its subsequent and pervasive, perverse use in our society that grants more power to the perpetrator than he could ever garner on his own. The tragedy of rape is therefore found in the action of the speaker of the word, since using such a word only serves to signify the diminished value of a woman. Or, more specifically, the reduced worth out of which some other man was cheated. As such, rape is not a crime against a woman, but the theft and vandalism of another man's property. Otherwise, rape would not be rape. It would be assault, just as the man in the bar had his eye and arm and head assaulted. If not for men's ownership of women, rape would not exist, since otherwise, such an attack would be classified as simple assault. Assault on the vagina, true, but assault all the same."

Her mother paused, but Clare continued to scrub the pasta pot without looking up. Her mother's speech was a variation of a theme (one, among many) that Clare had heard since her memory began. (Clare suspected her mother used such speeches in lieu of bedtime stories, but no proof existed to this fact.) Had Alice Lyndsay survived the next few weeks, such a topic would no doubt have become the subject of a classroom lecture in some dusty hall at Columbia University, or been transcribed into a chapter of her next book, the title of which may have read "The Actions of Words: Adam as the First Rapist," or "Nouns: How Verbs Travel Incognito," or the catchier "Beware of Verbs in Noun Clothing," or worse "Rape Victims, the Real Criminals."

Clare's mother thought best out loud and much of Clare's childhood had been spent perfecting the art of listening, sans contributing. It was a habit Clare would carry into adulthood, this skill of passive conversational response that eventually evolved into passivity, itself, as a lifestyle choice. It made Clare the target of needy friendships, subjugated work relationships, and more than one destructive romantic entanglement. Clare naturally attached herself to personalities larger than her own, content as she was to assimilate others' experiences for her own life story. (Not coincidentally, it was only when Clare decided to end her life that she learned to prioritize her story over others'. In death, it seemed, she would finally respond.)

During her mother's pause, Clare chipped the last of the pasta from the bottom of the pot and threw the hardened chunk into the trash. When she turned, Clare caught her mother's eyes which blazed, liquid catching light in twin explosions that made Clare look away. Clare hesitated, one hand over the trash, the other hand clenched in an awkward fist that sealed her open cut. Her mother was the only explosion that mattered that summer, Clare would realize later. Alice had been exploding by degrees for months, pieces torn away, debris flung from her innermost structures so that collapse was inevitable, once the foundation had been blown asunder.

When Alice spoke again, Clare knew the words were meant only for her. The unknown audience had vanished. Clare and her mother were alone in the room now.

"Haven't you ever wondered, Clare, why it is that all the trappings of being a woman, of appearing sexy or attractive, are the same things that make us vulnerable to men? Skirts and heels that make it impossible to run, long hair and jewelry that are easy to grab. Is that a coincidence, do you think?"

"We can shoot all the Christa McAuliffes we want into space. But as long as the worth of a woman is determined by the experiences of her vagina, nothing will ever change. Make no mistake, Clare. Society will always shuffle women into one of three categories—virginal enough to fuck, whorish enough to fuck, or not worth fucking. And every woman on the planet falls into one of those categories."

Clare's mother lifted her head from the doorway and what she said next, she said with such deadly certainty that Clare momentarily forgot about her bleeding finger. Her fist relaxed, releasing bright red drops that made tiny splatters on the kitchen floor.

"You think you can escape it because you see it coming. You think if you're smart, if you keep your eyes open, if you educate yourself, you can protect yourself, protect others. But you can't. All your smarts? All that insight? It only makes it worse. Just because you see it coming, doesn't mean you can stop it. And you realize, too late, that it would have been better if you had gouged out your eyes when you still had the chance."

4 DAYS

Saturday, June 26, 2010
3:11 p.m.

The trail was narrow and Albert led the way, forging a path through the wildlife that encroached on both sides. The woods rose up around the trail, blocking much of the mid-day sun, but the late June heat still penetrated the canopy overhead. Sweat seeped through the back of Albert's shirt, beneath his arms, trickled down the sides of his neck. There was no ignoring the spot at the base of his back that lit fire up his spine with every third step or so, and Albert listed to the left to compensate. He pulled out a handkerchief—a thick, cream-colored cloth with embellishments along the side, the last of a set Emily had bought for him—mopped his eyes, around his ears, and shoved it back in his pocket. The woods were silent, animals tucked deep inside whatever shelter from the heat they could find. Albert heard only the sound of footsteps crunching through the underbrush.

When he turned, he saw Clare lagging behind, head down, frizzy blond hair covering most of her face.

"You doing okay?"

"Yeah."

Albert stopped walking and unshouldered his canteen of water that hung from a long strap. He offered the canteen to Clare, who refused, then opened the cap and took a long drink. They had set out early enough, but at the pace Clare was setting, Albert worried they'd be walking home in the dark.

"Come on," he said, slinging the canteen back over his shoulder. "It's not far now."

Clare nodded but said nothing. Her eye was much more bruised today, Albert noticed. Yesterday's fall had left a scrape on her face from temple to chin, but it looked today like her eye had taken the brunt of the landing. A blotchy patch was forming, reddish at the eyebrow and fading into purple by her cheekbone.

Albert had not witnessed the scene at the side of the road the day before, but he'd heard the shouts and the squeal of tires. Ben had filled him in on most of the details, specifically, Clare's leap toward the road. If he hadn't tackled her, Ben was sure she'd have run straight into the traffic.

They walked in silence the rest of the way, Clare several paces behind Albert, head down, arms crossed against her chest, hugging herself, as if cold. The woods gradually fell away as the trail crossed into a soft field with waist-high grasses and tiny buzzing creatures that released into the air at the sound of their approach. The heat loosened slightly in the breeze that blew in from the water and Albert breathed in deeply from the base of his stomach.

"We're here."

Clare finally looked up, and for a moment, she almost smiled. Albert watched the tension drain from her face as she took in the sight. Her eyes widened in amazement, her lips separated, her entire countenance opened. Bruised as she was, the transformation was startling. Something like joy passed over her face, if only for an instant—a searchlight passing across a darkened night. And as he had been that night by the pond, Albert was taken aback by this change in Clare. She seemed a different person. Beautiful. Powerful. Unfearing.

(They had reached Tirol Farm, a property less than a mile west of Old Clevedon Road, a farm that once included nearly 3,000 acres of grazing land, vegetable crops, and fruit trees. Now though, the property was nearly abandoned, including its lake, which, in all actuality, had always been abandoned. The water was too murky for swimming or fishing, the shore too marshy for picnicking, the lake's proximity to the fields too inconvenient for irrigation, and its volume simply too large to drain and fill in any cost-efficient manner. So there it sat, more than five acres of water, unusable by any human standard and nearly forgotten by the owners of the land.)

By Albert's count, there were two, perhaps three hundred geese at the lake on the day he and Clare walked out from Old Clevedon Road. Many of the birds were cooling themselves in the water, bobbing along the surface in the shade of the red oaks at the water's west end. Other geese wandered beneath the trees, picking at the grasses, snatching up the occasional water beetle or catching the springtails as they jumped along the marsh. Most of the geese were sleeping, though, waiting out the long, hot afternoon. The birds curled together in large plush piles on the high grounds along the marsh. A few males stood guard nearby. Here and there a mallard duck or blue heron nestled in with the group, but it was obvious that it was the geese who belonged to the lake.

And nearly all the geese were purple.

Albert watched Clare take in the sight, silent for a moment. After yesterday, Albert had wanted nothing more than to show her this place and share with her the experience of hope that had been given to him upon his discovery of the lake, just a few days ago. Up until that moment, Albert had been uncertain of the outcome of their walk, but watching Clare watch the geese confirmed his decision.

"How...?" Clare said, still scanning the area. She had uncrossed her arms and stepped past Albert to the top of a little rise for a better view.

"I just stumbled up on it one day. Turned a corner and there they were." He pulled the canteen from his shoulder, took a drink, and offered it to Clare. "For everything we think we know, there's always so much more."

"The blind man and the elephant," Clare said, taking the canteen.

"What's that now?"

Clare took a long swallow and handed the canteen back to Albert.

"The last author I worked with before..." she paused, looking back at Albert. He nodded, understanding. "Anyway, that was the title of his book. Blind Man and the Elephant. More of a metaphysical rant, actually. All about how the most dangerous thing in life is not what we don't know, it's what we think we know, and don't question."

"It's a pillar, it's a rope, it's a basket." Albert screwed the cap back onto the canteen and slipped the strap over his shoulder. "I remember that book. Author had a Hindu name, I think. Jazir, something."

"Jivraj Syed." Clare looked back at the lake. "His real name was George Geoffrey Stacks. He almost killed himself last year."

"I remember that now."

"Bathroom cabinet full of pills," Clare said in a flat tone. "I saw it myself. But in the end, he used a gun. Not very successfully."

They watched as a small group of geese paddled across the lake and waddled onto the shore. Tails shaking, they dried themselves and then found a spot near the others to lie down. In the shadows, the birds' feathers were nearly gray. It was only in full sun that their true color could be seen.

"She would follow you," Clare said. "And they would follow her."

"Yes. That was my thought as well."

Albert and Clare stayed as long as they could at the lake, watching the geese, wandering the field, resting in the shade. They sometimes talked, but mostly they simply enjoyed the silence. When the shadows deepened and the sky began to turn pink, Albert led them back the way they had come through the woods. The trip home took half as long, now that Clare kept pace with him and the sun's heat slanted toward regions west. Clare moved quickly, her earlier lethargy consumed in a silent energy evidenced in the way she brushed aside wagging branches and stepped without hesitation along the cluttered trail. They cleared as much as they could, widening the path, pulling fallen branches into the woods. Clare did not speak to Albert as they worked, barely looked at him when they took a break to drink from the canteen. Albert let her be. By the time they reached Old Clevedon Road, the canteen was empty, and the sky was ablaze with color.

"Ben tells me Elwin and the dogs will be back on Saturday," Albert said, raising his voice to be heard above the noise of the passing cars. "Then they'll work every day until the fourth. That gives us a week."

"Six days."

An eighteen-wheeler blew by, kicking up road grime and blowing Clare's hair away from her face. She watched the road, but Albert could tell she was seeing something else.

"She won't pass at night," Clare said.

"Dusk, it's the only time we can do it."

"Rush hour."

"That's right."

Clare walked a few steps along the shoulder of the road and peered through the trees at the glimmer of lights reflecting off the water. Albert had already walked the distance himself. The west end of Honock Pond laid a good three hundred steps from Old Clevedon Road. Less than a quarter mile, he guessed.

"Even if we managed to get them to the road, they'll never make it across," Albert said. "Not all of them anyway."

Clare didn't reply. She looked north, where the road wound through the woods, narrowed and became Shalott Drive, continued into the town of Kinderkamack and eventually met up with Interstates 80 and 95, taking commuters across the George Washington Bridge and into New York City.

"The noise alone will scare her away," Albert continued. "She's smart, Clare. She knows it's not safe."

Clare turned and walked past Albert without responding. She watched the cars coming from the south, where, less than a half mile down the road, a single-lane bridge spanned the Kitane River that fed both Honock Pond and the lake at Tirol Farm. Beyond the bridge, Old Clevedon Road changed names several times before joining the Garden State Parkway and emptying commuters into west Newark.

"I know what you're thinking, but it'll never work."

Albert had come up behind Clare and now put his hands on her shoulders, turning her to face him. "We have to move them ourselves, at least across the road. It's the only way."

"How do you think you're going to do that?"

"A truck. Here, come look." Albert pulled Clare away from the side of the road and toward the entrance to the trail where the remains of a driveway were still visible below the overgrown brush and debris. Albert walked a few paces down the driveway and turned back to Clare. "We can back a truck up through here at least a hundred feet or so. We'll walk them the rest of the way."

"That's crazy."

"It could work."

"Fine, say we get a truck, somehow. How are you going to get them in there?"

Albert raised his arms and took a few dancing steps, winking at Clare. "You forget who you're talking to."

"She's never going to follow you into the back of a truck, are you kidding?"

"She might. If we're careful. If not, we can try—"

Clare laughed, but the sound was harsh. "What, you're going to catch her now? Give her a go at your other hand? Drag her. Forcibly. Into a truck."

A memory flew to the surface of Albert's mind, a flash of panicked flesh, knobbly limbs flailing, and his own hands, scrambling for purchase. It was twelve-year-old Clare's face he saw, screaming at him as he dragged her from under the bed. Clare's face, covered in blood.

Albert's legs weakened. For a moment, he could not speak.

"You'd scare the life out of her, and she'd never trust you again."

Albert started at the sudden shift in Clare's tone, anxious that she'd somehow also seen the vision from his memory. Albert tried to catch her eye, but she was staring back at the road, arms wrapped tightly around her body. It was getting dark and the headlights from the cars lit up the woods all around them.

He sighed. "Ok, then what's your idea?"

So Clare told Albert her idea—the dogs, the sinkhole, the pills, every detail of her plan, in a measured manner lacking any hesitation. While Clare spoke, her eyes never met his, as if the scene she was describing had already played out in her head and she was simply telling him her experience of it. This was the thought that had occupied her mind on the way back from the lake, Albert understood now. This simple, potentially devastating plan.

When she finished, Albert was silent.

"Well?" Clare waited, finally looking up at him.

"No."

"It'll work."

"That's not the point."

"So?"

"I can't let you do that. We'll find a better way."

"This is the better way, Albert. You know it is." Clare stepped away from him and turned back to the road. "Get rid of the cars or get rid of the dogs. It's really just a math problem."

"How's that now?"

"X equals A or B. They both solve the equation."

"I taught history, Clare. Never did care for math."

"Well, you don't need to know math to know that the shortest distance between two points is a straight line."

"Machiavelli. Didn't know you were a fan."

Clare turned to him then, and Albert saw he was starting to lose her. Years of teaching taught him not to ignore the hardened stare Clare was giving him now. He stepped forward, reached out to put his hands on her shoulders again, and then let them drop to his sides.

"We still have time, Clare" he said. "Let's just try the least crazy thing first. Okay? That's all I'm asking."

Clare said nothing for a moment. Then she nodded. "Okay. Sure."

"You still in?"

She returned his smile, if only a little. "Yeah, I'm still in."

Clare turned and walked down the shoulder of the road, toward home. Albert watched her, seeking some sign from the straight angle of her back, some hint or warning. There was nothing.

After a moment, Albert followed.

3 DAYS

Sunday, June 27, 2010
2:42 p.m.

Penelope lifted the handles of the wheelbarrow to roll it closer to the fence, but the load was piled high and placed unevenly in the tray. The wheelbarrow tipped sideways, spilling its contents onto the lawn. Penelope knelt in the grass to retrieve the items. She was aware she was being watched. The past five minutes or so, Penelope had felt the curious presence at her back, but had, until now, chosen to ignore it.

"You want to come help? Or are you just going to stare."

There was an uncomfortable silence from behind the fence.

Penelope turned. "Well?"

Cee-Cee came around from behind her hiding spot. Flowered t-shirt, shorts, grubby knees. And for a reason Penelope couldn't fathom, there was a purple feather wagging from her ponytail. "What are you doing?"

"What does it look like I'm doing?"

"Are you moving away?"

The question sounded so hopeful, Penelope had to hide a smile. "Nope."

"Then what are you doing with all the gnomes?"

"Getting rid of them."

"But why?"

"I don't need them anymore."

Cee-Cee frowned but said nothing. After a moment, the girl came around the bushes, crossed the front lawn, and stood beside Penelope and her fallen pile of garden gnomes. All in all, the gnomes had survived the fall rather well, Penelope thought. One had lost a nose. Another had suffered a few scratches.

"There's a bunch more around by the bushes there. You know the spot, don't you?" Penelope said, watching the girl from beneath her sunhat.

Cee-Cee hesitated, twisted her hands into the bottom of her t-shirt, and looked around behind her at the empty cul-de-sac. It was still early afternoon, but the horizon was gray, heavy with humidity.

"There's a box on the porch you can use," Penelope continued, finally looking up at Cee-Cee. She met her full in the eyes and nodded gently. "Grab some tea while you're there. It should still be cold. Cups are on the table."

Cee-Cee dropped her shirt and backed away a few steps, then ran toward the porch, feather bouncing from her hair. Penelope watched her fill a paper cup full of iced tea, drink all of it, then bang the cardboard box down the porch steps onto the lawn. Turning back to the wheelbarrow, Penelope began restacking the fallen gnomes.

The afternoon waned, a hazy white sky pressing the world below in damp heat. Sweat trickled behind Penelope's ears. Across the cul-de-sac, a screen door squeaked open and the Schlingerman's dogs burst into the front yard, barking joyfully.

Penelope continued to gather up her collection of garden gnomes but stopped often to watch Cee-Cee work in the backyard. The girl was careful, Penelope noticed. Cee-Cee had arranged the gnomes side by side on the ground and was picking each one up with both hands to place it gently in the box. Once, as Cee-Cee picked up a gnome, Penelope saw the girl's mouth move as she made the little statue talk. Another time, Penelope saw Cee-Cee pat a little fat gnome on the head as she settled it in the box.

When Cee-Cee had finished in one area, she moved to another spot, pulling the box slowly over the grass so as not to jostle the contents inside. Cee-Cee began dismantling the fishing scene by the koi pond and Penelope watched her step over the water to reach the gnomes on the other side. *She has her mother's ease*, Penelope thought, and a familiar ache rose from her stomach. The feeling dissipated quickly though, as it had been doing these last few weeks. Penelope knew that ache would always be with her, but it was becoming diffuse, something through which she could move easily.

As she watched Cee-Cee throughout the afternoon, she found it difficult to remember why she'd felt such animosity toward the little girl these past few months. Hadn't Cee-Cee been just as hurt when her mother left? Hadn't she known the same loss Penelope felt when Odis left? This new feeling of kinship with the girl brought with it illumination, and Penelope now felt she understood Cee-Cee's thieving ways. She recognized the urge to reach out and take things, grab hold of them before they were ripped away from you. To consume anything within reach—barbecue potato chips and Ho Hos mainly—just to fill up the empty places that suck all the joy from life.

Penelope had felt a softening in her chest recently, where before had been a heavy weight. It might have begun with roses— Penelope smiled here, an image of Lenny's crooked face swimming to the surface—but she thought it started before that. With a casserole. She'd made a new friend, and at a time when she'd least expected to do so. Penelope was beginning to think that if something so unexpected and pleasant could happen, perhaps there were more unexpectedly pleasant things in store for her. This feeling (it was "hope," though Penelope had yet to identify it as such) made the days feel lighter and Penelope had decided to enjoy it, rather than think about it.

Penelope stood, lifting the wheelbarrow in both hands, waiting for Cee-Cee. A dense heat had gathered around her head and Penelope tilted her head back, so that her sunhat tumbled onto the ground. The air cooled her brow, and she closed her eyes briefly at this release.

"Got them all?"

"There's still some by the bushes," Cee-Cee said, pointing.

"Let's load up the car and then come back for the last."

Penelope rolled the wheelbarrow across the lawn and onto the front sidewalk.

"So where're you going with all of them?" Cee-Cee asked, as they lifted the box together and slid it into the backseat of the car.

"The thrift store in town said they'd take them. I figured they should go for a good cause."

"But why are you getting rid of them?"

"Well," Penelope said, brushing off her hands. "They aren't actually mine. They belonged to…" Penelope paused and saw that Cee-Cee had already figured it out. "…someone else. Actually, I always thought they were kind of creepy."

"What? No, they're not creepy, they're cool."

Penelope smiled. She picked through the box in the backseat until she found the gnome with the yellow flower. The one Cee-Cee had named Norman.

"That's why you're going to keep this one."

Cee-Cee looked down at the gnome, then back up at Penelope. After a moment, she took the gnome in both hands.

"Really?"

Penelope smiled.

7:56 p.m.

Albert raised his hand to knock on the door, paused before his knuckles touched the wood, and lowered his arm to his side. The seed made a nervous rattling sound against the paper bag as Albert turned toward the street. It was dusk and the cars passed steadily along Shalott Drive, commuters returning home after a long day's work. There was nothing different about the day. The sky held the same heavy humidity it had all weekend. The air was damp with the promise of rain that had been predicted three days in a row but had yet to manifest one drop. Albert had spent the afternoon reading and then turned on the news when early evening came, as he always had. Nothing was different.

It was the first day, though, since he and Clare had begun to walk to the pond together at dusk, that he came by her house and didn't find Clare waiting for him on the porch. Her front door was closed. The windows, curtained.

Taking a breath, Albert raised his hand again and knocked on the door. Five sharp raps, then another seven when she didn't answer.

"Come in."

Clare's voice was nearly too soft to be heard, but Albert was listening for it and immediately opened the door. It was dim inside the house, though some light came from a small lamp in the corner of the room. Albert stood in the living room for a moment, letting his eyes get adjusted to the gloom.

"Is it time already?"

Clare sat at the kitchen table, a newspaper opened in front of her. She turned toward Albert.

Albert hadn't been inside Clare's house since the night he'd lifted the gun off Jared, and he was glad to see she'd unpacked many more of her boxes. A framed print hung on the far wall, books stacked on the floor, and her laptop was open on the coffee table. The print on the wall was new and Albert stepped closer, trying to discern the shapes in the darkness.

"You like it?"

Clare flipped on the light and stood by the kitchen doorway. She had on jeans and over her tank-top, wore a thin, white robe that reached past her knees. She leaned against the wall, arms folded across her chest.

Albert saw there was a woman in the picture. The woman sat on a stone bench in the midst of what seemed to be the ruins of an ancient garden. Her gown gathered in draped material around her legs, and her breasts and feet were bare. The woman, the decaying garden around her, and the sky above shared varying hues of taupe. The only real color in the painting was the brilliant yellow of the flowers which sprouted in new buds by the woman's feet.

"It caught my eye from across the store. Beautiful, isn't it?" Clare was saying, but the tone in her voice was unconvincing.

"Looks like a Waterhouse."

"That's what I thought too. I found it at the flea market a few weeks ago."

Albert continued to gaze at the print, but he wasn't seeing it anymore. He was remembering Clare on that first night. The night he had talked his way into using her oven. The night they had shared the casserole at Albert's kitchen table. Clare had slumped in the chair across from him, drunk, exhausted, hair hanging past her darkened eyes, fork dangling from her pale fingers, mostly ignoring whatever Albert's conversation had been that night, inane as it was. She nodded her head at times, grunted occasionally. When she did speak, there was very little breath behind her voice, as if something had knocked all the air out of her lungs and she was having trouble filling them again. And her tone was flat, unemotional.

In fact, her tone that night was very much like what Albert was hearing now.

Albert turned, facing Clare directly. "What's going on here, Clare?"

She flinched, just a slight flutter of her eyelids, but Albert thought he'd caught a glimpse of the storm blowing behind Clare's carefully set face. She stared at him, unmoving, eyes wide, lips pressed together. Then she left the room.

Albert followed her into the kitchen where Clare picked up the newspaper from the table. She folded it in half, held it between her hands for a moment, and then handed it to Albert. Albert took the paper, but he didn't look at it. On the table beside where the newspaper had been was the three by five photograph.

"They killed them a few days ago," Clare said in the same flat voice. "They came in the middle of the night. They gassed them all."

Albert stared at the photograph for another moment. He'd first seen the photo from across the room, standing in the doorway and over Clare's shoulder, but he knew this one was the same. The photo depicted a powerful scene, beautiful in the way only the simplest things in life were. The colors of the photograph were muted, the shadows, deep. Clare slept on her side, a tiny bundle curled against her middle. There was a vulnerability in Clare's face that Albert had not seen in her before. An intimacy in the moment that made him wonder who had taken the picture.

Albert finally moved his eyes away and lifted the newspaper.

Scanning through the articles, Albert stopped when he reached the headline: "400 Park Geese Die, for Human Fliers' Sake." Quotes from city officials and outraged park-goers followed. The article stated that the bird carcasses had been dumped in a local landfill.

"They're calling them the 'Prospect Park 400'. There's going to be a vigil." Clare grunted, and something broke at the back of her throat. "Maybe Elton John will sing."

Albert looked around the kitchen but saw no bottles on the counters or above the refrigerator. Clare was drunk. He wasn't sure how he'd missed it when he first came into the house.

He set the newspaper on the table beside the photograph and backed away. Clare sat down in the chair, letting her head fall back a little. She looked exhausted.

"I'm so sorry, Clare."

"Why?" she said, eyes closed, face tilted toward the ceiling. "Did *you* kill them?"

"I never should have brought you into any of this." Albert rubbed his face with both hands, blew out hard through his lips. "I don't know what I was thinking."

"It's fine, Albert. It doesn't change anything."

"I don't know about this, Clare."

She opened her eyes and frowned at Albert. "Don't know about what?"

"This—" Albert said, "This thing that we're doing. Look at you. Look at us. Over some…birds. This is crazy, Clare."

Clare leaned forward and pushed herself to her feet. She picked up the newspaper, threw it in the trash beneath the sink, slammed the cupboard shut. When she turned again to Albert, he saw the exhaustion on her face had been replaced with something else.

"What do you mean?" Clare's anger shook her words and Albert reflexively took another step away from her. "'Just some birds.' You're the one who started this, Albert. *You* came to *me*."

"I know I did, Clare. But I didn't know it would come to this."

"So, what, you're backing out now?"

"No, that's not what I'm—"

"Then what?"

Albert looked down at his hands, choosing his words carefully. "I'm saying that sometimes, we lose. That's all. We might want to rethink what we're doing here, before it's too late. Because you and I, we might lose this one, Clare."

"'You rarely win, but sometimes you do,' right?" Albert could feel Clare's fiery gaze, but he didn't look up. "Courage 'isn't a man with a gun in his hand. It's when you know you're licked before you begin but you begin anyway, and you see it through no matter what.'"

"I'm no Atticus Finch, Clare."

"You started this, remember? Me? I thought you were *nuts*. But you went and waxed poetic about how not saving them all is no excuse not to save one. You said that." Her voice faltered and Albert heard the restrained sob behind her words.

"I know what I said, Clare."

She was silent for a moment, only stared at him over the kitchen table. Albert began to speak again but stopped himself and stared down at his sneakers. Blue whales on the sides. They were the first pair of sneakers he'd bought for himself in forty years. He'd found them in the discount bin at the Pathmark. They were hideous, he knew.

The refrigerator kicked off with a loud clang of metal. The sound seemed to spur Clare to action.

"No."

The word reverberated through the room. Deafened all other noise. Filled every empty space.

Clare left the kitchen, brushing past Albert with a chilled breeze. He heard her in the living room, rummaging through boxes, peeling tape from cardboard.

"'Stand up for the stupid and the crazy'," Clare said when Albert came into the room. A copy of *Leaves of Grass* flew through the air and onto the couch, where it bounced off the cushion and fell to the floor.

Ignoring Albert's surprise, Clare dropped to her knees in front of a box and pulled out several more hardbound books, throwing them to the side where they fell open and scattered across the carpet. She held out a copy of *Walden*. "'A thousand hack at the branches of evil for every one that strikes the root.'" Rifling through several more, Clare pulled a book from the bottom of the box. "'Be an opener of doors to those who come after you.'" Thoreau and Emerson joined Whitman on the floor.

"Oh, here we go," Clare said, dragging another box closer to where she sat. She slid out a massive volume. "'No matter how small, we fight injustice to preserve our humanity.'" She hefted Mandela's *Long Walk to Freedom* onto the coffee table where it landed with a bang and nearly knocked over her laptop. Clare's hands were shaking.

"If one is lucky, a solitary fantasy can transform a million realities.'" She threw Maya Angelou on the floor. "It's the little bits of good that overwhelm the world.'" Desmond Tutu joined the pile. "She who has conscience on her side, has a majority against the universe.'" Frederick Douglass fell open, splaying its yellowed pages.

Albert stood by quietly while Clare stumbled to her feet and went to the stack of books on the shelf beside the couch. She picked them up one by one and heaved them to the floor.

"'If a woman wants to change the world, she starts first with herself...Wrong is wrong no matter who says it or who does it...Be ashamed to die until you have won some victory for humanity.'" The books piled up by her feet, hard corners landing on her bare toes.

Finally, Clare grabbed a ragged paperback near the end of a bookshelf, sending several others to the floor.

"'No one starves while I eat!'"

She threw the copy of *The Kingdom of God Is within You* at Albert but missed and hit the lamp instead.

There was a warble, then a crash.

Then darkness.

Silence held the room for a long while. Time seemed to vacillate on the horizon outside the living room windows. Light dying so slowly as to not be noticed.

Albert could make out only a vague outline of where Clare stood at the base of the stairs, a slumped figure, small and childlike. When Clare's voice came again, it was as if the sound traveled from a much farther distance than the few feet between them. The words she spoke also reminded Albert of the small girl Clare had been. There was a terrible plainness to what she said next, a simplicity that was crushing. As he listened, though, Albert sensed something slide into place, some old, broken piece that finally fit snuggly. Incredibly, even while Albert's eyes teared up in the dark as he heard what Clare had to say, Albert felt a sense of relief. (The storyteller in Albert might have used the word *dénouement* to describe this sense of resolution, this untying of some final knot. Three days before his death, Albert would learn the answer to a twenty-five-year-old question he had never had the courage to ask.)

Clare finally shared her secret.

"I could hear her breathing."

The shadowy figure moved so that Albert knew she was staring into the nothingness at the top of the staircase. "Before the storm came. Before the sun went down and it got so cold, I could hear breathing. For a long time under the bed, I couldn't hear anything. I couldn't see anything. I smelled blood. There was…this little draft coming up between the boards in the floor, and I put my nose to it. I couldn't breathe the blood-air, so I pressed my face against that crack."

She went silent for a long while. The room chilled as night gathered around the house. The refrigerator kicked on in the kitchen and Albert started, his heart recoiling against his chest.

"At first, I thought it was my own breathing. The ringing went away, and the sound was so soft…like branches against the roof." Another long, painful silence.

"She told me once that they used to use leeches on women. In the nineteenth century, if a woman was unhappy, or depressed, doctors would put leeches on her uterus because they believed the problem lived in a woman's blood. 'Letting out the trouble,' they called it. And I remember thinking...that was what she'd done. The branches kept scraping, and the blood-air...it was so...thick I thought I would drown, but I...I couldn't move. She was...still breathing...alive...but I couldn't do anything. I just...I kept thinking, *she let the trouble out.* Little rasps...they got softer and softer until...I couldn't hear them anymore. And I couldn't...move...I..."

Later, after Albert brought in a lamp from the closet and screwed in a new light bulb, and after he helped Clare sweep up the glass and pick up the books, Albert left Clare's house to feed Violet and the four remaining goslings at the pond. Albert and Clare would meet the following morning. Nine, sharp. They would drive together in Clare's car to rent the truck. Albert would drive the truck back to his house and Clare would follow him in her car. Then they would spend the day at the pond, keeping watch on the island. And when dusk came, they would do what they could. Albert could no more turn his back now than Clare could. He had made his choice the moment he picked up the dead gander from the road and buried it in the woods. The moment he'd knocked on Clare's door with that Shepherd's Pie.

And so, they would do what they could even if they would most likely fail. Clare was right. It wasn't about saving Violet or her goslings. It was about getting the truck. Hacking at the branch. That little bit of good. It was about doing what they could.

Nonetheless, as Albert stood with Clare on her porch, making plans for the following morning, he sensed how things had changed between them. She smiled up at him, her eyes dry but pink around the edges. She seemed subdued, shaken in the wake of her outburst and a little shy as she spoke.

"Nine o'clock," Albert repeated, hesitant to leave her on the porch.

Clare nodded and then smiled again, but all Albert sensed was sadness. "Don't be late."

"Sure you don't want to come with me?"

"Tell Violet I said 'hi'."

So Albert had left her there, standing on the porch and staring after him as he went down the front walk and across the street. He turned twice to wave his goodbye. Clare waved back both times.

When he turned a third time, she was still watching him, her hands tucked into the pockets of her jeans, her thin white robe wrapping around her body in the breeze like a winding sheet. He turned the corner, and she was gone.

Later, Albert sat by the second-floor window of his study, looking down into Clare's kitchen windows. He saw her make a sandwich. Watched her eat it quietly at the kitchen table. And he waited, his book open and unread on his lap, for the lights to turn off in Clare's house. She had disappeared from the kitchen right before ten o'clock. The shadows in the living room flickered until nearly two o'clock and then the lights turned off. One by one, the windows darkened until Clare's house lay in total blackness. With no small feeling of relief, Albert sat back in his chair.

After a while, he slept.

2 DAYS

Monday, June 28, 2010
2:31 a.m.

Clare had waited until two o'clock before turning off the computer. She had never bothered to connect the cable to the house, and so she watched movies online until it was time. The images flickered on her computer screen and when the credits rolled, she found another title to load, but mostly, she gazed at the print above her couch. At the woman with the bare feet.

When it was finally two o'clock, Clare shut down the computer, rose from the couch, and turned off the lamp Albert had retrieved from the closet earlier in the evening. She turned off the kitchen light, the hall light, brushed her teeth and turned off the bathroom light, then went to her bedroom. Sitting on the bed, Clare faced the blank wall in front of her, looked down at the half empty box of clothes on the floor, turned toward the blackened window. She reached beneath the bed, pulled out a pair of old sneakers, and slipped them on her feet without socks. Then she'd turned off that light too and left the room.

Outside, the air was cool and sweet, the humidity of the day like silk against Clare's skin. No stars shone through the clouds that hung unseen above. A veiled, sparkling blanket, hidden behind a night that pressed down in blackness. Even the crickets were silent in this early morning hour. The lightening bugs had long winked out and found shelter for the night. An owl hooted once overhead. A breeze wound through the fattened leaves of trees (...*swush*) and then fell silent.

Clare stood at the bank of the pond, looking toward the water. The island was completely hidden at night, lost within a pool of shadows. Clare imagined the goslings curled against their mother's side in the nest Violet had made with her own soft pin feathers. They would be warm within their mother's heat and protected by the morning dew beneath her body. Clare thought that Violet would not sleep but would watch her goslings slumber instead. Clare imagined she felt Violet watching her as well, black eye gazing across the black night. She wondered what she might look like to the goose, a pale figure, floating along the pond's shore.

Kneeling on the grass, Clare placed the photograph face-up on the surface of the water. She stared at it for a moment. Pushed it out into the darkness.

MAY 31, 2008

The *Rolling Stones* crackled softly from the radio on the day Clare drove her car into oncoming traffic. She did not swerve, but rather, and in keeping to the minimalist purity of the idea to which she was drawn—*nature wants death, it is we who strive vainly to avoid it*—Clare simply did not abide a right-veering curve in the road and instead, continued along a straight path. It was into the side of a mountain that Clare directed her little hatchback, and in that moment, the idea had grown so large in her mind that the thought of hitting another car, of killing another person, aside from herself, had no room to form into possibility.

On this day, Clare had been returning to Seattle along Steven's Pass through the Cascade Mountains. On the seat beside her were the manuscript pages of George Geoffrey Stacks who was, in all biasness, her least favorite author. That Clare was the author's favorite editor was a double-edged, job-securing benefit in the tenuous economy that was the 2008 recession. That Mr. Stacks belonged to the class of author who found fame and fortune on the heels of a famous marriage and an even more famous divorce, that the man had a taste for the talk show circuit like an alcoholic craves a half-empty beer left out the night before, and that he was able to churn out the kind of self-aware-pseudo-spiritual tomes that bookstore windows coveted—*Food for a Soul-deprived Tech-ciety*, as Clare had shamefully penned herself for his latest back cover—and on a bi-yearly cycle, no less, made Mr. Stacks a sort of demigod in the publishing world.

According to news reports, Mr. Stacks had recently spent a month at a meditation retreat in Bodhgaya, India where he'd enjoyed a great "spiritual awakening" in between book signings and several dinners with a Bollywood pop star, one of which included a paparazzi Vespa chase through the city and ended with full-color photos of the two being escorted from the Mahabodhi Temple.

Clare did not see the news reports, she'd not, in fact, watched news of any sort, nor read the paper since losing faith in the media at large after the investigation into Anna Nicole Smith's overdose during the week of February 8th, 2007, trumped coverage of both the Mecca Agreement in Gaza and the first large-scale trial of an HIV vaccine in South Africa. (That Clare watched coverage of the woman's apparent suicide from a 13-inch television in the basement morgue of the Virginia Mason Medical Center, while her own death lay just beyond the glass in the next room, was a variable Clare did not believe factored into her decision in any way.)

What Clare did know, however, was that Mr. Stacks had returned to the states in a kurta and now insisted everyone call him by his new pen name, Jivraj Syed.

"It means 'a life of happiness' which is what we all deserve," he'd told Clare, kissing both of her cheeks, and bowing in a confusing blend of newly acquired cultural rituals. Along with abstaining from meat or eating after the noon hour, Jivraj had also, supposedly, overcome his highly publicized chemical dependence and forgone most forms of technology, including email.

Hence, Clare's three-hour drive to retrieve the manuscript pages.

When Clare hit the oncoming car, she did not hit it straight on, but instead, clipped the car's front right bumper with her front right bumper. The sound of the cars connecting triggered a group of feasting birds to take flight from the shoulder of the road, a mere half-second before they might have met a quick and rubbery end. Some loose gravel, along with three perfectly placed patches of ice created a near Olympic-grade skating surface upon which the two cars collided and then rotated around each other. (*You can't always get what you want*...was the soundtrack from the radio that accompanied this performance, a detail that Clare would not remember. She would, however, develop an inexplicable aversion to the song from that day forward.) A front wheel of the opposite car—a four-door sedan whose bearded driver stared gape-mouthed at Clare through the windshield—caught firmly on an area of dry pavement around which Clare's car pivoted, completed its circle, and executed what in the world of championship pairs figure skating would be deemed a near flawless death-spiral.

The engine of Clare's car died just before the car stopped moving and Clare braced for impact, too late remembering that she had not unbuckled her seatbelt. But the car simply glided to an anticlimactic skid onto the shoulder of the road. Only the manuscript pages suffered minor damage when they slid out of their manila envelope and onto the floor.

PART THREE

...and in my breast
Spring wakens too; and my regret
Becomes an April violet,
And buds and blossoms like the rest.

Lord Alfred Tennyson,
"In Memoriam A. H. H."

2 DAYS (CONTINUED)

Monday, June 28, 2010
9:06 a.m.

"Is the victim breathing?"

"What?"

"Is she breathing?"

"I can't—I don't see—"

"Sir—"

"She's not moving, please you have to—"

"We have a unit on the way, but I need you to—"

"—come. Please tell them to hurry, I just got here and—"

"Sir, listen to me. Can you hear me?"

"Yes."

"I need you to tell me if she's breathing. Set the phone down and put your ear up to her mouth."

"Yes, okay. Hold on."

Albert knelt on the floor beside the couch, his house phone still clutched in one hand. He'd gone back for the phone the moment he found Clare, and its signal was weak, causing crackles in the background. He bent down. For a moment, all he heard was the sound of his own rasping breaths. He held his breath and then came a pounding heartbeat in his ears. He waited, listening...listening...

"Yes, yes. I can hear it. But just barely. It's very slow."

"Good. That's good, she's breathing."

"Is the ambulance coming?"

"Yes, they're on their way. When did you find the victim?"

"We were—we were supposed to meet at nine."

Albert looked up and stared dumbly at the clock on the microwave but could not understand the time it read. "The door was open, and she was, she was just lying here. She's so pale. I—I think she's cold. Should I get her a blanket?"

"You know the victim?"

"Yes."

"What's her name?"

"Clare."

"And her last name?"

Albert looked toward the open front door, strained to hear sounds of a siren approaching. There was nothing.

"Sir, do you know her last name?"

"Lyndsay."

"Good. That's good. And what is your name?"

"I don't know her middle name."

"Sir, can you tell me *your* name?"

Albert shook his head. "Sorry. Albert. It's Albert."

"Okay Albert, now I need you to look around for me. What do you see? Is there anything disturbed in the house? Any chairs tipped over?"

"No."

"Did Clare fall? Do you see any blood?"

"No…" Albert spotted the pill bottle under the couch just as the word came out of his mouth. "There's a bottle of pills."

"Are there any pills left in the bottle?"

"No."

"Okay Albert, read me everything you see on the label, starting at the top."

Albert read the label to the operator, struggling to gain control of his voice in order to properly enunciate the unfamiliar terminology. The prescription's list of warnings ran the length of the bottle and continued in two more columns. Albert was only mildly surprised to see that the name on the bottle read *G. G. Stacks*.

"Is that them? I think I hear the ambulance."

"Yes, they're pulling in now. You did good, Albert. You can hang up."

"You're welcome," Albert said.

Albert placed the phone on the coffee table without hanging up and looked away from the open door to where Clare lay on the couch. Her arm had fallen off the cushion and Albert picked it up at the wrist and placed it on her stomach.

A police car pulled up to the sidewalk, lights flashing. And behind it, a fire truck. Albert struggled to his feet, grabbing onto the table when his hip threatened to give way. He thought he would meet the ambulance in the yard outside, but he didn't want to leave Clare alone on the couch.

Albert stood in the living room, uncertain.

7:43 p.m.

Most of the hospital workers at Hackensack Regional Medical Center were familiar with Ben, and several of the nurses behind the admitting desk greeted him when he walked through the automatic double doors. The old Pascack Valley Hospital had been closer to his patrol and his home, but after it closed in 2008 (a poorly timed expansion, followed by bankruptcy), patients from Kinderkamack were now brought to the newer, farther facility. It lacked the charm and appeal of the older hospital, Ben thought, designed, as it was, for simplicity—just four gray walls, each wing of the hospital like four gray towers. Pascack blended with Hackensack staff, which meant that a few of the nurses knew Ben not only as a police officer, but also as the boy who received a rabies shot after being bitten by a wounded groundhog one summer, and also as the asthmatic kid who frequented the emergency room from October to March every year.

"Eddie's back." The admitting nurse shot Ben a sympathetic look as she tapped on her keyboard. Her name was Sheila, and she always wore an animal scrub top, though her days as a pediatric nurse were long over. That day it was frogs. "They brought him in last night from the park. CCR on roller skates. Neighbors called from two blocks away."

"'Proud Mary'?"

"'Fortunate Son'."

Sheila moved her wireless mouse, using a stack of patient charts as a pad. She clicked several times. "What was the last name again?"

"Lyndsay."

"Here we go." Sheila turned the computer monitor so Ben could see the list of patient names.

Ben jotted down the room number in his notepad. "Roller skates," Ben said. "That's new."

"Still naked."

"Variation on a theme." He smiled. "What happened with Shorebrook House?"

"They haven't seen him in a week over there."

"I'll give them a call."

"It's a volunteer program, Ben. There's nothing you can do if he doesn't want to go."

Ben nodded, turning toward the stairwell. "Thanks, Sheila."

"You can't save everybody."

"It's just a phone call," he said as the door shut behind him.

In the stairwell, Ben wrote a few more notes to himself, then slipped the notepad into his pocket. He began up the steps at a brisk pace, grateful for this short workout to the twelfth floor after spending most of the day sitting in his cruiser. It was cool and dark in the stairwell, empty, but for the sound of his echoing footsteps.

You nobody hero… Sheila's voice came back to him in his mother's dark eyes, each word sharpened by her broken English. *You think you superman? You think you Sánchez del Río? Look, no wings. No fly.* Ariana would hold Ben's skinny arms away from his body to prove her point. *You my boy, gonna get hurt.* They spoke English everywhere, even at home, since his mother believed English was the language of freedom and prosperity—the life she wanted for her son.

For years, though, it was Todd Middleton, a bigger, older boy, who brought the Spanish out in Ben. Todd enjoyed kicking Ben's classmates in the legs and driving them to the ground when no teachers were looking. During Ben's third grade year, Ben came home nearly every week with a ripped shirt, bleeding from some cut or another on his body. *You nobody hero*, his mother would say, her brown face wet as she wiped dried blood and dirt from Ben's face. By the time Ben reached fifth grade, Todd had moved on to the junior high where, Ben heard, he had been thrown into a gym locker by some eighth graders one day and forgotten about for most of an afternoon.

It was around this time when Ben began losing weight. Always a scrawny kid, even a few pounds lost hollowed out his face and sucked the flesh around his ribs like tissue on the back of a fan. Horrified, his mother brought him to the clinic where Ben confessed that for the past few weeks, he had left the packed lunch his mother made him every night with the homeless man who lived behind his school. Then there were the bedsheets he gave to a neighbor who'd had a fire—the good ones, *mijo, why the good ones?*—the trips to the store for blind Mrs. Ortega across the hall who mistook Ben for her dead husband and often wacked him in the shins with her cane, and also the summer Ben spent walking Mrs. Vega's tiny shih tzu who enjoyed people-watching at the park nearly as much as Ben did. For months,

Ben and his mother had listened to the fighting upstairs, but Mrs. Vega had pleaded with Ben's mother not to call the police for fear they would both be deported. When the police finally came, little Dulce was dead, Mrs. Vega, unconscious, and Mr. Vega was crying in the tiny courtyard downstairs. No one in the building ever saw the Vegas again.

It was the animals, though, that brought the Spanish out in his mother. Ben brought home injured robins, starlings, swallows, finches—whatever happened to fall from the trees of the park around the corner from where he and his mother lived. He found a box of kittens behind the A&P during the fall of his first year of junior high. It was the day before Hurricane Gloria hit, a point that became a persuasive argument with his mother. *They'll die in the storm!* he'd pleaded, hugging the box tightly to his chest. And so Ben spent two weeks chasing the mewing creatures out from behind the refrigerator, beneath the couch, and under the kitchen chairs while his mother shouted a string of threats—*te voy a guindar de los dedos del pie con una cadena!*—that were exponentially more effective in her native tongue.

But it was when Ben brought home a possum that he'd found on the side of the road that his mother finally said, *no.* Arms full with what felt like a furry sack of rocks, bones rolling along Ben's hands, Ben had kicked at the front door lightly with his sneaker and his mother had opened it. She looked down at the unconscious animal wrapped in her son's jacket, held out from his body in both hands, like an offering. Then she looked at Ben. Her expression was one he didn't recognize. Anger, he knew. Frustration, dismay, worry, were all well-worn countenances within his mother's emotional repertoire. But not fear. Though he didn't understand why at the time, he did understand that her fear was not of the wild animal Ben carried in his arms. Her fear was for Ben, himself. *No.* She finally said. His mother shut the door and Ben weakened with relief. He hadn't wanted to bring this one home. Hadn't wanted to find it. Had hoped, actually, that it was already dead when he saw it there, curled up by the gutter. Ben took the possum behind the apartment building where he made it a bed of dried pine needles and sat vigil with it into the evening.

Mi pobrecito, his mother would tell the ladies who gathered in their kitchen every Sunday to roll tamales. *His heart so big, his body so little.*

It shamed Ben to hear that. He knew he was no hero. He knew he was just a scared little boy who had often hid from Todd in the bathroom stall at school, who had dragged his mother's telephone into his bedroom closet and called the police the night he heard Mrs. Vega beg for her life through the walls, who had whispered, shaking with fear and grief, *die, why won't you just die* to the failing possum whose matted fur quivered on and on and on while the sun sunk behind the trees.

He was nobody's hero.

Ben reached the twelfth floor, only slightly out of breath, stopped at the doctor's lounge, and emerged a moment later with two steaming paper cups. He passed an open patient door with at least six girls draped about the room, wearing matching red and blue lacrosse uniforms. They giggled in a chorus of adolescent tribalism. One of the girls by the doorway caught his eye and she raised her hand in mock salute. Soft catcalls dissolved into more fits of shushed laughter that followed Ben as he walked away.

At the end of the hall, Ben found Mr. Hallam standing outside of Clare's room. The man leaned against the window that looked into the room, hands in his pockets. His back was to Ben, so he couldn't see the man's face, but Ben could tell from down the hall that the news wasn't good. The slump in Albert's spine made his old teacher's body appear wilted, smaller in some way than what it had been only days before.

"Mr. Hallam?"

He turned, visibly startled by Ben's voice. Ben looked down, shying away from the raw expression on the man's face.

"Ben. Yes," Albert said, as if reminding himself of who Ben was. "No coffee for me, thanks."

The man's voice had fallen so soft and deep, Ben barely recognized it. "It's tea. All year in your classroom, I never saw you drink anything else."

Albert took the paper cup in both hands and returned Ben's smile with a twitch at the corner of his mouth. The man's face had grayed, eyes sagged at the corners, his shirt untucked, his hair a frizzled black and silver mess. Ben took a long drink from his cup of coffee, startled himself, to see his former teacher in such a state.

"So what's the update?"

Albert sighed, then shrugged, a slow, tired gesture.

"Wait and see." He turned back to the window. "Wait to find out the extent of the damage. See if she wakes up."

Ben came around to stand beside Albert and looked into the room. The sun was beginning to set in the long window behind the bed and it lit the small space in rich tones of red and gold. The shadows in the room were already turning black. Beside the bed was a blinking heart monitor that flashed slowly in the dim light. An empty chair sat by the wall, a bit of white stuffing showed at the ripped vinyl. On the nightstand was a plastic water pitcher with two cups beside it, still wrapped in their sterile packaging.

Clare laid on the hospital bed in the center of the room, her arms at her sides, palms facing the ceiling, a white blanket pulled to her chest. Her hair appeared nearly black in the low light and trailed alongside her face. Her cheeks and neck shone nearly white as the sheets. Her chin was tilted upward, eyes closed within their darkened pits. Ben watched the blanket at her chest but could discern no movement to indicate breath. He was struck by how disconnected she seemed, cutoff somehow, from the room, from the two of them watching in the hall, from the sun setting outside the window. She was no longer a part of the world that chattered cheerfully at the nurse's station behind him or sobbed quietly in the room next door. The idea held Ben strongly. She'd been untethered and was floating, drifting on a current, even as he watched, farther and farther away, toward regions unknown.

You nobody hero…

Ben took a deep breath and shook himself slightly. "Is her family coming?"

"No."

"Were they called?"

A long silence. "There was an aunt, her mother's sister in Seattle. I think it was cancer, a while back…no, there's no one to call."

Ben frowned and turned toward Albert.

A burst of laughter suddenly jostled the quiet in the hall. Two or three of the staff gathered around one of the nurses who held out her cell phone. There was a muffled gasp. Hushed giggles.

Ben wiped his mouth, not sure how to ask his next question. Though this was his investigation, the question felt anything but routine.

"I should have seen this," Ben said instead. "The way she ran out in front of that car—"

Albert put his hand on Ben's arm, stopping him silently. The old man didn't look away from the bed in the room, but the pressure on Ben's arm was there, steady.

"Do you know, I mean..." Ben paused, started again. Stopped. He swallowed. "We didn't find a note at the house, on her computer, any indication..."

"You want to know why?"

"Do you know?"

Albert sighed, a slight wheeze ending in a tiny rattle at the base of his lungs.

"There was a baby. Her daughter," Albert said. "But I think she's been looking for a reason for a while."

Ben closed his eyes briefly, listening to the continued quiet laughter behind them.

"There has to be someone who can come. A friend from work..."

Albert turned then, his watery eyes narrow, and Ben was suddenly sitting again in the back row of Mr. Hallam's third period World History class. Ben at sixteen was a jokester and full of teenage hubris, and Mr. Hallam had allowed him a certain range during his lessons, tolerated Ben's sometimes inappropriate comments, overlooked a degree of witless humor. It was only with a look, though, that his teacher could reign in Ben's foolhardiness. A slight narrow of Mr. Hallam's eyes that made Ben aware of all that his teacher knew and all he had yet to comprehend. This was the look Albert was giving Ben now.

Ben turned away, looking back at Clare on the bed. "How does that happen?"

The heart monitor continued to blink. The blanket on her chest did not move.

"Easier than you think."

8:16 p.m.

Albert stood beside Clare's bed, his hands on the bedrails, as the last of the sun set in blazing colors across his face. The long window was too high for viewing the ground, but it offered a scene of sky that was dazzling. Golden beams stretched across a purple expanse in a kind of ethereal bloom that Albert knew, after nearly eighty years of New Jersey summers, meant a storm, and one that would leave its mark on the town when it finally hit. The dark clouds glowed, etched in unearthly light. Near the western horizon, a narrow shaft of sun broke through the bruised firmament and spread out like a starburst. The entire sky suggested movement. Some giant, lumbering behind a curtain, waiting for a cue.

The windows in the Pascack Valley Hospital had been bigger. They had a wide ledge and were set low in the wall so that the space doubled as extra seating for the room, granted that the sitter moved aside all the get-well cards, stuffed animals of bears and rabbits and chicks, and the brightly colored flowers (good cheer mixed with desperate hope in a pot, had been Albert's unshared thought). On the northern side of the hospital, the windows offered views of the town—the back alley behind the shopping mall, the parking garage next to the train station, the used car lot beside the daycare center. On the southern end of the hospital, all the rooms faced the greenlands that bordered the entire southern parameter of the town. Oradell Reservoir fed several tiny streams and at least one major creek that all wound without direction through the countryside, dead ending in various marshes and backyard swamplands. The windows near the western wing of the hospital looked out over the woods, a lush canopy of green and blooms of pink and white during the springtime months.

The windows at the eastern wing of the hospital looked over the cemetery.

The trees around the cemetery were cut back, and the landscape had a sculpted appearance, green clay molded, rough edges smoothed into perfection. A creek widened into a long pool at the base of the cemetery, and headstones spanned across the hills in orderly, neat rows. Death made organized.

In February, of course, there had been no green outside the windows. The leaves on the trees had long since withered and died beneath the mounds of snow that had come the first week of November and accumulated every week since. The water in the creek iced over quickly that year, surprising the wildlife and causing early death along the banks. Frost glazed the frozen hills, encasing everything in its path. The trees at the horizon sparkled dangerously, branches sheathed in ice. The cemetery was barren tundra.

Emily had been transferred to the eastern wing of the hospital in early February of 2007. Her cold had started before Christmas, just a bit of stuffiness in her head. A slight dip in her voice. By New Year's Albert had wanted to bring her to the doctor, but she'd brushed aside his concern in her usual, chastising way. *I've been taking care of myself for seventy-six years, Al. If I need to go, I'll go.* A week into the new year and Emily seemed better. They had shopped together for the after-Christmas sales at the outlet mall, and she'd teased him when he asked to stop at the ice cream parlor. She knew he needed to sit and rest his back. She ate both scoops of her mint chocolate chunk and finished his vanilla bean—'old fart flavor,' as she called it—tapping his foot under the table and chatting about Nancy Pelosi's recent win for Speaker of the House. *When will it stop being news for a woman to land a high-power position?* Emily had wanted to know, and they argued over the merit of the news story while Albert watched the white tendrils of her hair that had broken loose from her bun and were dancing by her eyes.

The second week of January Albert noticed a lag in Emily's walk. She sighed going up the stairs to their bedroom at night and in the mornings, she spent too long in the bathroom. But she shushed him with a look, put her crooked finger to his lips, trapping his concern inside. By the end of January, she was in bed most days and Albert was frantic with fear and angry at her stubbornness. They had talked about the hospital many times during the last three years, had had many heated discussions on the porch that ended with one or the other of them slamming back inside the house.

—completely irrational, Emily. You're a grown woman, you know better.
So you're calling me a child?
When you act like one, that's exactly what I'm saying.
I'm taking the medications, Al. I'm doing everything they tell me. But you have to promise.

I won't. And you can't make me.

Now who's being a child?

You can't just—

It's not your decision. Please, Al. Please try to understand. It's not what I want. For me or for you.

They were years away from such a decision, Emily would assure him when they both tired of fighting. Surely when the time came, they would know what to do. And yet, here they were, and the issue went unresolved. Emily wanted him to let it pass, this illness that had taken hold of her, certain as she was that a trip to the doctor led inevitably to the hospital. *I won't come out, Albert,* her voice firm though her eyes drooped with fatigue. *I'm not scared, I'm not. I just don't want to die in there.* His pleas went unheard, and Albert wandered the house during the day, banging about like a fly trapped in glass, keeping watch on his wife who slept more than she was awake. It was the first of February when Albert woke to find their bed sheets wet with urine and Emily crying softly into her pillow. He held her in his arms, her thin bones rolling beneath his hands, her nightgown damp against his legs. Three hours later, she was lying in a bed in the eastern wing of the hospital with a view of the cemetery behind her.

It chilled him to see his wife, backdropped against such death.

She got better, then worse, then better again. Her kidneys failed, then her liver. Her heart rate rose, her blood pressure dropped. She developed pneumonia in her left lung. Her fingers swelled, so Albert pulled off her wedding ring and slipped it onto the chain she always wore around her neck. Her feet turned club-like, cold slabs of meat that would not stay warm no matter the blankets Albert piled on top of her. Albert lifted his shirt and sat at the foot of her bed, hugging her cold feet against his bare stomach. Her skin became translucent, veins coursing along her forehead, her neck, her chest. She woke only to smile at him, his worry, his hovering. Eyes unfocused and roaming, she drifted off again.

Is it the leukemia? Albert asked so often even he tired of hearing it.

Hard to say. Sepsis can originate from any number of sources. Infection, disease...patients already at risk are most susceptible.

So she could have got it here, at the hospital. Is that what you're saying?

You need to decide how aggressive you want us to be.
But if it's not the leukemia, she could get better?
There's no way to tell.

Emily's doctor would flip her chart shut, signaling the end of the conversation. The man worked at a computer station most mornings, saw patients in the other rooms, and then disappeared for the rest of the day. Often, Albert caught him watching the television in the nurse's lounge where news coverage of Anna Nicole Smith's drug overdose aired wall-to-wall without commercial break. Albert hated Emily's doctor with the kind of senseless passion he'd once hated peas as a child.

As it turned out, Albert was at the Pathmark when Emily died— the freezer aisle, specifically. In the years that followed, Albert had much time to think about that last day. How she woke, how she seemed to be his Emily again for just a moment when she smiled. Did she send him away that day? Did she know how it was hurting him to watch her die? Could she see, through the fog of her illness, how he was dying in bits and pieces right along with her? Albert spent some time being angry with his dead wife—stubborn to the end, she was. He spent more time being angry at himself for so easily escaping her room that afternoon. But eventually Albert learned that grief overcomes anger, if you let it. And slowly, Albert let it. He was still waiting to find out what overcomes grief.

When Emily woke that afternoon, her eyes had been clear for the first time in a week. She smiled. She lifted her hand slowly, and he rushed forward to take it in between his own.

How are you feeling? Are you okay? What can I do? Albert had said all of this in a rush that he wished immediately he could take back. His words felt so clumsy and intrusive around her quiet space. *What do you want me to do?* he needed to ask her but couldn't. *We're here now, Emily. The time finally came. Please tell me what you want, and I'll do it,* he begged silently with his eyes. *I promise this time. Just tell me what you want me to do.* Words that died in the tears that would not stop flowing down his cheeks.

She smiled, ever gracious. When she spoke, her throat closed around her words in spasms and her voice was someone else's— some ancient, desert wanderer. But her eyes held his, and twinkled, incredibly, with her old mischief.

Ice cream…Al. Find me…some.

So Albert fled the room to find her some ice cream and then had stood in the freezer aisle, not unironically, frozen by indecision. Emily liked mint chocolate, but it was only available in a half-gallon container that Albert would never be able to smuggle into the hospital. He could get a package of the little ice cream cups that came with wooden spoons that he could slip into his pocket, but the only flavors they had were strawberry or fudge ripple, not even chocolate. Chocolate chunk was available in a quart container that might fit under his coat, but it was a frozen yogurt and Albert couldn't clearly recall Emily's position on frozen yogurt. Maybe he could crumble a bit of peppermint patty on top? Could she swallow it? He tried to calculate the time and distance to the bigger grocery store on the other side of town. Tried to remember if the ice cream parlor by their house was open all year or only for the summer season. But Albert couldn't decide and thankfully, perhaps, Emily died before he had to.

"Albert?"

He jerked, clutched the bedrails and shook the mattress slightly. An arc of fire soared down his spine. The sun had set without Albert noticing. The sky beyond the window was black.

Clare was awake.

1 DAY

Tuesday, June 29, 2010
1:34 a.m.

The doctor nodded at Albert, nodded at Clare and then left, flipping his clipboard shut. Albert stood in the doorway, watching the man walk down the empty hallway, his footsteps echoing, pounding to the beat in his head. The crying woman in the next room was gone, as was the patient who had been in that room. One dozing orderly sat at the nurse's station, foot resting on a filing cabinet, his head propped up against his hand. The mechanical whir of a floor-buffer could be heard in some distant hallway.

When Albert turned back to Clare her eyes were closed, but he knew she wasn't sleeping. The bruise on her eye from Ben's tackle had turned nearly black. There were dark smudges around her lips where the charcoal the paramedics had forced into her body had seeped out of her mouth. There was a rashy scrape along her arm where her skin had caught some sharp edge of the gurney, and a swollen area by her wrist where an earlier IV had slipped out of its vein. Around the fading bruise of Jared's hit, red splotches marked her upper chest where emergency workers had performed CPR—once in the ambulance and again when they'd reached the hospital.

"How long?"

Clare's eyes were still closed, and Albert thought at first, he'd only imagined she spoke. Her lips barely moved. She whispered, like air moving through sand, the voice of an ancient wanderer.

"You've been out all day," Albert said, and checked his watch. "It's one-thirty. Early Tuesday."

"No...the trucks."

Understanding washed through Albert's body like icy saltwater in his gut. He'd had his suspicions. From the moment Albert found Clare on the floor that morning, he'd had his suspicions as to why Clare had done what she did. It was a fire she'd suggested that day after he'd taken her to Tirol Farm. Just a small one in the kitchen, she'd said, so they could

218

factor in the timing of the trucks, but Albert had told her it was too dangerous. And so instead, she'd done this. All night long Albert had been trying to decide which reason he hoped had caused Clare to take such a drastic action—to save Violet, or to destroy herself. But he hadn't yet figured out which reason he hoped to be true.

Neither, Albert thought now. Definitely neither.

"I cannot. I cannot believe you did this."

"How long?"

Clare opened her eyes and Albert cringed, looking away. The doctor assured him the redness around her pupils would fade in a day or two, but it was hard to look at her. She looked ghastly, poisoned. Albert turned toward the hall.

"I can't believe I dragged you into this."

"Albert," Clare said slowly, a note of chastisement in the word. A familiar tone. "How long?"

Albert looked down and kept his eyes on the floor. "Between the ambulance, the fire truck, and the police, traffic was blocked for nearly an hour. They redirected to Route 4."

Clare took a deep breath. She let it out slowly. "Okay."

"We would have found another way."

"We're running out of time."

Albert spun around to face Clare, sending a roar of pain down his back. He crossed the room in two long strides and without thinking, slammed his hands on the bedrails. Clare looked up at Albert, unflinching.

"You took the whole bottle, Clare. You could have done the job with half of that. What the hell were you thinking?"

Clare held his stare until Albert turned away. The anger had taken hold of him so quickly, so violently, he felt his insides actually shake with the emotion. She was so stubborn, so childish, so completely single-minded. But the anger withdrew, quick as it came and left his stomach a hollow pit. Albert had known this about Clare all along. There was something of her mother about her, something of Alice. Intractable. Unmovable. It took a singular mind to plan one's own death. Down to the very last boxed-up detail. Anyone could hurl themselves off a bridge in a fit of irrational passion, but Albert understood that only a particular intellect could plot the disposal of one's own body. And how long ago was it that she'd planned that? Weeks? A month maybe? He'd let himself forget. Fooled himself into thinking something had changed. And he'd been vain enough to imagine he had been an agent of that change. But it was he who was so stubborn, wanting to believe against all evidence to the contrary. Here was his proof, staring up at him, red-eyed and unblinking.

Emily was wrong. Seasons change. People don't.

Albert lifted his hands from the bedrail and took a step back.

"You okay, Albert?"

"Am I—?" He breathed in slowly, let it out through his mouth. "Yes. Clare. I am okay."

She watched him quietly for a moment longer. Then she nodded.

"Good, because we still have a lot to do. Why don't you sit. You look tired."

Albert took another deep breath, stretching the very bottom of his lungs. When at last his heart decided to behave, he looked back at Clare. "First, I have to tell you something."

Clare listened silently as Albert told her what Ben had told him about Jared and the girl who had died. Then he explained how they had made a serious mistake in not telling Ben about Jared breaking into Clare's house. Clare's lips tightened as she absorbed the information. When Albert was done, Clare said nothing for a moment. Her eyes roved across the ceiling.

"We can fix this, Albert. C'mon. Sit down."

Albert sat in the ripped vinyl-covered chair beside Clare's bed, his hip collapsing in relief, as Clare talked about their plan for saving Violet and the goslings. He peeled off the wrapping from the plastic cups and poured them each a cup of water while she spoke. He answered her questions, asked a few of his own, and nodded whenever it seemed she needed his agreement. He heard nothing, however. Her words blended into the pounding at the back of his head, a humid pressure that rose and fell with the cadence of her voice. The pounding became louder as the time wound toward the wild hour of 3 o'clock. Clare seemed untouched by the late hour, or the dampness in the air. She spoke quietly, sometimes holding her swollen throat with one hand. A sense of urgency laced everything she said. Her eyes burned with it. Feverish,

Albert thought at first. But Clare wasn't sick. This wasn't illness he was seeing. Then again, she wasn't exactly well, either, was she?

"I wish we had more than three days," Clare said finally, resting her head and staring up at the ceiling. "Can you bring my laptop in the morning?"

Clare paused, looking at him. "What?"

"Nothing. They'll never let you out of here before the weekend. If then."

She rolled her head away. "I'll take care of it. Just get my laptop."

Albert paused, staring into the bottom of his nearly empty plastic cup. There was a black flake of something floating in the last sip of water. He wondered about other flakes he'd inadvertently swallowed.

"Where's your laptop?"

"On the table, in the kitchen. Albert, what is it?"

There was no way not to tell her, but Albert hesitated all the same. He had been a fool to bring Clare into this. He knew that now. For as much as he'd wanted to believe what Emily said was true, he knew now she was wrong. Albert had watched Clare from his second-floor study, had witnessed, during those early spring months, her descent from grief and sorrow into something like madness. His first mistake was thinking he could save her. There was no saving what had already been lost.

Albert tipped the cup to his lips until he had swallowed the last sip. He set the cup on the nightstand. He turned to Clare, looked her full in the face.

"Ben said something else. They're bringing the dogs back tomorrow, not Thursday," Albert said. "We've only got two days."

His second mistake was believing the worst had already passed.

7:31 p.m.

Albert left again late Tuesday afternoon, having delivered Clare's laptop and having gone over the plan twice more. In Albert's front pants pocket, he held Clare's prescription.

"*L.A.T Rentals*," she reminded Albert before he left and he promised, however wearily, to return in the morning.

"You're okay to drive?" Clare asked him.

"What kind of question is that?"

Now, alone in her hospital room, Clare picked up the telephone from her bedside table and placed it on her lap. The heaviness of the phone surprised Clare, and her arm shook as she lifted it. The phone's weight pressed heavily into her legs. She felt the ridged surface of the mattress against her back and legs. She felt the hospital gown rub against the grain of the fine hairs on her arms and shoulders. Clare felt everything.

A nurse had raised the head of Clare's bed and left the overhead light on, making it difficult to determine the passage of time outside her hospital window. Swollen clouds had lumbered by the glass all afternoon. Clare smelled dampness in the air, even as it was pumped in through the hospital's ventilation system.

The clock on Clare's laptop read 7:32 PM. Nearly sunset. Only twenty-four hours left.

"Let's get this apple juice down you, okay?" the nurse said, who'd begun speaking before she entered the room. She breezed around Clare's bed, shoving the chair back against the wall and pulling the IV stand closer to the window, smiling all the while, but never quite meeting Clare's eyes.

Clare took the plastic cup and "got down" the colored liquid, smiling into the nurse's neck as she did so.

The nurse's name was Kimi—with an "i" according to her name badge—and Clare found her cheery in the blank way of Christmas cards, wishing generic happiness to anyone who happened by a holiday display. Good cheer bestowed arbitrarily, until properly addressed. Clare guessed Kimi might spend all her life without ever being properly addressed.

Kimi motioned to Clare's open laptop, a tiny hill appearing along the plump perfection that was the girl's forehead.

"We're not working, are we? You remember what Dr. Gully said?"

"Oh no, just getting in touch with a friend."

"Good! Good!" Kimi beamed with pride and again Clare wondered at the unspoiled landscape that was the girl's face.

"And what about your mother, have you heard back yet?"

"She's on her way."

"That's wonderful! Dr. Gully will be so happy to hear that, won't he?"

"Yes, he will."

"You might just get to go home this weekend. Maybe Saturday. Plenty of time for the Fourth. Wouldn't that be great?"

"Saturday. Great."

The lacrosse team suddenly exploded in joyful shouts in the hallway. Girls in red and blue rushed by the hallway outside Clare's room.

"I'd better go see what that's all about, shouldn't I?" Kimi asked, still beaming as she hurried toward the door.

Clare shifted the weight of the phone across her legs and pulled her laptop closer. Three browser tabs were open at the bottom of the screen: "Truck Ignition Switc…" "dosage canines calc…" "TOTALLY LEGAL pyro…" Clare clicked on this last tab and a Craigslist page sprang up. Her internet search had brought back 27 hits—ten with dates too old and twelve with locations too far. Of the remaining five posts, only three used the machinegun-like syntax Clare knew well—Killer explosions! More bang!—and only one post encouraged customers to call Trent Reznor, lead singer for Nine Inch Nails. Clare lifted the phone receiver and dialed the number.

The phone rang once. Twice. Three times. Clare waited.

A gruff voice cut off the sixth ring. Clare recognized it immediately.

"Yeah?"

"You want it back?"

"What? Who is this?"

Clare cleared her throat and winced at the sharp fire that lit down her throat. She lifted the heavy receiver closer to her mouth.

"I have it. Do you want it back?"

"Do I want what—? ...*Clare?* Is that you?"

"Come tomorrow. At the house. Four PM."

"You stupid bitch, what game you playin' at? Cause I swear to Jesus—"

"Don't be late."

Clare hung up.

FINAL DAY

Wednesday, June 30, 2010
12:47 p.m.

Kimi finished her rounds and sat down at the computer behind the nurse's station to check her messages. She'd been quietly stalking Stephan in pediatrics on Facebook since last month and she saw that he'd just posted four new photos to his wall. Kimi bent over the screen, examining the angle at which Stephan's arm was draped across a blonde in a group photo at what appeared to be the bar across the street. Sister? Kimi wondered. Surely the angle was too casual for a girlfriend.

Kimi glanced up as one of the lacrosse girls hurried past the desk, *Kinderkamack Pride* printed across the back of her red t-shirt. Kimi had played lacrosse in high school, when she wasn't cheering, and her team had brought home the championship three years in a row. Kimi remembered how it felt to be a part of that team. She had an entire album of lacrosse photos posted on her profile. Kimi secretly believed that most of the sad people in the world were only sad because they had never belonged to something special. Like the Lyndsay woman in room 301. Kimi would bet she'd never played lacrosse in her life. No wonder she got so old and sad.

Thinking about the patient in room 301 reminded Kimi that it was time for meds. Nearly a half hour had gone by while she'd checked Stephan's Facebook page. Kimi quickly copied the photo of Stephan, cropped out the blonde, and saved the newly single Stephan to the folder named "Yummy."

When Kimi entered room 301 a few minutes later, tiny plastic cup of pills in one hand and an apple juice box in the other, she stopped in the doorway with a tiny "oh!"

The bed was made. A hospital gown was folded and placed neatly on the pillow.

Room 301 was empty.

3:03 p.m.

The house was quiet. No movement fluttered the curtains in the front window. No light brightened them either, though the sky was so heavy with clouds it was surely dark as night inside. The storm was coming. It had been coming for days now, but that morning brought a fine edge of coolness in the air, a faint scent of seawater.

Jared sat in his rig, two blocks away, watching Clare's house through binoculars. The scene before him jumped and skittered. The ice he'd smoked had smoothed out his thoughts into a fine, crystalline line, buff edges all around, but it hadn't touched the pain in his tooth which now wound a tightening path through his ear, and his hands…they wouldn't stop shaking.

Jared had parked his rig behind a moving van—one of those do-it-yourselfers—with *L.A.T. Rentals* written in block letters across the side. The truck provided sufficient cover for Jared's surveillance. A steady stream of cars passed, two joggers and a dog-walker had gone by, but in the twenty minutes Jared had been watching, he'd spotted not one police cruiser. He checked the time again. An hour early, just as he'd planned.

Jared swung open the truck's door and (out of habit) reached for the glove compartment. He cursed Clare under his breath (not the first time that day) and started to get out of the truck before he leaned over again and reached back inside the glove compartment. From beneath a stack of maps and old receipts, Jared pulled a box cutter, which he mostly used to open mail. After shaking the box cutter free of cracker crumbs, Jared shoved it into the front pocket of his jeans.

He slammed the rig's door shut and walked up the sidewalk toward Clare's house. The box cutter rubbed against his thigh as Jared walked. It felt small, insignificant. Not at all like the purposeful weight of the .22 against his lower back. Jared tried to ignore the tiny rubbings of such an insufficient weapon. He would have his gun back soon enough.

At the driveway of Clare's house, Jared paused. He looked down Shalott Drive in one direction, then the other. No police cars. No one sitting in a parked car either. No one crouched behind the shrubs at the front walk or hiding behind the house. Even so…there was something…

Jared turned a full circle at the end of Clare's front walk, watching the street, watching the cars, watching the houses. There was nothing.

The windows in the front of Clare's house were all closed, but her car was in the driveway. *She's home.* Jared felt this certainty and didn't doubt it. Jared had no doubts, in fact, as he made his way to the back of the house. The meth helped with that. *It is only indecision that makes one weak, action creates strength.* Jared thought he'd read this quote somewhere and made a mental note to write it in his notebook when he finished at Clare's house.

(That the cellar door at the back of the house was still unlocked, even slightly ajar, when Jared had already used it twice to gain entry to the house was something else Jared didn't question. Neither did Jared question the recycling and trash bins that had been set aside, clearing a straight path to the cellar door. Jared's mind discerned nothing out of place. Rather, the ease with which he broke into Clare's house only further assured him that the decision he'd made was, in fact, the right one.)

One chapter of Jared's life would end today, the chapter where he lived in the basement of his mother's house and lied to the girls he brought home, sneaking them into his mother's bed when his mother was at work. The chapter where he spent his days chasing after unpaid property, sitting up nights, alone in his rig and hoping not to get caught while he sometimes masturbated into a sock to the low lights of the dashboard. The chapter where, according to his brother's contact, the Kinderkamack police force was hunting him like a dog for illegal weapons possession, first-degree assault, sexual assault—*aggravated* sexual assault, only because that silly bitch from Hunter had seen the gun in his pants—and now, second-degree murder. (That Lacy had died, actually *died*, was something Jared could not yet fully comprehend. The word simply floated beneath his drug-drenched thoughts, bumping to the surface every so often with a gasp.)

Jared was eager to reach the end of this chapter of his life. He would soon be on his way to Canada and living like a man should— off the land. (Jared was currently reading *White Fang* and had only a reader's idea of what "living off the land" actually meant). He would sleep under the stars with only his notebook and his thoughts for company. He was done with women, finished, for now at least. He would finally write a book, finally have time for himself, without all the female distraction, though he had heard that French girls were all prostitutes in disguise (and from what Jared understood, Canada was packed full to brimming with French girls), but otherwise Jared would focus only on his work. Yes, he would leave all this nonsense behind him, live off the land, sleep under the stars, and depend on only himself and his gun.

His gun, yes.

Jared had only to wrap up this storyline with Clare and the old man before turning the page on his new life. Hopeful novelist that he was, Jared knew he would enjoy the end of this chapter, since the end of this chapter brought a cliffhanger for the protagonist— an exciting choice laid before the lead character: would Jared shoot Clare first when he got his gun back? Or would the meddling old bastard get it between the eyes while Clare watched?

Jared thought that wasn't bad for a cliffhanger.

3:12 p.m.

A massive shadow suddenly filled and then disappeared from the bay window of the kitchen as Jared passed through the backyard. Clare heard a soft thump on the cellar door and then felt the air in the house shift as Jared opened it. The wooden steps creaked under his weight. Clare had already slipped out the front door, though. She turned the doorknob, closing it silently behind her.

On the street, Clare looked back only once, but saw no movement behind her curtained windows. She tripped on an uneven block of sidewalk, caught herself, and ran toward the parked tow truck. She didn't look back again.

It's best to catch 'em unawares. Clare remembered this line mostly because of its odd mix of colloquialism and slight Middle English syntax. High as Clare had been for most of the time she'd spent with Jared, her interior editor rarely took time off. Jared had been lounging beneath her sheets, naked but for his pinky ring and telling her his strategy for repossessing vehicles. Clare had been wishing he'd shut up and leave. *You set an appointment,* he told Clare, and she heard notes of pleasure in his voice, pleased as he was with his technique. *You tell 'em you want to reappraise the car. Whatever. Get 'em a better rate. Lower their payment. They're desperate. They buy it. But you come in an hour early. Nab it before they know what hit 'em.* Jared had then sat back and bent his leg so that the sheet slipped down from his knee and left him completely exposed. Pride made him begin to swell again. He shifted his hips toward Clare and put one hand behind his head, staring at the ceiling, still talking. Clare got up to take a shower. She shut the bathroom door firmly behind her, but Jared's voice still managed to reach her from down the hall. *Sixty minutes, that's the sweet spot, I'm telling you.*

Clare's watch read a few minutes past three o'clock. She smiled.

Two cars passed going north on Shalott Drive. Four more passed going south. Clare caught her breath as she waited for a break in the traffic. After the battering it had taken over the last few days, her body still felt strange, heavy in a way that reminded her of dream movement, as if the air were too thick to move through. She took a deep breath, then jogged across the street, a bottle of pills and a ring of keys jangling in her deep pocket. It was only then, when she heard the rattling, that Clare realized she forgot to change her clothes. She still wore the bright red t-shirt and dark blue running pants she'd lifted from an open lacrosse team duffel bag at the hospital that morning. Dread twisted her stomach. What else had she forgotten?

At the tow truck, Clare stopped short, all thoughts of her fatigue and inappropriate dress draining from her mind. The dread in her stomach quickly boiled over into flat-out panic as she took in the scene before her.

A packed knapsack sat on the passenger seat of the truck, one that bulged around the middle and was unzipped at the top. Rolled clothes, granola bars, and a motorcycle magazine spilled from the knapsack, onto the seat. A camping stove leaned against the backseat, along with a propane tank, camping tent, a tattered copy of White Fang, a jar of peanut butter, three packages of ball-point pens, and a pair of slippers. Two cases of beer were stacked against the driver's seat, a fishing pole bent wildly along the roof of the truck, roadmaps, rolls of toilet paper, and a black flashlight heavy as a lead pipe littered the floor behind the seats.

Clare's eyes took in these items without meaning or context. Her mind focused only on the small back window of the truck. Clare had never ridden in the truck, but she had seen the truck twice before—once when Jared pulled into her driveway and Clare had been drinking on the porch, and once the night Albert took Jared's gun. Clare remembered the sound the plastic made when the wind caught it, that sharp snap—a clap of cupped hands, or a muffled gunshot. Jared had taped up the window after discovering the broken glass last month. He'd told Clare a long story about how the system was rigged and the insurance refused to pay (mostly because Jared had not renewed his policy), and so the window had remained unfixed.

Clare touched the new glass. The plastic, the tape, all of it was gone. In its place was this sparkling clean pane of fresh glass. A sticker in the lower right corner.

Clare hesitated only a moment before she turned, bent slightly at the waist, and began scanning the ground. There had to be something, a rock, a brick, a heavy stick… She moved quickly along the sidewalk, not caring that she'd attracted the attention from a man in an SUV who watched her from where he sat, waiting for traffic. He had creamy-white hair and wore some sort of bunched tie at his neck, the name of which Clare, in her distracted state, did not recall. Ignoring his blatant stare, Clare continued to search the frustratingly pristine grass along the sidewalk. There was nothing, and Clare felt her stomach tightening again. This was taking too long. Jared would see her through the window any moment now, come tearing out of her house, pounding down her front walk. Clare jumped, spinning around to check the street behind her, nearly certain she'd heard him shout her name—

There was no one. Only the man with the neck flourish who was trying not to stare.

Now that she'd turned around, Clare saw the lavish garden in the front yard of the house adjacent to the tow truck. The garden housed a cornucopia of early-summer blossoms—bluebells, white and red baneberries, mountain laurel, scarlet beebalms, sweet Williams, Indian apples—all of which strained against a flimsy, mesh-wire fence. A row of smooth landscape stones, each roughly the size of a squashed cantaloupe, lined the base of the fence.

Clare was in the yard, scrambling at the fence, and running back to the truck, dirt and grass dangling from the stone cupped in her hand, before realizing the man in the SUV was watching her intently now. Clare paused, turned away from the truck, inspected the sky. She tried to breathe normally. The man shook his head and turned his attention back to the traffic, which had begun to move again.

With the man gone, Clare stared at the tow truck's door handle. Would it be that easy? With a quick breath, Clare grabbed the handle and pulled.

The door opened.

Once inside the truck, Clare dropped the stone by the curb, yanked open the glove box, and thrust both of her hands inside. Papers, pens, a tiny bottle of mouthwash, a tire pressure gauge, an open bag of potato chips and there…at the very bottom, the extra set of keys hooked onto a bottle opener Jared had once gone to the truck to get when Clare lost her own. In her rush, Clare dropped the keys, and they landed on the floor of the truck between a dirty sock and a tube of women's anti-wrinkle cream (expensive looking, judging from the label). With two fingers, Clare picked up the keys without touching the sock, left the glove box open with all its mess spilling out, and slammed the truck door shut.

Coming around the tow truck and into the street, Clare held Jared's keys high above her head, silver keys against a silver sky, then continued quickly to the moving truck. She exchanged Jared's heavy key ring for the truck keys in the pocket of her running pants. There were only two keys on this metal ring—one for the ignition and one for the pad lock. A dirty piece of plastic wrapped around the ring that read "L.A.T. Rentals" with a phone number and website at the bottom.

Clare checked her watch. She smiled. It was early. There was still plenty of time. Turning the ignition, Clare started the moving truck, then pulled away from Jared's tow truck and onto Shalott Drive.

3:13 p.m.

Albert watched Clare run down the front walk, pause for traffic, then jog across the street. She was quick, her steps surprisingly light given the fact that it had only been less than forty-eight hours since Albert had found her passed out on her living room couch. A shudder crept up Albert's spine.

Moving closer toward the window, Albert continued to watch Clare hurry up the sidewalk toward the moving truck. Albert and Clare had picked up the moving truck that morning, after he'd broken her out of the hospital. Albert drove Clare's car back to the house, while Clare followed behind him in the truck. Nearly twenty years it had been since Albert last drove a vehicle. He forgot how much fun they were, like the go-carts he'd driven at Coney Island as a kid. Albert had rolled down the window and stuck his arm out, thumping out a beat and singing loudly, all his worries vanished, if only for the moment. *I look for my heart it's Perdido, I lost it way down in Torido...*

Albert watched as Clare finally reached the rental truck. She disappeared behind it. Albert waited a few seconds. Clare had to have reached Croker's truck by now. He waited for Clare to reappear with the spare set of keys. Waited. Waited.

Leaning into the windowpane, Albert watched Clare's house. Her door was closed and he could detect no movement from within.

When Albert looked down at his hands, he saw that he'd picked up the revolver from the telephone table. It was heavier than it'd been this morning, though Albert knew that couldn't possibly be true. Its black steel shone dully in the cloudy light. It was loaded. Albert had checked. Four bullets. He'd taken them out last night, rolled them around in his palm. Replaced each one into its chamber. Could he really fire it? Not that he would have to, their plan called only for the absence of the gun, not its use. But as Albert waited for Clare to reappear from behind the rental truck, he watched Clare's house and asked himself the question again, as a purely hypothetical exercise. Could he really point such a thing at another human being and squeeze the trigger? Albert flipped the safety off. Flipped it on again, watching, waiting.

Finally, Clare emerged from behind the rental truck. She held up the keys so that Albert could see them, then quickly climbed into the truck, and drove away.

"911, what's your emergency?"

"Yes, I need to report a break-in at my neighbor's house."

Albert held the phone receiver between his head and his shoulder, lifted up the back of his shirt and slipped the revolver inside the waistband of his trousers. Its weight fit perfectly at the small of his back. This also was not a part of their plan, but Albert paid little attention. He only wished he could be there when they hauled that bastard away in handcuffs. Albert hoped Jared would resist, just a little. Just enough to deserve a kick in the stomach, a blow across his jaw perhaps. He would have enjoyed taking that story back to Clare, but Albert knew he had no time. When Ben showed up, he would have questions—lots of them.

But Albert had places to be. People to see. And things still left to do.

3:16 p.m.

Cee-Cee pushed her balled hands deeper into her pockets and stretched the zipped front panel of her yellow sweat jacket so that it flapped like a wing with each step. It had been warm and sticky when she left with her father for the dentist that morning, but now the clouds were darker, and the wind was blowing. Cee-Cee could smell the pond before she left the house, and the cold-pond smell reminded her of fall, of school. Seventh grade would begin for Cee-Cee in only eight short weeks, and those weeks would see the girl undergo one of many transformations into maturity. No longer the rowdy little girl whose mother had run off with a neighbor's husband, Cee-Cee would return to school subdued. Less concerned with how others perceived her, more focused with how she saw herself, and with a solidity to her personality that even Cee-Cee's teachers would notice. Great moments of tragedy changed a person, as did great moments of bravery. By the end of that summer, Cee-Cee would experience both.

That she was late made Cee-Cee tramp through the brush of weeds and broken tree limbs with less care than was necessary, causing Cee-Cee to throw out her hands often to keep from falling over a jutting rock, or into a leaf-covered pool of mud. She'd had to wait at the dentist office with nothing but old issues of Highlights to keep her occupied since she forgot her cell phone at home. Cee-Cee had to wait again in the dentist's chair as the oral hygienist flipped through the channels of the television mounted in the corner of the room, looking for a daytime talk show she liked (two male doctors demonstrated a breast self-exam with animated computer visuals that made Cee-Cee's face hot where she lay, reclined in the chair between the hygienist and the dentist with drool seeping from her mouth). Then there was a line at the post office, road construction on the parkway, and finally, Freddie, banging at her bedroom window and begging to go with her while Cee-Cee was racing to get ready. She promised Freddie they would meet up at his house later to play the video game he got for his birthday. Cee-Cee felt a twinge of guilt over the lie, imagining him home and eagerly setting up the game while he waited for her, but Cee-Cee saw no other choice. Freddie wouldn't understand what she had to do today. And he definitely wouldn't keep his mouth shut about it.

Cee-Cee pulled her cell phone from her pocket and checked the time. She had recently added Mr. Hallam's home telephone number to her contact list and Cee-Cee scrolled down to his name, confirming again that the number had been saved. A little thrill fluttered her heart as Cee-Cee remembered Mr. Hallam's words—*a small job, but very, very important*—and Cee-Cee hoped she hadn't already disappointed Mr. Hallam by being late. Today was the day they would save Violet and her babies. Nothing could go wrong.

Thunder rolled through the clouds beyond the tree line, slow and powerful. Turning all her concentration to the uneven ground at her feet, Cee-Cee half-ran, half-tripped through the woody area that surrounded the park. She took a more direct, steep route, cutting straight through in her rush to reach the pond, crossing the trail several times as the path wound back and forth, descending down and down to the water.

She reached the pond in a third of the time it usually took her and immediately saw Mr. Hallam on the opposite shore. Cee-Cee had spied on the old man many times that summer, sneaking away from her house after her father settled in front of the television, and watching him from the hideout she and Freddie built together. It was only when Cee-Cee discovered the purple feather at the hideout that she realized Mr. Hallam had known Cee-Cee was spying on him all along.

Mr. Hallam didn't see her at first and Cee-Cee paused a moment before going to him. She loved to watch him dance. Until that day, Cee-Cee had only seen Mr. Hallam dance at night with Violet and the babies. Sometimes with Clare, but mostly by himself. From the neighborhood above, the darkness was too complete to see a lone old man moving around the shoreline. At water level, though, in the deep weeds by the hideout where Cee-Cee often crouched, watching, the night shone off the pond and cast a warm glow on Mr. Hallam's nocturnal activities.

Cee-Cee never saw Mr. Hallam dance in the daylight before. She'd never seen his face as he moved to the music in his imagination. Watching now, a giddy sort of happiness rippled down Cee-Cee's spine, making her forget (if only for a moment) the important job at hand. There was something about his movements that made Cee-Cee want to dance to whatever music it was that Mr.

Hallam was listening to. She wanted to leap and spin and twirl across the water. (Though Cee-Cee could not properly articulate what she was feeling, the emotion engendered by the sight of Albert waltzing silently around the pond was one of joy. Deeper and more firmly rooted than happiness, lighter and less tightly binding than contentment, it was a feeling of joy, however brief and unexamined, that would alter the course of both Cee-Cee's and Penelope's thoughts that afternoon. Joy, which suddenly brought a singular moment of life, stunningly, amazingly into focus.)

Mr. Hallam turned in his dance and saw Cee-Cee standing opposite the pond, watching him. Still dancing, he smiled and raised his arm in greeting. Cee-Cee raised her hand in return and ran toward him.

3:58 p.m.

Penelope lowered her cell phone from her ear but didn't put it back on the table right away. She held the slim device with loose, curved fingers and stared out of her living room picture windows, watching the sky. Afternoon had come and the storm that had boiled across the sky all morning had yet to release a single drop of rain. Even where Penelope stood, in her dark, air-conditioned hallway, she could feel the thickened atmosphere outside. The clouds simmered, threatened to bubble over. Steam trickled down on the neighborhood, fogging the streets, and layering everything in a thick vapor that smelled of pond water. Penelope's underarms dampened beneath her sundress. A thin layer of sweat had collected above her eyebrows and was immediately chilled by the artificial air blowing through the vent above her head. She shivered, shaking to the base of her spine.

A loud clatter broke Penelope's gaze from the sky outside the window. Her cell phone lay in pieces on the floor, and she crouched down to retrieve the battery, the tiny plastic backing, the numbered front panel. She snapped the pieces back in place and pressed the red button. The phone lit up with a musical tune and Penelope let out a sigh of relief.

The nurse's name was Kimi, and Penelope wondered vaguely how old the girl was. Not more than twenty, by the sound of her voice. It seemed like the older Penelope got, the younger everyone else became. Just the day before at the grocery store, Penelope was short-changed by the cashier—a little ding-bat with a half-shaved head and an inability to subtract two-digit numbers in his head— and when the manager was called, Penelope almost laughed, thinking someone was playing a prank. The manager-boy had baby fat and pimples down to his neck. The two of them worked with the computerized cash register for nearly five minutes, unable to make it perform the simple function of subtraction. The line behind Penelope grew longer and more irritated, as the pocket of the manager-boy's pants ringed, dinged, and whistled its many electronic alerts.

Young Kimi had much to learn about patient confidentiality. That Clare was in the hospital was something Penelope had to find out from the Carlyles across the way. Mr. Carlyle had been part of the traffic jam created by the fire truck that blocked Shalott Drive for nearly an hour. Penelope tried to shrug off the sting of not having been informed of whatever illness had befallen her friend. Clare would call her when she could.

That Clare hadn't called, though, and that Penelope had to learn of her friend's suicide attempt from some teenaged rent-a-nurse who couldn't spell confidentiality, let alone keep it, hurt Penelope deeply. She had misjudged their friendship. She'd talked herself into believing she meant more to Clare than she apparently did. It had been the same with Odis. For years, Penelope had fooled herself into thinking she held the most central position in her husband's life. Just as her entire existence revolved around her husband, Penelope had assumed she held a similar role as his wife. As it turned out, there were other people who filled that role for Odis, Cee-Cee's mother among them. Penelope had barely skimmed the periphery of her husband's world. It would eventually be the same with Lenny.

Penelope's stomach turned and suddenly felt hollow. In fact, her whole body suddenly felt as if it might crumple in upon itself. Without pausing, Penelope yanked on her bathrobe from the back of the hall door, slipped the cell phone into the pocket of the robe, and went to the kitchen. In the refrigerator she shoved aside the bags of vegetables and moved the pitcher of orange juice out of the way to reach the clear plastic container in the far corner. The kitchen darkened again as she shut the refrigerator door with her foot. Penelope set the container on the counter, peeled off the lid, and picked up one of the foil-encased chocolate cakes. The smell of chocolate reached her senses before the taste and Penelope immediately felt her stomach relax. Leaving the container open on the counter, she wandered through the shadowed rooms of her house. She chewed slowly, licking cream and brown crumbs from her fingers.

In the living room Penelope paused. Frowning, she lowered the cake from her mouth and squinted at the scene before her. Still not able to understand what her eyes were telling her, she picked up her binoculars, fumbled with the lenses, grasped her half-eaten cake between two fingers and focused her view on the pond below her house. When the blurry colors finally sharpened, Penelope let out a tiny sigh. Cake crumbs embedded in white cream hung precariously from her bottom lip. She moved closer to the windows, barely feeling the pain as she banged her shin against the coffee table.

Standing directly before the floor to ceiling windows, Penelope continued to watch the scene at the pond. (She had seen Mr. Hallam feed the geese many times from this same window, through these same binoculars, but what Penelope saw now was a part of the show she had always missed, coming, as it did, after the sun had set and the park settled into full darkness.) After a few moments, Penelope smiled. The bobble of crumb and cream broke free from her lip and disappeared onto the floor.

There was a summer vegetable casserole she had been planning to try, one with six kinds of cheese and a crumbly topping with just a hint of zing. The cheeses were all low-fat and the vegetables were hand-picked and sold at the roadside stand by Tirol Farm. If Penelope started the casserole now, she had just enough time to shower and change before it finished cooking in the oven. Watching the incredible scene out the window, she found it no longer mattered that Clare hadn't called her. Sometimes life could be simple. Clare was her friend. And something horrible had happened to her friend. Penelope would be there for her. She'd bring the casserole and they would sit and talk. Or not talk. It would be enough to simply show up. To let Clare know she wasn't alone. Penelope knew what alone felt like. She knew that too much alone changed the way a person thought. She'd hidden herself away all her life because she was afraid of being alone. Something about what she saw through her binoculars, though, reminded her that she had a choice. There were people who could fill her life, if she chose to let them.

Sometimes life could be simple.

Penelope set the binoculars back on the coffee table and went to the kitchen, tossing the last of the cake in the trash.

5:44 p.m.

Clare was headed back toward her house, barreling down Old Clevedon Road behind the wheel of the *L.A.T.* rental truck. On the other side of the grassy median, a police cruiser traveling in the southbound lane passed. Clare let off the gas pedal, too late realizing she had exceeded the speed limit by nearly twenty miles per hour. She checked the truck's side mirror as a loosely articulated prayer slipped from her lips. The cruiser continued on.

Everything Clare had accomplished that afternoon had taken longer than she planned. Thirty-five minutes wasted on the Garden State Parkway behind a bottleneck of traffic and a slow-moving construction crew, fifteen minutes at the gas station trying to locate and then decipher the directions for unlocking the fuel cap, twenty minutes at the grocery store, most of which spent behind a woman who locked herself out of three debit cards before finally giving up on the pin and paying with credit, and nearly half an hour crouched and hiding from Elwin in the bushes behind the dog pen. The Border Collie named Satan returned sleepily to Clare's hiding place twice while Clare hid, nuzzling her hand for more of the laced ground beef. *Tell me they didn't actually give you a prescription for sleeping pills*, Albert had said, shaking his head in stunned disbelief.

Had Elwin jumped down from the back of the camper truck to investigate the canines' sluggishness, he would have found Clare where she hid behind the honeysuckle, sweating, shaking, hands covered with damning smears of hamburger grease and white powder. As it was, Jared's brother was more concerned with the baggie of weed on his lap through which he picked meticulously, than with his dogs' unexpected afternoon naps.

Only Clare's business with the shed at the rear of the Croker property had gone (mostly) as planned. Jared's key worked without incident and the door opened to a heavy stench of sulfur. The shed was larger than the one in Clare's backyard, and windowless. Only a single crack of useless light from a split in the roof pierced its darkness. Clare felt around on the wall on either side of the door for a light switch and, finding none, flailed her arms at the ceiling, stumbling over scattered objects on the floor, until her fingers found purchase on a dangling shoestring. She gave the string a tug and a dirty light bulb illuminated the room.

A man's gotta have his space, Jared had told her, describing the shed as a place where he went to think, where he stored items too valuable to be trusted at his house, and where he went to work (Clare hadn't cared what Jared meant by "work"). Stacked floor to sloped ceiling with sagging cardboard boxes, splintered milk crates, and flaccid strips of some black material she could not name, Clare couldn't imagine spending any amount of time in such a space, let alone working there.

Mostly, the shed was where Jared kept his stash, along with boxes of syringes, scales, jugs of purified water, bottles of alcohol, all stacked high and cleverly hidden behind a tarp that blended in with the wall. Or so he had proudly told Clare.

The shed door swung inward and so this area had been kept fairly clear of debris. Now, however, Clare struggled to venture further into the room, following a path between the stacks of boxes, and cringing at the scuttling sounds that had been frightened by her approach. Clare hugged her body and tried not to breathe too deeply. The aisle she followed snaked toward one wall, then the other, and finally dead-ended at a heap of filled garbage bags. Clare retraced her steps, searching for an outlet through the maze, and finally came upon a slight opening between two towers of boxes she'd passed earlier without notice. Through the opening, Clare saw a small, cleared area with an old television and VCR balanced on the back of a car bumper in front of a stuffed, legless chair. Dingy light filtered through greasy glass at the back window.

Shutting her eyes, Clare shoved herself sideways through the opening, coughing on a puff of mildewed dust knocked loose from the boxes. Another light bulb hung above the cleared area and Clare yanked it on. There were two things Clare had come to Jared's shed for. And it was here, finally, that Clare found the first item.

A sheet of black tarp hung crookedly against the wall beside the back window. Clare stepped closer, pulling back the tarp to examine the contents of the hidden shelves behind it—open boxes of hollowed-out tennis balls, ping-pong balls, tin foil, alcohol, water, and bottles of potassium nitrate labeled "Stump Remover." Along the highest shelf Clare saw dented metal pots, dirty spoons, open bags of white sugar, boxes of baking soda, bottles of colored dye, cardboard tubing, packing tape…

And there, beside the tape and sitting atop an old green tin that had long ago housed an herbal tea, directly at eye level, as if it were waiting for her, Clare found her rock. The rock was unmistakable—a sharp, cutting edge at one end, round and smooth at the other. It fit into Clare's palm with the weight and balance of a bird's egg. She let it settle in her hand for a moment, remembering the day Jared had found the rock, this member of Clare's childhood pet rock family. She remembered how she had watched Jared pick up the rock from the floor in her closet. How he had slipped the rock into his pocket. How she had said nothing to stop him.

Albert had not understood why, in the midst of everything else they had planned for that day, Clare insisted on stopping at Jared's shed. Clare hadn't tried to explain. She couldn't explain it to herself, but she knew now it was good that she had come. Clare slipped the rock into her pocket, and its slight weight against her body had an inverse effect. She felt lighter. She almost smiled.

Turning, Clare discovered a picnic table, half-camouflaged within mounds of debris, on which several plastic bins had been stacked. The bins shone newer than anything else in the shed and along their sides Jared had written with careful penmanship in magic marker: DRIVERS, GIRANDOLAS, WHEELS, SAXONS, TOURBILLIONS/HELICOPTERS, STINGER MISSILES, HUMMERS, SPOLETTES, AERIAL SHELLS, M-80'S, M-100'S, SILVER SALUTES… She rummaged through each bin and knocked some of the items onto the picnic table where they rolled off the wood and into the shadows on the floor.

Clare found the bin she was looking for and heaved it to the stuffed chair to examine its contents in better light. *Orange, blue, red, green, purple*…Clare cursed under her breath as she searched for the correct color. The sound of a truck engine suddenly broke the silence inside the shed.

Desperate, Clare tipped the bin upside-down on the chair. Tiny tubes rolled everywhere, and Clare crouched down to grab several from the floor. Thrusting them into her pockets, and inside her shirt, she fled the shed, wiping her hands on her shorts as she ran.

5:44 p.m.

The silver coupe with Pennsylvania plates swayed toward the shoulder of the road and onto the solid white line. It then drifted left toward the dotted white line and slowed too late for a curve that wound around a near forty-five-degree turn. Tire rubber shrieked against asphalt.

Flipping on the cruiser's lights, Ben pulled beside the car, matching its speed. He briefly made eye contact with the driver—an older woman with heavy lipstick who immediately dropped her cell phone in her lap. She smiled nervously, slammed on her brakes, and turned on her windshield wipers. Ben passed her vehicle, watching in his rear view mirror as the coupe's hazards came on and then its high beams in the woman's fumbled attempt to pull to the side of the road.

"10-1. Can you 10-9 that last transmission?"

"Standby for additional, 359."

Ben flipped off the cruiser's lights and left the silver car behind him. There was no time for cell phone ticketing today. He thumped his thumb against the steering wheel, waiting.

After a moment, Marcy's voice broke through the radio again, much louder and with more breath. Ben heard the fatigue in her voice. It had been a long day for all of them.

"Base to 359, can you respond to a Signal 4, Century Road and the GSP. Officer at scene reports this may involve our B and E from this morning."

"Black tow?"

"Unclear. Interviewing witnesses now. No injuries at the scene."

"10-4. You can show me 10-51, I'm maybe ten minutes out," Ben said. "And Marcy?"

"Yeah Ben?"

"Why don't you get yourself a coffee."

"Oh, 10-4 that."

Turning down the dial on the radio, Ben continued south along Old Clevedon Road toward the parkway. He worked the situation again in his mind, cataloging vehicles on the northbound lane while he drove—*tan, late-model pick-up, standard cab; early '90's 4-door station wagon, New Jersey plates; moving truck, 2-door, yellow, L.A.T. Rentals; white sedan, luggage rack, Connecticut plates…*

Something didn't fit about the call they got that morning. In truth, something didn't fit about the way the entire day was unfolding, but Ben focused on the particulars of the 911 call. Why would Croker break into the Lyndsay house? And in broad daylight, no less. The house had been tossed, top to bottom, Ben had seen that for himself. Croker was looking for something, but what? The local news had run the story two days ago, so surely the man knew by now that half the police force of New Jersey was looking for him. The DNA had been rushed after the Landryes woman died, and the results confirmed what Ben already knew.

What Ben hadn't anticipated, however, was the witness that came forward. Rosamond Pennell, a Hunter student, home for summer break, who lived in the same apartment building as Elizabeth Landryes. She'd seen the news report and walked into the station yesterday morning with a chilling story. When asked why she'd waited to report the crime, she said she hadn't considered it a rape, since she'd agreed to sleep with Jared the first few times. She thought the police should know about Jared's gun, though.

Ben felt as if he'd been running in circles all day, asking all the wrong questions. Mr. Hallam could have answered a few of them, Ben was certain, but damned if the old man had up and disappeared as well. Why had the man called 911, told them about Croker breaking in next door, only to vanish before Ben could talk to him?

From there, Ben's wild goose chase led him back to Croker's mother's place, where the woman threatened to set the dogs on him. (This, while Clare waited behind the woman with the bad pin number at the grocery store. Had Clare not been held up, she would have encountered Ben at the Croker house and the day might have ended immediately for all of them.) Ben then drove up to the hospital, meaning to question Clare, if she was up for it, and hopefully run into Mr. Hallam, but the nurse on duty told him Clare left sometime that morning. *I won't get in trouble, will I?* the nurse wanted to know—Cyndi or Bambi. Ben had written her name in his notes. *It's not my fault she left before the 72-hour hold, I have other patients, you know?* Clare and Albert were both gone, but where? Ben spent the rest of the afternoon tracking down one black tow truck after another, when he would have rather been searching for the two people who could most likely answer the more important questions of the day.

"Base to 359, come in 359."

Ben turned the radio back up. "359 here, go ahead base."

"Ben, we just got a call about some dogs. I wasn't sure, but it seemed like something you ought to know."

"Dogs?"

"An Elwin from the Goose Guard just called in a non-emergency. Said someone might've dosed his dogs."

"Dosed? As in drugged?"

"Not hurt, just sleeping like babies. That's our suspect's brother, isn't it?"

Ben trusted Marcy's instincts nearly as well as he trusted his own. "Send Chasseur," Ben said. The man surely needed to redeem himself after letting Croker slip away from the Lyndsay house that morning.

"Tell him to cover his rear this time," Ben growled.

"You want him to radio it in?"

Ben slammed on his brakes and pulled quickly to the far right shoulder of the road to avoid being hit by the minivan behind him. The cruiser's tires crunched noisily as they slid to a stop. Ben hit the lights again and twisted in his seat to confirm what he'd spotted in his rear view mirror.

"Tell him to call me direct," Ben said. He threw the cruiser into reverse and waited for a break in the traffic. "Who's the officer on scene at that Signal 4?"

"Jerry's out there."

"All right." Ben thought for a moment. "Tell him I'll be there in a bit. There's something I want to check out."

"Want me to send somebody?"

"Negative. Standby."

Ben backed the cruiser along the shoulder of the road until he found his break in the traffic. Turning the wheel and throwing the cruiser back into drive, Ben sped across the southbound lane and onto the grassy median, bumping along the uneven terrain and bottoming-out the steel frame of the car twice on hidden ridges and rocks. When he reached the northbound lanes, Ben hugged the shoulder of the road, rolling slowly in the gravel until he reached the area he'd spotted in his rear view mirror.

Two lines of flattened grass, like racing stripes, crossed the median from the southbound to northbound lane. They looked much like the path Ben had just made with the cruiser a few hundred yards south. These stripes were wider, though, their impressions deeper. They were obviously created by a much heavier vehicle with dual rear tires.

Directly across from the lines of deeply flattened grass was the tiny gravel road that led through the brush and trees and down to Honock Pond.

It was that day by the pond that sprang to Ben's mind when he'd slammed on the cruiser's brakes. That day a few weeks ago, while Ben was responding to a complaint call and shamefully patrolling for a certain elderly bird feeder. A day long before the business with Lacy, when Ben had come across Jared at the pond. The Schlingerman boy had been with him, and while Ben could clearly see what was happening, he'd no cause to search them, so he'd run them off instead. Ben remembered the growl of the truck's engine as it bounced along the ground. The truck had dual rear tires and had left a wide trail in the grass behind it. Twin lines of deeply flattened grass.

It was a long shot, Ben knew, but a cop's instincts often were. Ben checked the traffic, then shot across the northbound lane and onto the gravel road, red and blue lights still flashing.

5:56 p.m.

Clare maneuvered the rental truck as close to the sidewalk as she could manage, rubbing the truck's front right tire against the curb. She waited for a break in the traffic, slipped out through the driver's door, and slammed it shut behind her as she hurried toward her house. Albert would be waiting for her at his house, that was the plan, but Clare felt entirely too conspicuous in the red t-shirt and blue running pants, not to mention the *Kinderkamack Pride* stamped across her back. It would only take a moment to change her clothes.

Clare pulled the cardboard tubes and the rock from her pockets and was reaching for her house keys before she remembered that the police had probably left the door unlocked after arresting Jared. As she'd suspected, the doorknob turned. Once inside, Clare flipped on the living room light and tossed the tubes on the coffee table. She walked past the overturned couch cushions, sidestepped a pile of books that had been knocked to the floor in Jared's desperate search, and set the rock on the kitchen table. She would grab a snack for them both—something simple, sandwiches maybe—and then head over to Albert's house. (In Clare's rushed and distracted state, her eyes had moved over Penelope's casserole dish on the counter but had not actually *seen* it.) Clare couldn't wait to tell Albert how easy it had been with the dogs. He'd worried over that part. They both had.

But first, she would change.

At the top of the stairs, Clare stopped short. The door to the second bedroom was open. Her mother's bedroom. In all these months, Alice's door had remained shut up tight, ignored, as Clare came and went. Clare puzzled over the light in the hallway. With the door open, the light in the hallway was all wrong.

She took a step into her mother's bedroom and in the instant before Clare's thoughts stopped altogether, she was just beginning to understand that there was a leg on the floor behind the bed. A bare leg, with a bit a flowered skirt at one end and a bright pink flip-flop on the foot at the other end. A leg and a foot that looked a great deal like Penelope's.

But then there was Jared. And all thought stopped.

7:09 p.m.

When Albert woke, sweaty and half-smothered beneath a couch cushion, the light in the living room had fallen into an early evening hour. Shadows clung to the corners of the room. More shadows draped across the framed photos along the wall and gathered within the viney foliage across the desk. The sheer curtain behind the couch billowed inward with a breeze, bringing with it the scent of impending rain and the sound of pulsing traffic.

Wush-wush, wush-wush-wush, wush-wush…

He had taken his nap in the living room, after returning from the pond where he'd chatted up Cee-Cee while waiting for the police to be finished next door. Leaving Cee-Cee with her shift on watch at the pond, Albert had gone home, stretched out on the couch beside the telephone table, whale sneakers lined up together on the floor, as his thoughts spun happily around an image of Jared being taken away in handcuffs. Albert had fallen asleep quickly, having hardly slept since finding Clare two days earlier, and he slept hard, forgetting even the revolver tucked inside the waistband of his trousers. Its barrel bit into Albert's left butt cheek, and Albert felt it now that he was awake, but he didn't move.

Cee-Cee had not called. The dogs had not come. For the first time since Clare articulated her plan, that day he'd taken her to Tirol Farm, Albert believed it might work. They would save Violet. And the goslings too. This story would have a happy ending.

Albert lay on the couch for several more minutes, thinking about the evening ahead, working through each detail in his mind, and trying to ignore the nagging feeling he was forgetting something. Sleep was slow to release his old bones and it was only when Albert forced himself to sit up and turn on a light that he remembered why he was surprised the day was so late.

Where was Clare?

Through the gauzy curtain behind the couch, Albert saw the dark outline of the rental truck parked by the sidewalk. The light was on in Clare's living room window. She was home. Why hadn't she stopped by as they planned?

The Roman numerals on the clock above Albert's desk read just past seven o'clock. They had less than an hour, and here he was, snoozing away. Albert flexed his foot, slipping first into one whale sneaker, then the other. He grimaced at the arthritic pops his ankles made. Clare should have woken him. He'd planned a meal for them—sandwiches and a salad. He hadn't eaten since breakfast, and he doubted Clare had either. The bread was still where he'd taken it from the pantry and set it on the kitchen counter.

A fingertip of fear brushed against Albert's stomach. Why hadn't Clare woken him?

Minutes later, Albert hobbled up the porch steps to Clare's house, stopping only once when it seemed his popping right ankle might give way. He tried the door, found it unlocked.

"Hello? You here, Clare?"

SEPTEMBER 28, 1985

7:26 p.m.

"Hello? You here, Clare?"

On that long ago day in 1985, it had been forty-eight hours since he or Emily had seen Clare, either coming or going. That was when Albert had finally gone over to the house. That they had not seen Alice was not unusual, especially during these last few months. The woman kept odd hours—smoking on the porch at three in the morning, rushing to her car, fully clothed, but for the slippers on her feet, at ten at night, bundles of papers in her hands and headed, apparently, to the university.

He and Emily had watched quietly, warily, since the afternoon in August when Albert had found the purple house choked with gas fumes and every window on both floors shut up tight. The summer of 1985 was the summer their block got a new mailman, a young kid who transposed numbers and shuffled the neighborhood mail like a blackjack dealer in Atlantic City. Albert had crossed the yard that afternoon and knocked on the Lyndsay door, a rubber-banded stack of Alice's mail in his hand. He caught the sour scent almost immediately, as it permeated the house so thoroughly that it seeped from around the wooden frame of the front door. The door was unlocked, the house empty, and in the kitchen, Albert discovered with his shirt pulled tight over his nose, all four burners and the oven were turned on. The pilot light was out. Alice gazed up at him, disinterested, through a cloud of cigarette smoke from where he found her, sitting quietly in the back yard. Albert had never been shaken by anything so completely as he was by the emptiness in that woman's eyes.

That they had not seen Clare in the last forty-eight hours, however, *was* unusual. Against his wife's wishes, Albert had called social services and reported the incident with the stove. *This is more than we can handle*, Albert told his wife firmly. *The woman needs professional help*. But social services had come and gone, and the only

251

result had been that Alice stopped waving hello when they passed in the yard. Emily pleaded with Albert to visit the woman, invite her over or otherwise engage Clare's mother in some way that would encourage a relationship. *She just needs to know someone cares*, Emily insisted, but Albert dismissed her argument as so much feminine nonsense. Mental illness cured by friendship? Albert ignored her, asserting, for the first time in their marriage, the sort of male dominance he'd witnessed in his own house as a child. Albert forbade his wife any contact with the troubled woman next door, and he and Emily fought bitterly. Albert conceded when it came to Clare, however, and Clare continued her visits to their house, having dinner and often stopping in for breakfast before school. He couldn't let the child go hungry, could he?

Albert had kicked aside the small tree branches and other debris that still littered the sidewalk as he strode toward the Lyndsay house that late September evening. Hurricane Gloria, for whom the whole neighborhood had braced—windows taped, porch chairs dragged inside—had left behind only a few pulled shingles and a single uprooted mailbox in her wake.

"Hello?" Albert had called again, pushing open the door. The purple house was silent.

Albert had been a different man that day. Young. Foolish. Certain of himself, certain of the world. Just certain, in the cold way that only young people can afford to be. (At seventy-nine, Albert occasionally missed that sort of certainty. He remembered the time when he could so clearly find the line between one thought or another. Between right or wrong. Should or should not. As Albert grew older, he began to find the world ironic, but later he realized that what he'd mistaken for irony were actually cycles. Terrible, beautiful, looping patterns, a societal organism stuck on repeat, a phenomenon seemingly visible only to the very old and the very old at heart.

(And that evening in 1985, Albert was still caught in the most powerful pattern of them all, that constant struggle for dichotomy—yes or no, black or white, pro-life or pro-choice, Republican or Democrat, American or alien, colored or white, gay or straight, *support the troops while opposing the war? Impossible!*—it was an effort that was foolishness incarnate, Albert saw now, when even the ocean itself could not determine a shore. Built into the mind of the young, it seemed to Albert, was this incessant need to split things in two and then stand firmly on one side or the other. Was it fear that so threatened allowing the unknown? Was it really better to be *wrong*, if it meant being *sure*? The whole world seemed so terribly young to Albert sometimes. Had always been so young, so terribly certain of itself, when it occurred to Albert that only the line between life and death held such a sharp edge. And even that edge was blunted when he so clearly heard his dead wife's voice woven between his own thoughts.)

But on that cool, wet evening in 1985, Albert had been fifty-six with no idea how young he really was. On that evening, Albert had been sure. Certain in his ability to make the right decisions. Childishly believing there were right decisions to make.

A whimper had returned his call into the house—soft, bird-like—and Albert leapt up the stairs to the second floor of the purple house without hesitation, his long, lean legs taking three steps at a time. When he burst into Alice Lyndsay's bedroom it was the words the hit him first—*CULTURE IS PERSONALITY WRIT LARGE*—and then there was only the smell. It overpowered him, immediately eclipsing the strange text on the wall. Before Albert's mind took in the blood or the body on the bed, the smell caused bile to rise in the back of his throat, and he covered his nose and mouth, squinting, as if the air might be toxic. This wasn't the sour scent of gas, but the putrid, vaguely spicy odor of death.

The tall windows on either side of the bed were shut up tight, curtainless, untaped against the storm. Alice Lyndsay had never been one to follow the news, much less the weather, so Albert was not at all surprised when he learned later that Alice had left a message with the school that Clare was to go to the Hallam house when the bus dropped her off Friday afternoon. A message that was, of course, never delivered, since the school district had shut down in preparation for the advancing hurricane. And so, the Lyndsay house stood alone on the block in its unprepared state. Completely vulnerable to the storm that hit it.

The bared bedroom windows poured unbiased light onto the ghastly scene before him.

Alice Lyndsay lay on the bed.

Her body was arranged carefully, silk nightgown pulled down to her ankles, feet together, bare toes pointed toward the ceiling. Her head rested on a pillow, dark hair gathered over one shoulder. Her right arm lay straight at her side, palm up. Only her left arm lay askew, its hand dangled off the edge of the bed, thin fingers cupped. The bed was still made, corners tucked, top sheet folded down. The sheet, the pillows, the down comforter, the nightgown Alice wore, and the throw rug by the foot of the bed were all the same shade of midnight blue.

At first Albert could not understand why the floor at the foot of the bed was slippery. Why he'd almost fallen in his rush to enter the room. But then it became agonizingly clear. Alice had done her ankles first.

Along with the slices at her lower legs, another long incision traced the inside of Alice's left arm, splitting open the pale skin from wrist to elbow. The gash on her right arm was less clean. It trembled upward, toward the middle of her forearm, took a sharp inward turn and stopped.

Alice's eyes, half-open, indifferent, had rolled toward the bedroom door. They stared at Albert.

A razor blade wrapped in tissue lay on Alice Lyndsay's stomach. The tissue was soaked in blood. The blue nightgown, stained in blood, had turned a deep purple. The sheets, the down comforter, the mattress, the floor beneath Alice's dangling hand, the pool that Albert had nearly slid into, were all soaked in blood. Albert had not known a woman's body could contain so much blood.

The whimper came again. From under the bed. Louder now. It was clearly a human sound and Albert jerked, astonished that anything could still be alive in such a room.

FINAL DAY (CONTINUED)

Wednesday, June 30, 2010
7:26 p.m.

"Hello? You here, Clare?"

Albert glanced around the disheveled living room. Thrown couch cushions, splayed books. A lamp teetered in the corner. Even the rug by the window had been thrown aside. Jared's search for his gun had been thorough.

Through the archway into the kitchen, Albert saw a casserole dish on the counter. His stomach rumbled. Footsteps creaked the floorboards upstairs, and Albert decided to wait for Clare to come down before helping himself to whatever was in the dish.

Glancing at the coffee table, Albert saw that Clare had been successful at Jared's shed. Scattered across the table were the canisters they would use soon. Picking up one at random, Albert read the print on the back of the canister. *Tactical grade, use extreme caution, blast wire pull.* He flipped it back to the front and frowned at what he found there.

"Why in the world did you get the—"

But the noise from upstairs cut him off. It wasn't a whimper, exactly, more like a muffled grunt, but it was a whimper that Albert heard. Soft, tearful, stretching across twenty-five years from the past to reach Albert like a punch in the gut. And before Albert realized his body was moving, he'd dropped the canister on the floor and was again leaping up the stairs, ignoring the splinters of pain that shot through his hip with each step, wobbling a bit on his throbbing ankle when he reached the landing.

Albert saw Clare first. Before he noticed the heavy-duty flashlight that had rolled partway under the dresser. Before he saw the crumpled body of Penelope in the corner to his left. Before he saw anyone else in that room, Albert saw Clare sitting quietly on the corner of the bed.

And then he saw the room.

The writing on the wall had long been removed. The walls of the room were now a soft cream, and the bed was bare, just a clean white mattress. It had been twenty-five years since Albert had seen this room, but as he stood in the doorway, chest heaving from his sprint up the stairs, Albert saw it all again. The bloody mattress, the slippery pool on the floor, the blue walls. And the writing—*CULTURE IS PERSONALITY WRIT LARGE*—those words that would forever sound like a threat to Albert.

Clare looked at him, bleary, tired, turning her head in an oddly stiff motion. Albert took little notice of Clare's strangeness, however. Every cell in Albert's body had suddenly become tight, alert. They were not alone in the room.

"Finally."

Albert staggered backward as if the word itself pushed him off balance. The memory of Alice's bedroom was instantly eclipsed by the sight before him.

Jared stood in the shadowy corner to Albert's right. Pale, shaky, pitted eyes, stinking of sweat, wrinkled Metallica concert shirt hanging from his thin shoulders, dirty jeans stained black at the knees. *Life on the lam does not suit this young man*, was Albert's wildly thought rhyme before he spotted the box-cutter in Jared's trembling left fist. And as if Albert's gaze propelled him into action, Jared lifted the box-cutter and took a lunging step toward Clare. He grabbed Clare's shoulder with his free hand.

With his other hand, Jared angled the razor edge of the box cutter toward Clare's throat.

Albert took another stumbling step backward and slammed his hip into the wall. Now he saw Penelope's body, her legs by the bed, flowered skirt raised over her chubby knees. An arm splayed. Dark hair covering her face.

Albert's lungs collapsed at the sight of Penelope lying so still on the bedroom floor. The sound of the air as it escaped through Albert's throat—*moh!*—hit a falsetto note Albert did not know he could make.

Jared followed the direction of Albert's gaze. He suddenly let go of Clare's shoulder to point accusingly at Penelope's body.

"Now tha-that," Jared stuttered, "*that* was an accident."

7:21 p.m.

Prior to Wednesday, June 30th, 2010, Ben had pulled his service revolver only once in the line of duty during his entire sixteen-year career as a New Jersey state policeman. Ben was proud of this accomplishment in the way that other men might be proud of a bench-press weight or pulling a clean off-tackle. That these sixteen years included a four-year stint as a street cop in Newark was a further point of pride. Ben had talked down everyone from a drunken husband wielding an iron frying pan, to a strung-out crack dealer with a stolen ballistic knife, to a would-be car thief with an aerosol can full of bug killer (*twice*, incredibly). Ben's secret was simple. He made conversation. It was Ben's experience that people wanted to talk, they needed to be heard. Even the most hardened souls, Ben learned, couldn't help but reach out in times of great duress. And so Ben made conversation. They each had a story. They all had a past, a road that led them to where Ben found them. All he had to do was listen. Though Ben was not so arrogant, and not so lapsed a Catholic, as to assume that luck (if not some old-school divine intervention) played no small part in his sixteen-year record.

Ben had been guarding Bunty's Dock at the base of the George Washington Bridge in the early morning hours of September 12, 2001 on the only day during his long career, prior to June 30th, 2010, that he pulled his weapon. He had been alone, but for two police boats from the Marine Unit in New York City that floated nearby on the river. The waters had been closed to all recreational and commercial craft, and the bridge closed to all traffic, save for emergency vehicles. The night sky was an empty, black expanse, where all planes in the country would remain grounded for another twenty-four hours. Behind the canopy of trees, a string of green bridge lights linked the shores of New Jersey to New York. Beyond the lights, Manhattan smoldered.

When he first heard the screaming, Ben's ears tricked him into thinking it was a mechanical sound. No human could have uttered such a noise. The noise was not unlike metal rubbing against metal. The sound of bending steel maybe, buckling, then failing.

Ben walked the length of the dock, patrolling the stretch of pavement along the boat ramp where the night's darkness was complete. It seemed Ben could almost touch this darkness, an oily material, cool and slippery against his skin. The moon shone off the water and the sky gave off a smoky glow above the tree line, but at the dock was a darkness Ben had never experienced. The depth of this darkness absorbed all light, all sound. His ears seemed to pound from its force.

When Ben heard the scream again there was no denying its human quality. The strange silence at the dock stunted the shriek at both ends, the reverberations trapped by the darkness, like shouting into a glass jar. But it was human, nonetheless.

Ben stumbled, turning in time to see the girl burst forth from the bushes across from the dock. Her robes fluttered furiously at her sneakers and her ripped headscarf hung around her neck. A mass of black hair blew away from her face. Her cheeks were round and firm, swollen with her youth. Blood dripped from the gash on her chin and smeared down her neck. Her black-ringed eyes met Ben's. She screamed again.

The service revolver was in Ben's hands and pointed at the bushes in the space of one breath. There was no decision involved in the pulling of Ben's weapon. There was only the terror he found in the girl's face. As she screamed, the girl tripped and fell onto the dock. She pulled herself into a fetal position and buried her face in her scarf. Ben took three long steps, positioning himself between the girl and the bushes. He leveled his weapon. Based on the girl's reaction, Ben had fully expected to fire upon a grizzly bear or lion that would spring from the trembling bushes. Ben was sure it was some wild, crazed beast on the attack.

On the day of the second time Ben pulled his service revolver in his sixteen-year career, the bushes were trembling again. It had been more than an hour since Ben had pulled in behind the black tow truck, leaving the cruiser's lights on as he approached the vehicle with one hand on his sidearm. Ben had completed a search of the area, circling the pond twice, crisscrossing in a methodical grid pattern through the surrounding woods, feeling the day slip away from him with every step. Marcy was running the tow's plates, but Ben had no doubt of the truck's ownership. It was Croker's. The driver's door was open, and Ben had mentally cataloged the items inside the cab—backpack, camping supplies, books, maps—

as a McDonald's wrapper blew out from the cab of the truck and into the underbrush.

There was no sign of Croker's firearm.

The breeze was brief and when it was gone, silence descended again. The storm was just outside of town, circling slowly and gaining strength, but its proximity had had a clearing effect. The woods had emptied. Creatures scattered to far corners in deep hollows to wait out whatever trauma Mother Nature had in store. The air was unmoving, heavy with moisture, thick with pressure. The air swallowed all sound left in the woods—the slam of his cruiser's door, the crunching gravel under his feet. Once again, Ben's ears pounded.

On the other side of the truck, the bushes trembled, and Ben instinctively took cover behind the open driver's door. His service revolver had slipped unthinkingly into his hand. Ben had no memory of unholstering his weapon or disengaging its safety. He'd been standing by the cab of the truck, an open hand covering his weapon, and with one sharp inhale, he was suddenly crouched behind the vehicle, his weapon ready.

But it was the bushes at the dock on that dark, long ago September night that Ben saw now. The bushes from which wild animals *did* emerge, though not ones he'd been expecting. These animals were filled with rage and an insane sort of anger fueled by ignorance and hysteria—two men, boys really, drunk on whiskey and hate who had spent the day cursing at the television set. Two boys who had, in the early-morning hours of September 12, 2001, decided to "patrol the neighborhood" with a hunting rifle stolen from one of their fathers and with which they'd chased a young woman into the woods. She was nineteen years old and getting off the bus after a late shift at the Wawa when she had happened to cross their path. She was their neighbor, two years prior she had been their classmate. Later, the news would report that one of the boys had gone to a YMCA camp with her the summer they were both twelve.

Ben had ordered the boy who held the shotgun to drop his weapon, but the boy seemed not to hear Ben at all. There would be no conversation this time. No sharing of stories. Ben had fired a warning shot over their heads.

The boy had fired a shot into the girl.

"Who's there? Identify yourself!"

Another tremble shook the branches of the honeysuckle bushes by the tow truck, and then suddenly it was coming toward Ben again, charging forward through the brush, flattening branches and snapping twigs in a flurry of flailing limbs, stampeding toward Ben as if to crush Ben as well under its rushing feet.

"Stop or I'll shoot!"

It happened too fast. Ben saw the flash of purple feather, the snatch of firm round skin, but the crazed animal stampeded forward, and it was too late to stop his finger from pulling the trigger. The reverberation of the gunshot rang out into the tree canopy. A moment later, it was silenced by the coming storm.

7:22 p.m.

"Sh-she came at me. She screamed. What was I supposed to do?"

Albert leaned against the wall, thankful for its support. His heart made awkward leaping motions in his chest and Albert waited for the feeling to stop. One breath. Two. It seemed the muscle was intent on pulling itself apart. He forced himself to look away from Penelope.

"An accident?"

"Yes," Jared said with obvious relief. "She wasn't supposed to be here. What's she doing here?"

Albert slowly motioned toward Penelope. "...may I?" Surprisingly, Jared nodded. The man seemed eager to find out himself.

Albert pushed away from the wall, pausing to see if his legs would hold him. When it seemed that they would, he moved to bend over the woman. He lifted Penelope's hair away from her face. Slipped two fingers into the folds of her neck. Nothing. Moving his fingers, Albert felt again. Nothing. He tried her wrist.

"Sh-she just came at me," Jared said again.

Albert let go of Penelope's wrist. He watched her chest. Willed it to move. His thoughts flew to the casserole dish he'd spotted in the kitchen and with a sting at the back of his eyes for the terrible irony of it all, Albert suddenly understood why Penelope had come to Clare's house. He saw Penelope knock on the front door and then cautiously try the knob when there was no answer, saw her shock at the state of the living room in shambles, saw her set the casserole on the counter in the kitchen, and then, concerned for her friend, go searching for Clare upstairs, only to find Croker. *No one should die for being neighborly*, Albert thought.

Penelope's chest was moving. Albert held the back of his hand against her nose. His skin warmed.

Albert let out his own breath in a hot burst. "She's not dead."

Relief loosened all the features of Jared's face and for a moment, Albert thought it might all be over. He stood, making his slow way back to the doorway. They might all walk out of here together. Well, not Penelope, someone would have to call about Penelope.

They could stay with Penelope until the ambulance came, and then he and Clare, they could still—

"Where is it?"

Jared's snarl ground up Albert's fantasy and, in that moment, Albert understood two things: first, there would be no walking out of here, not together anyway, not without someone in handcuffs or a body bag, and second, regardless of what Jared said, the man had *not*, in fact, come for his gun.

"I said, *where* is it?"

The trembling blade of the box cutter caught a stray band of light from the window and played radiant shadows across the ceiling. The refrigerator kicked on downstairs with a startling clamor of metal. Cars passed on the street outside—*wush, wush-wush, wush.* A goose honked in someone's yard.

"Don't you fucking call me a pussy. *You're* the fucking pussy, you hear me?"

Albert froze at the man's strange words. He didn't blink, tried not to breathe. It was as if the air between them was charged with explosives. One small move could light the fuse.

Jared seemed to shake himself and blew hard through his lips before he spoke again. Even from where Albert stood, motionless in the doorway, he could smell the foul air that passed through Jared's mouth.

"I'm gonna give you the count of three."

That the gun was far from irreplaceable was apparent to Albert. A discount store special at best and probably bought online. Its faux-metallic finish was chipped at the handle and around the barrel. Jared ransacked Clare's house earlier in the day and had probably found enough money between her purses, dresser drawers, and couch cushions to pay for the cheaply-made thing several times over. Fleeing at the sound of the police sirens, Albert saw Jared in his mind's eye, Jared waiting for the coast to clear before circling back around to lie in wait for Clare to return. Albert knew that a man wouldn't risk what Jared was risking—a box cutter at Clare's throat, a possible manslaughter charge on the bedroom floor, police in the driveway at any moment—for the hunk of Taiwanese junk currently lodged in the back of Albert's trousers.

"One…"

As a teacher of history, Albert understood that all of the conflicts of the world and throughout time were always about something else. Albert had instructed his students on this pattern of misdirection: the Palestinians' Gaza Strip, Napoleon's Mount St. Jean, Mao's Huai River and the Lung Hai Railway, Pizarro's Cajamarca, William's Senlac Hill—battles fought and won or lost, not for land or resources, but for religion, for language, for a way of life, for ideas about the world and why it's here, why *we* are here. Gandhi found freedom in a grain of salt. Western culture found power drilled from the earth. And so, Albert first taught his students to peel back the wrappings of a conflict to reveal some sense of the ideology contained inside. Who are these people? What do they want? What do they fear? What do they believe? Questions that had no simple answers, but rather, challenged his students to consider what *they* wanted or feared or believed.

Albert watched Jared, watched him intently. But he was not watching Jared's grimacing face, nor the man's trembling body, which was no doubt hyped up on an unholy mix of adrenaline and alcohol, or whatever else was making Jared's pupils shake in such an alarming way. Albert also ignored Jared's shaking left fist that held the box cutter at Clare's pulsing throat.

Instead, Albert watched Jared's right hand, the hand that lay on Clare's right shoulder. There was a quality to the placement of Jared's hand that Albert had been slow to ascertain, but now he saw it clearly—intimacy. For all his months of watching Clare's house, Albert of course knew about Jared's late-night visits that never lasted until dawn. The two had been intimate, yes, in whatever way a man like Jared could be close with a woman who was plotting to kill herself. (And Albert had very carefully chosen *not* to think too long on that sort of intimacy.) The casual placement of Jared's fingers along Clare's clavicle, the way Jared rested his palm on the soft tissue of Clare's shoulder, there was a familiarity there. A sense of possession. *Ownership*, was the feeling emitted by Jared's right hand.

For whatever else their relationship had been, Jared had claimed Clare as a result. Albert peeled back Jared's desire for his gun and found the betrayal Jared believed he'd suffered at the hands of Clare's rejection. There was betrayal, hurt, the sting of longing, feelings overwhelmed and drowned in the anger which shown plainly in the tightened knuckles of

Jared's right hand (for what is anger, but a façade behind which all other faces hide?).

And anger such as Albert was witnessing, there in the bedroom of Clare's long dead mother, soon needed an outlet, an explosion.

A good teacher learns with his or her students, and so Albert asked himself the same questions he posed in the classroom. What did *he* hold true about the world? After all of the events of the last few weeks, all of those evenings at the pond, all of the changes he thought he'd witnessed in Clare, what did Albert believe? And what did he still fear?

Albert knew the answer. He feared that people don't change. Even when the world around them changed, at their core, Albert still believed that people remained the same. It was Emily who believed differently. And he feared that Emily was wrong.

"Two…"

So here was Albert's problem: It wasn't Jared, who pressed the blade of his box cutter ever harder into the thin skin below Clare's jawline and who had created this childishly contrived 'ticking clock' by his ridiculous count of three. Albert's problem also wasn't Penelope, who might wake at any moment and whose confusion and fear would cause further liability to the situation. Neither was Albert's problem the police, who were destined to return to the house in their search for Jared, and whose sudden presence at the door might propel Jared into action sooner than either of them were planning. Even the fact that Albert had never fired a weapon in his life was not the problem.

The problem was Clare.

When Albert first entered the room, Jared had been standing in the far corner, a few feet behind Clare and to her left. Upon Albert's entrance, Jared took a long step forward and to his right, positioning himself behind Clare and holding the box cutter against her neck with his left hand. Clare was sitting at the foot of the bed, facing Albert. The bulk of Jared's weight was still to Clare's left, which created an opening behind Clare's head and right shoulder. Clare had only to throw her body weight backwards and to her right to slip cleanly beneath Jared's right arm and thereby escape any damage made by the blade of Jared's box cutter. If Jared moved at all, say because Penelope suddenly awakened or the police pounded at the front door, this opening would disappear, along with Clare's opportunity to escape.

That this ordeal was playing out in the room where Clare's mother had killed herself was an irony not lost on Albert. Clare had hidden under this bed some twenty-five years ago, listening to her mother slowly die above her. (Well, not this exact bed. This bed had been left by the renters Clare had kicked out last November, but for Albert it was, indeed, the *same* bed.) And Albert had a sense that the long road that ultimately led Clare to plan her suicide began in this exact space that the three of them shared now.

Only weeks ago, Clare had plotted to end her life. Would she now take action to save it? It was one thing to pull the trigger, take the pills, but quite another to have someone else do it for you. (*All that is necessary for evil to triumph*, Mr. Hallam's students had been taught, *was for good men to do nothing.*) And Albert knew the editor in Clare would discern this difference keenly—action through inaction.

And so, Albert's problem was simple: had Clare changed? Would she throw herself backwards and onto the bed when Albert drew the gun? Would she jump out of harm's way so that Albert had a hope of taking down Jared without taking out Clare in the process?

As Albert had watched Jared intently, Clare had watched Albert intently from the moment he came into the room. Albert felt her eyes on him. He'd not been able to look at Clare, though, what with the woman on the floor, the jittery man in the Metallica shirt, and the brilliant blade of the box cutter distracting Albert's attention. But in the remaining seconds before Jared shouted *"Three!"* Albert was looking at Clare. Her eyes were steady, dark.

Goddamn unreadable.

Had Clare changed? Albert knew what Emily would tell him. And Albert knew what he believed. It seemed they would all soon find out who was right.

"Three!"

Albert drew the gun.

7:22 p.m.

One of Freddie's more irritating skills, at least in Cee-Cee's opinion, was his talent for knocking her on her ass. *Have a seat!* he'd yell maniacally, thrusting his knees into the backs of hers and toppling her to the ground. They'd be standing in line for the movies, or making popcorn in the kitchen, or enjoying a perfectly pleasant afternoon of stalking the neighborhood ice cream truck when out of nowhere Cee-Cee's legs would collapse beneath her, sending her rear to the ground and a shot of stunning pain up her spine. *Ha-ha! Have a seat!* That the trick would not work on Freddie was a deeper source of Cee-Cee's irritation. She stood three inches taller than her friend, and her knees met the backs of his thighs, which meant that any attempt at retaliation only threw Freddie forward. Cee-Cee schemed other devices of revenge, though none as yet satisfying as landing Freddie on his ass.

When Officer Light's gun went off, Cee-Cee had been running toward the man. She'd hidden from him at first, unwilling and equally unable to explain her presence in the woods that afternoon. Cee-Cee took cover behind the honeysuckle bush and watched Officer Light walk slowly from his police cruiser and then search the black tow truck. Cee-Cee was afraid—afraid of being caught, of jeopardizing the mission to save Violet and her babies, but mostly she was afraid of failing Mr. Hallam who had trusted her and treated her like an adult, and thus Cee-Cee's fear bubbled out of her like steam escaping a pot. The fear shook her body, which rattled the branches of her cover, and the more Cee-Cee tried to quell her trembling body, the more violently the branches of the honeysuckle shrub shook all around her. By the time Officer Light shouted, Cee-Cee's fear had boiled over completely, causing her to rush forward through the brush and straight into the line of fire. There was an explosion (Cee-Cee had never heard a gunshot in real life and so her mind conjured visions of Fourth of July fireworks), and her legs crumpled like wet noodles. *Ha-ha! Have a seat!* She could almost hear Freddie's laugh echo through the canopy of trees above her as she fell.

After Mr. Hallam left her at the pond, Cee-Cee spent the better part of the last few hours watching Violet's island. That Violet's island was invisible to the other park visitors was a source of secret pleasure for Cee-Cee. The cluster of reeds that comprised the island was not so different from any other cluster in the pond. One had to peer closely, be patient, and allow the imagination to conceive the pond beyond the boundaries of what appeared at its surface. The pond appeared round in form, though it was not. The pond also suggested a basin shape beneath its waters, and this impression was an illusion as well. If one peered closely at Violet's island and if one were as patient as Cee-Cee had learned to be that summer, a solidity in the movement of the reeds could be detected. Where other reeds floated in the pond's waters, swayed back and forth in the currents of waves and wind, the reeds of Violet's island bent rather than swayed, betraying the solid ground into which they were rooted. And once the island was discerned, the physical makeup of the pond changed irrevocably in the mind's eye. Now mountains could be imagined beneath the water, and the island became one of an ancient archipelago that had flooded long ago, yawning valleys cut winding paths along the depths of the pond, slices of earth fell away leaving steep cliffs that overlooked murky vistas, wide canyons and deep caverns and miles and miles of caves housed mythical sea creatures whose sleek, translucent bodies had never once felt the warmth of sun.

Cee-Cee thought about these creatures as she'd sat at the bank of the pond, the rear of her jeans soaking in moisture and a hank of loose hair fluttering across her face. Did they have fins? Flippers? Laser-like green eyes that could pierce through the watery darkness to seek out their prey? But mostly Cee-Cee thought about Violet and her babies. She watched the reeds on the hidden island and smiled to herself. Snatches of yellow fuzz sometimes appeared between the stalks of plants. Every so often she saw a flash of purple.

Cee-Cee touched the feather on the back of her head, pushed it farther down into her ponytail, shoved her bangs out of her eyes again. Her bangs were getting long, too long to sweep out of her face, almost long enough, but not quite, to pin back in her ponytail. Her mother was the one who trimmed her bangs. In the beginning, at least once a month, she'd sit on the edge of the bathtub in her mother's new condo on early Saturday mornings before Mr. Homerton woke up. Mr. Homerton—and it would always be "Mr.

Homerton," not "Odis" which the man repeatedly urged her to use—enjoyed sleeping in late on the weekends, so these were rare moments she could spend alone with her mother. While her mother drank coffee, letting Cee-Cee sneak an occasional sip, she hummed softly to herself as she worked on Cee-Cee's hair. With her eyes closed, wet hair clinging to her forehead, she breathed in her mother's soft breaths that warmed her face. When the cool blade of the scissors slid against the bridge of her nose she always shivered. Her mother liked Cee-Cee's bangs short, just below her eyebrows, *so everyone can see your beautiful face*, and so Cee-Cee liked her bangs short as well.

The wind picked up and with it, Cee-Cee detected a trace of ocean air. Brisk. Salty. The clouds at the horizon hadn't moved, but they had darkened, thickened. The sky above the pond began to gray.

Cee-Cee shoved her hair out of her eyes again, pinning her bangs against her head with both hands. Bending her legs, she rested her elbows on her knees and held the position, watching the island. Cee-Cee's mother had been gone since the spring. First, there was the wedding and Cee-Cee in a princess-cut silk taffeta which, for all her complaining, she'd secretly loved. It floated out like a flower when she spun around. Then there was the honeymoon—the postcards from Santorini came nearly every day. Cee-Cee liked the one with the white donkeys the best. Then home just long enough to miss her end-of-school recital before Mr. Homerton's mother had fallen up some stairs and broken her hip. Cee-Cee could have gone with them, even Mr. Homerton had extended the invitation, his thick fingers awkwardly patting her head, but Cee-Cee had declined. *How do you fall* up *stairs anyway?* Cee-Cee had wanted to ask but didn't. Several times she'd tried to direct her anger toward this faceless old woman, but it never stuck. Not to the old woman, not to her mother, not even to Mr. Homerton and his irritatingly clumsy bloodline.

Indeed, there seemed to be no target for Cee-Cee's anger, but there it was, nonetheless. Her mother was happy. She would miss Cee-Cee, and it would be difficult to be away from her daughter for such a long period of time, but even Cee-Cee could see that this difficulty was easily surmounted. There was Mr. Homerton after all, the new man in her mother's life who followed her mother around the room with his eyes and who was nearly always in physical contact with her mother, even if it was just to brush pinky fingers together at the dinner table. And to this as well, Cee-Cee could not get her anger to stick, as her mother was so obviously and joyously happy.

And so, on the morning of Cee-Cee's twelfth birthday, she had cut her hair. Cee-Cee had watched the stylist in the mirror with her tongue firmly between her teeth where she could bite down when she felt the tears begin. Ten inches of her blonde hair, hair her mother used to braid and twist and pin, all fell to the floor with a soft whisper. Her birthday had fallen on Memorial Day that year, a slow day for the stylist, and the silence in the shop led Cee-Cee to think she could actually hear her long, beautiful strands hit the polished floor beneath the chair (*swish, swish, swish*). The woman had left Cee-Cee's bangs far too long, but Cee-Cee had said nothing.

Shoving her hair out of her face again, Cee-Cee watched the island, thinking about Violet and her babies. She knew that Violent would never leave her babies. Even if the dogs came. Even if the men with the nets and the poison came. Violet would stay with her little ones for as long as they needed her. Life on Violet's island was simple, harsh, perhaps, but simple in a way that Cee-Cee and her growing maturity quietly envied.

After her mother moved out, her father spent a lot of time alone in the bedroom he'd shared with his wife. He sat on the bed and looked out the window (his gaze had settled almost permanently on the Homerton house across the circle, but Cee-Cee hadn't known about Mr. Homerton at the time). When she dared to enter the room, she saw her father wasn't crying, just sitting. His face was hard. The lines around his eyes and mouth chiseled deep. He didn't speak much during that time, only rubbed the back of her hand with his thumb to let her know he knew she was there.

The weeks passed and eventually her father came back to her. His hardened shell appeared to crack, perhaps under its own weight, leaving a vulnerability in his face that made Cee-Cee hug him more often than she usually did. His words were softer now, slower, and she perceived an ease in his walk that she'd never seen, even before the divorce. And so no, Cee-Cee wasn't all that sad to see her parents split up. She was a bright child after all, and insightful beyond her years, perhaps, in understanding that life often means loss, but that loss nearly always opens up new ways for love. She loved her father with a strength she never could have, had her parents not separated. Her mother too, she loved now with the compassion of an adult child who sees her parent as a person, fallible, needing, floundering.

And though this insight triggered in Cee-Cee a capacity for acceptance that was rare, even in adults, she could not deny the simple wish that refused to be silenced in her heart. She sat by the pond all during the afternoon they were to save Violet and her babies with sour tears in the back of her throat. She watched the island. Pushed the bangs from her eyes.

When Cee-Cee first heard the truck rumbling down the gravel road on the west side of the pond, she thought for sure it was the *Goose Guard*. She'd already begun to dial Mr. Hallam's phone number, when the noise of the truck abruptly stopped. Cee-Cee waited, watching the tree line, her chest drumming with anticipation. After a few minutes, she dropped her phone back into the pocket of her jacket and set off for the woods. She kept off the road, dodging the bramble and fallen logs and slipping only once on a moss-covered rock. (From the air, as a bird—or goose—flew, one would see that during this time Cee-Cee and Jared passed within twenty feet of each other. Jared, who snaked through the brush back toward the neighborhood after having slipped out Clare's cellar door just as the police arrived earlier in the day, and Cee-Cee, who crouched behind the thick overgrowth and made her slow way toward what she thought was the *Goose Guard's* truck. They heard each other as they passed. A rustle of leaves. A crunch of twigs. *Deer*, Jared thought, angry again for his missing gun. *Rabbit*, Cee-Cee thought, hoping she hadn't scared it.) When Cee-Cee came upon Jared's truck, she recognized it immediately as the one parked outside Clare's house.

Here. Close. The possible proximity of Jared Croker spurred Cee-Cee to rush back toward the pond (this time she did slip on the rock and caught herself with both palms). Back at the park, she paced along the water's edge. She followed the bank all along its western shore to its southern tip and then turned back toward the northern end. She kept the island within her sights as she walked and a wary eye on the tree line. Confusion, mixed with a vague sense of dread muddied her thoughts, and Cee-Cee struggled to sift through the muck for some plan of action.

What did it mean, Jared's truck in the woods? Cee-Cee knew he was with the *Goose Guard*, but where was the *Goose Guard* truck? Where were the dogs? Should she call Mr. Hallam, or would he think she was being a silly child for panicking so easily? Cee-Cee was to call Mr. Hallam if the *Goose Guard* came. That was her job, and she very much did not want to fail at that job. But the impression of *here, close*—not even words in Cee-Cee's rattled mind, just a physical reaction—very much made her want to go home instead. (Cee-Cee was unaware of the finer points of Clare's plan, Jared's arrest among them. Nor was she aware of just how spectacularly that plan was failing at the moment.)

Cee-Cee's thoughts flew back to the night she'd first seen Jared Croker, weeks ago, the night she and Freddie stole Clare's mailbox. The night she'd met his gaze, where he'd sat in his truck across the darkened street. It was Officer Light who had warned Cee-Cee and Freddie about Jared Croker, told them the name of the man in the black tow truck, had given them his police card and told them to call if they ever saw anything suspicious or *dubious* (Cee-Cee had liked that word especially, since it conjured feelings of international espionage.) She told Officer Light about the gun she'd seen when she stumbled across the man waiting on Clare's porch. But Cee-Cee had not told the officer about what Jared had said. She was trying to forget what he had said, how Jared had shouted that word at her—*nobody* fucking *asked you*—and how it left her feeling somehow lost and despondent for the rest of the day.

Call, or don't call. Call, or don't call...

Through the muck, Cee-Cee rolled this decision in all possible directions after returning to the pond. Her decision-making process deteriorated from there, however, as her precocious mind spun in useless circles. By the time Cee-Cee finally made up her mind to call Mr. Hallam—better she call and be a fool, than not call and ruin the plan—Cee-Cee knew that far too much time had passed since she'd first heard Jared's truck in the woods. And it was then, as she reached for her pocket, having finally decided to make the call, that Cee-Cee learned her phone was no longer in her jacket pocket.

Fireworks?

Now, Cee-Cee lay on her back, staring up at the gray sky, wondering if the fireworks explosion was actually the sound of her legs breaking. She couldn't feel her legs. She couldn't feel her arms. She had traced and retraced her steps through the brush and hadn't found her phone. Cee-Cee wished she had listened to her father about not keeping her phone in her pocket. *Fireworks*, she thought just before the gray sky went black.

But the fireworks came out of the gun.

"Why do you think you had sex with this 'gravedigger,' as you call him?" Dr. Johnson asked on the day of Clare's last visit.

"What else would I call him?"

"Groundskeeper, custodian, I'm sure he had a name…?"

There was a bird in the window opposite from where Clare sat. The day was late, and a thin pink light filtered through the glass into the tiny office, casting the otherwise nondescript gray bird in an ethereal, nearly heavenly glow. The bird was utterly round, ball-like, in fact. It bounced along the windowsill outside as if jolted by electric shocks.

"And this wasn't your first risky sexual experience. From what I gather, intimate partner violence is something of a pattern?"

"He was…there. I don't know."

"But I think you do, Clare. You chose a stranger, a 'gravedigger.' Why do you think that is?"

In the year since the Incident on Steven's Pass, as she'd come to call it, Clare had analyzed a number of errors she'd committed that day, not the least of which was endangering the life of another human being, as well as the business with her seatbelt. Clare was not a rash woman. She was a careful thinker, slow to act, often slower to react. Even in Clare's questionable state of mind, she understood that the irrevocable nature of the idea demanded a more thorough examination.

And so, Clare began where she was most familiar, with research. She studied the seminal works of Kübler-Ross, explored all five stages of grief and then cross-referenced each against her own experience. Clare found few points of comparison and concluded that either the research was faulty or that she was so deeply immersed in the stage of denial that she was unable to recognize any points of comparison, which made the entire paradigm an exercise in frustrating futility, something akin to proving the existence of God by not *dis*proving it. Moving from Kübler-Ross to Freud's "Mourning and Melancholia" and Klein's "Mourning and Its Relation to Manic-Depressive States" Clare found that she agreed with both and that she did, in fact, feel quite physically ill. After that, Clare discovered *A Grief Observed*, by C.S. Lewis and then fell prey to a maddening detour of candy-filled self-help books before righting herself with Joan Didion's *The Year of Magical Thinking*.

"I know you're a writer—"

"Editor."

"—but I think you use literature the way some people use drugs," Dr. Johnson had told her when Clare reported her findings. Her health insurance covered twenty visits to a psychologist, and so Clare had felt this was a necessary, if time-consuming, angle to explore.

"At some point, you'll need to tell me why you're here," Dr. Johnson said at the end of Clare's tenth visit.

"I told you."

"You told me what happened, yes. But you haven't told me why you're *here*."

Clare's psychologist had a cloudy-white mane and the sadly thoughtful gaze of an Old English sheepdog. His nose, which he often twitched in lieu of an answer, was appropriately red and wet looking. After trying three other psychologists, Clare liked Dr. Johnson as soon as she entered his office, if for nothing than the extraordinary mess that was his workspace. Volumes of books and notebooks filled shelves that reached the ceiling, while more books and papers were scattered across every available surface of his office, including the cushioned chair where she would sit. As Clare watched him moving the stacks around on that first day, she detected an order to the chaos, and this, combined with Clare's irrational trust in fellow fanatical readers, signaled to Clare that she would spend her remaining seventeen visits in his office.

"Why don't you tell me?"

Dr. Johnson smiled and cocked his head slightly in an expression that was equal parts humor and irritation.

"Well, I can tell you what I see. Massive intrapsychic conflict, perhaps a borderline personality disorder. Then there's the psychic trauma and somewhat poor identity formation which indicates severe childhood damage, most likely some sort of violence, since all the signs of long-term PTSD are apparent—anxiety, depression, hypervigilance, and a certain numbing of responsiveness."

He waited, tapping his fingers against his rounded belly, his eyes searching out some sign of reaction on Clare's face.

"I'm not depressed."

Dr. Johnson's nose twitched.

After being sidetracked by a number of Chinese philosophers, Clare had returned to the Western world with Pals's collection of *Eight Theories of Religion* then read Marx on alienation, Eliade on the sacred, and Frazer on animism and magic. Because she was tiring, Clare went to Blackburn's little book on *Being Good* next, then skimmed through Žižek's thoughts on Violence—it was everywhere, and all the time, and could be found even within the act of reading the very book she held in her hands, an idea that struck Clare as uselessly inspired. After taking a break with Annie Dillard's Holy the Firm, Clare delved into the psychoanalytic texts, mostly to irritate Dr. Johnson, who had advised her against it.

"How are you sleeping?" Dr. Johnson asked her that last day in his office. This was his fallback question, leading Clare to suspect there was a classic Freudian lurking within, waiting for her to tell him about her sex-filled dreams.

Clare turned back to the window, letting both questions rest on the cluttered desk between them. The bird bounced another lap along the windowsill. She watched it silently. Dr. Johnson sat back, creaking the joints of his leather-tufted chair. He watched Clare watch the bird.

When Clare was young, there was a game the elementary school children played at recess—Superpower. Everyone took turns sharing what superpower they would choose if ever bitten by radioactive spider or experimented on by aliens—x-ray vision, super speed, shooting lasers with your eyes, whatever. Clare had always listened intently to the children play this game, knowing she would never be asked. But Clare always had her answer ready, just in case.

Flying.

"What are you thinking about?"

Clare startled out of her reverie just as the bird took flight from the windowsill and into the pink sky. A tiny black dot, then it was gone.

When Clare turned back to Dr. Johnson, whatever he saw on her face made him sigh. "How about if you just tell me about your day."

"I still don't see how telling you about my day does any good."

Dr. Johnson nodded, noncommittal, allowing her to go on.

"What can you tell about a person's day? It's pointless. 'A single revolution of the sun.' There's no such thing as a tragedy in a day."

"True, Aristotle had some odd ideas about tragedy," he said, rising easily, as he always did, to her literary challenge. "But it's also true that all our lives are lived in a day. In hours. In every minute, every moment. Each one of us playing out our own Greek drama. Battling our own demons. No man is an island, Clare."

Clare left Dr. Johnson's office for the last time that day, satisfied that she'd exhausted this line of inquiry. There was only one thread left for her to explore, and though Dr. Johnson had strongly advised against it, it was, in fact, his literary analogy on that last day that provided a path for what Clare would do next. Clare saw then that she needed to complete her hero's journey to the center of the earth, to the belly of the beast, to sail deep within the demon's mere. She would follow the circles round and round until she at last fell into the ninth one. She would listen to the siren's song and finally respond to her call. Clare felt something deeply romantic in the literary symmetry that was the last part of her plan.

She would go and do battle with the monsters. And she would live, or she would die. Either way, this part of her journey would, at long last, be mercifully over.

So in November of 2009, and not caring much how her story ended, so long as it ended, Clare Lyndsay went home.

FINAL DAY (CONCLUDED)

Wednesday, June 30, 2010
7:23 p.m.

"Three!"

The brain's security system is swift and deadly, Albert had once read in a magazine article. *It takes no prisoners and makes no apologies.* When confronted with mortal threat, the brain releases the floodgates above the kidneys and dumps adrenaline into the body's bloodstream, which raises the heart rate from a steady 60 to 80 beats per minute, to a mind-numbing 145 beats or more. And the effect is truly "mind-numbing," according to the article, since the rush of adrenaline-rich blood is diverted to the vital organs—heart and lungs—leaving the brain, or at least the prefrontal cortex, in a wash of painkilling endorphins. The Reptilian Brain then takes over, the oldest part of the brain that cares little for those pesky moral concerns—"thou shalt not kill," for instance—and is purely in the business of its own survival.

While our more newly-acquired higher-reasoning skills are trampled beneath webbed feet, along with our peripheral vision and ability to decipher right from wrong, those old instincts kick in. We run faster, jump higher, hit harder, and are suddenly, however fleetingly, capable of lifting large vehicles off small children.

What the article failed to mention, however, and what Albert was in the midst of tragically discovering firsthand, was that the powerful instinct to preserve life was also, occasionally, arbitrary.

Oh Emily, how is it that we were both wrong?

Albert squeezed the trigger of the gun again. Again nothing happened. He pressed down on the safety of the gun, but the safety was most definitely disengaged. The trigger of the gun was not jammed. The gun itself was not malfunctioning. The malfunction was Albert's index finger. Albert watched his finger in amazement as he squeezed the trigger.

His finger did not move.

The three people in the bedroom also did not move. Jared stood empty-armed and stunned at the foot of the bed. The box-cutter in his fist trembled, sending a shard of light across the ceiling.

Clare sprawled on the floor, hair in her face, where she'd landed. With the appearance of the gun in Albert's hand, Clare had hurled herself away from the box-cutter and backward into the empty space beneath Jared's arm. She'd landed backwards on the bed and immediately rolled to the floor, her face tight, prepared for a blast. When no blast came, Clare's eyes widened in dismay. Her mouth drooped open, allowing a tuft of hair inside.

And Albert stood before them both, gun in hand, finger on its trigger.

Albert, who had once pulled a trapped mouse from behind a bookcase and allowed it to bite him several times as he hurried down the stairs and through the house to release the squealing rodent into the backyard. *You old softie*, Emily had teased him, dabbing his swollen palms with a salve of turmeric powder.

Albert, who caught and released all manner of bugs and insects and creepy crawlers who were unlucky enough to stumble or fly into their house during the summer months.

Albert, who had already been thinking of the money in the sugar bowl, long before Emily placed it in Hawtrey's hand.

And Albert, who now stood before an armed and dangerous man, who pointed a loaded weapon at this man, and who could not force himself to pull its trigger. *See Emily*, Albert thought beneath the shouting in his head—PULL THE TRIGGER! SHOOT THE BASTARD!—*people don't change*. If only Jared weren't so large. Albert might have trapped him under a glass.

And on the heels of that thought came another, brightening every one of Albert's dopamine-drenched synapses—*Clare ducked!* A feeling that was not unlike fatherly pride road the waves of adrenaline through Albert's body, even as he looked down at Clare and realized she might die anyway, since Albert was apparently unable to shoot Jared. *Clare ducked!*

Jared's shock paralyzed him for only the briefest of moments before he lunged at Albert, box-cutter slicing through the air toward Albert's chest, while Jared's other hand reached for the gun. Clare too, sprang to action, leaping up from the floor to hurl her body again through the room, this time toward Jared.

Only Albert stood still, idiotically basking in the joy of his own error.

Clare ducked!

Even as the gun went off, there was still a trace of smile on Albert's old, cracked lips.

7:23 p.m.

"Stop or I'll shoot!"

But Jared had just kept coming, giving Ben only enough time to silently curse the man's stupidity before firing off the shot. The bullet was already in the air when the figure emerged from the bushes. The figure, who was not a wiry, thirty-something drug addict, but a little blonde girl in a yellow jacket with a purple feather jutting from the back of her head.

"Cee-Cee?"

The name flashed brilliantly across his mind, but Ben could not be sure if he'd said or only thought it. For an instant she locked eyes on Ben, her face all white eyes and open mouth, then her muscles relaxed, and her body crumpled to the ground.

Ben holstered his handgun as he ran to the girl. Her legs had twisted as she fell so that she laid face down in the muddy earth. Ben turned her gently as he'd been taught, keeping her spine in line with the base of her skull. When he had Cee-Cee safely on her back, Ben began examining her body, searching for the entrance wound. *I aimed high, I aimed high,* he hissed to himself (unaware that he spoke these words out loud) and, finding no wound, Ben raised Cee-Cee's limbs one by one, running his fingers along her jacket, her jeans, under her arms, as if his fingers might reveal what his eyes denied, and all the while fighting off a wave of nausea at the sensation of rolling bones beneath loose skin. It seemed Cee-Cee's slender bones connected to nothing, not muscle, not ligament. They rolled along each other and against Ben's hands like (the dead possum) potatoes in a sack.

There was nothing. No ripped clothing, no blood, not a scratch anywhere along the girl's body. Ben put his ear to Cee-Cee's mouth and felt a relief all the way to the hollow of his stomach. A tiny breath of air warmed his cheek.

"Cee-Cee, wake up."

Ben peeled a wet leaf from the girl's face and slapped her cheek lightly.

"You're okay, wake up. You fainted. Cee-Cee, wake up," Ben said several more times.

The girl began to rouse. Her eyelids fluttered. Her mouth opened and closed. Finally, she looked around, a slight frown on her pale face and said, "Freddie?"

Ben put the girl in the front seat of his cruiser, gave her a bottle of water to drink and a clean cloth to wipe the mud from her face. Cee-Cee drank obediently, head resting against the seat, feet dangling out the car door. Her purple feather lay at Ben's feet, where he knelt by the girl. It was splattered with muck but otherwise undamaged.

Ben picked up the feather and pointed it accusingly at Cee-Cee. "Now are you ready to tell me why in—"

"Base to 359, come in 359."

Another burst of static sprang from the radio clipped to Ben's belt. Marcy's voice came again. "359, come in 359."

Ben tossed the feather onto Cee-Cee's lap. "Slide in," he said. Cee-Cee drew her feet into the car and Ben shut the door.

"This is 359, what's up Marcy?"

"We have a 911 call and possible shots fired or…explosion, on Shalott, 1842."

Ben's chest tightened when he heard the address. *Goddamn bastard doubled-back on us…*

"Well, which is it?" Ben growled. He was already in the cruiser and starting the ignition. Reaching across Cee-Cee, he snapped her seatbelt in place before throwing the car in reverse.

"Unclear at this time. Should I show you 10-76?"

"Yeah, I'm on my way. Pull Chasseur and send Jerry too. It's gotta be our guy."

"10-4." There was a pause while Marcy left the microphone open. Ben heard muffled conversation, a disagreement of some sort, and then Marcy's voice came back loudly over the radio.

"359, we've got 911 calls lighting up the street now. There's…"

Ben waited, but there was only static and more muffled voices.

"—sort of disturbance," Marcy's voice came back to the microphone. "It sounds like we'd better call in hazmat."

It was then that he noticed Cee-Cee staring at him. The girl's eyes were huge.

7:37 p.m.

The smell of gunpowder seemed to fill the cab of the rental truck, and though Clare knew this could not be so, since Jared's tiny firearm was surely not that potent, the stench of burnt paper and something like chalk filled her nostrils, nonetheless. She drove one-handed, wiping the shaky hand that had held the gun on the leg of her sweatpants.

Clare sped south on Old Clevedon Road in the rental truck, weaving between the rush hour commuters as fast as she dared. The time on the truck's radio clock told Clare she was a full fifteen minutes late. Nearly tapping the bumper of a particularly slow-moving compact car, Clare veered to the left, cutting off the van behind her that moved into the left lane at the same time. She sped up and passed the car. The van's driver blasted his horn and waved his arm angrily behind his windshield.

Minutes later Clare was forced to slow down and finally stop, as the two lanes of traffic merged to one just before inching across the southbound bridge. As she waited, Clare wiped her other hand on her leg. Her palms were damp. Her shirt clung wetly against the vinyl seat. Her body buzzed with unspent energy. Clare clicked on the radio and swung the dial crazily from left to right blasting a cacophony of static, voices, and music into the cab of the truck.

She crossed the southbound bridge at a crawl, the wheels on the truck making a low whirring sound against the grated platform. On the others side, Clare made the first left, raced down a residential street, with a silent prayer that no children would jump out from behind the many parked cars, then made another left.

Clare was at De Vries Crossing a minute later, facing north, where the town of Kinderkamack laid just two miles ahead and Honock Pond less than a mile north and slightly east. Clare drove the truck to the highest point of the bridge, at its exact midway point.

She completed a full stop. Engaged the emergency brake. Shut off the engine.

Sitting behind the wheel of the truck for a moment, Clare took a slow, deep breath in an effort to clear the pounding in her head, the fluttering in her stomach. This was the plan, her plan. The time had finally come to save Violet and the goslings.

Reaching below the steering wheel, Clare pried open the panel with her fingernails and found the ignition fuse exactly where the website had said it would be. She yanked out the fuse and slipped it into the pocket of her sweatpants.

Clare opened the truck's door slowly, since the girth of the truck made it impossible to open the door all the way without slamming it into the guard rail of the bridge. She slipped through the narrow opening, shut the door behind her, and side-stepped along the guard rail until she came out at the front of the truck.

Clare looked out over the river. The traffic was lighter going north and so for the moment, she was alone on the bridge.

She checked her watch. Jared had slowed them down, but there was still enough daylight left. Dusk lingered in the summer, even if the sky had been dark all day. They still had time. A raindrop landed on her arm.

Jared.

Clare shivered.

7:37 p.m.

"Okay, sir, can I have your name?"

"Just hurry."

Albert replaced the phone receiver on its hook, having completed his third 911 call in as many days. He stood by his upstairs study room window where he'd stood many times before, watching Clare's house. The extraordinary view this evening though, was one Albert had never seen, nor ever hoped to see. Albert watched the amazing sight that was Clare's house for a moment, transfixed. Then with a jolt, Albert remembered the day was far from over.

It was time to go, past time to go, in fact, since Jared had delayed them far too long. Albert heard the shot again, felt the gun kick back in his hand. Had that really happened? Had he and Clare really done this? The scene in Alice's bedroom now seemed to Albert like something he'd once seen in a movie.

Shaking off these thoughts, Albert made a frantic search of the upstairs, muttering under his breath, before finding the book in the medicine cabinet of the bathroom. Albert retrieved it from the shelf, not bothering to question the logic that had caused him to place it there. Turning it over, Albert traced the gold leaf with his thumb. He'd found the book at the drugstore just last week, placed it in the shopping cart without understanding why. Well, that wasn't altogether true. Clare's face had flashed before him when he saw it, sitting there on the shelf. So Albert had known it was for Clare, but it wasn't until later that Albert understood the reason. Now, the reason was obvious.

Downstairs again, Albert pulled his notepad from the breast pocket of his shirt. He wrote quickly, ripped the sheet from the pad, and laid the note on top of the book, arranging both on the table so they would be easily spotted by anyone entering through the front door. After a moment, Albert anchored the note with his pen. It wouldn't do for a breeze from the door to blow away this part of his plan.

Having completed this task, Albert slipped into his yellow slicker and retrieved his paper bag of seed from the kitchen counter. He put the bread back in the pantry, closed the kitchen window, and shut off the light in the hallway. Back at the front door, Albert paused at the table, checking again that his plan was secure. Albert's keys lay beside the book and his note. Albert stared at his keys. Then he looked up, gazing at the image that stared back at him in the mirror.

Albert was forty-seven when he planted the first rose bushes in the front yard, roses whose descendants would, thirty-four years later, be given to the mailman for purposes of romantic subterfuge. Albert had gone to the nursery that afternoon in 1976 to buy some mulch for the rhododendrons in the side yard, but a sale on rugosas had caught his eye. While browsing the plants, a girl of perhaps three or four ran down the aisle toward him, screaming. Albert still remembered how wide the girl's eyes had been, how her pain and fear had spread them to perfect spheres. Like oceans, Albert remembered, tiny blue oceans, impossibly deep and sparkling, pure. The wasp had stung her twice by the time she reached Albert. He could see already, the splotchy swollen areas on her arm. She had startled upon seeing Albert, either by his size or by his color, and opened her tiny lips for a different kind of scream. Albert acted without thinking, swatting the insect off her skin where it then circled Albert's head several times in angry flight before lighting on his forehead, just above his left eye, and injecting the last of its poison into Albert's dark skin. He could still feel the spindly arms around his pant leg.

Albert stared into the mirror, seeing the darkened blotch the wasp's sting had left after it healed. The blotch had only darkened with time. Below that mark, Albert stared at his eyes, at how his eyes, once perfect almonds, now sagged tiredly at the corners. Years of smiles and tears and laughter and worry had carved deep, dark fissures above his cheekbones. The skin around his mouth had also loosened over time, pulling away from the bone, thinning with age. Tuffs of white hair grew for no good reason at all from the tip of his right ear. Below the ear was a cluster of freckles that he'd been born with, and which had grown lighter and lighter as he'd aged. The freckles formed the shape of the Little Dipper on Albert's neck. Sometimes, when they were lying together, Emily would whisper, *I have all the stars I need, right here* and then trace that pattern on his neck, sending a shiver down his spine that landed pleasantly in the base of his stomach.

Albert's back ached from years of sitting at a desk and grading papers, from standing by the blackboard and watching over his students as they bent over their tests, from leaning over ovens, from kneeling at his flowerbed. In the winter, it was his wrist that reminded him of the tumble he'd taken at one of the Teotihuacan pyramids (he could never remember if it was the sun or the moon) on the trip to Mexico he and Emily had taken in 1992. Two years later, Albert had stepped on a piece of coral while he and Emily snorkeled in the Sea of Japan, which left a crescent-shaped scar on the inside of his left foot. More scars speckled Albert's forearms, burns from his years of cooking, minor burns for the most part, with the exception of the mark across his right palm. Albert had served as a cook during his deployment in 1951, had volunteered for the job in fact, having never boiled water in his life, but preferring a paring knife in his hand to a rifle. On his third day, he'd made the rookie mistake of bare-handedly grabbing a pot of beans that was erupting its contents all over the mess hall floor. The burn across his palm had turned nearly silver over the years.

Albert turned his hand over, examining the beak-shaped mark that was still healing, the most recent addition to his collection. He gazed back at the mirror, a slight smile pulling at the corners of his mouth. Albert's body was a living testament to the life he'd lived—frayed in some places, thinned in others, marked and scuffed, well-worn and much loved, like a favorite book read again and again.

A siren rang out in the distance, still several blocks away. First one, then another, ringing in a harmony of alarm.

"I hear you," Albert murmured. "I'm coming." The door swung shut behind him.

Albert left his keys on the table.

7:52 p.m.

Even after Marcy explained to Ben the situation currently underway at the Lyndsay house, as best she could under the circumstances, Ben was unprepared for the scene that greeted him as he approached Shalott Drive. The cars had already begun to back up, so Ben parked his cruiser a block away, told Cee-Cee to stay in the car, and headed on foot toward Clare's house.

A possible "shots fired" call meant that fire and rescue were waiting for Ben before entering the house, and as Ben approached the house, he saw several firefighters standing idly in the street. The fire truck stopped traffic at one end of the block on Shalott Drive, the ambulance, at the other. Drivers had emerged from their cars. Some of Clare's neighbors had ventured onto the sidewalk for a better view. Save for the roar of the fire engine, the street was eerily silent.

Everyone stared at the house.

Red and blue smoke poured forth from the front two windows, a side window, and the open front door of Clare's house. The winds from the coming storm held steady just outside of town, so barely a breeze stirred on Shalott Drive.

The colors rose from the windows and door, and mixed together along the front porch, roof, and yard. Clare's purple house was now enveloped in a cloud of purple smoke.

"Sputtered? Like a blurp-blurp-blurp sound?"

"More like a blumble-blumble-blumble."

"Huh. Did it shimmy?"

Clare touched the ignition fuse in her pocket, turned it between her fingers.

"A little, maybe? Then it just died."

He was a big man wearing a baseball cap too small for his head. The cap balanced atop the shiny dome of his head, seemingly affixed only by a thin sheen of sweat. The name sewn onto his shirt read AAAL's Mechanics.

"Lucky I came by, I guess," the man said, removing his cap and running his fingers down his bald head—the gesture of a man in deep denial, perhaps. He plopped the cap back on his head and grinned at Clare. "Let's open her up and see what we've got."

Yes, lucky, Clare thought, following the mechanic to the hood of the truck. Cars had started to line up behind Clare's rental truck. First the mechanic's white pick-up, then an apple-green SUV, a couple of black sedans, a rusted minivan, and a flatbed truck carrying a load of metal pipes.

As Clare watched, two more vehicles pulled up behind the flatbed.

"Too bad I don't have my rig today. Could have hauled you outta here just like that." The mechanic snapped his fingers, still grinning.

"I called for a tow," Clare said. The honking had begun from behind the rental truck, so Clare wasn't sure he'd heard her.

"Moving in? Moving out?" The mechanic lifted the hood of the truck and wiggled the wires around the truck's battery as he talked. "Just passing through?"

"Oh. Well, I was—"

"What's the problem, lady, you know you can't just block the road like this."

The driver of one of the black sedans was sidestepping between the guardrail and Clare's rental truck. As he came out around the hood of the truck, he smoothed his shirt and fixed Clare in an angry gaze. He seemed to Clare somewhere between a businessman and a nightclub bouncer—biceps bulging against his black silk shirt, wet-black tie, charcoal-grey slacks. He was young, twenty-five, twenty-eight at most, with a moussed mane of carefully tousled and highlighted hair.

"That's just what we were trying to ascertain," said the mechanic, without looking up from the engine. "Wanna give me a hand?"

The moussed man seemed shocked at the suggestion. Clare tried not to smile.

"I have a meeting in half an hour. What I want is for you to haul this piece of junk off the road." The driver glared at Clare as he spoke to the mechanic.

"You just hang onto your panties for a minute." The mechanic straightened, wiping his hands on a rag he'd pulled from his pants pocket. He nodded at Clare. "Go give her a turn, see if she's starts up now."

Clare walked around the driver of the sedan, who appeared frozen at the mention of *panties,* and climbed back inside the rental truck. Two more drivers had emerged from the line of cars and were headed toward the group gathering on the bridge. The woman in the apple-green SUV leaned out her window as they passed. The honking continued.

Clare turned the key in the ignition and when nothing happened, the mechanic motioned for her to stop. He reached back under the hood and busied himself for a moment before motioning to Clare to try the key again.

"I hate to say it, but Slick there is right," the mechanic told Clare after she'd joined him again at the hood of the truck. He nodded at the other two men, ignoring the driver of the SUV who had turned his back on them all and was tapping vigorously on his cell phone. "The three of us can push, if you wanna hop back in and steer, uh…sorry, I didn't catch your name."

"Clare."

"Danny. Make sure the parking brake's off, okay Clare? We'll take it slow, just head for the shoulder up there and——"

"I called for a tow, they should be here soon." Clare checked her watch. She still had twenty more minutes to keep them all on the bridge. And that was only if everything had gone as planned on Albert's end. Cars were still passing on the southbound bridge.

"Well, until then, we've got to get you off the road," Danny said, moving away from Clare. He called, waving at one of the men. "You go around, we'll meet you in the back."

The woman in the apple-green SUV had gotten out of her car and was making her way along the guardrail toward Clare. She wore a simple cotton sundress with a white sleeveless bodice and pink skirt. Her face and arms and hair were a golden hue, glowing with summer warmth. Her progress was slow along the rental truck, hampered by the large swell of her belly beneath the pink skirt of her dress, which brushed up against the side of the truck as she waddled forward. She smiled at Clare and raised a hand in greeting.

"Keep your foot off the brake, just let her coast in," Danny was saying. He spoke over his shoulder as he gave Clare directions.

"No."

"—wanna give the horn a quick tap if—"

Even Clare had barely heard her own voice, and so she drew a deep breath and used it all to say the word again.

"No."

Danny stopped and turned back toward Clare. "What?"

Clare wrapped her arms around her stomach and stared down at her feet. The sight of the pregnant woman's belly had somehow sapped the last of Clare's energy. The events of the day came flashing back—the hospital, the dogs, Jared… The back of her head throbbed, and Clare felt weary, drained, and simply too exhausted to lie anymore.

Clare looked up at the undeniable swell of human life beneath the woman's cotton dress and heard herself speaking as if she were listening in on someone else's conversation.

"I said we're not moving the truck. I said. No."

7:52 p.m.

The grayed sky above the pond had thickened with clouds and streaks of near black now traced their curved bodies in long, arced lines across the firmament. Rain fell just beyond the horizon in the south, darkening everything in its path as the storm moved north along Old Clevedon Road, approaching town. In the west, though, a spectacular sunset beamed its last rays across the park, casting brilliant shadows along the hills, and setting the waters of the pond ablaze, glowing with amber and deep bronze.

But when Albert looked up at the sky, he saw only blue. A deep, summer blue that warmed his face and prickled his arm hair with heat. The breeze was soft. The grass beneath his bare feet was soft. And the voice he heard was soft, melodious, just as he remembered.

"May I have this dance?" Albert extended his hand and bowed with a flourish.

"Always."

He took Emily in his arms, holding her at the small of her back and breathing in the rich scent of her body lotion. Jasmine? Lavender? He'd always meant to ask. It was the summer of 1951, and they were driving through the Pocono Mountains. The meadow they had found was filled with sun but hidden from the road by a circle of trees, their own private paradise where later, Albert had made love to her beneath a weeping willow with tears in his eyes for the sweetness of that moment. Before that though, they had danced in the sun, slipping out of their shoes, and swaying back and forth on the warm grass, while Albert kept time with a little tune he hummed deep in his throat.

"I'm proud of you."

"She's going to be okay, I think."

"Because of you."

"No," Albert said, nuzzling his face against her hair. "I only did what you said."

Emily laughed, the sound like music notes on Albert's ears. "You old softie."

Albert had taken the more direct route to the pond (similar to the one Cee-Cee had also taken, earlier in the day). He'd fought his way through the thick brush at a steep downward angle, cutting his travel time in half. The pace he set put a crick in his back that sang out each step. Albert heard the gunshot explode in his ears again and again as he stumbled forward. Twice, he lifted his arm to smell and wonder at the scent of gunpowder that clung to the material. Jared's terrified face floated before him.

But when Albert reached the edge of the pond, the pain in his back, the sound, the smell, all of his thoughts were silenced by the sight of his wife at the shore, waiting for him. When Albert had first started coming to the pond to feed Violet and her goslings, Albert was careful to remind himself that this image of his wife, standing at the edge of the water in a soft white dress, scooped at the neck with sleeves that ruffled in the breeze, was firmly rooted in his imagination. Albert had long conversations with himself about this at night, reminding himself of friends who had succumbed to the same sort of fantasy Albert was now allowing himself. Friends who now entertained those fantasies within the comforts and confines of a nursing home.

As the weeks went on, though, these conversations turned to argument, specifically, the argument of harm. There was no harm here, Albert decided, to allow himself this small luxury. No harm in indulging the fantasy, as long as Albert understood it for what it was—fantasy, his imagination, grief incarnate. And that's exactly how Albert understood it…all the way up until he saw Emily at the water, until he reached for her. Then Albert understood nothing but the feeling of his wife in his arms.

As they neared Old Clevedon Road, Albert strained to hear the sounds of cars approaching from the south. They would come fast, swerving around those deadman curves like the devil himself were on their tails, silent one moment, bearing down on them the next. But Albert heard nothing. Clare had been successful on the bridge. The road to the north was also silent. Empty. The emergency vehicles had done their job.

Violet and the goslings followed Albert only a few feet behind him. In the stillness, Albert could hear their little webbed feet scuffling across the forest debris. The new surroundings worried Violet, Albert could tell, though she continued to follow. Her feathers had fluffed to twice their size and her long neck swung round and round, taking in the new sights and sounds. They were late, and so Albert hurried their progress, taking them directly west toward the road.

The first drops of rain splattered across Albert's face.

The scent was jasmine, yes, that was it.

"I miss you."

Emily only touched his cheek with the tips of her fingers in response.

7:54 p.m.

Long before scientific studies suggested that the sight of a woman's tears can lower a man's testosterone levels, aggression, and even sexual desire, Alice Lyndsay wrote an article titled "Weeping as Weapon: A Woman's Tactical Advantage," which took aim at this particular male complaint. In times of conflict, her article argued, opponents deploy whatever arsenal they have at hand. A man's arsenal—height, speed, agility, sheer muscle bulk—lends him an advantage over a woman, at least in physical conflicts. This is why, according to Alice's article, men tend to escalate verbal conflicts to physical confrontations so quickly. They lure the enemy into home territory. During non-physical confrontations, however, it is a woman's arsenal—conversational skills, including a much larger vocabulary, and various methods of non-verbal manipulation—that often prevails. Alice's critics predictably balked at the idea that a woman's tears might be deemed "non-verbal manipulation" and used the article as further proof of Alice's anti-feminist and possibly communist leanings. But Alice held firm. No one cries foul when men use their bigger size and deeper voices to intimidate and subdue women. In the battle between the sexes, there is no doubt, Alice argued, that tears are a weapon, a uniquely feminine weapon, and one women should not hesitate to utilize if it brings them a win.

That Clare found herself crying—doubled-over, chest spasming, salty-tears-in-her-mouth crying—was as much a shock to her as it was to the others on the bridge. Clare was not a crier. She detested the reddened eyes of her female coworkers who found all matter of life's events—births, deaths, breakups, engagements, performance reviews, the list was endless—weep-worthy. Disappointment or despair called for action, not the sort of emotional atrophy that sobbing induced. Alice's daughter had learned well that women who cried were weak and lacking and generally too brainless to organize their feelings toward some more productive intent. Tears may be a weapon, but they were the most shameful weapon of all.

"I'm sorry, hon, what did you say?"

Danny half-knelt, one knee on the pavement and one by his chest, in front of Clare who sat on the front bumper of the truck and continued to weep steadily. He reached for her face, fingers twitching inches above her skin, pulled away, hand fluttering around her shoulder and arm as if Clare might be too hot to touch. All confidence had disappeared from his voice, and his face opened in deep concern and a bit of fear.

The two other men stood a safe distance away, gaping at Clare and folding their hands, perhaps subconsciously, over the vulnerable area between their legs.

"I don't understand, why is it we can't move your truck?"

Clare used the back of her fist to wipe her face, but the tears just kept coming. She tried to speak, choked on the snot streaming down the back of her throat, and fell into a coughing fit.

"Leave her be a minute. Here, take this."

A bottle of water materialized in front of Clare's face, and she accepted it gratefully. The pregnant woman sat beside Clare, ankles crossed, her skirt arranged carefully beneath her, the material clinging wetly to her belly. For the first time, Clare realized not all the dampness on her face was tears. It was raining now, heavy sheets that blew sideways in the wind. Clare's teeth chattered. The temperature had dropped ten degrees in the last ten minutes and her bones rattled together in violent shivers. The car horns continued to blare from the line of vehicles behind Clare's truck, calling to each other in a way that was not unlike the honking of geese.

"Just take your time." The pregnant woman put her arm around Clare's shoulders and pulled her close. She caught the citrusy scent of the woman's hand lotion.

Clare swallowed several times from the water bottle and then set it down in the hollow of her stomach. She took a ragged breath, pinned her shaking hands between her knees, and in a voice far from her own—high, shaky, often broken by sobs—Clare began to explain.

7:54 p.m.

In the academy, Ben learned what is known as Command Presence. There was a chapter in the manual and a two-hour seminar during a weekend training session: *Look Sharp, Act Sharp, Be Sharp.* The enemy will perceive you as you present yourself to him. Authoritative and confident or hesitant and apathetic. Ben's tactless roommate—a spry, twitch of a man—dubbed the seminar *Look Shit, Act Shit, Be Shit* with a bark of laughter that made Ben cringe.

Command Presence, Ben quickly learned, is the ability to assert authority and control without the use of force or coercion. Whether encountering a suspect or entering a crime scene, Command Presence lets others know immediately that you are to be trusted and obeyed without question. It begins with a clean, pressed uniform, polished shoes and badge, and a spotlessly maintained police cruiser. It is found in the arrow-sharp line of an officer's back and the unyielding stride of an officer's walk. Often, the officer alone is the beacon of reason in a storm of chaos, and so he (yes, "he," as stated in complete ignorance of the six women who were in attendance), he must always stand firm against the sea, if he is to protect those who lie at its shore. The trainer, an ex-navy admiral, offered a variety of maritime metaphors—beacon of reason, sudden squalls of danger, breakers of indecision—and so in Ben's mind's eye, it was from the deck of a ship that he commanded every police scene in his 16 years on the force.

The seminar ended with the dramatic playing of the 1985 black box recording from Delta Flight 191. Specifically, the last two minutes of the recording, before the plane crashed. While the voices of others in the cockpit and from the tower betrayed the fear that grew quickly to terror, the voice of the captain could be heard clearly above them all. This voice never faltered, never weakened, even unto impact. And this, the ex-navy admiral emphasized, is the voice of Command Presence. The voice that steers straight through the storm, without hesitation, without fear, even as the ground rises up at you at 200 miles per hour.

So as Ben entered the scene on Shalott Drive—purple smoke spewing from the Lyndsay house, flashing emergency vehicles flanking its property lines, an entire neighborhood gaping from the street—his face betrayed neither surprise nor alarm. His gait was hurried, not rushed. His voice was loud, clear, and decisive.

"You all need to back it up," Ben said to the crowd gathered on the sidewalk. He tossed a roll of police tape to Chasseur. The man had run up behind Ben, panting from the two-block sprint from where he'd parked his own cruiser and wide-eyed at the sight of purple smoke pouring from the Lyndsay house. But Ben was glad to see that otherwise his officer was unruffled.

"Move. Now. Behind the fence."

The crowd scattered unquestioningly in response to Ben's command, some lining up behind a sagging picket fence, others taking position behind parked cars. Several of the bystanders held cell phones in the air, recording the fantastical scene playing out before them. It had finally started to rain and others in the crowd held jackets over their heads. One woman had ripped apart the plastic casing of a newspaper circular, fashioning for herself a sort of rain hat that tied beneath her chin, unwilling, apparently, to miss even a moment of drama to duck inside her house and retrieve her umbrella. As Ben walked away, Chasseur began taping up the scene.

Ben spoke briefly with the fire truck crew and verified the report Marcy had given him over the radio. He was coordinating with the paramedics when a voice behind him suddenly interrupted.

"Hey, are you going to move these trucks out of the way and do your job, or do I have to do it for you?"

An older man with a thick plumage of white hair had crossed beneath the police tape and was striding toward Ben, holding his umbrella high in the air. He wore a double-breasted grey suit and a paisley ascot tie which gave him a European flair that Ben was certain was intentional.

"Sir, get back behind the tape. This is a police scene."

"Well then why don't you *police*." The man flashed air quotes in front of Ben's face. "And stop scratching your ass so that we can get out of here. Maybe you people don't know what it means to keep a schedule, but mine is already *ten minutes late*."

Ben took a single step forward, bringing him beneath the man's umbrella and within inches of the man's nose. Ben caught a whiff of expensive cologne and old coffee.

"Sir, get back behind the tape," Ben repeated, without raising his voice. "Get back in your vehicle and close the door, or I will cuff you to the back of my car where you will wait until I take you to the station."

Shock gave way to anger, gave way to grudging acceptance all within an instant on the man's face. Clearly, men cowered in this man's presence, not the other way around, but Ben held his ground and his gaze until the man turned away. Striding back toward the tape, the man ducked beneath it, and turned back toward Ben with a defiant glare.

When Ben was confident of the paramedic's position, he spoke quietly into the microphone. "Chasseur, you take the front, come in low," Ben said. They would not wait for backup. With a possible shots fired call, it was Ben's decision, and Ben had decided immediately upon arriving at the scene that they would enter. It was a decision based on equal parts experience and hunch. Neither the craziness of the day, nor the sight of purple smoke slowly engulfing the neighborhood dissuaded Ben from believing that Jared was either inside the Lyndsay house or had recently been on its premises. And if Jared was involved, they could not afford to wait.

Ben pressed the radio's talk button again. "Wait for my signal."

Drawing his firearm for the second time that day, Ben crouched low and proceeded along the north end of the property toward the rear of the Lyndsay house. The first droplets of rain that had splattered his windshield as he sped back toward town with Cee-Cee in his passenger seat, now sprayed almost sideways in the wind like a busted pipe. A terrible clatter rang around his ears where the water met his hat. The lower areas of the Lyndsay yard had flooded quickly, causing Ben to sink with each step. The rain did little to dissipate the smoke, though, and as Ben approached the thickest layers of what now appeared to be purple steam, his eyes began to sting and the lines of a long-forgotten war poem from Mr. Hallam's class suddenly invaded his thoughts—*Stormed at with shot and shell/ Into the jaws of Death/ Into the mouth of Hell.* Ben looked back only once before the rain and purple smoke swallowed him entirely.

What Ben saw when he looked back through the hellish haze was Cee-Cee. She'd not stayed in his cruiser as Ben had instructed her and was instead standing with the crowd on the street. She peered between the adults to look at Ben, shielding her eyes from the rain with her hands, and what Ben saw in her expression nearly stopped him cold. Her face was alight with so much anticipation and glee, biting her lip and grinning with so much delight and eagerness, that all at once Ben felt like the hero of his own action movie. And it was then that Ben understood that for all his confusion surrounding the events of the day, Cee-Cee knew exactly what was going on.

And from the top of Cee-Cee's head, the purple feather rode again.

8:02 p.m.

There was silence, and Clare, who'd spent her childhood reading various types of silences—her mother content and working, her mother festering with some glum idea, her mother simmering in a rage—found it difficult to discern the mood of the crowd that had gathered at the hood of the rental truck. Clare kept her head down, not daring to make eye contact with any who stood above her. The pregnant woman (whose name Clare had been told twice and still could not remember) had withdrawn her arm from around Clare's shoulders but continued to sit close, nodding hesitantly as Clare told the story.

Others had emerged from their cars, creating a gathering of nearly a dozen. Clare stared only at their shoes, conjuring images of the people in them based on the style and condition of their footwear. Even the man with the cell phone had momentarily paused in his angry texting—over-priced loafers perched on a mound of uneven pavement to avoid the rain runoff—to listen to Clare's crazy tale. The rain made a great clatter along the guardrail of the bridge, and umbrellas had opened above where the women sat on the truck's front bumper.

Somewhere in the telling, Clare had stopped crying.

"So…there's this goose…"

This was Danny, rocking back into a puddle on the heels of his work boots.

Clare nodded, wiping her chin.

"Purple, you say?"

Another nod.

"And it dances."

There was a snort of laughter, cut short by a hissing *shh*. Clare wasn't sure who the laugher was, but she thought the shusher might have been the pregnant woman. With her head down and the drumming rain, though, Clare couldn't be sure.

"I'm sorry, hon, but you've got to know how this sounds."

"I do," Clare said, her voice raw, breaking on each word. Clare had counted three uses of the word "hon" since she'd first begun to cry. Danny sounded very much like he wanted to pat Clare on the head.

"Why don't you go wait in my truck, get out of this rain. We'll take care of this."

"Why don't you just leave her be?"

This from the pregnant woman whose arm had found its way around Clare's shoulders again. Her fingers gripped Clare's upper arm tightly, holding her secure as she might a child. A world of irrationality waited within the woman's swollen stomach. Children brought with them all sorts of delusions, all of which parents were called upon to indulge, accept, and manage to greater or lesser degrees. Clare guessed she'd decided to start practicing early.

Danny stood suddenly, his patience lost at the prospect of now handling two crazy women. He removed his hat and ran his fingers through his imaginary hair, flicking rain from the dome. "So what do you suggest, we all stand around here in the rain just 'cause this lady wants to play fairytale?"

"No, but you don't have to be so heartless about it, can't you see—"

"*Heartless?* Are you serious—"

"What does it matter? What harm will it do to wait a little while, even if it seems a bit illogical?"

"Illogical? This isn't illogical, it's nuts—a purple goose? Were you even listening?"

"It wouldn't hurt anything to wait a while longer, she's obviously having some sort of…*trouble.*" The woman said this last in a voice that very much made the word sound like *breakdown.*

"Well, she can have her 'trouble' somewhere else. We're moving her out of here."

Danny motioned to several of the men as he spoke, and they moved in toward where Clare and the pregnant woman sat on the truck. Clare had a brief flash of herself looping her arms around the truck's bumper, sixties protest-style, while the men pulled at her ankles.

"Hold up a minute."

A new voice. Polished black loafers stepped down from the pavement mound and into the stream of water that gushed down the slope of the bridge. It was the angry man with the cell phone who now approached the front of the truck, stepping between Danny and the women.

"How much time are we talking here?"

"You can't honestly be considering this," said Danny.

"Practically-speaking. Five more minutes? Ten?"

The man addressed Clare directly, ignoring Danny and the rest of the crowd. He bent over slightly, his phone in one hand, the handle of his umbrella in the other. "On the outside, how long?"

Clare turned her head upward from the rain-splattered loafers and charcoal-grey slacks to the man's face. All traces of irritation had vanished, leaving only a kind of open curiosity that made him appear almost childlike. And as he spoke, he seemed to grow younger before Clare's eyes. Clare had never realized how the presence of calculated thought aged a person. The editor in Clare ticked off details as usual—a high brow that meant early hair loss, a faint lightening around the eyes where protection had been placed prior to an artificial tanning session, a thin scar along his jaw line that looked like the repair of a serious childhood injury by a very expensive plastic surgeon—but the writer who'd been emerging in Clare during the last few weeks sensed a story. Was it a parent? An uncle? A teacher, perhaps? Someone in this man's life had shown him what it meant to suspend disbelief. Someone had taught him the value of letting some things just be…without imposing judgment or understanding or any of the other petty mechanisms adults needed to justify the world. Someone had read this man stories as a child, or helped him build blanket forts, or had otherwise encouraged him to believe that dragons and heroes are real and that saving one life *really might save the world.*

He smiled down at Clare, beamed, really. And through that smile, Clare saw the boy he had been, the gapped teeth, buzz cut, a sprinkling of freckles across his nose.

And, impossibly, Clare grinned back.

8:02 p.m.

Ben read the note again. They had decided to leave it taped on the man's chest when they cut him free from the chair—"evidence," or so Ben had called it, knowing the chief would get a good laugh. They could all use a laugh today.

Jared Croker sat in the back of Ben's cruiser, hands pinned behind his back with Ben's handcuffs, sweaty hair plastered to his forehead, glaring darkly out the window. Ben had removed the duct tape from Croker's wrists and ankles, slicing carefully between the skin with his pen knife. They'd banged into Clare's house, guns drawn and shouting *police!*, only to find the man taped neatly to a chair and sitting at the kitchen table. Duct tape bound his hands and feet and mouth with more tape wrapped around his chest, securing him to the chair. (His clothes were greatly disheveled, and the man was missing a shoe after having been roughly dragged down the stairs by Mr. Hallam and Clare, or so Ben would learn later.) Croker's chest heaved and his eyes went wild when Ben and Chasseur burst into the room. After clearing the house and determining that the threat had been "contained"—Chasseur's word, a smile in his voice—Ben had leaned over the grunting Jared to examine his suspect more thoroughly.

A soft sheet of stationery, lavender flowers etched at one corner, had been affixed to the front of Jared's torso. Duct tape held the paper at the top, wrapped several times around Jared's chest and the back of the chair, and pinned the man's arms to his body. More tape held the paper at the bottom around Jared's tiny potbelly. Two lines of small, familiar script were written at the center of the stationery. Even if Ben had not recently seen the script on a note addressed to his chief, Ben would have known that handwriting anywhere. And Ben had not been at all surprised to find this script on this particular piece of stationery, fastened to this particular squirming, growling man in this particular kitchen. *Which perspective are you missing?* this same handwriting had asked him from the margins of his history papers, years ago. *You are circling a good idea, zero in on your point…Where is your support for this claim?...Words have meanings, be careful with both.* Or the rare, but highly-prized *Exactly! Now you're thinking!* or *Beautiful, Ben.* or simply *Nice!* with a triple underline.

Ben reread the note taped to Croker's chest, and this time he couldn't help but smile.

This is the second time I've broken into Miss Lyndsay's home today.
Please arrest me this time.

They found Penelope on the floor upstairs, a bed pillow placed under her head, a blanket pulled over her body. Paramedics had taken Mrs. Homerton to the ambulance just as she was waking. It looked like the woman had suffered only a mild concussion.

They found Jared's gun on the kitchen table, its chamber open and empty. Three bullets lay on the table beside it. Chasseur discovered a single round lodged in the coils of Clare's refrigerator—shot clean through the floor of the bedroom upstairs, through the kitchen ceiling, and into the refrigerator, where it punctured a head of crisp lettuce on the top shelf. From the sound of things, Ben doubted the refrigerator would survive.

"Take a look at these."

Ben turned away from the glaring man who still wriggled against his cuffs and shouted through the glass—*gonna arrest that black psychopath!*—and moved to stand beneath Chasseur's umbrella. The crowd had not dissipated with the onslaught of the rain, eager as they were for more potential spectacle. A burst of applause had traveled along the sidewalk when Ben emerged from Clare's house with the handcuffed man. Applause that was led, Ben suspected, by Cee-Cee, herself. Someone had whistled.

Chasseur held out his hand, revealing two burned-out cardboard tubes—one scorched red, the other, blue. *Tactical grade, use extreme caution, blast wire pull.*

"We found some more 'round the side there, propped up in the windowsill."

"Smoke bombs."

"Military grade, looks like." Chasseur rolled the tubes in his hand. "You know we found some of these up at Croker's earlier on that call. The dosed dogs? There was a shed 'round back. All sorts of crazy stuff."

Ben looked back at the house, scratching his head and knocking his hat askew. It had been Ben's experience that every crime scene told a story, complete with major and minor characters, conflict, climax, and resolution. It was how Mr. Hallam taught history: Who are the players? What do each want? How do each go about getting it? History was first and always story—people creating plot by playing out their needs and desires and fears and envies—the significance of which, the lesson, the larger worldview, the what-have-you, was for future reader-descendants to decide. As a student of Mr. Hallam's, Ben learned that the record of human events nearly always began at the end. The victory or defeat, the great invention, the catastrophic famine. To understand what had happened, you had to ask the right questions, which meant tracing events back to the story's beginning.

Being a cop also meant entering the story at its end. You arrived on the scene and worked backwards from whatever you found when you got there. You examined each piece of story until it could be placed in sequence, and, if you're lucky, a theme emerged. Meaning surfaced.

Which perspective are you missing, Ben?

A loud beeping pierced Ben's thoughts as the fire truck backed up to the sidewalk and bounced onto the front yard of the house next door. The first car in the long line of traffic inched past the fire truck's front bumper, climbed the curb, made a sharp turn behind a parked SUV, and accelerated noisily down the road. A second car followed.

Chasseur was still talking "—clear the roadway here. They reamed us a new one with that last Lyndsay call, guess the mayor was late for dinner—" but Ben wasn't listening. He was watching Cee-Cee. Or, more accurately, Ben was watching Cee-Cee watch the fire truck. The girl still stood on the sidewalk, thirty feet or so away from Ben. Someone had been holding an umbrella over Cee-Cee's head, but she'd stepped out from beneath the shelter as the fire truck began to back up. Rain pelted her face, pasted her hair to her cheeks, dripped from her nose. The purple feather sagged at the back of her head, heavy with water. As Ben watched, the feather slipped from its hold in her ponytail and fell into a puddle at Cee-Cee's feet.

This had been a day of questions, and all day long Ben had had the nagging feeling he'd been asking the wrong ones. Chasing Croker, searching for the tow truck, fixated on why the man had broken into Clare's house in the first place this morning. But Ben had known from the start that there was another perspective here, some major conflict Ben had failed to zero in on.

When the first car began to make its way forward past the fire truck, Cee-Cee's entire body began to shake. Her eyes opened to white circles, blue sparks flashing. She took a step back, drowning the feather under her sneaker.

Ben crossed the distance between them in a half dozen swift strides.

"Where are they?"

When Cee-Cee didn't answer, Ben grabbed the girl by her shoulders, giving her a shake that was harder than he'd intended. "Cee-Cee, where are they?"

Cee-Cee pointed at the road, at the third car that had squeezed past the fire truck and was speeding out of the neighborhood, heading south toward Old Clevedon Road. Tears filled the whites of Cee-Cee's eyes, pooling at her dark lashes, spilling down her already wet cheeks.

Ben had finally asked the right question. And before the girl opened her mouth to say the words, Ben knew what she would say. It came back to Ben in a rush, that last day in Mr. Hallam's class. Nearly twenty years ago, there was one lesson Mr. Hallam had tried and failed to instill in Ben. The last lesson of the year. Ben saw his teacher again, tall, strong, perched on the edge of his desk. It was hot in the classroom and the blinds had been pulled against the early June summer heat. Ben had been daydreaming, half lulled to sleep by the darkness and the heat, but the sound of a book hitting the floor jolted him awake.

"I hope you will remember that this book," Mr. Hallam pointed at the history textbook they had used all year, the one he'd dropped on the floor, "was written by us. Every word. Every event, every war, every treaty, every king and queen and peasant revolt—all of it, written by us. People create history. People create the world we live in. People, like you and me and your mom and dad and your friends, everyone you know. Individuals, who are right now writing the history that other generations of students will study. And while some of us will write violent stories with our lives, selfish stories of greed and power, of ignorance and fear, so many of us are writing stories of compassion, of heroism, of sacrifice and bravery. The books aren't written yet, they're waiting for your

story. And so that is your job. You do what you can, when you can in this world. And you write a good story."

Ben heard again that wretched, inhuman scream, saw the girl on the dock crumple like a puppet with its strings cut. And for the first time in nine years, Ben breathed calmly into the memory. He had failed that day. He'd failed her. He'd failed himself. He'd failed that childish vision of the hero he'd always wanted to be. But that was the work, wasn't it? And the work is all there is.

Our job, each of us, is simply to do what we can. When we can.

All summer, Ben had dismissed Mr. Hallam's feeding of the geese as pure stubbornness. The foolish fancies of an old man. But his was the perspective Ben had missed all along.

"It's Vi-Violet," Cee-Cee said. "They're taking her home."

8:07 p.m.

Clare sat with the pregnant woman in a comfortable silence. Cars continued to honk. The gathering of men continued to talk in a huddled, wet circle. An occasional sideways glance of male consternation was thrown in Clare's direction, a tightening of the brow, a shake of a head. The river continued to rush by beneath their feet, swollen with the storm. But the sound of the rain against the pavement, against the bridge's metal guardrail, against the umbrella the pregnant woman held above their heads, this sound was deafening, muting all others. It isolated the women where they sat on the bumper of the truck, creating a space around them that made Clare feel oddly relaxed, safe.

When three or four minutes had gone by, Clare became aware that she was staring at the woman's swollen belly. The wet material of the woman's dress revealed raw, pink skin in patches across her middle. Clare became aware, also, that the woman had noticed her stare. Still, Clare couldn't look away, and the woman made no movement to discourage her.

"Do you have children?"

There was more silence, within which Clare forgot to breathe.

"One," Clare said, finally. She took a breath. Then another, feeling as if she balanced atop a high, high building. The dizziness was familiar, something she was learning not to fear. She dangled a foot over the edge, looked down. "Once."

The woman nodded, a quick, stunted motion as if confirming something she'd already suspected.

"It's a crazy thing, having a child," the woman said, speaking softly but forming the words carefully. She watched the huddle of men as she spoke. "Knowing what we know."

Clare saw the cemetery again. Saw the sun glare off a row of stones. Saw Lance, a dark, broken figure among the headstones. The world tilted, lurched forward. Clare's fingers tightened around the edge of the bumper.

"I almost didn't. It seemed so ridiculous at the time. I actually…I made an appointment to take care of it." The woman's fingers traced the bulge of her stomach, circling the life inside. "My sister found out about it and just went crazy. *You can't play God!* She screamed at me. She was so…angry."

The woman sighed, fingers still rubbing her belly. "But she didn't get it. Nobody does. Not really, do they? You play God either way."

When had the question occurred to Clare? Before the cemetery, certainly. Before the hospital, before that quiet room and the stench of ammonia and the broken fluorescent light, or that other room, the one filled with all those rushing people and the sounds of Clare screaming. (This had actually been the same emergency room, but its qualities changed for Clare at such a foundational level in the aftermath of her loss, in the presence of such absence, of the tiny, unmoving bundle they'd placed in her arms, that Clare remembered it as two different rooms.) Though never clearly articulated in Clare's thoughts prior to that day she'd steered her car into a mountainside, the question had arisen in her months, years before these events.

As Clare sat on the bumper of the rental truck that was blocking De Vries Crossing and within the circle of the pregnant woman's umbrella, it was another bridge Clare thought of. She'd left the doctor's office the day she found out, bursting with the need to find Lance, tell him the news, watch his face alight in happiness. Unexpected or not, Clare knew Lance would be ecstatic when she told him. It was something she'd already identified in him, the possibility of his fatherhood, his capacity for love, gentleness. The steady, deep resonance of a male voice in her home. Something Clare had only dreamed of, but something her child would know.

But on the afternoon she'd found out she was pregnant, Clare found herself driving north, away from home. She wound along Puget Sound on Magnolia Boulevard, taking in long, dangerous gazes at the water as she drove. She circled back on Emerson, then Nickerson, meaning to return home, wanting to be with Lance and rejoice in this surprising turn in their lives, but she turned onto Queen Anne Drive instead, and drove up to the bridge with no more thought than she did driving to work or to the grocery store. Clare was at the doctor's office, and then Clare was suddenly on the bridge, getting out, closing the car door, walking up to the railing.

She would have the baby in May of 2006, on a rainy morning after a foggy night that would end with a spectacular rainbow on the east side of town that the entire hospital would comment on, and that Lance would only half-jokingly tell Clare was sent just for them. The baby would die (just pass away in the night, under her moon and stars plush mobile, as babies still sometimes do) in February of the following year. And so this was November of 2005, and the leaves on the trees around the bridge had been falling for weeks, jamming Wolf Creek in soggy clogs along its banks.

Clare had leaned over the bridge's handrail. The ravine was not so far below, but there were rocks to think about, and tree limbs that would catch and snap and break. A car slowed behind her, and Clare leaned back, taking in the view, just out for a walk this cold November afternoon. The car passed.

Now Clare would be forced to decide, and that hidden, stubborn part of herself, the part that had enjoyed the freedom of *any time I want* felt resentful at being cornered into finally making a decision. (While Clare called it "freedom," the feeling she truly experienced would be better named, "escape." Her secret passageway, her way out.) Clare knew she would not bring a child into the world, only to leave it. She would not do as her mother had done. And so for Clare, having a child meant creating a tether that would tie her to the world, permanently. Would she allow it? Could she? It was only there, on the bridge, that Clare understood the question had existed in her for a long while—before this baby, before Lance, possibly long before she'd reached adulthood—whether or not she'd asked it. To stay or to go. To live or to die. Creation or destruction. She would indeed play God, whatever her decision.

The rain continued. The silence descended from all directions, and there, beneath the shelter of the woman's umbrella on another bridge, five years and three-thousand miles away, Clare realized there were other ways of tethering a person to the world. People made good tethers. Kindness. Compassion. Sometimes a Shepherd's Pie. And some days, most days lately, Clare didn't mind.

"You must be cold," Clare said, turning to the woman, meeting her eyes. "Let's go wait in the truck. I think I have a sweater or something—"

And as Clare spoke, the silence around the women was broken by the sound of a passing car. Confused, Clare turned, still clutching the water bottle in both hands, and peered past the truck where the long line of cars still waited, horns honking, behind them. Clare heard another car pass, its tires making the sound of a wave against the flooded pavement. Clare grabbed the edge of the umbrella and thrust it upwards so she could see across the water, just as another car passed by on the southbound bridge.

"What is it?"

But Clare was gone, running into the rain. The water bottle clattered against the truck's bumper, landed in the stream of water, and floated away.

8:14 p.m.

It was a garbage bag. Or a sheet, Ben thought. No, a garbage bag, he decided. Large, bright yellow, odd, but there was a definite plastic quality to the way the material crinkled. The way it flew up and over the road when the black SUV hit it. The way it folded, spun, flared out like a parachute as it reached the pinnacle of its flight. The landing was all wrong, though. The weight, too solid. The material struck the pavement heavily, bodily.

Ben had already flipped on the cruiser's lights, his hand reaching the switch instinctively when the SUV in front of him began to hydroplane. Ben made a small groan in the bottom of his throat to see the driver overcorrect to the right, then to the left. Then the vehicle began to spin, all the while its brake lights blazed in desperation.

Cee-Cee began screaming in the seat next to Ben the moment the yellow garbage bag came into view. Ben had put his hand against her collarbone, securing Cee-Cee to the seat as he tapped the cruiser's brakes. Ben began to say something reassuring, incorrectly assuming that the child's terror sprang from a fear for her own safety—they would not crash, not even with this vehicle making wild circles in the road ahead of them—but as he began to speak, Croker interrupted from behind the wire mesh in the backseat—"can't you shut the hell up already? For fuck's sake she's"—but the rest of the man's words were overwhelmed by the sight of the garbage bag landing so heavily on the pavement.

The cruiser's windshield wipers washed waves of water from the glass, and so the scene unfolded for Ben only between these surges. *Swipe*—the yellow garbage bag appeared from the shoulder of the road. *Swipe*—the black SUV glided across the road as if the pavement had become ice, hit the garbage bag with the corner of its front bumper at what Ben estimated was roughly sixty miles per hour, and sent the bag flying into the sky. *Swipe*—the bag crashed back to earth as Ben steered the police cruiser toward the grassy median to avoid hitting the SUV. *Swipe*—a woman ran through the grass, materializing out of the rain, hair plastered to her face, mouth open in a scream like some urban legend, and veered into the trajectory of the cruiser's impact.

Ben cut the steering wheel hard to the right and slammed on the brakes just as another wave washed over his view.

8:53 p.m.

Of course, they all had to make a big deal. Put up the police barricades. Tape off the road. Call in the goddamn paramedics when it was clear to anyone with half an eyeball that it was all purely superfluous—procedure, he guessed (but the word that bounced into his thoughts was *ritual*), and all the while, he's trussed up like a farm hog in the backseat of the cop's car with some freak bird staring at him like he was about to eat it.

"Fuck off," Jared growled to the bird. But the bird didn't move.

The cop had left the driver's door open when he jumped out of the car, and so through the wire mesh that blocked the front seat from the back, Jared could clearly hear the rain that had lessened only in wind strength. The crying had not lessened at all, nor the constant clickity-clack of police radios.

Purely superfluous procedure, Jared thought, wishing he had his notebook.

Two ambulances had parked in front of the cruiser, their back doors open, the lights from inside illuminating a large swatch of the grassy median where several uniformed officers stood in government-issue, yellow rain slickers and hats, taking statements from the drivers and passengers that had witnessed the event on the road. Beyond the ambulances, a tow truck pulled the black SUV from the ditch where it had landed, wedged against a tree. The sounds of crushed steel screeched across the darkness.

To Jared's right, a spotlight from a fire truck lit up the southbound lanes of Old Clevedon Road bright as day, where police tape blocked off a large square area. In the center of the square, a black tarp had been laid over the pavement to cover the body.

"I can't believe this, I can't believe this is happening, I can't believe…this isn't happening, this can't be happening—"

There was a man sitting at the back of the ambulance who rocked himself slightly, wet white hair pushed back into a helmet on his head, hands on his knees, elbows out, in something of a throne pose as he ignored the paramedic's attempts to take his blood pressure and babbled quietly to no one in particular. *Fruity-ass tie*, Jared thought, glaring at the bit of silk fluff at the man's throat. *What self-respecting man wears paisley?*

The man in the ambulance quieted for a moment, blew hard through his lips, shook his head in an attempt to regain composure. His gaze fell on the police car where Jared sat and the men made eye contact, though the man in the ambulance could not have seen Jared within the darkened space where Jared sat. Jared met his eyes, however, and immediately flushed into his chest, prickles of heat warming his underarms where the sweat broke through. It was as if he'd walked in on the man, naked. Pink flesh exposed and raw, dangling, flaccid. This sense of nakedness (vulnerability) manifested itself physically in Jared, like a current racing through his body, triggering his heart into a soft whir, whirling in his chest like a playing card against bicycle spokes. His breaths came faster, shallow, skimming the surface of his lungs. His fingers tingled. Bright spots appeared at the edges of his sight. (Later, Jared would attribute this panic attack to the meth wearing off, arguing about it first with himself and then, with the New Jersey State Prison's court-appointed group therapist. An "epiphanic" experience is what she wanted to call it, and while Jared was certain the word was purely a creation of the shrink's hippy-dippy mind, Jared couldn't deny a certain transformation in his thinking at that moment.)

It was the sense of nakedness that Jared couldn't shake. The sense of exposure, of helplessness. Jared found it disgusting in a man. In a woman, Jared had taken pleasure in such defenselessness. Had reveled in their vulnerability. His doing, his creation. But Jared would never be like women—laughed at, exposed, splayed open, bared to the elements and whatever errant whim of the universe (so long as he controlled the cosmos and the goings-on of a woman's body. It was fear that Jared had faced, the hippy-shrink would later insist. Fear and not disgust that Jared had felt when he'd met the man's eyes.)

In the darkened cop car, Jared had waited, watched the man's inflamed eyes, felt the strength drain from his own body through the whirring efforts in his chest, waited for the worst to manifest— an explosion, lightening, a heart attack—as a result of such stark helplessness. But there was nothing. Just this weakened man staring sadly into the night. Jared looked away (ripped his gaze from this mirror vision of himself), and immediately fell upon another set of eyes.

"I told you to fuck off," Jared said to the bird, but his voice had lost its hardened edge. His tone was loose now, yielding, and the bird drew nearer the open door of the car, as if he'd summoned it. The grass between the north and southbound lanes of Old Clevedon Road had grown tall in the summer rains, no longer stiff and erect, but long stalks bending, looping under their weight, soft mounds creating tiny caves, under one of which Jared saw the shivering shapes of smaller birds. Three, maybe four tiny babies.

"Get as much as you can from the couple in the minivan, and then we'll finish up at the station." This from the cop, standing in the cruiser's headlights. He also wore a yellow slicker, collar turned up, rainwater gleaming across his face. The cop spoke to his partner, but the man's attention was clearly elsewhere.

"Any word from Lushington?"

"On his way," the partner answered. "Ten, maybe fifteen minutes."

The crying was finally subsiding, its original intensity muffled by exhaustion. Now there was only a steady sob, a low, deep groan broken by occasional gasps of air. The cop looked toward the ambulance as he spoke, where the little blond girl straddled Clare's lap, her legs and arms wrapped around Clare's middle, her face buried beneath the blanket that covered them both. From Jared's angle, the girl appeared an enormous pregnancy.

"See about getting some of these cars moved out when you're done."

Nodding, the partner moved away, but the cop stayed where he was in the rain-soaked headlights, watching the ambulance, watching Clare.

Clare had only screamed once. Not when the cruiser had nearly knocked her down—Jared was certain Clare hadn't even seen the police car, all her attention had been fixed on the road—but when she'd caught sight of the old man sprawled on his back on the pavement. She'd screamed—a wild, shredded noise Jared would never forget—lunged forward, was bodily stopped by the cop who'd jumped out of the cruiser. Collapsing on the ground, Clare had then gone silent. For seven minutes Clare knelt by the body, not crying, not moving, while the cop performed CPR and the girl wailed on and on in the front seat of the car. Jared had kept track with the cruiser's digital clock, cursing each minute and cursing the handcuffs that trapped him with her loud hysterics. He'd shouted at the girl to "shut it" several times, had even kicked the back of the seat, but this only resulted in louder, more startled wails.

When the paramedics arrived and took over, Clare rose without a word and went to the cruiser to retrieve the wailing girl. Eleven more minutes passed before one of the paramedics went to the ambulance and came back with the black tarp. Jared heard later that the old guy was dead before he hit the pavement—neck snapped in mid-air. He died "in flight," which, regardless of how he felt about the old coot, would later strike Jared as hopelessly poetic.

Now the cop stood, unmoving in the headlights, rain beading on his face, watching Clare. Clare stared only at the black tarp on the road, ignoring the comings and goings of the emergency workers, the shrieking noises from the tow truck, even the weeping child in her lap.

Clare's face had changed. A lack of expression made her features appear to Jared...unfamiliar. She seemed not Clare, but some stranger who wore Clare's frizzy hair and little body. Jared found he could not look directly at her for more than a moment at a time. Like staring at the sun, or moving magnets together, Jared tried to look at Clare, decipher whatever transformation had so drastically altered her appearance, but he ended up looking at the cop or the kid or the black tarp instead. Another peek and Jared was suddenly thinking of the *memento mori* photographs he'd browsed one late night at some chick's apartment. (It was the "Hunter chick" that Jared was remembering, whose name was actually Rosamond Pennell. Along with Russian literature, Ms. Pennell had an interest in the Victorian age, and it was a picture book set next to the wooden ducks—babies draped in roses and black garb, dead grandmothers leaned awkwardly for grim family photos—that flashed in Jared's mind.) Clare's face had that sense of *arrangement*, as if someone had propped open her eyes and added a rosy tint to her cheeks. Even her lips, which had once wrapped around him in such pleasure, now hung limp and lifeless. (Jared fought down a swell of bile then, which he would later, also attribute not to guilt, but again to the waning effects of the meth.)

The cop, however, could not seem to look away from Clare. He moved slowly, as if not to startle a wild animal, and went to the ambulance. He stood close to Clare but did not touch her. He said something, a few words Jared couldn't hear. Clare didn't move. The cop leaned in closer, just an inch or two. He said it again, waited. Finally, Clare looked away from the black tarp, but she didn't turn to the cop. She stared at the grass, straight ahead, straight at Jared, and now Jared was the one who couldn't look away. There was something happening in her face. It was changing again, features moving in and out of focus, colors and textures sharpening, a bit of lens flare.

The cop said it one more time, and Clare finally turned toward him. The transformation in her face was complete. She was crying. Silent. Unmoving. Only crying. She was Clare again, but a Clare that Jared had never met. Open, exposed, vulnerable in a way Jared had never managed to position her, despite their late-night tussles, his subtle indecencies. He'd slapped her once, as he'd slapped others before her. She didn't cry, though. Only stared at him with a sort of…indifference. (It was Jared who'd fled that night, running from the house in confusion, and only later filling with rage at how easily she'd manipulated him.) Even with a goddamn blade at her throat, Jared had failed to render her helpless.

But here, with the *cop*, here was the Clare Jared never managed to capture, though instead of anger, it was envy Jared felt. Clare turned toward the man, tears wetting her cheeks. She closed her eyes, more tears gushing, lowered her head. Now the cop sat beside her, reaching over the girl to place his hands on Clare's back, to lower his chin to her hair. There was nothing sexual about their embrace, nothing fatherly either. There was only comfort, solace, some rare form of strength that was only found in the loving presence of another human being.

Jared's envy twisted and hardened, ached in his chest like a sucking wound. It sharpened, squeezed. He could hardly breathe. Not once in his thirty-seven years had anyone leaned on him as Clare was now leaning on the cop. Jared tried to push the ridiculous thought away, actually shifted physically in his seat in an attempt to get away from such a sentimental idea. He tried to stretch, to loosen the tight feeling in his chest, but was stopped by the cuffs and succeeded only in infuriating himself, banging his head several times against the back cushion of the seat. The anger was familiar, safe, and Jared struggled to grab hold of it, use it to make sense of the other feeling, to simplify his mind once more into concrete regions. But the anger slipped away, black and oily, slithering beyond his reach. Jared was left floundering and suddenly terrified. He was crying. *Actual tears sliding down his face.* He wiped his face on the shoulder of his t-shirt, but the tears wouldn't stop. He jerked in the seat, looking behind him and all around, certain someone would spot him. For all the accusations against him, for all the crimes he'd committed, it was the charge of crying that Jared now feared most.

(Here, it was the kitten Jared was remembering, the one they'd found in the weeds behind the A&P, though he couldn't have told you himself. That day, so long ago when his father had been packing his things and his mother had screamed some ugliness at her son, making him feel trapped and helpless and terrified of such overwhelming and violent emotions and eventually causing him to flee the house. Jared had been crying when he came upon the older boys. *Pussy!* they'd called him. They'd pointed. They'd laughed. The kitten was crying too. Trapped, helpless, terrified. She'd peed in the bag. Jared could smell it from where he stood. And before Jared had seen Clare down the street, watching him, Jared had snatched up the bag. Without thinking, he'd grabbed the bag. Without thinking, he'd slammed the bag on the ground. He had wanted only to make the noises stop, to silence those terrified wails. And they did stop. After the first hit on the pavement, the kitten's cries stopped. After the second hit, Jared himself had stopped crying.)

But in the back of the cop's car, Jared's tears wouldn't stop, and he flailed frantically against his cuffs, searching for something, anything to smash and shatter and destroy. He threw his body hard against the seats, bouncing the car on its tires, bucking and grunting and sweating. He was trapped again, helpless, and utterly terrified. Now he *wanted* someone to notice, he was beyond the point of caring. There was no pride here. No pretense. He wanted only for someone to come, and laugh if they must, as long as they put him out of his misery. But no one noticed. No one came. And as he thrashed and flailed and moaned against the seat, it was then that

Jared's tooth fell out. The rotted piece of enamel cracked with the sound of a potato chip when his cheek connected with the edge of the front seat. Once freed, Jared's tooth slid across his tongue and shot to the back of his throat, silencing Jared in mid inhale.

For a moment, Jared didn't move. The rain continued to beat against the glass and darkness pressed in on him from all sides. Wherever the tooth had lodged in his throat had created a tight seal. Jared felt it there, no longer in his mouth, but much, much further down, dangerously low within the region of his neck. He felt his lungs contract and begin to ache with the urge to inhale, but for the moment, Jared fought against it. For a moment the world stopped. For a moment, a blackness Jared had never experienced began to eat up his peripheral vision, and in that moment, Jared saw himself take a deep, long, final breath. He imagined what it might be like for it all to be over. Finally finished, here on this night, in the back of the cop's car.

But a moment later and with a split-second decision that probably saved his life, Jared violently expelled the last of the air in his diaphragm, bending tightly in his stomach with a wheezy grunt. The tooth shot out of his mouth and hit the floor between his feet with a phlegmy pink splash.

The coughing fit lasted a long time, but just as Jared thought his lungs might explode, he began to breathe normally again. In the silence that followed, Jared explored the new opening in his mouth with his tongue. The gums around it were swollen and tender and the pain that had plagued Jared these past few weeks had changed in quality. Instead of the throbbing ache that emanated from deep inside the bone, an ache with which Jared had become miserably familiar, this new pain had a bright edge to it. Jared imagined it as shooting sparks through the gap and exploding in beautiful bursts of white light, but even as this image grabbed hold, the pain began to subside. Jared took another deep breath, soothing himself by rolling his head against the car window. Back and forth, back and forth in a rocking motion that calmed his weary heart and warmed his clammy skin. Back and forth, back and forth, as the taste of blood and salt seeped down the back of his throat.

"Daddy!"

Through his swollen eyes, Jared saw the girl disentangle herself from Clare's lap and run full speed toward a man who'd just gotten out of his car. The girl hit the man's body and she was picked up and swung into the air with one smooth motion. The man held her tightly, his head buried in her hair, her legs wound around his torso. Backlit by the spotlight on the fire truck, they appeared one darkened body. Tall. Massive, like a mountain.

A fresh flood of emotion washed down Jared's cheeks, but this time he didn't fight it. It flowed through him like a river, cool, cleansing, loosening the last of the ache in his chest. When it was over, he felt lighter somehow. Newer. He relaxed back into the seat.

Clare stood now, beside the cop, both of them watching the girl with her father. Others had stopped to watch as well. Paramedics and police officers and the drivers who'd been detained for questioning and even the tow truck workers—for a moment, all eyes were on the father and child. There was silence, a sort of communal sigh for this open display of love. The girl's father held her, unspeaking, unmoving for an indefinite amount of time. Jared too let out his breath, aware that this moment was special, rare, but only because it was being witnessed. In his newly heightened emotional state, Jared sensed the connection that ran between everyone at the scene, some invisible tether that linked each of them. He understood suddenly that the tether existed always, generally unseen beneath the distractions of living, but here, between the child and her father, the connection had shifted into full view and the effect of its presence was one of collective, unabashed awe. (Later, Jared would try to blame the meth for this wild thought, as he would try to blame the drugs for all of the strange ideas and feelings that came over him that night. Thankfully, the others in his group would not allow Jared to ignore what happened to him, how he had changed or had *been* changed by the events of that night. Even when Jared told the group the incredible tale of what happened next, they insisted it was real, if only because it was what Jared perceived to be real. Real or not, the Jared who was driven back to the police station that night was not the same man who had broken into Clare's house that morning.)

Finally, the girl's father turned slowly and walked back to his car, with his child still in his arms. And as if a light had flickered and went out, the darkness of the evening descended once more, while the police and paramedics and everyone else returned to whatever business had been occupying them.

"—let's get these cars moved out—"

"—need the gurney from the back—"

"—have to get home, how much longer—"

"—open up the northbound—"

"—always such a sweet old man—"

Jared was alone again, sitting in the back of the police cruiser with his hands cuffed behind his back. The people outside the car and the world beyond had moved on without him. There was only Jared, his sweating, beating head, and the taste of blood in his mouth. Whatever connection Jared had sensed between himself and the others was gone, and Jared was already well on his way to believing it had never existed at all.

He was alone, as always. Only Jared.

And the bird.

She held Jared's eyes. Blinked once, bottom eyelids rising to meet the top lids, as if the bird were upside-down. Or Jared was.

Jared's heart once more began to pound. He opened his mouth and screamed as loud as he could.

"Hey!"

Jared turned his full attention to the bird that still stood by the open door of the police car. It had retreated a few steps during the full fury of Jared's rage, but had returned, closer now, nearly poking its head inside the car, feathers matted and blackened with rain. It stared at him. Unblinking.

As the three of them had sped south along Old Clevedon Road, before her obnoxious screams and before she went mute altogether, the blond girl had rattled out enough of the story for Jared to understand most of what had happened that night on the road. Rescuing a bunch of park geese. The old guy was a fool all right, just as Jared had said. And he'd dragged Clare into this nonsense with him. At this, Jared was surprised. Clare had never struck Jared as the sentimental type.

A door closed with a slam. The ambulance where Clare had been sitting pulled away, bumping slowly over the grassy median, before driving up onto the road. The cop motioned to his partner and the three spoke briefly before the partner guided Clare toward another police cruiser that was parked by the fire truck. The yellow emergency blanket still covered Clare's shoulders and she pulled it tighter around her body, shivering a little as she walked away.

Jared's chest once more began to pound. He looked from the bird, to the flashing eyes beneath the grass, to the rescue workers who were all beginning to pack up for the night. Without thinking, Jared shouted out again, louder. "Hey!"

From the other ambulance, a stretcher was rolled out. Two paramedics carried the stretcher over the grass, across the gravel shoulder, and to the road where the black tarp covered Mr. Hallam's body. A bag was rolled out onto the ground, and the tarp was removed. Quickly, deftly, the paramedics transferred the body into the bag and zipped it closed.

"Hey!" Jared shouted again, this time much louder. "What are you doing? Hey!"

The cop turned, gave him a disapproving look, and turned away.

At the other side of the median, police officers had begun to wind up the yellow caution tape. Other officers were moving the barricades. A police cruiser made a U-turn in the street, turned off its flashing lights, and drove back toward town.

"Wait, what are you doing? Hey! *Hey!*"

The cop was on him in three long strides, leaning down into the open passenger window. "I'm going to have to ask you to settle down, Mr. Croker. You'll be headed to the station in just a minute."

The cop was gone before Jared had a chance to speak. "Wait! Wait, you can't do that!"

Jared kicked the back of the driver's seat several times, then slid sideways and shouted again. "Clare! Clare, hey! You can't leave! You can't just leave her here!"

Immediately, the cop was back at the window, this time positioning himself so he blocked Jared's view of Clare. "You've made enough trouble for yourself for one day, don't you—"

"Clare! Clare! *You can't leave her here! Clare!*"

Jared had been frantic. Panicked, and for no good reason at all. When he told the story to his group, he had tried and failed repeatedly to convey the feeling that gripped him that moment in the cop's car. The best he could do was explain it as a sense that something horrible was about to happen. Something truly terrible, perhaps more awful even than the death that had occurred on the road that night, and that he, Jared, was the only one who saw it coming. And he was the only one who could stop it. Jared tried to explain why it suddenly became so desperately important that he make this right. This one, small thing that, for whatever reason, had to be corrected.

(Jared had also heard Albert's speech that long ago afternoon in June during one of the few days he'd attended eighth period World History, though for no other reason than because it was slightly cooler in the classroom than in the alley behind the school where he usually got high. For Jared, doing what he could, when he could, that night in the cop's car was a *redemptive* act, a word with implications Jared wouldn't learn until a long time later. And it was one of the last words Jared wrote in a list in his notebook before the sentences took over. After the first two years in prison, Jared began to write pages and pages of sentences—beautiful, painful, often surprising sentences built from the collection of words he'd gathered over the years. In time, Jared threw away his old notebooks and used new words to write new sentences, new stories for himself. By the time of his release, thirteen years later, Jared's journals filled every shelf, every surface, every available space of his prison cell. And on the day he walked out of his cell for the last time, he left every single one of his journals behind.)

Jared tried very hard to explain to his therapy group how he had felt that night in the cop's car, but knew he failed, even as the words passed his lips. In the end, Jared could only tell them what happened. As he saw it.

And so, this was the story he told:

Clare had heard Jared and stopped. The cop blocked his view, but Jared could still see Clare's small figure from beneath the cop's arm. Slowly, Clare turned and Jared edged toward the window. Clare came closer to the cop's car but paused a few feet away. She gazed at Jared through the window. Met Jared's eyes. She was still crying, puffy face, wetness around her nose, but now Jared saw something else. Clare saw him. For all the time they'd spent together, both in and out of bed, Jared couldn't remember Clare ever looking directly at him. Her eyes always focused on his brow, his chin, the space just above his head, never his eyes. But now he'd entered her cool, still gaze, and Jared knew that Clare saw him for everything he was—the shame, the fear, the confusion, the bottomless grief. And Jared saw Clare too, as if for the first time. Recognized something in her sad, plum-colored eyes that opened a feeling in his chest that felt as soft and warm as feathers. (It would take years before Jared would be able to describe such a feeling as "love.")

And when Clare spoke, Jared thought he might have seen a flicker of a smile on her face.

"Jay's right."

It was from high above that Jared remembered what happened next. As if he watched from a tree, high up over the road, perched on a branch and looking down at the humans below. Or at least this was the only way he could describe it. He saw Clare, the cop, the rescue workers, even himself, sitting in the back of the cruiser. Jared saw everything and when Clare came around the car and approached the bird, he saw this from his place up in the tree as well.

Clare lifted her arms, the blanket balled in each fist so that it unfolded into a sort of cape behind her.

"Okay, ol' girl," Clare said to the bird. "Come on."

Clare stepped forward with her left foot, stepped out to the right, brought both feet together. She then stepped back with her right foot, back again and to the left, brought both feet together.

The bird watched Clare for a moment. Looked back at Jared as if checking to see if it were all right with him. Jared nodded, whispered, *"go"* to the bird, and the bird began to follow Clare. (This bit he left out in his retelling to the group. Even to himself, Jared could not admit to talking to a bird, let alone the bird seeming to understand.)

The bird shook herself, flicking rainwater from her back. Between her feathers, in the dry areas closer to her body, Jared saw the soft down of what appeared to be purple patches—a trick of the light, surely, created by the headlights, the moon that had begun to break through the clouds, the reflection of the rainwater. Geese don't have purple feathers. A mirage, Jared told the group. It was the only explanation.

The bird followed close behind Clare, her long neck straightened to its uppermost height, head erect, beak pointed at Clare's yellow blanket. The smaller birds, the babies, tottered out from beneath the grass and tumbled in behind the bird. A sort of slow procession began. Clare stepped forward with her left foot, stepped out to the right, brought both feet together. They crossed the grassy median in this slow, circular way and approached the road.

The cop joined her then, still wearing his yellow raincoat. He walked slowly around the birds to fall in beside Clare. He matched her slow gait, if not her intricate footwork. The cop's partner soon joined them. And a paramedic. The firemen. The girl's father, holding his child's hand, both of them wrapped in yellow blankets.

Before Clare and the birds reached the other side of the road, a crowd had joined the procession. And from high above, his vantage point in the tree, Jared watched as a flock of yellow figures waltzed the goose and her babies into the woods.

CODA

A warmth within the breast would melt
The freezing reason's colder part,
And like a man in wrath the heart
Stood up and answer'd "I have felt"

Lord Alfred Tennyson,
"In Memoriam A. H. H."

VIOLET

(Of course the geese came back to Honock Pond.

Right around the time the sinkhole by Trinity Street finally settled, but still weeks before traffic toward southbound Old Clevedon Road resumed as usual, New Jersey recorded four consecutive days of triple-digit heat. And while the town retreated into air-conditioned living rooms or swarmed the beaches, we sought shelter beneath the boughs of the red oaks by the lake at Tirol Farm. We mostly slept in the shade during the day, waking only to use the lake in shifts, dipping our heads deep beneath the tepid water to feed on pondweed, watermeal, and the occasional tadpole, before returning to the shore to spread our wings, hoping to catch a cooling breeze between our feathers. With molting season over, the adults flew short distances in scouting runs, but never ventured far from the farm. The chicks could fly by the end of the summer, and practice runs took place over the water where splashdowns were frequent.

As the leaves turned and the nights cooled, we welcomed our migrating neighbors from the north—American Tree Sparrows, Dark-eyed Juncos, Redpoll Finches—all huddled together in a great diverse mass against the strengthening winds and dipping temperatures. The new year began with the snowiest January New Jersey had seen in sixty-two years, but within the down-filled community beneath the red oaks, only a half dozen casualties would be counted before the thaw arrived.

Two more seasons would pass before I found a new mate. During that time, I enjoyed the amenities at Tirol Farms—my sunspot in the back of the pumpkin patch where I meditated away the summer afternoons, my daily spa routine in the center of the lake where I splashed and flapped and scrubbed my body clean before diving deep beneath the surface to spread my wings wide and soar through the dark waters. In particular though, there was a swath of eelgrass just over the rise at the far end of the farm, beyond which grew the most scrumptious blueberries I've ever tasted. The first of the berries bloomed in April, carried on a night breeze that breathed into my dreams and woke me with a grumble in my belly. The berries grew low to the ground in a thick carpet, but the ancient rock that lay beneath the soil broke through the surface in a path that afforded unfettered access to the crop. After an evening at the berry patch, I often returned for the night much later than the others, my beak and long neck stained dark with juice.

On the evening of October 29th, 2012, just as Hurricane Sandy was making landfall south of Atlantic City, I sheltered in the hollow I had claimed upon my arrival at Tirol Farm. The hollow was small, just large enough for me, its opening barely noticeable at the base of one of the oldest red oaks at the lake. When I procured the hollow for myself, I went unchallenged. Whether for my age, or perhaps for my health—I would carry a limp for the rest of my life, a forever reminder of the night I lost my mate—or possibly for a general respect for my grief, I was granted privileged status among the geese. They yielded me the hollow whenever I chose, allowed me a central position in the bird huddle where it was warmest in the winter, and they kept their distance at the blueberry patch. So, I was startled when the goose entered my hollow that evening. The cracking trees and stinging wind and blowing water made me burrow my head deep into my back, but when he entered, I extended my long neck, ready to attack. The male stood his ground, though, curling next to me against the tree, opening his wings to enfold my body beneath his warm feathers.

And just like that, where there once had been room for only one, now easily held two.

In the spring, we flew together back to Honock Pond, soaring over Old Clevedon Road with no more thought to this arbitrary boundary than any river or cliffside or fence or wall. In the spring, the road could barely be seen from the air for all the new blossoms and young leaves that colored the world below, and excited me in a way I hadn't felt for the past two seasons. I was pleased to find my island much unchanged. The water had receded a bit on the sunny side which widened the beach area, but the camouflaging tall reeds, the cattails, the fox sedge, the water willows that would bloom pink in the next few weeks and release the tastiest seeds, the mud plantains that obscured the borders of the island, the water lilies where tiny frogs rested and sang me to sleep at night…all of this remained as I remembered.

During that first season, I wasn't sure if I would see Clare at the pond, but as the years go by, I come to expect our yearly reunion. I look forward to my first glimpse of her through the reeds, where she sits on the bench by the water's edge and waits for me to emerge. On the back of the bench where Albert and Clare used to sit together, there is now a plaque. Several of Albert's neighbors, former students, and even some of the hospital staff where Emily used to work gathered funds for the plaque, leaving enough left over to care for Honock Pond for many years to come. Contrary to what Albert might have thought, it turned out that many people marked Albert's absence when he was gone. A whole community, in fact.

Clare sometimes traces the letters with her fingers as she sits on the bench, though from the way she stares at the pond while she does it, I doubt she is aware.

In Memoriam A.H.H.

I recognize Clare now regardless of what she wears. I know the gait of her footsteps as she approaches on the path, I sniff out the scent of her shampoo. I greet my old friend with low grunts, and sometimes we still dance along the shore. Other times we sit together and watch the goslings play in the water in comfortable silence. I still miss Albert, his deep voice, his gentle walk. I miss the sound of fragrant seed rattling in his paper bag. Like all geese, I have a long memory and so the vision of Albert's kind face lingers forever in my mind. Though I am grateful for Clare's friendship.

Also, she brings me blueberries.

Clare still thinks about the question at times, still stares into the darkness above and senses the abyss grinning back, but those nights are fewer and farther between now. More often, Clare is too busy for such distractions. She sometimes fills her evenings cooking with Penelope, who has cheerfully departed the mailman's company and is now busy running the Kinderkamack Book Club. Shortly after the funeral, she also began a blog, *Penny's Picks*, a running list of her favorite books, along with thoughts on the meditative impact of reading on the mind/body connection. George Geoffrey Stacks, who has long since dropped the Jivraj Syed, is a frequent guest contributor.

Other evenings Clare sits with Ben on the porch, quietly talking on the swing she bought from the new owners of the Hallam house. Often, she and Ben spend comfortable, silent hours together as Clare grades papers. Clare knows there is something growing in those silences, some bright, warm light that occasionally passes between them. Silences in which she senses Ben in his later years, greying hair, crinkled eyes, smiling down at her. For now, Clare is content in the silences, his hand on hers, the gentle rock of the porch swing, the warmth of his presence beside her.

Clare never returned to *Running Brook Press*, and instead made the career move Albert had always known she would. Clare's students at Kinderkamack High School sometimes call her "Mrs. Lyndsay, the Grammar-Nazi," and complain that such errors should be overlooked in a history class. But Clare corrects the epithet on both counts—three, if she includes the lazy rhyme.

In the fall, Clare teaches her students 2,000 years of stories about men and their wars and their curious inability to recognize foreshadowing in their never-ending quest to change the settings of other people's stories. In the winter, they study the story of one man's vision of a war to end all wars, a Final Solution that would people the world in homochromatic characters. In the spring, Clare's students learn of a new way to write a story for the world. In this story, the setting moves from the bloody battlefield to the salty shores of the Arabian Sea, to lunch counters in North Carolina, to factory grounds in Poland, to the red stone streets of the Plaza de Mayo, to Rosenstrasse, to Tiananmen Square, to Leipzig, to the day a quarter of a million women descended on Washington D.C., to every location around the world where a diverse cast of characters took hold of their story and rewrote the ending. Mothers and children and students and soldiers and workers and fathers, the poor, the oppressed, all those huddled masses who yearned to breathe free wrote long into the night to derail the rising action and craft a new plotline toward denouement.

When Clare is done and the heat in the classroom has gotten so bad, she's had to start shutting the blinds against an overzealous June sun, Clare drops the book on the floor and gives them the speech. It's not as good as Albert's, Clare knows this without ever having heard it, but Ben gives her the highlights, and she does her best.

Clare found the book the morning after Albert's death. It was sitting on the table, just inside the front door of Albert's house. On top of the book was a note, written on a small sheet of lavender stationery. On top of the note was a pen, which kept the note from blowing away when she opened the door.

Write yourself a better story, Clare.

The words dipped and swirled across the sheet in a cursive hand Clare knew well. Clare opened the faux gold-leaf cover to reveal the pages inside. The beautifully blank pages. Clare bent the pages and fanned herself with the sheets, cooling her wet face, smiling.

As it turned out, there never was a need to drive the geese from their home, to change their setting, as Albert might have put it. In the end, the solution to the goose problem at Honock Pond was easily solved—first with a weed-whacker, then by some gardening. The grass around the playground, the picnic areas, and the benches at the north end of the pond could be kept at six inches tall, which discourages us from grazing, since we are well aware that any number of low-bellied predators might lurk within the shaggy stalks. *Additionally*, a certain newly minted seventh grader would go on to tell the Kinderkamack Town Council, *planting a few bush and plant barriers around the north end of the pond will interrupt the geese's line of sight, which will keep them from roosting in the area.* That these ideas were readily available on the internet and that Cee-Cee, just barely twelve years old herself, had to explain these ideas to a roomful of adults was a fact Cee-Cee believed they should all be ashamed of. But it was also a fact that Cee-Cee's father had suggested she leave out of her presentation to the council. Instead, Cee-Cee smiled as she showed them the sketch she'd made with her computer and some colored pencils, demonstrating how her ideas would create a clean outdoor recreation area for the park-goers at the north end of the pond, and a close-cropped open space for us to enjoy at the south end.

It was the same sketch Cee-Cee would show her crowd of cheering and crying supporters, some twenty-three years later, after having won her second term in the United States Senate. Senator Cecilia Anne Lushington would hold the yellowed sheet of paper high over her head and tell again, the story of the extraordinary summer she was twelve. The summer that inspired her life of public service. The summer that taught her ignorance is always the enemy, and that compassion is always the answer.)

The End.

Author's Note

Thank you for picking up my book and giving it a try. I truly hope Albert, Clare, and Violet have found a special place in your heart, as they have in mine. As a writer, trust me when I say that there is no greater pleasure in life than to know that someone enjoyed your story, so thank you.

If you want to support this book, and other indie books like mine, please leave me a review and let others know what you think! Reviews are the lifeblood of indie authors. Every. Single. Review. Counts.

And here are some other easy ways to support authors everywhere who are struggling to put good stories in front of readers' eyes:
- Request their books at your local library
- Follow them on social media
- Like and share news about their book on your social media
- Suggest their book at your book club
- Attend book signings and readings at your local venues
- Subscribe to their newsletter (I have a book blog you can subscribe to here: https://samanthaleighmiller.com/blog/
- Give their book as a gift
- Add their book to your TBR on Goodreads
- Tell your friends about the book!

Acknowledgements

The Goose Waltzer began as a simple sketched plotline on the back of a paper napkin, at a place called Dutch Haven Shoo-Fly Pie and Bakery in Ronks, Pennsylvania. (If you don't know what a Shoo-Fly Pie is or don't have a strong opinion about the wet-bottom ones, you haven't met this quirky southeastern part of the state.) It was Thanksgiving of 2006, and I'd flown to Philadelphia from Arizona for the holiday. My dad and I slipped out for a quick road trip the day before my flight home. We talked on the phone every Sunday, but it had been years since we'd had in-person time. When he picked me up at the airport, my fears had been relieved, since he was as I remembered him—strong, tall, a commanding presence. For as long as I can remember, people quieted when he spoke, sensing the authority. He embarrassed me as a silly child, but I grew to appreciate his deliberate and powerful way of speaking. He was a scholar and a poet and he spoke as he thought. He wrote as he spoke. As he'd taught me to think and to write. He'd be coughing on our Christmas phone call. Telling me it was allergies. By Valentine's Day he'd be gone.

But that afternoon at the little table outside the bakery, drinking hot tea against the November cold, it was just us. No illness, no divorce, no distance. Not even any family. Just two writers working out a story, creating characters, a simple conflict, a possible resolution. All the best parts of storytelling, when the possibilities are still endless, before the characters take over and a timeline hems it all in, that point at the very beginning when the writer still plays the part of God. We chatted and wrote until we lost the light, then came home late and missed dinner. I wish I still had that napkin. I wish I had that afternoon.

And for the record...purple geese do exist. I've never seen one myself, but my dad did. There was a little pond down the road from where my dad lived, and he walked there every day with a paper bag of seed and cracked corn. "Those geese always know when I'm coming," he told me. "They hear the paper bag and they're lined up at the shore by the time I get there." In the spring of 2005, he rescued a goose that'd been hit by a car. Holding up his hands like a traffic cop, he told me he stopped traffic as the injured bird limped to the side of the road and then flapped off into the trees. He referred to the goose as Violet because that's what she was. In researching for this book, I discovered the goose was probably an American Lavender Ice, but clearly a genetic anomaly. Possibly a pet. I can still hear my dad's voice on the phone when he said, "it was the most remarkable thing. In that low light she was as purple as a plum."

In the story it's Violet who inspires Albert and Clare to set off on their adventure. But in my life, it's always been my dad.

Table Mountain, South Africa

Samantha Leigh Miller is a Social Studies teacher whose creative work has appeared in several literary magazines including *Talking Writing*, *Indolent Books*, and *Raving Dove*. Miller has also co-authored research in peace pedagogy for *Teaching of Psychology* and presented her work at conferences around the country. Along with writing, travel-on-a-budget is her passion, having already visited five continents. She is currently working on a historical fiction novel based on a real-life 1855 unsolved murder in her hometown of Pottstown, PA.

To learn more about the author, along with a complete list of works referenced in *The Goose Waltzer*, upcoming releases, and much more, visit SamanthaLeighMiller.com

The Goose Waltzer

A Novel

Samantha Leigh Miller

A READER'S GUIDE

Ties To Tennyson

Growing up, my dad filled our house with literature from around the world, from the weary blues of Langston Hughes and Sun-tzu' thoughts on war, to Chekhov's short stories and the poets of England—Keats and Coleridge, Wordsworth and especially Tennyson. My dad believed Tennyson's, "In Memoriam A.H.H.," to be the most accurate reflection of grief he'd ever read. I'll never know what grief of his he might have compared this poem against. I never asked.

- Clare's boyfriend (with whom she breaks up at the cemetery before the beginning of the book) is named Lance. Tennyson draws heavily from the story of Lancelot and the struggle between relationships and isolation in his 1833 poem, "The Lady of Shalott."

- Tennyson's 1884 poem, "Lady Clare," tells the story of a woman who is loved for who she is, not for what society tells her to be. "Lady" Clare's mother in the poem is named Alice. Not coincidentally, our protagonist's mother's name is also Alice.

- As we learn during his 911 call, Albert's full name is Albert Henry Hallam—A.H.H. Tennyson's poem, "In Memoriam A.H.H." documents the poet's 17-year struggle with the death of his friend and muse, Arthur Henry Hallam.

- Tirol Farm is where Albert and Clare believe Violet will finally be safe. Arthur Henry Hallam and his father were on their way to Tirol, Austria when Arthur suddenly died in Vienna.

- Clare and Albert live on Shalott Drive where the cars "neither stopped, nor gained speed; they glided, nearly silent…as if boats on water…" The "Lady of Shalott" dies on the water on her way to town.

- Albert's wife is Emily Nosynnet (check that backwards) before she became Emily Hallam. Tennyson's sister, Emily was engaged to A.H.H. when he died.

- Officer Ben Light struggles with the ethics of following orders, versus doing what he knows is right, reflecting a theme of Tennyson's famous and tragic 1854 poem "The Charge of the Light Brigade."
- Craven Hawtrey, Albert's former student and the draft-dodger who shows up on Albert's porch is named for the headmaster of Eton College where A.H.H. was a student.
- Tennyson based "Lady Clare" on Susan Ferrier's novel, *The Inheritance*, in which the male character who was truly in love with the protagonist is named Edward Lyndsay—hence Clare's last name, Lyndsay.
- Clare's neighbors are contemporaries of Tennyson—the (Thomas) Carlyles and the (Matthew) Arnolds.
- The dangerous thoroughfare Albert, Clare, and Violet must traverse in order to reach Tirol Farm is Old Clevedon Road. A.H.H. is buried at St. Andrews church in Clevedon, Somersetshire.
- Clare's stalker/ex-boyfriend/childhood "friend" is named Jared Wilson Croker. One of Tennyson's harshest critics was John Wilson Croker, who, in 1833, wrote a scathing review of Tennyson's "Poems." Some historians believe this review contributed to the poet's rather unproductive decade after A.H.H.'s death.
- Cee-Cee Lushington, the papergirl whom Clare befriends, is named for Cecilia, Tennyson's sister who married Edmund Lushington. Cecilia and Edmund's wedding marks the end of "In Memoriam," leaving the poem on an image of hope.

Questions And Topics for Discussion

1. What does *The Goose Waltzer* tell us about the nature of grief and healing? In which way is each main character grieving?

2. Think about the use of color in the novel—the yellow slicker, the purple cloak, Clare's yellow bike, Alice's purple house, the yellow goslings, Violet herself. What are the relationships between these items and what meaning might be ascribed to these colors throughout the book?

3. What is your opinion of Clare's mother, Alice Lyndsay? Is she a feminist? Mentally ill? What do you think of Alice's writings and views of the world?

4. Both Clare and Jared are witness and are deeply impacted by the scene of Alice's death. How does this trauma inform the development of each character's childhood? Their adulthood?

5. On the day Clare rolls her childhood bike out of the shed, she also finds her mother's journals. While Clare doesn't open them, the narrator tells us that among the journals is one marked "CA," which recorded her mother's time during the year before Clare was born. This journal was empty. "Not blank-page empty, but sheets-ripped-from-the-spine-in-tears-and-rage-leaving-only-jagged-edges empty" (page 55). What do you think happened to Alice Lyndsay in California? What clues does the author provide throughout the book in answer to this mystery?

6. At the beginning of the book, we're told Albert brings his keys everywhere, even though he doesn't lock up his house or drive a car. Why does Albert leave his keys behind on the last day of the book?

7. What do you think of the end of the book? Does each character get the ending they deserved?

8. *The Goose Waltzer* opens and ends with Violet's story. Throughout the novel Violet also shares her thoughts on the happenings of the story or the motivation of its characters within the use of parenthesis. How was your experience of *The Goose Waltzer* impacted by this omniscient bird-narrator?

9. After Clare's apparent suicide attempt, Albert and Ben are
    talking at the hospital. Ben is shocked to learn Clare has no
    family or friends to be with her and asks Albert how that can
    happen to a person. Albert replies, "easier than you think"
    (page 174). Think about your own circle of support. How
    might you build on it? How might you find ways to support
    others?

If you enjoyed *The Goose Waltzer*, please tell your friends and consider leaving a review! I'd love to hear from you.

For updates on upcoming novels, promotions, events (and occasional silliness), follow me here facebook.com/sleighbooks/ and check out my website: SamanthaLeighMiller.com

Thank you for reading!